THE CALDER BOATS

THE CALDER BOATS

Gabrielle Ross

HEADLINE

This book is dedicated to the many canal lovers,
and those who sail on them in this modern
New Canal Age.

First published in Great Britain in 1988
by HEADLINE BOOK PUBLISHING PLC

*All characters in this publication are fictitious
and any resemblance to real persons, living or dead,
is purely coincidenial.*

British Library Cataloguing in Publication Data

Ross, Gabrielle
   The calder boats.
   I. Title
   823'.914[F]   PR6068.0818

   ISBN 0-7472-0064-5

HEADLINE BOOK PUBLISHING PLC
Headline House
79 Great Titchfield Street
London W1P 7FN

Printed and Bound in Great Britain by
Richard Clay Ltd, Bungay, Suffolk

PART ONE

1811–1829

Sweet Spring, full of sweet days and roses

George Herbert

Chapter One

Life in England, before Queen Victoria's era of smug respectability and simpering gentility, was a roistering, robust affair. Stagecoaches linked town and country, and steaming horses drew up outside the hospitable coaching inns, wherein all was light and warmth. Away from the turnpikes, however, roads were all too often impassable once the autumn rains set in, and families were obliged to visit each other on horseback, ladies riding pillion.

But there was another form of travel. Across the Midlands spread a network of canals, narrower than the water-ways of the south and north, and on these still and tideless waters sailed equally narrow wooden boats, with tall rudder-posts suggesting the ships of the Norsemen, but with gaily painted sides picked out with patterns of old castles and roses, suggesting the gipsy. They brought colour to England, these bright birds of Paradise, and on these boats people lived, loved and died. It was a world within a world, unsung and forgotten.

Tamarisk Calder was born on the day the Chilverton Canal came into being. There were four years to go before the victory at Waterloo, and George Augustus Frederick had recently been sworn in as Prince Regent. But battles and princes were far from the thoughts of the crowds who watched the water gush merrily into the new canal. They cheered and stamped and hoped that the waterway would bring prosperity to the area.

Outside the town, in the large house of mellow brick, with grounds sloping to the canal side, a man stood watching the gurgling water. Jamie Calder was short, stockily built, around forty years of age, and although well dressed, there was a look about him that told in some indefinable way that he was of the people. Chilverton town recognised this and wondered how such a man came to have for a wife the daughter of a peer of the realm, if indeed she was – for why then had she dropped her title?

Tongues wagged busily about the Calders of Cherry Trees. They didn't mix with any of the townspeople, was it because the wife was in the family way? And anyway, who would they mix with? Only the Squire perhaps, Sir William Fargate, and he was a hard man, had driven his son away to

1

America and his wife into an early grave, so 'twas said, and wasn't given much to socialising. The only other people of note were the Warings, merchant weavers who had made money, so that John Waring was building himself a grand new house, and his wife putting on airs indeed. But John Waring was a good fellow, he had something to do with the canal, and this new man, Jamie Calder, had a bit of interest in it too, some way or another. A company had been formed, and Sir William would know a bit about that, no doubt; he owned all the land and the coal mines and the farms round about. No one knew exactly how it all was done, but there it was, the new canal, and the three men involved with its birth, Sir William, John Waring, and the newcomer, Jamie Calder.

Jamie knew nothing of Chilverton gossip. He turned from the window as the door opened and a short dark-haired little body of indeterminate age entered. Abby could have been thirty or fifty, she never had, and never would look any different. Calm and capable, with purposeful tread she approached the master. 'It's a girl, Mr Calder,' she said.

'Thank you, Abby.' If Jamie felt any emotion he did not show it. 'Is my wife recovered?'

'Indeed, yes, Mr Calder. If you'd like to come up . . .'

He followed her up the flight of stairs into the large bedchamber whose furnishings spelled money spent to indulge it owner's extravagant tastes: satin curtains were looped back from the windows, firelight glinted on the silver candlesticks standing carelessly on the Sheraton table. In the four-poster bed, its hangings picked out in blue and gold mesh, the new mother lay. Annabel Calder was a beauty, with red hair, full pouting lips, and eyes that could flash like summer lightning. Jamie walked to the bedside and there was a world of tenderness in his voice as he asked 'How are you, my love?'

The young woman stretched her weary body. 'I suppose I shall survive,' she said. 'Though faith, there were times in the night when I thought I wouldn't.'

'You must rest now,' he soothed.

'Oh, pshaw, Jamie, rest indeed. As soon as I'm up I'm going back to the stage.'

'But, Annabel – '

'But what, Jamie? Do you think to keep me in this house? It's *your* house, Jamie, it's what you wanted, where you wanted it – '

'I was going to say, my love, that you should wait a few months at least, to get your strength back.'

Annabel moved restlessly, and the dark little woman moved to the bed.

'Now, Miss Bel,' she admonished. Abby had been Annabel's nurse, dresser on the stage, and was said to be the only person who could handle her. 'It's quite true. You must wait a few months.'

'But I'll be quite well tomorrow, Abby.'

'Not yet, Miss Bel,' she said sternly. Then her face softened, 'Besides, it would be a shame to leave the baby so soon, poor little mite.'

'Oh stuff, Abby. Poor little mite, indeed. We have a nurse ready and waiting. Heavens, my mother never took much heed of me, as well you know.'

'Don't get excited, Miss Bel. A few months is neither here nor there.'

'Well, it will only be a few,' Annabel grumbled. 'You hear that, Jamie? Just a few months. You've got your bargain, and nowhere did it stipulate that I become one of these middle-ranking wives.' There was scorn in her voice.

'You'll have the child to consider,' he said.

'Oh, pooh. Abby, bring her to me.' The tiny, red-faced baby was placed in her arms and she looked at it for a moment with a strange, scrutinising glance. Then she held the child to Jamie. 'Don't you want to see her too?' she asked mockingly.

He took the baby, staring down at the tiny face with its fluff of reddish hair so like its mother's. He sighed, then, as one tiny hand curled itself round his finger, he smiled, and walked to the window. 'There,' he said, holding the baby high. 'There it is, the Chilverton Canal. There's my dream, there's the reason I came to live here. It's the beginning of a new world, baby, and it's all yours.'

Tamarisk's first memory was of walking to the canal with Papa. It was a beautiful day, the sun glinted on the water, and on the old house with the mellow brick. In the distance was the church spire and the huddle of buildings that was Chilverton, surrounded by the meadows of the Warwickshire countryside, filled now with wild flowers, daisies and buttercups, delicate meadowsweet, ragged robin. Somewhere above a lark poured out its soul to the sky. When Tam thought of heaven it was always the mellow brick of Cherry Trees, and the green, flower-filled meadows around the canal.

They came to the water and a narrow boat passed slowly, pulled by a dreamy, slow-moving horse whose brasses gleamed in the sun. The woman at the tiller wore the traditional full-skirted black dress and had a black sunbonnet on her head. Then came the sound of a horn, and Papa said 'This is one of my boats coming now, the *Queen*.'

Tam's mouth became a round O as the *Queen* approached. She was a magnificent sight. Seventy foot of gleaming hull; cabins worked with roses and castles, glass windows, and merrily smoking chimneys, all pulled by two horses at a gallop, the second ridden by a postillion who flourished his whip and sounded the horn again. People looked over the side, laughing and waving to the child.

'It is a packet boat,' said Papa. 'Carrying passengers to Stratford-on-Avon.'

Tam pointed in astonishment at the great curved knife-blade mounted on her bow, then turned her face up expectantly to her father.

'That is to cut the towline of any boat that fails to give way,' explained Papa. 'A packet boat has precedence over all others.'

Tam smiled as the happy faces of the travellers glided from view. To the child it was the epitome of romance, flying steeds carrying happy people.

Later, she would take Celia and baby Juliet and explain to them that Papa owned packet boats to carry happy travellers. She had no memory of the birth of her sister Celia, being but one year old at the time. Indeed, it seemed that Celia had always been there, always trying to keep up with Tam, always complaining when she could not. There was a definite recollection that after Juliet was born Mama did not stay home any more, and sometimes fragments of a conversation would pass through her mind, when Mama and Papa were arguing.

'I think I've done my duty to you, Jamie. I'm going back to the stage.'

'But, Annabel, just wait till the girls are a little older.'

'That's what you always say, Jamie. And then before I know where I am I am stuck with another child. No, enough is enough.'

'Juliet is so delicate – '

'She'll outgrow it. Anyway, I don't aim to go immediately.'

'I would have liked a son.'

'I daresay, Jamie. So would I. But I don't intend to go on forever trying to produce sons, my family don't seem to be able to get many boys, I have but one brother. No, no more babies.'

'Very well, my dear.'

Tam did not remember the conversation word for word, but the essence of it stayed with her: Mama did not care for babies; Mama wanted to go away; only Papa remained. She learned at a very early age to be self-reliant and to look after herself and her younger sisters, for Celia never did have any ideas of her own, just followed Tam grudgingly and after much disagreement. Juliet was a different matter entirely. She was delicate, given to chesty colds which, if not checked, soon developed into bronchitis or worse. But there was more than that. As the baby sister grew, it was obvious that she was intelligent and could read and write easily, but she was somehow different. Loving and generous to a fault, she was entirely lacking in cunning or selfishness or any form of self-protectiveness, and moreover would talk to herself and, crowned with daisy chains on her head, would wander around singing like a small Ophelia.

Celia was not very interested in the canals, and Juliet was too often confined to her room with a cold, so Tam was alone for hours, when she would gather the rushes from the bank, and the tall yellow flag-irises, then she'd forget them, letting them drop into the canal to drift along in the wake of the boats. She marked the flash of blue that was a kingfisher, watched the water voles swimming along to their little homes in the banks, saw from her window foxes running at night under the moon. Childhood for Tam was a dreamy sunny time, with occasional winters jutting into a perpetual summer. And even winter was exciting, the canal ran dark between rimy fields; sometimes it would freeze over and the ice-breaker would crash its way through.

She never thought her childhood was unusual because she did not know any other way of living. The fact that her mother was away so often did not affect her very much at first. Papa was there and always had time for little girls which Mama did not even when she came. She would flutter into the

4

house like some bright butterfly with arms full of presents for the three girls.

'Dearest ones,' she would coo, clasping them to her scented bosom. 'See what I have for you. A grand doll for Tam, one for Celia, and a baby doll for baby Juliet.'

'Tam's is bigger than mine,' Celia invariably cried.

'Nonsense, Celia, don't be so cross. Oh, and I have some ribbons for your hair. Now, the blue for Tam, I think, it would look well in her red curls.'

'I want the blue,' whined Celia.

'But, dear one, the red would be just as well for you, your hair is fair and will take any colour . . . and oh, so straight. However did I come to have such a plain child?'

'My eyes is blue,' Celia whimpered. 'Tam's eyes is funny.'

'Tam's eyes are hazel,' said Annabel. 'And hazel eyes are most beautiful, they change colour. See the flecks of green that light up – '

'That light up when she's in a temper,' put in Abby.

'And then become a lovely smoky brown when in repose,' said Annabel, a smile on her face as if she were thinking of other things.

'My eyes is blue,' repeated Celia. 'Blue is pretty.'

'Celia can have my ribbon,' lisped Juliet.

'No, really, baby, there is no need. Oh dear, why do I always have this trouble?' Annabel asked plaintively.

'It would help, Miss Bel, if you brought the same gifts for each child,' said Abby.

'Oh, pshaw, Abby, if I have a pretty child, then I want to give her pretty ribbons. Now, tell me what you have been doing while I was away.' And without stopping to listen, Mama would be whirling round the room, talking to Abby, to the servants, to Papa if he came in.

Memories of childhood were strung like beads on a chain. The time when Mama was home, and they were sitting outside on the lawn, taking tea. It was a pleasant sunny day in late spring, the cherry trees were in blossom and sometimes a little breeze would stir, and the pink petals would come gently wafting down around them. Juliet ran to catch the falling petals and seemed to forget the family and wandered singing down to the water.

And Mama said, with a frown on her lovely face, 'Tam, you are a sensible girl. Will you do something for me?'

'Yes, Mama,' said Tam, wanting to please this beautiful, elegant lady who came so seldom.

'Always look after Juliet. Promise me, Tam.'

'Yes, Mama, I promise.' Tam was a little puzzled, she could not, as yet, envisage a world without Mama and Papa, and so could not understand why the promise should be made, but it was given, and she never forgot it.

And then the wind rose strongly and the pink petals whirled down like a summer snowstorm, and Juliet ran back to Mama and hid her face in her lap, though they all knew she was not afraid. Juliet had no fear.

5

A few days with them, and Mama would depart, but Papa would be there to talk to Tam about the canal, when his work was done, walking in the summer twilights with the swallows swooping round the eaves, or in his study, filled with books and maps.

'I bought another boat today,' he might say.

'Do you own the canal, Papa?'

'No, but it was my idea.'

'Was it, Papa?'

'Yes. I saw that another small cut was needed between the Worcester and Birmingham and the Coventry Canals. But I hadn't the money to do anything, and I didn't live here then.'

'Where did you live, Papa?'

'I was born in Scotland, where we scratched a bare living from the land around a tiny croft. When all that was taken from us, we moved to England, to Yorkshire.' He laughed mirthlessly. 'And we weren't any better off there. Not at first.'

Tam blinked, uncomprehending. She had never been into the poor parts of the town.

'There was no schooling for me, though my father taught me how to read and write,' said Papa, his face grave. 'Then he heard that navigators were wanted and he got a job with them. And that changed my life.'

'What's navigators, Papa?'

'They were the men who dug the canals. I saw it all, Tam. The Leeds and Liverpool first of all. That was a bold and magnificent venture, nothing like it had ever been seen in Britain before. A miracle of engineering. Look.' And together they pored over the map, and Papa traced the line with his finger, showing the aqueducts, the summit, the great tunnel. 'I was a baby when it was started,' he went on. 'I grew up with it. My father helped to dig it. And it was finished only a few years ago.'

Tam's face glowed with pride, her Papa's father had built that canal. 'Go on, Papa,' she said, loving him.

'Miracles of engineering,' he repeated, dreamily. 'Three giant canals, crossing the Pennines. See this one, the Huddersfield, the highest in the kingdom. Miracles . . .' his eyes were far away. 'That's when I wanted to work with canals, when I cursed my lack of education. But I studied, learned all I could.'

'Did you, Papa?'

'Yes. Wishing I were one of the engineers who had designed them. James Brindley was untaught, too, but he was a genius.' Papa smiled ruefully. 'As I grew older I worked as a clerk for the Leeds and Liverpool, first of all. I came down here simply because I wanted to see all I could, and that's when I saw what was needed here. A new canal.'

'So you built one, Papa.'

He smiled again. 'No, I didn't. I couldn't. Because it needed a lot of money, as I said. But before that an act of Parliament had to be passed.'

'Yes, Papa.' She didn't understand, but wanted to hear more.

'There's isn't a Member of Parliament for Chilverton, so that meant

6

lobbying, and that needed influential men. I approached several people, and one of them was Sir William Fargate.' He looked into the distance, while Tam waited. 'I told him his interests would benefit by having a canal here; he owns coal mines, he'd be able to sell more coal if he could send it away from the area. He wouldn't listen at first, he pointed out that Chilverton lies on the edge of the East Warwickshire Plateau, he said a canal couldn't be cut through that. Imagine, Tam, he said *couldn't*, after what I'd seen. I said the only way was to take the canal round the plateau.'

'Did you, Papa?'

'So he approached an engineer and agreed in the end. Then Sir William floated a company.'

Tam wondered hazily how a company could float, and imagined it drifting down the canal.

'Yes. John Waring saw the sense of it too. But it was my idea.'

'You are clever, Papa.'

He smiled wryly. 'Little use being clever without money. But your Mama helped me. We must always be grateful to Mama.'

Tam pulled her lip mutinously. She didn't want Papa to love Mama so much, she wanted him to love her, Tam. He was her god, her protector, the one who knew everything, the omnipotent.

'You said you didn't own the canal,' she said.

'No. In a company so many people own shares, you see, Tam. I had thought that Sir William might have offered a few to me as a little reward, but he didn't.' Papa was serious now, his face set in worried lines. Tam waited.

'Oh well. John Waring managed to get hold of some. And I wanted to run boats, and canal companies cannot act as carriers, so . . . I bought boats. I'm not sure that Sir William was best pleased about that, I don't know why.'

'They are lovely boats, Papa,' she said loyally.

'Come to the table, Tam, let me show you what I dreamed of.' He unrolled a larger map of England, and together they looked at it. 'See, there is already a countrywide network of canals,' he said, and she saw the lines spread over the map like a huge spider's web.

'The canals have opened up the world to us,' he said. 'The rivers have always been navigated, men sail the sea. But here in the Midlands it was a closed society, villages working at farming and hand-loom weaving, goods could only be moved by packhorse or turnpike, both expensive. Men like Josiah Wedgwood wanted to move their goods, he makes fine pottery you know, Tam, and he and others wanted to send to London, even to the ports to be sent overseas.' Now he was staring dreamily through the window. 'So men started building canals, and helped develop the industries of this country. We are no longer land-locked. Here is the Oxford Canal, see it, Tam, and the Grand Junction that leads right down to London. Here's the Worcester and Birmingham, and the Coventry Canal which takes you to the River Trent and so to the northern ports, Liverpool and Hull. It could be possible to sail to the River Severn and to Bristol.'

7

She stared fascinated seeing the wonder of boats and ships and far-away places where East Indiamen with billowing sails carried spices and silks, and she understood his dream.

'But,' Papa said, as though she had spoken aloud, 'not everyone understands the way the future will be. Why, maybe they will be making goods in Birmingham to be sent all over the world, so we must first get them to the coast. Yet each man builds his own little canal for his own little area, as Sir William here, narrow boats on narrow canals. We need a grand plan, all the canals the same size, so that all boats can pass freely.'

'Maybe someone will do that one day, Papa.' She did not fully understand, but Papa had said so.

He sighed. 'If not, it could be our undoing. John Waring sees this too.'

'Then why can't you do something, Papa?'

He sighed again. 'We are powerless, Tam.'

But she couldn't believe that. Not Papa. 'Maybe you'll make a lot of money some day,' she said hopefully.

'It's not money alone, Tam, it's power. And some people are very powerful.'

She strove to comfort him. 'I'll do it, Papa. When I grow up, I'll make it all as you want.'

He laughed, but kindly.

'I will, truly, Papa.'

'Yes, Tam, maybe you will,' and he brushed her hair lightly and went to stand at the window, and Tam felt he didn't really believe that she would do these things to help him and wondered why. And why did he look so sad? He often looked sad. And now, oddly, she felt a strong desire to protect him, for she thought that he was too kind and too lenient, as he was with Mama.

Once he took her down to Chilverton wharf, perched before him on his bay mare. And the wharf was a splendid place indeed, with offices and warehouses, and many boats in the basin. Though early morning, already it was a hive of activity, sacks of flour were being loaded into one of the boats, while farther along, a tramroad brought waggons of coal. Papa went into one of the little offices, but Tam wandered along the wharf, coming to where a group of children played, and she joined them, running and shouting and rolling around till they were all gloriously dirty.

'Where do you live?' she asked the children, and they said, 'On the boats.'

'All the time?' she asked. 'You live there all the time? Oh, I wish I did. I wish I lived on a boat.'

As she sat there on the dirty ground she saw someone coming to the office, she thought he was a man, he was so big and strong. 'What are you kids doing here?' he asked. 'Move away, you little ragamuffins.' And the children put out their tongues rudely, and Tam did likewise.

'Who's that?' she asked, and the children said it was one of the Warings, Mr Charles, and he wasn't a man, he was only a youth, and training to be canal agent.

Papa took her home, tired and dirty, and she thought it was the most wonderful day of her life. She was so excited that she told Mama about it when she came, and Mama immediately said she was not to go to the wharf again.

Tam was mutinous, her eyes flashed green. 'Why not, Mama?'

'It won't harm the child, Miss Bel,' Abby remonstrated.

'What? Rolling around on the wharf? The very idea,' said Annabel. 'She might be drowned.'

'But, Miss Bel, it's not right that the girls should be left like this. Never seeing other children. They'll grow up odd.'

'Nonsense, Abby. I only had a governess.'

'But you saw other children, Miss Bel, there wasn't a week went by but you visited, or went to a child's party.'

'But, Abby, there are none here they can mix with, are there? And besides – '

'Yes, Miss Bel, besides . . .?' Abby asked, ominously.

'Oh nothing. No more, Abby. The girls stay here,' said Mama.

There was a succession of governesses, all merging into one in Tam's eyes. All old, plain and dull, compared with Mama, but none bothering too much with the children, so that Tam could always find time to drift to the canal. Very occasionally they would order the carriage and go to church, but when Mama was away Papa didn't seem to care about it, and when she was home she only seemed to recollect that they should go – the children and governess – out of a sense of duty. Tam knew nothing of the town where she lived and nothing of its people. Had she been told that in some of the cottages the tenants threw their slops into the open gutter in the roadway she would not have been shocked, the world of 1821 was not easily shocked.

'When I grow up,' she said to her sisters, 'I shall live on a boat.'

'You can't,' said Celia, flatly.

'Of course I can. Why not? Papa owns them.'

'Because we don't live on boats, we live at Cherry Trees,' said Celia.

'You're just a Miss Prim,' said Tam.

'I'm not Miss Prim, I'm Celia,' and she would begin to howl, and Tam would escape to the canal again.

But when Juliet fell in the water Mama realised that something would have to be done. It had been a pleasant morning, they'd had lessons with Miss Grant, who had then mysteriously disappeared as she so often did, to the children's delight. They wandered into the garden, down to the canal. For a time they were content, waiting for the boats to pass, seeing the water sucked out towards the middle only to rush back in a wave, and Tam would venture out, running back lest the water caught her. And the boatwoman would laugh and move the tiller sometimes to make more waves and splash her. But as always, when the children were together for long, a quarrel ensued. Tam walked along the bank, muddy after the spring rains, picking the yellow flags, and Celia set up a howl.

'I want some flowers.'

'Then get some,' said Tam.

But the flags were growing in the mud and one had to be sure-footed.

Celia made one attempt then drew back afraid, setting up a monotonous cry.

'I want some flowers.'

'I'll get some for you,' said Juliet, and stepped straight into the mud. It squelched, and she lost her balance falling into the water, flat on her face, where she lay, floundering. Tam, with great presence of mind, pulled her legs, and she was borne, dripping and choking, to the bank. Celia, frightened, ran for help, screaming. Miss Grant was not to be found, Papa was out on business, one of the servants came running, and the child was put to bed. She developed bronchitis, it was feared pneumonia might follow. Annabel was sent for.

'This is the end,' she said, when Juliet was on the way to recovery and Miss Grant had been dismissed for being out with a man when she should have been supervising the children. 'The girls must go away to school.'

'Juliet is too delicate,' protested Jamie.

'Well, Tam and Celia then, Juliet won't get into mischief on her own. Not another word, Jamie. Nor you, Abby. You've been telling me long enough that the girls should meet other children.'

'I thought,' murmured Jamie, 'you might stay at home now – '

'I cannot, Jamie. I am the best Shakespearean actress they've seen at Drury Lane for a long time. Heavens above,' she cried, 'I think sometimes you'd like to go back to the days when women weren't allowed on the stage at all.'

'I don't want to go, I don't want to go away,' shouted Tam. 'Papa, don't let me go,' and she ran to him, sobbing.

'You must be educated,' he said. 'See what I lost by not being educated.'

'But, Papa, I could not be an engineer.' Even at ten years, Tam knew that.

'No, my love, but you can learn far more at school than with a governess,' Papa said.

'Shall I learn about canals?' asked Tam.

'I'm sure you will,' said Jamie, whose knowledge of girls' schools was as limited as that of his daughters.

'But I want to stay here with you, Papa.'

'Your Mama thinks it best,' and this she could not fight, the fact that whatever Annabel did or did not do, her father would not oppose her. Never put his foot down, order his butterfly wife to stay with her children, he just stood there, sad and silent, and Tam loved him the more and her mother the less. Not that she felt her mother should stay at home for the children's sake, such things were not done, but she knew that Papa wanted her mother at home, and this she could not forgive, that Papa's wishes went unheeded.

Her feelings towards her mother were, by this time, ambivalent. She knew she was an actress, and studied the programmes she brought home with avid curiosity, heard her talking about Mr Kean at Drury Lane. Tam admired her for her beauty, her elegance, her charm, but disliked her for holding Papa's affections, she was her rival, one who won without even

10

trying. Tam felt that, if she must go to school she must learn all she could and then come home to work with Papa, till in the end he would love her more than Mama.

Yet, almost imperceptibly, her love for her father had changed. He was no longer her omnipotent god, her grand protector, he was fallible, unable or unwilling to cross Mama. She felt more protective towards him than ever, but something had been lost. 'Some day, Papa,' she said, 'I'll come back to you and *I'll* live with you all the time.'

But he only smiled, and put his hand on her hair, ruffling her curls.

So abruptly, the carefree existence of childhood ended. Tam and Celia were packed off to Miss Laker's Academy for Young Ladies, not to be allowed home until the summer holidays.

Chapter Two

The Academy was a large building standing in its own secluded grounds in the south of Warwickshire, well away from the coal pits of the north of the county. The girls were driven in the carriage, accompanied by John Dexter, the butler, and Abby's husband, then delivered to Miss Laker, a thin, grey-haired spinster with a forbidding expression and steely grey eyes behind rimless pince-nez.

And now they were in a strange world of little girls: girls of all shapes and sizes, who talked and whispered, and pulled each other's hair when the mistresses were not looking, and who gathered round the newcomers plying them with questions.

'Who are you? Where do you live? What does your Papa do?'

'He owns boats,' said Tam.

'You mean he's a sea captain?'

'No, boats on the canal.'

'Whatever are boats on the canal?' And there were giggles, something else they had to endure. Oddly, Celia settled in first, accepting the order and discipline and the correct way of doing things as Tam never could. It was Celia now who was the favourite, who smiled at the mistresses and sat straight in her place, while Tam fidgeted and looked through the window and thought of Cherry Trees and the canal.

The girls asked other strange questions too. 'Where do your grandparents live? Have you many cousins?'

The parents of Miss Laker's young ladies were mostly abroad, either on Government Service in the colonies or wealthy traders from the East India Company. Their home life was as haphazard as the Calders', they seldom saw their parents at all, but they did seem to have grandparents and cousins in England, and only now did Tam realise her own loss.

'We haven't any,' she said.

'You must have grandparents, everybody does. Unless they're dead.'

So when the longed-for summer holiday arrived, Tam asked her mother, 'Where are our grandparents?'

12

Annabel stopped walking and stood quite still. 'We don't see them,' she said.

'Why not, Mama?'

There was a pause. 'My mother is dead, and my father quarrelled with me, I'm afraid. We do not meet.'

'But why not, Mama?' Tam persisted.

'That's enough, Tam.'

'But who is he, where does he live?'

'He is the Earl of Sandford, he lives at Trentham Hall, a long way from here.'

'But doesn't Papa have any relations, either?'

Again Annabel paused. 'He doesn't see them.'

'Did they quarrel with him, too?' asked Tam, puzzled.

'I said that's enough, Tam.'

She intended to ask her father about these mysterious relations, but when she saw him she was so pleased to see him, so overjoyed at being home again, near her beloved canal, that she completely forgot. Mama soon went away again, so she was able to live her life as before, hugging Juliet, gazing into her grave, self-contained little face, asking innumerable questions 'Do you miss us, baby? Does your governess take proper care of you? She mustn't let you fall in the canal again.'

And Celia said spitefully, 'She won't fall in the canal when you're not here, Tam.'

'Oh, Juliet, you are so lucky not to be sent away,' said Tam, then took herself to task; you could not be envious of Juliet. Her nature was so sunny, she was always so ready to help others, that though her sisters might quarrel with each other, they united to love Juliet, everyone loved Juliet. Her mother noted her goodness with disquiet, wishing she had some of Tam's temper, of Celia's awkwardness. Like most mothers, Annabel believed that good children were not long for this world.

'Are you not happy at Miss Laker's, Tam?' Juliet asked, troubled, when Tam wished she might stay at home longer, and she replied, 'Happy enough, baby,' though she felt that going back was like going to prison.

The Academy was in fact, more isolated than many prisons. As the young ladies had parents in very high positions, Miss Laker took no chances, and the girls were kept as secluded as any nuns in convents, and were never allowed out of the grounds, not even to go to church. They had the Vicar visit them and he was very old, as were the gardener and the physician.

'Lord,' said Amanda Fotheringay. 'I don't think the old witch knows what a real man is.'

Amanda was Tam's age, and the granddaughter of a duke whose pastimes were a national byword. He loved three things: watching prize-fights, hunting, and women. He would go hare-coursing with the peasants on his estate, looking and talking as coarse as they, yet, should one of the self-same peasants dare to poach a single rabbit from his grounds, he would personally see they were transported to the colonies for seven years. His granddaughter would tell the girls some of the old reprobate's sayings till their hair stood on end. At twelve years the girls were moved from a dormitory to a smaller room, Tam and Celia placed with Amanda and a girl called Elizabeth Winters, and Tam learned more about life from Amanda than she had in all her previous years at Cherry Trees. And, with the resilience of childhood, she began to enjoy herself, but only up to a point. She could never forget her home, the freedom she enjoyed there, and she looked forward to her father's letters eagerly.

'I have bought my sixth packet boat today,' he wrote. 'The *Princess*, she is a fine sight. She averages ten miles an hour, with the two horses changed every four to six miles. There are two cabins, giving first and second class accommodation, and they are very comfortable. A luxury after stagecoach travel. The fare to Birmingham will be six shillings, and she will hold sixty passengers. I have put it in Mama's name, I thought it would be a pleasant gift, though, of course, in law all Mama's possessions are mine. I often think that it is a strange law which says a woman's property belongs to her husband, but many of our laws, and the way they are made are strange. Everything is geared to the landed gentry, you see, Tam, and all this will have to change someday. Have you heard about the hoped-for Parliamentary Reform at Miss Laker's, when all men will have votes? You must be receiving a very good education there.'

They had not heard about Reform at Miss Laker's. They were taught music, dancing, a little religion, mademoiselle taught French, and Miss Laker herself taught the correct writing of English and the little arithmetic that was considered sufficient for young ladies. Their history was a list of bygone kings and queens and battles long past. Of the present day they knew nothing. When Tam asked in class about the proposed bill Miss Laker was shocked.

'These are not fitting subjects for ladies,' she said frostily.

'But my Papa told me – '

Miss Laker pursed her lips and said nothing; her silence was eloquence enough.

'My Papa is a gentleman,' Tam said, then hesitated. Was he, in the world's eyes, a gentleman? He might be the dearest, kindest man in the whole country, but was he a gentleman? Miss Laker was going on with the lesson.

'This gives me the opportunity to instruct you in the art of conversation. At a dinner party one might discuss light topics in mixed company, the weather, travel, and so on. When the ladies withdraw and leave the gentlemen to their port wine, it is to enable the menfolk to discuss serious matters.'

'Oh stuff,' said Amanda Fotheringay in the privacy of their bedroom. 'The ladies withdraw so the gentlemen can piss in the pots, I've heard my grandfather say so.'

But the incident had started Tam wondering about her parents' marriage and how it had come about; at thirteen she was more introspective than she had ever been, or would be again. Annabel never talked about

14

lords and ladies; she accepted that all people had their place, like the poor, and those middling people like physicians whom one was forced to have in the house, but would be sent to the housekeeper for a repast if necessary, and with whom one didn't mix socially. But Papa had said that his parents were poor, so how had he come to marry Mama? It was unlikely that such a couple should meet, let alone marry. so how had it all come about? Was it a passionate affair such as Amanda Fotheringay talked about? She thought it unlikely, when Mama was always away, and when at home, seldom, if ever, gave in to Papa's wishes. There were great gaps of mystery in her parents' lives, and it was useless asking them about it, they would not tell.

At each holiday Papa always met them with the carriage and Juliet, and she could not wait to get home. She'd run out of the Academy, Miss Laker's teachings forgotten, rush to fling herself into Papa's arms. 'Papa,' she cried. 'Dear, dear Papa,' and then the drive through the lanes of Warwickshire, on the turnpike, with Tam talking nineteen to the dozen, clasping her father's hand, never wanting to let him go. As soon as she arrived at Cherry Trees she ran down to the water, while Papa smiled. 'It's still there,' he said. And it was, just the same, with horses, and packets, and flyboats, those fast carriers that travelled non-stop, night and day.

Now the wharf was forbidden, Papa always found time to go for long walks with Tam. It came about quite naturally, for Celia didn't like walking and Juliet wasn't strong enough, she stayed with her governess. So Papa and Tam walked through the leafy lanes, and Tam would pick flowers, or berries in the autumn, and they'd talk about the countryside and the boats. Sometimes it seemed Papa was almost talking to himself, for she didn't understand the half of what he said, though oddly, his words remained in her mind to be remembered years later. She was proud he talked to her instead of Mama, though everyone knew Mama wasn't interested in canals, she only talked about plays in London and her latest gown, and how fashions were being worn that year. Why couldn't Papa realise what a silly woman Mama was? Why did he have to love her?

They were in the garden watching the boats when Tam cried, 'Oh look, Papa, that packet boat has soldiers in it. What are soldiers doing here, Papa? I thought the war was over.'

'It is. They are going by boat to Liverpool, and they stay overnight in Chilverton.'

'Is that your boat, Papa?'

'No, I wouldn't carry soldiers unless I were desperate for a load.'

'Why not, Papa?'

'They are taking them to Ireland.'

She did not understand this answer, and asked, puzzled, 'Don't you like fighting, Papa?'

'Sometimes we have to fight. We had to fight Napoleon.'

'Was it bad, the war?'

'War is always bad, Tam. Though the strange thing is, people can always make a lot of money in wars.' He was talking to himself again and she strove to bring him back to her. She tugged at his hand.

15

'Did you make money in the war, Papa?'

'Well, yes. Canals gained a lot of traffic because there were French privateers facing the coastal trade. Of course trade slumped afterwards on my canal.' Papa would often say *my canal* and smile at his own vanity, and she'd smile too, but staunchly, because she believed it was Papa's canal. He had had the idea, and no one loved it as he did.

'The weaving benefited, too, because no foreign silks were allowed in the country. Now they're talking of letting French ribbons in again and I fear there will be trouble in the town. But come, Tam, that's all above your head, isn't it?' And he would tell her things to make her laugh; how the sexton rang the church bell in the mornings to wake people up at six o'clock, and how, last week, he rang it at three by mistake and everyone woke up early. And she quite forgot to ask what trouble there'd be in the town.

They walked away but she still turned to look at the soldiers, their splendid red coats shining in the sun, and she thought about how on the boats you see all the world. In the middle of the country you see all the world.

'Come,' Papa said. 'We must meet Mama. Isn't it splendid that Mama is coming back just when you are here?' And she frowned, wanting to keep him with her, to talk, even about things she didn't understand. For when Mama was here she would lose him.

They'd return to Cherry Trees and Mama would come down for the evening, dressed in silk and smelling nice. And they would sit round the table, but now Papa no longer belonged to Tam, he would talk to Mama, and if she moved away his eyes would follow her. And Tam would talk and try to hold Papa's attention, but she never could, not against Mama. So she would sit, finally, in mutinous silence, until Celia would ask, slyly, 'What is the matter, Tam? Why are you sulking?' and Tam would shout, 'Be quiet! Leave me alone!' Then Mama would frown and tell Tam to stop making such a dreadful noise. Tam would pinch Celia, Celia would squeal, and finally Tam would be sent to her room, smiling triumphantly at having won the attention of Papa, who was no longer looking at Mama.

The girls at Miss Laker's were dubious about Annabel Calder.

'Actresses,' said Elizabeth Winters, 'are not always respectable. I heard my brother say they are of easy virtue.'

'Easy virtue?' asked Tam.

'She means they're whores,' said Amanda Fotheringay. 'And what is wrong with that, pray? I think it would be a fine thing to be a whore.'

'What are whores?' asked Celia.

'They go around with a lot of men,' said Amanda. 'And make a lot of money. But they're not respectable.'

'My Mama is a lady,' cried Celia, angrily. 'And most respectable. Her father is – '

'Yes, we know,' said Elizabeth Winters from the superiority of a respectable family with a mother who stayed with her family. 'But it seems a peculiar life for a lady.'

16

Tam said nothing. She'd never questioned Mama's absences and did not want her at home all the time anyway. But she forgot about it until they went home again, then she asked her father, 'Why doesn't Mama live with us?'

'She is busy, Tam, you know she is an actress. I'm sorry she can't be here to see you, I know you miss her.'

But Tam didn't. And was immediately afraid that Papa might beg Mama to come especially to see them, and she'd take him away from her again.

Celia said nothing. But she badly wanted a Mama who was the same as any other.

Celia spent her childhood, and indeed her life, trying to catch up with Tam, to go one better; but Tam was always one step ahead, and neither sister understood that the year's difference in their ages meant that Celia could never catch up until they were grown up, by which time it would be too late. Tam could run faster, could jump higher, and no one pointed out that it was because her legs were one year older and longer, and she was also prettier, already showing some of their mother's elegance and poise. And Celia was not; nor could she even boast of the same lead over Juliet, because Juliet was delicate, and so could not be expected, or even allowed, to run and jump. So with Tam always ahead, always walking with Papa, taken notice of by Mama when she came, either being given a bigger doll or being hauled over the coals for naughtiness, and with Juliet spoiled and petted by all, parents and servants alike, poor Celia felt aggrieved and unwanted.

At Miss Laker's Celia learned that there were other ways to win friends and influence people, that if you were determined enough you could do well. She was not by nature a rebel – unless her eccentric family made her very conformity a rebellion – and the teachers preferred conformists, preferred little girls to be quiet and work prettily with heads bent over watercolour painting or embroidery. It did not matter too much if the work was not very good, the effort was being made. So Celia settled in happily, reflecting that if she could never earn a smile at home from Mama, it was easy enough here if you always remembered to bring a little present from home for your current teacher, always sat quietly with hands together. Nor was she too unpopular with the other girls, she took care never to give offence, and although Amanda Fotheringay both shocked and frightened her, she was accepted by that young lady as she was Tam's sister.

So Celia blossomed in the secluded air of Miss Laker's Academy, but the sense of inferiority she'd learned at home never left her, and she developed as compensation what, to Tam, was an unbearable superiority complex, talking whenever possible of her grandfather the Earl, making derogatory remarks about tradespeople, trying, in every way she could, to put Tam down. Tam, who had no idea of the root of her sister's discontent, and would not have cared greatly if she had, thought Celia the most disagreeable person she had ever known.

Tam fought her way into her teens, watching her body change and develop, standing for long periods before the looking glass in their bedroom. She had been told so often she was pretty, yet she felt doubt as she studied her reflection. Her eyes in repose might be two smoky pools, but how often was she in repose? Too often they sparked green fires, while her mouth was smiling and stormy by turns. Her hair, reddish-brown now, curled softly into her neck, and her figure . . .? She frowned, twirling this way and that. The classical line was on the way out, her new dress had a lower, tighter, waist. *Was* she pretty? She felt restless and wondered why. She found a new interest in the girls' whispers. 'Lord Byron,' breathed Amanda. 'See his picture, was he not beautiful?' They read Byron's poems in the privacy of their room and sighed. 'Just imagine,' said Amanda, 'if he had kissed you on the lips,' and the girls shuddered with ecstasy.

'He had to leave the country,' Amanda told them. 'There was a scandal.'

'Ooh what? Do tell,' cried the girls.

Amanda drew them closer. 'He fell in love with his sister,' she whispered.

'You can't fall in love with your sister,' objected Elizabeth.

'He did, she was his mistress.'

'What is a mistress? You mean like the mistresses here at school?'

'No, muttonhead. All rich men have mistresses; my grandfather had dozens. And you must know about the King, everybody does, when he was Regent. And the Duke of Clarence lives with an actress and has ten little FitzClarences.'

'Men shouldn't do these things,' said Celia, primly.

'Ladies do too,' said Amanda. 'Both Lady Bessborough and Lady Lembourne had several illegitimate children, and the Countess of Oxford had such a mixed family that they're known as the Harleian Miscellany.'

'What do you mean, a mixed family?' asked Tam.

'All different fathers,' said Amanda. 'My grandfather was one of them, I shouldn't wonder.'

'I don't believe ladies are like that,' said Celia.

'Neither do I,' said Tam, united for once with her sister in upholding the virtue of aristocratic ladies.

'But what do they *do*?' asked Elizabeth, puzzled.

'Don't you know anything? You do know when a man is married he gets children from his wife?'

'Of course.'

'And do you know how?'

'Because they sleep in the same bed.'

'They do something else too. At least if he has a mistress.'

'What? Do tell, Amanda.'

'Have you ever seen a naked man?' she asked.

The girls squeaked. 'No.'

'Wait a minute, I'll show you. Now, don't tell anyone I have this book or Miss Laker will expel me. Look, *Great Works of Art*,' and she opened it.

The girls pored over pictures of nude ladies which bore little resemblance to great works of art.

'Where did you get this?' asked Tam.

'I got it here, in school.'

'Oh no, you couldn't.'

'I did. A woman came, pretending to buy cast-off clothes from the servants, but selling these books. Miss Laker would die if she knew.'

'Oh look, there's a man.'

'After David, by Michelangelo,' read Tam, staring in wonderment.

'See that down there,' said Amanda, pointing. 'It is with that a man gets the mistress with child.'

The girls stared blankly. Tam, who had no idea as to what use the appendage would be put, nevertheless nodded knowingly.

'I'm going to be someone's mistress one day,' announced Amanda.

'You mean you're not going to get married?' asked Elizabeth.

'Oh yes, that too. But it won't be such fun.'

'I'm going to get married,' Celia said virtuously. 'I don't want to be a mistress, it seems uncommon vulgar to me.'

'But suppose,' Amanda was whispering now, 'suppose Lord Byron was with you, naked like this . . .' and they all laughed self-consciously and looked away and then returned fascinated to the picture before them.

'I wish I could meet some young gentleman,' said Tam, boldly.

'Why don't you come home with me for the holidays?' asked Amanda. 'I stay with Grandfather.'

'I'll ask Mama,' said Tam.

She wrote home, but Mama said she must stay with Celia, so she could not go, and Tam felt more animosity towards Mama and towards the luckless Celia.

And now the older girls waited restlessly to emerge into the big world, their 'coming out'.

'Balls and parties,' said Amanda dreamily. 'I wonder who'll marry first.'

'I hope it will be me,' said Celia.

Tam said nothing. She wanted to return to Papa, to help with the boats, but she was a normal girl, and was caught up in adolescent fever. She stared out of the window more than ever, dreaming of handsome men like the late Lord Byron and puzzling over the naked David of the picture. Amanda talked of kissing and the raffish London society and the girls put on their tight stays and wondered why they felt so hot.

Chapter Three

For birthdays at Miss Laker's the girls were allowed the celebration of a cake, with candles, paid for by the parents. Tam surveyed her seventeenth birthday cake impatiently, knowing it was nearly the summer holidays, wondering what Papa had bought her. Mama had sent her gift to the school and it was a new dress, white silk with pretty ribbons around the neck. Miss Laker had eyed it disapprovingly and said she could not of course wear it until she got home. But Tam tried it on in her room and the other girls said it was beautiful. Even Celia said grudgingly it looked well.

'I wish I could put my hair up,' Tam said.

'You're not out yet,' objected Celia.

'Let's try it,' said Amanda, and they swept her hair back and up, fastening it with pins, and Tam pirouetted in her new dress, feeling quite grown up.

'Listen,' whispered Amanda the next day, 'Miss Laker is going away two days *before* the holiday. Her sister is ill.'

Tam sat, digesting this news. Miss Laker always superintended their departure, standing near the door as each girl left, seeing she was properly dressed. But now . . .

'Put my hair up again,' she said to Amanda as the time came, and the girls saw she was wearing her new dress.

'The other mistresses will tell,' said Elizabeth.

'Never mind.' And Tam sat while they pinned her hair, then covered it with a cloak with hood. She wanted to surprise Papa, to run to him as a grown-up young lady. Grown-up, like Mama. How he would admire her.

She waited and Celia, posted as look-out, ran up to her. 'The coach is here,' she hissed, and Tam, holding her cloak around her, ran quickly down the stairs. Out to the coach where she let the hood fall, threw the cloak back, and halted in disappointed shock. 'Where is Papa?' she asked.

'He couldn't come, Miss Tam,' said John Dexter. 'He has a business appointment with Mr Waring.'

She scrambled into the coach, hearing a mistress call behind her. She felt sick with disappointment, as she watched Celia get in behind her.

'Papa never makes appointments for the days he meets us,' she said as they drove home.

'No, Miss Tam, Mr Waring came to see him, unexpected like. Your father said he was sorry.'

The coach rumbled up to Cherry Trees, and still there was no sign of Papa. She wanted to show him her finery, her hair . . . and if she once took it down she'd never get it back again. She kissed Juliet absent-mindedly, let John take her trunk to her room, waited till he'd gone before walking down again.

But Papa's study door was closed. From inside came the rumble of voices, and she had to wait another half an hour till the visitor had gone.

She sat in the parlour: a pleasant room, with its comfortable chairs with faded covers, and a faint smell of pot-pourri mingling with scents from the flowers. Annabel always insisted that flowers be put in every room whether she were there or not. She heard the voices again, louder now, the door opening, steps. And then Papa was with her, coming to her side, but she did not move.

'I'm sorry, Tam, I could not meet you. I had a visitor.'

'So I heard.' She sat waiting, hoping he would notice her finery.

'It was Charles Waring. He brings sad news. John Waring – his father – is ill.'

'Really?' Tam asked politely.

'John Waring is a good friend of mine.'

She could no longer keep up her reserve. 'I'm sorry,' she said. 'Though I've never met Mr Waring.'

'No,' his face clouded a little. 'We don't meet many local people socially, do we?'

'We don't meet any, Papa – ' she stood up now, her emotions churned by disappointment into bravado. 'Would you not be happier with someone who stayed with you, and worked with you, and entertained? I would – ' she broke off, appalled at her daring.

He turned away to the window. It was raining now, and the canal was covered with little round circles like coins thrown into the water. He said nothing and, emboldened, she went on. 'Other people have friends to the house, visitors, we have no one.'

He moved a little and when he spoke his voice held pain, 'Aren't you happy, Tam?'

'Oh, Papa, you know how I hate Miss Laker's.'

'But young ladies have to go to school, Tam. It is fitting.'

'I wish I were a boy,' she said hotly. 'Then I could ride down the wharf every day, whether Mama was here or not.' She did not want Mama here all the time, she wanted to take her place, and she was sad that he did not understand. 'I'll soon be home, Papa,' she persisted. 'And then I shall do as I please.'

'Yes, of course.' But he looked doubtful.

She took a step forward. 'Papa, look at me. I am quite grown-up now.'

'So you are indeed,' he said. 'And quite surprisingly like your Mama. I can see you'll be breaking a number of hearts in the years to come. I wish you could have met Charles Waring.'

But she did not want to meet Charles Waring. It was her father's love she needed, and the loss, real or imagined, would stay with her for many years.

'Now, let me see, where is the birthday gift I have for you?' And he pretended forgetfulness, still treating her like a child, while she fumed impatiently.

But at last she was able to open the little box, and inside was a gold locket. She opened it and saw the space for a keepsake. 'You must give me your likeness, Papa,' she said. 'I'll wear it always.'

'No, no, Tam. I have no likeness.'

'A lock of hair then.'

'I haven't much hair now. No, Tam, the locket is for your future husband.' He sighed a little. 'It won't be long before you find that husband, I'm thinking.'

But she threw her arms around his neck and cried, 'No, Papa, I don't want a husband. Only you.'

When Tam was home Papa always went to the wharf in the mornings, saving the afternoons for their walks. But the next day Tam was up at six, and she dressed carefully in her riding habit before going down to breakfast.

'Good morning, Papa,' she said.

'Why, good morning, Tam, you're up early. Are you going riding?'

'Yes, Papa.'

'I am going to the wharf. Then we can walk this afternoon.'

'Take me with you to the wharf, Papa.' she said.

He hesitated. 'Your Mama wouldn't like it.'

'But Mama wouldn't know.' Her mother's spells at home had grown less with the years, only at Christmas could they be sure she would be with them. 'Besides, I aim to work with you when I leave school, so I can start learning now,' she said.

'You're a minx, Tam. Very well, but don't tell Mama.'

So they rode together to the wharf before the rest of the house was astir, and Tam strove to look like a business partner. At the wharf she dismounted and went with him to the little wooden shed that was his office, where the flyboat steerers waited for directions.

'Now, Joe,' said Papa. 'I went over to Rugby yesterday, and there's a load of wood to go to their company in London.' He spread out his map and worked out the route. 'There are ribbons to take down, not a full load, but better than nothing.'

'Yes, Mr Calder.'

'And Will, a load of flour for Warwick. See it's well sheeted up, it looks like rain. Tom, stone from the quarry for Fenny.'

And so it went on. The flyboats departed, the steerers' wives and children waving goodbye before returning to their homes, then passengers began arriving for the packets. Out on the wharf other boats were loading as always, pulling in, going out. Tam loved it all: the bustling activity, the

22

smells, the shouting and the constant echo of splashing water.

They went to eat in an inn beside the water, and again Tam felt very grown-up to be sitting here with Papa. Mama, she knew, would frown upon her being at an inn, and this gave her greater pleasure. In the afternoon they rode to the quarry, where Papa enquired about loads of stone for other areas. It was a wonderful day. They rode back tired and happy. And as they entered Cherry Trees Tam saw a black-clad figure inside. 'Papa,' that's Abby,' she whispered.

And Celia came to meet them. 'Where have you been?' she asked. 'Mama is back.'

Tam slipped up to her room and quickly changed. But she did not see Annabel till dinner, when she glided in smelling of violets and roses, dressed in a silk gown. And Tam, wearing her new dress, felt gauche beside her. Annabel kissed Tam and asked how she did.

Tam pulled away from her scented bosom. 'I am well,' she said ungraciously. 'Thank you for your gift, Mama.'

'It looks fine,' said Annabel carelessly.

And then they went into the dining room and Mama was talking to Papa with hardly a word to spare for her daughters. Tam felt that, after her enjoyable experience of this day, it was hardly to be borne that she was treated like a child again, to be seen and not heard. She could not bear the looks Papa gave to Mama, so she said, loudly, 'There are a number of new boats on the wharf now.'

Annabel, silenced at last, looked at her horrified. 'You have been to the wharf again, Tam?'

'Yes. Why not, Mama? I am older now, I would not play with the boat-children or roll in the mud.'

'What purpose does it serve, your going to the wharf?'

'I like the boats, Mama, and when I am home for good I shall work with Papa.' Tam's voice was triumphant.

There was an appalled silence. 'Jamie,' Annabel said, 'I am amazed.'

And for once Papa answered back. 'Why so, Annabel?'

'Letting my daughter go to the wharf.'

'I see no harm, Annabel.'

'My daughter,' said Annabel, 'is not to be a boatwoman, Jamie.'

And her peace-loving father retorted, 'Then you should stay and see to your daughter, madam. You go away, you take no heed of what they do, any of them. In short, you fly your own kite but frown on your daughter wanting to do the same.'

Annabel stood as if struck. 'I will not have it, Jamie.'

'And I will not refuse to take her, Annabel.'

'You are treating her as if she were a boy – '

'If I had a son then I would be taking him to the boats, yes. But I don't have a son, Annabel.' There was reproach in his voice, and Tam applauded her father for at last fighting Mama. But he lost, as he was bound to. Annabel refused to let them come home again, except at Christmas, when she was there. Tam argued and battled, but Annabel was adamant.

23

'But I can come home, can't I, Mama?' Celia asked, and her mother pondered.

'You might,' she said, 'but it's hardly worth the trouble of sending the carriage just for one.'

'But, Mama,' cried Celia, outraged. 'I've done nothing.'

'Well, there it is, you both stay,' said Annabel. 'And not another word, I beg.'

And now Celia's long-standing envy of Tam was fanned into definite enmity. She was happy enough at school, but not to be allowed home in the holidays was so unfair it was unbearable. She blamed Tam, and the girls went back to Miss Laker's arguing bitterly.

Six months later Papa wrote: 'John Waring is dead, and I am sorry, for he was a good man and a good employer, and I needed him in my fight.' What fight, Papa? Tam asked silently. 'He has two sons, Geoffrey and Charles, and now Geoffrey inherits the weaving business, and I suppose the canal shares, which is a pity, I think, for he does not seem strong enough to battle for what we need, looks a bit foppish that young gentleman, over fond of the ladies. And of course, as long as his father was alive he could influence Sir William with the canal troubles. But Geoffrey's the eldest, so it had to be, I suppose – ' and Tam fretted that she was not home.

When, just after her eighteenth birthday, she was called to Miss Laker's office, she was excited, thinking it would be the long awaited summons home. Amanda Fotheringay had already left, with promises to write, but Annabel was, as always, vague about the date they would finish school.

'I have heard from your mother,' Miss Laker told her, peering through her pince-nez. 'She wishes you to go for a year to an establishment in Belgium. There you will be finished, made ready to come out.'

'Oh.' Tam knew better than to argue with Miss Laker. 'And Celia, will she come too?'

'Not till next year.'

'So you'll be left alone then,' Tam muttered angrily to Celia. 'I don't think Mama wants us home at all, she makes any excuse to keep us away.'

'No, because when we do go, she'd have to stay and launch us into society,' Celia said wisely. 'So she's putting it off as long as possible.'

'Oh, it's monstrous. I don't want to go to Belgium. I want to go home. Faith, I'm eighteen now, I'll be nearly twenty when I do get home. That's if Mama ever allows us out, I think she plans to keep us shut up like mad people.'

'Oh hush,' said Celia. 'I confess I'd like a year in Belgium.'

Tam wrote an impassioned letter to her father, but he did not answer. She went home before going to Belgium and was surprised to see how old he looked. Never a tall man, he was now quite stooped – or was it that she'd grown? – and his hair was quite white. Why, Tam thought, horror struck. He must be sixty. She had never thought of her parents getting old, and she fretted anew at the wasted years spent away.

It was spring, and the cherry trees were in flower. Looking at their rich redness and the meadows of gold where the buttercups grew, and the clear waters of the canal, Tam wanted to cry with love for it all.

'I don't want to go to Belgium,' she muttered.

'A year will soon pass, Tam,' said Papa. 'And Mama would like you to have the advantage of a year in Belgium.'

Always Mama. The old antagonism returned. Would she never win? She wondered why none of them ever went to see Mama act. The nearest they came to her world was when she brought programmes from Drury Lane. Otherwise, Tam thought, crossly, I'd never believe she was an actress at all. Though where else would she be?

'You're quiet, Papa. Is everything all right?'

'Yes, of course, Tam.'

She stared at him quizzically. He was usually so enthusiastic about his latest venture, packet boats or fly-boats or whatever. Now he said nothing, and when she asked him to take her to the wharf he shook his head.

'Mama would not approve,' he said.

'But I shall come with you next year when I'm home,' she argued. 'So tell me about everything, Papa.'

'What a very headstrong young lady you are,' Papa said, with a ghost of a smile.

'Are the boats doing well? What are you carrying now?' she asked.

'Soldiers,' he said.

'Soldiers? But I thought . . . Have you no other loads, Papa? Was it the bad winter?'

'Yes, it was bad, the boats couldn't run, though I had to pay the men.'

'But that's over now. Is it what you said about the silk weaving? Does that affect you?'

'Chilverton is a silk town.'

She had never seen him so downcast. She put her strong young arms around him and hugged him. 'Everything is going to be all right now,' she said. 'The winter's over, maybe the silk weaving will improve . . .' and as he didn't answer, she repeated, 'Won't it?' uncertainly.

He didn't smile. 'Yes, Tam. Except – '

'Except what, Papa? Papa, tell me what is worrying you.'

'The old problem, Tam. We had men of vision who built the canals, we need men of vision to make them into a countrywide network, as they do in Europe, easy for boats – and ships – to travel from coast to coast.'

'Can't they be made to see this, Papa?'

'I fear not. They are limited to the needs of their own little piece, they cannot see that England is changing and that they must change with it. We must have a uniform policy or England's trade will pass us by. That way we need not fear competition.'

'What other competition could there be, Papa?'

'There is this new steam-engine.'

She said nothing, for she knew nothing about it. She patted his hand.

He smiled ruefully. 'Perhaps I worry too much,' he said. 'It comes of being too much alone. Sometimes a man needs someone to share his misgivings.'

25

'You'll have me next year,' Tam repeated. 'Because I shall work with you, you know that.'

He smiled sadly. 'You've always been like a son to me,' he said. 'Strange that, when you think . . .'

Tam did not think it strange at all.

She went to Belgium, chaperoned by Miss White, the English mistress at Madame Lefevre's establishment. And it was on the ferry that Tam discovered young men, or rather perhaps young men discovered her. They were walking along the deck and were passed by two young dandies, who both stared boldly into Tam's eyes. Tam surprised, stared back, and the young men made as if to stop. Miss White, horrified, pulled Tam's arm. 'Whatever are you doing?' she hissed. 'You were *looking* at those gentlemen, Tamarisk. Where is your modesty?'

Where indeed, wondered Tam, and as they returned, her eyes were cast down. But she glanced upwards and sideways as they passed, though her face was quite impassive, her arms folded in front as demure as a nun. Tam was learning.

She settled in another, foreign, Miss Laker's, where she had to speak in French, and was taught how to sit, to move, to dress, taught manners of good society, which she bore with ill grace. The girls whispered here too, but her French was not sufficient for her to understand their innuendo, nor did she make any effort to comprehend. The days slid by one after the other, each marked carefully on her calendar, each meaning nothing to her except one day nearer returning home. When the girls were allowed out, to go to church on Sundays, Tam, not being a Roman Catholic, did not go with them, but stayed, fretting, under Miss White's eagle eye. There were no other English girls at Madame Lefevre's, so Tam felt very much the outsider. So she marked her calendar and waited.

It was too far to go home for the summer holidays, Mama had said, but Tam was surprised at first, and then alarmed, when she did not get any letters from Papa. She knew he did not find it easy to write even now, she had seen him poring over his books, a frown on his brow, as he struggled with the pen. But he had always written before . . . She confided her worries to Miss White, and was pleased when the mistress, who did go home to England, came back with a letter from her father.

'You called at my home?' Tam asked, touched with this concern. 'How very kind.' She opened her letter.

'My dear Tam,' her father wrote. 'I hope this finds you well. There is much to tell you about the boats, and much I should have told you before this, but I will wait now till you come home, you are young and strong, and have as much, perhaps more, courage than many men. You will need it.' Then some lines were crossed out, and when the letter started again there were many smudgings and blots making it almost unreadable. Puzzled, for this was so unlike her neat, tidy father, she carried on.

'There will be much for you to do, Tam, in the years ahead, and I hope and pray you will be equal to the task. I fear he is out to get me. Take care of yourself. I remain, Your loving father.'

And then there was a postscript and this, unlike the letter, was carefully printed, as though he had painstakingly forced his hand to make these words so clear because they were important. 'KEEP THE BOATS RUNNING. KEEP MY CANAL OPEN.' it said.

Tam studied the missive in growing bewilderment. What did he mean? Who was out to get him? She was worried. Something was wrong. She must go to him, immediately. She went to Madame Lefevre, poured out her worries, showed her the letter. Madame was sympathetic but unable to act.

'I cannot send you home unless your parents instruct me,' she said.

'Was my father worried, upset?' Tam demanded of Miss White. But that lady – who had seen her father for one half hour only – said that he certainly had said nothing to her. Perhaps it was just a temporary worry . . .?

Tam returned to her room, fuming. I'll go myself. I'll run away, she thought. And stopped, struck; she couldn't go home, she didn't know the way. She knew they had taken the boat to Ostend, where a carriage awaited them, she knew the name of the nearest town – but that was all. She hadn't the faintest idea of how to get into that town, much less out of it. She hadn't bothered to learn French as she should have done, and might not make herself understood. And finally, she had no money. She was furious that she, a grown-up young lady, should be as helpless as the tiniest child. Unable to travel without a chaperone, unable to walk alone, forbidden to go to the wharf, being a young lady seemed being a fool.

'Just wait,' she vowed, through gritted teeth. 'Just wait till I'm home, I'll have no more of this . . . I'll have my freedom just as if I were a man.'

'You'll be home again quite soon,' Miss White consoled, seeing her distress. 'Only a few more months.'

More months . . . Tam's tempestuous nature fumed at the prospect of more months of restraint. Her ready temper flared, her eyes shone green sparks, her French became more eloquent as she raged at any girl who crossed her. She was not surprised when, in early September, Madame herself sent for her. She went to her office, knocked, and was bade to enter, where she stood, defiantly.

Madame surveyed her for a long moment, then said, 'Sit down.'

Tam sat and waited, hoping she was about to be expelled.

'My child,' Madame spoke in English, and this was so unusual that Tam was alarmed. 'I have bad news for you.'

'What is it?' asked Tam.

'There has been illness in the family,' said Madame.

'Juliet?' asked Tam, jumping to her feet.

'No, but you will have to return home,' Madame said. 'It is your Papa.'

'Papa. I knew it. What is it? Is he ill?' Tam ran towards Madame, clutched her arm, and that lady took hold of her hand.

'I am so sorry,' Madame said quietly. 'Your Papa is dead.'

27

PART TWO

1829–1832

And you shall wander hand in hand in Summer's wonderland
Alfred Noyes

Chapter One

When Tam reached Chilverton from Belgium, the funeral was over.

She had not cried when Madame had told her the news, she had been too shocked; there had been a hard lump in her chest that was almost a pain and would not be moved. She was tormented by thoughts of Papa dying alone, perhaps needing someone . . . perhaps wanting her, Tam, and she was not there. She felt she had let him down, and anguished that maybe he didn't know how much she loved him. And that now he'd never know.

She travelled with a chaperone to the coast, was put on the boat, then there was an inn, and another coach, and still she did not cry. And here she was in Chilverton, tired and weary.

A figure moved from the shadows and she saw it was Abby. 'I have a hackney coach here, Miss Tam,' she said, and Tam was angry that they had not thought to send the carriage. Did no one care now Papa was dead? But she was pleased to see a familiar figure after so long, and when Abby said, 'Would you like to see the grave, Miss Tam?' she nodded wordlessly.

They walked into the quiet churchyard, and she stood by that new mound, still covered with flowers, and somehow it seemed so small . . . Why had people always seen Papa as small, in life as in death? Only then, as she turned to Abby, did she cry for the loss of the father she loved. Abby held her in her arms, and led her to the coach, and when all her tears were shed Tam had gone home to Mama and her sisters, with resolve in her eyes. Papa would be remembered. She, Tam, would see to that. She knew what he wanted, and she would carry out his wishes.

She greeted her family, noting how Juliet had grown in the past year. She would be sixteen now, and her oval face, sad and serious, was quite beautiful; her dark hair was combed straight back with no heed of the fashion of the day for curls and ringlets. Celia was as plain as ever, and no amount of crimped hair would ever make her different, Tam thought, ungraciously. She studiously avoided her mother, saying she wanted to retire early, she was tired. So she went up to her room under the eaves and watched the leaves falling from the trees like great brown tears. They matched her mood: summer was over; the perpetual summers of childhood were gone.

A knock at the door broke her reverie, and she called, 'Come in,' hoping it wasn't Mama, she didn't want to face her yet. Because in her heart she blamed her mother for leaving Papa alone, for sending them away, and all the old animosity returned in full force; it would be hard to forgive her now.

Abby came in with a tray.

'I'm not hungry,' Tam said.

'Come now, Miss Tam, you must keep your strength up. There's much to be done.'

'Yes, I suppose so.' Tam looked at the hot soup, the meat and vegetable dishes and said, 'Thank you, Abby. I'll be down early in the morning.'

'Aye, you'll feel better then,' Abby said.

'I – don't want to see anyone else tonight,' Tam said. 'I – I'm going to bed.'

'Very well, I'll tell them,' Abby said equably. 'Get a good night's rest, and we'll see you in the morning.'

Tam sipped at the soup, and realised to her surprise, that she was indeed hungry. She ate sitting by the window, watching the boats hurrying by, the women wrapped in shawls, the canal whipped into grey waves by the rising wind. Whatever happens, she thought, I'll always have the canal, they can't take that away from me.

The girls sat in a line in their drawing room, dressed in heavy black. Behind them the window looked over the lawns, sloping down to the water, and the sun was shining today; voices of merriment came from a packet boat travelling to Coventry. They sat silent, waiting for Annabel to speak.

'Girls.' Annabel seemed nervous as she brushed her elegant, upswept hair with one hand, and let her eyes rest on her daughters. 'I fear I have bad news.'

She stood up, and her black dress showed her figure, with its still tiny waist, to perfection. She paced to and fro while the girls waited patiently for their cue. Annabel stopped and said dramatically, 'Your father has left us penniless.'

The girls looked up, startled. Tam opened her lips as though to speak, but said nothing. Juliet seemed quite unmoved. It was Celia who asked practically, 'What do you mean, Mama?'

'I mean,' said Annabel, a little annoyed at this downright bringing back to earth, 'precisely what I say, Celia, we are penniless.'

The girls, who had no understanding of money, strove to take this in. Tam said, 'But Papa owned the packet boats, we have the house – '

'I saw the lawyer,' said Annabel. 'He told me that when your father died so tragically, he was already ruined.'

'But the house – ' cried Tam, wildly. 'Cherry Trees – '

'The house,' said Annabel, a little waspishly, 'though bought with my dowry, has been so heavily mortgaged that we shall be obliged to leave. The boats are sold to pay his debts, all but one he bought for me as a gift.'

The girls blinked, still hardly taking it in, knowing their mother's

30

fondness for dramatics. Annabel went on, a clenched hand at her brow.

'We spent money, true, but your father never breathed a word to me of any troubles. Instead, he mortgaged the house . . . He didn't think he was going to die.'

Now they stared in shocked surprise.

'But Papa had a thriving business. How was he ruined?' Tam asked.

'I have no idea,' said Annabel.

'We should have been with him,' Tam cried. 'Poor Papa, having to bear all this alone . . . none of us here except Juliet. Did you know nothing, Juliet?'

'No. Papa never talked to me about the boats.'

Tam felt almost gratified, she was the only one in Papa's confidence, and yet even she had failed him at the end by not being with him. 'Well, at least we know now why he was pushed into such a small grave,' she said bitterly.

Annabel drew herself up, affronted. 'What do you mean, a small grave? What else could I do, Tam, please tell me? That small grave is not yet paid for.'

'But, Mama,' cried Celia, outraged. 'Do you mean that I shan't be able to go to Belgium, as Tam did? That's unfair.'

'I know it,' replied Annabel. 'And there's nothing I wanted more for you. But it's impossible now. Ah – ' as there came a knock at the door. 'That will be Abby. Come in.'

'I couldn't come sooner, Miss Bel. I was busy, being all alone – '

'Alone? Where are the servants?' asked Tam, remembering that it was Abby who had met her off the coach, who had brought her a tray . . .

'Gone,' said Annabel. 'I have no money to pay their wages,' and this statement, more than anything else, brought home to the girls that they were indeed penniless.

'Sit down, Abby,' Annabel said. 'You must be here to listen to our plans.'

'What plans?' asked Celia. 'What are we going to do?'

'That is what we are here to talk about,' said Annabel. 'We have nothing but one passenger boat.'

'Surely your family will help us now, Mama?' Celia said.

'They will not. Even if I asked them, which I will not.'

'Then they're heartless,' said Celia, almost crying.

'Heartless indeed,' agreed Mama. 'I have often thought so. No, we have to manage alone.'

And Tam had to admire her mother then. If the world fell about her ears Annabel would accept it stylishly.

'Does Papa have no family?' she asked.

'They quarrelled with him for the same reason as did my own – for marrying me,' said Annabel. 'Anyway, they are quite poor, they could do nothing.'

Tam felt impatient. All these wasted years they had been stuck at Miss Laker's when they could have been here, helping . . . She moved suddenly

31

to the window. She saw the green meadows she loved so much, the sparkling water, a narrow boat with its patient horse. She heard Annabel say, 'I am an actress, first and foremost, I named you girls from Shakespeare's plays . . .' She was acting again.

'Why can't you take us all to London? ' put in Celia, eagerly.

'Because of Juliet's weakness,' answered Annabel. 'Dr Simmons says it would be fatal to take her away from the country air.'

'Then what are we going to do?' Celia's voice held panic.

'We – ell,' Annabel began, and Tam, turning to look at her mother, saw her uncertainty. *Mama.* Was it possible? She walked back to them her own mind made up, resolve shining in her eyes and voice. 'We have a boat,' she said. 'We must live on it.'

'Live on a boat?' asked Celia, horrified. 'With the common people? You must be out of your mind.'

'We have little choice,' said Tam. 'We have no home.'

'I don't want to be buried alive on a stupid boat,' cried Celia. 'I want to go to Belgium as you did. I want to go to parties and balls, to meet nice people, and young gentlemen. I don't want to live on a horrid *boat.*'

'We shall have to do something to earn a living,' said Tam.

'Live on a boat?' Annabel said. 'How very extraordinary. I would never even have thought of that, Tam. And yet . . .' She looked thoughtful. 'Yet it might be an idea – temporarily, of course. What do you think, Abby?'

'I confess I don't particularly want to live on a packet boat,' said that worthy. 'Are you planning to run the services? You and the young ladies? A lady like yourself, Miss Bel?'

'Well, I'm not sure about that,' said Annabel. 'I suppose it is hardly suitable.'

'Oh no.' Celia's voice choked with emotion. 'Whom would we meet? Whom would we marry?'

'Pshaw, marriage is highly overrated,' said Annabel. 'Look what it did to me, brought me to ruin.' She rose again with an air. 'Do you have a better plan, Celia? If so, tell it now.'

'I am sure I could ask some friends to take me in. Or I could be a governess.'

'A governess, pah,' said the independent Annabel. 'A drab, down-trodden servant, nothing more.'

'But respectable,' said Celia, primly. 'Which living on a boat is not.'

They waited for Juliet to speak and all looked with fondness at the baby of the family. She said now, 'Oh, I think it's a perfectly lovely idea.' She clasped her hands together. 'You've all been away,' she went on. 'I've been here all my life. I've met the boaters, and they're such good people.'

'Good people?' echoed Celia, aghast. 'I heard they were gipsies.'

'Oh yes, some of them are. Perhaps that's why their boats are such gay colours. But they are good, too. They know so much about the country, and they have such happy times. Do you know, they only go on land when they tie up at a waterside inn, and there they meet each other, boys and girls, I mean, arrange to get married. They dance, and play melodeons, and have such fun.'

'Juliet,' her mother said weakly. 'You haven't been inside those inns, surely.'

'Yes, Mama, occasionally. They are very nice.'

Abby gave a snort. 'What do you expect, Miss Bel? With you always gallivanting off to London?'

'I'd love to live on a boat,' Juliet ended dreamily.

The family stared with some perplexity, yet could not but be moved by her words. They all feared Juliet would not live long, they could not bear not to give her all she wanted. Tam was quick to seize the advantage point.

'I don't see why we should not run a packet boat,' she said.

'Well, where would we sleep?' asked Annabel, practically.

'The boatpeople sleep on their boats,' said Juliet.

'There's only a tiny cabin,' protested Celia.

'But it's all arranged so delightfully,' Juliet said. 'The table is made into a bed, boards pull down, it can sleep six or even seven.'

'Mama, I must have my own room,' Celia cried, outraged.

'Hush, ours is a packet boat, and bigger,' said Annabel. 'Though I admit we could hardly share, all four of us, with Abby and John. No, Tam, we cannot run a packet boat until we have somewhere else to live.'

'We could run it in the daytime and somehow make do at night,' said Tam.

Annabel pulled a face at the thought of making do, and Celia was horrified. Tam stared at the two impatiently.

'Well, all right, but what are we going to live on?' she demanded.

There was a pause, before Annabel replied. 'I have some jewellery. Not a lot, but I could sell it, and the proceeds should last us the winter. Then we'll have to see . . . But will it not be cold on the boat, Tam? How will Juliet survive?'

'Oh, there is a steam-pipe on the packet boats,' said Juliet. 'I don't understand how it works exactly, something to do with the stove, I think. It is quite warm in the kitchen.'

'And the stove needs coal,' said Abby, darkly.

'Well, goodness me,' said Annabel. 'All these boats carry coal, I've seen them myself. I'm sure we need never go without coal. Well, is that decided then, are we to move to the boat, for the time being? But we'll have to go as soon as possible, with no servants, we can't keep this big house going.'

'As I understand it,' said Abby, 'if we don't go, we shall be put out.'

'H'm.' Annabel sniffed, then stared thoughtfully at the little dumpy figure in black. 'We must keep costs down to a minimum. We'll need a man, indeed, we have the horses . . .'

'Yes, Miss Bel?' asked Abby, darkly, knowing already what would come.

'I wondered – your husband, Abby. I know he's been butler here, and I know it would be very different for him, but – ' Annabel's voice trailed away as she looked at the formidable little figure before her. Both knew

33

that a lot depended on whether John Dexter would condescend to lower himself from a respectable post as butler to a vagabond of a waterman. Neither thought it odd that the decision was put to Abby rather than to John himself.

At length Abby spoke. 'I've been with you all your life, Miss Bel,' she said. 'And I've watched you go into some harebrained schemes. You've always been wilful, and nothing I can say will stop you. But you're right when you say Miss Juliet must have country air, and you're right when you say you have no money. And – you have no offers for Drury Lane or anywhere else at the moment. I don't see what else you can do. So for that reason I'll be willing to go with you, and I don't doubt John will go also.'

Annabel bestowed her most charming smile.

'But you'll have to get permission, Miss Bel, to use the wharf and so on,' Abby continued.

'Indeed? From whom?'

'One of the Waring men, I imagine.'

'And who, pray, are the Waring men?'

'Mr Geoffrey is a very important man round here. He's a master merchant for the ribbon weavers, and seems to own part of the canal company. He has a big warehouse in London, and a town house. He lives in Chilverton with his mother.'

'I have to go to London to sell my jewellery,' said Annabel. 'So I'll call on Mr Waring then. You, Tam, shall come with me, and, of course, Abby.'

'Not me?' asked Celia, disappointedly.

'Not this time, Celia, I haven't the money for the fares.' Celia pouted, and Annabel went on, 'There is a new fast mailcoach I believe, starting from Chilverton at five in the morning. I confess I've never made the journey like this before, but no doubt we shall enjoy it. Well,' as Abby looked about to explode at the indignity of travelling by mailcoach, 'where is my copy of Shakespeare?'

'Mama,' Tamarisk said thoughtfully, 'if you named my sisters after Mr Shakespeare's characters, how is it I was named after a tree?'

Annabel started, and looked at her eldest daughter. 'That's quite another story,' she said, and hurriedly left the room.

Alone, the girls stared at each other.

'I can't bear to think of the life we'll have,' said Celia. 'And Mama's bought us only one black dress each. We'll soon be in rags.' She sniffed audibly.

'Don't cry,' said Juliet, gently. 'We'll be all right, you'll see.'

'I think Mama's relatives should help us,' Celia persisted. 'I cannot understand why she married Papa, she never spent much time with him.'

'You shouldn't criticise Papa,' said Juliet, troubled. 'He was the best man in the world.

'I know, but he shouldn't have done this to us,' Celia said bitterly. 'And, just when I was to go to Belgium, I can't, because we have no money. Oh, it's monstrous – ' she was crying now. 'And don't tell me money isn't everything because it is. I want to marry someone in good society – '

'Oh, don't prate on about marriage,' Tam said impatiently. 'You'll meet someone, somewhere.'

'Where?' wailed Celia. 'If we cannot get invitations to parties and rich houses, how can we get married? And what else can we do? Except be drab spinster governesses or live on a horrid boat.'

Her voice echoed through the still afternoon, and Tam walked to the window. The grey skies were clearing a little, a fitful gleam of sun showed itself low on the horizon 'It won't be so bad,' she said, but Celia had gone.

'It's dreadful to think Papa lost all his money,' Tam said to Juliet. 'Do you think it worried him to – ' she could not bring herself to say the fatal word.

'It may have helped,' Juliet said. 'But he was over sixty, Tam, much older than Mama.'

'Was he ill for long? Why wasn't I told?' Tam asked.

'No, it was quite sudden, he just collapsed, in the evening. We sent immediately for the physician, but when he got here it was too late. He said it was his heart.'

'And he'd been quite well until then?' Tam probed.

Juliet pondered. 'He hadn't been himself for some time, but it was such a gradual thing I didn't notice . . . I wish I had.'

'Don't worry, Juliet. It was no one's fault,' Tam said. Except Mama's. She should have known. She paced up and down. 'But how did he lose his money? He was prosperous, he was always cheerful. How could it be?' She felt she could not grasp this thing that had happened to them. That this dear old house, with its creeeper-covered walls, its mullioned windows, its attics with the delicious smell of apples stored there from the orchards, the trees in the distance that had once been part of the Forest of Arden and that filled the air with birdsong . . . All this would be lost. Surely something could be done. She stopped pacing, but she was still restless, her nerves strung up to a pitch that would not let her be still.

'Where is our boat moored?'

'Let's go down to the water, I'll show you,' Juliet offered, and wrapping their pelisses round them they stepped on to the terrace, to the lawn, and thence to the canal. The sun was still struggling with the clouds, and occasionally shafts of light would break through. A narrow boat approached, its horse walking briskly along the towpath, as though it sensed it was near its night's lodging, the woman at the tiller wrapped in a heavy shawl. She called something to Juliet in a dialect Tam could hardly understand.

'Yes, we're coming aboard,' Juliet answered. 'Wait for us.'

The woman called, 'Whoa,' to the horse, and turned to the man who stood balancing on a plank that ran the length of the boat, over the empty hold. 'Hold out,' she ordered, and he picked up a pole, pushed it with all his might against the towpath side, and the boat slid towards the girls. Juliet picked up her skirts and stepped aboard. Tam, after a startled look, followed suit.

They stood in the tiny area next to the tiller, and while Juliet talked to the boatwoman, Tam looked into the cabin. It was incredibly tiny and amazingly clean, brasses gleamed, cupboards shone with the same gaily painted pictures as on the outside. A small coal range was on the left, with a crockery shelf next to it. Every inch of space was utilised, with hinged cupboards which fell back to make the beds, as Juliet had said, and cleverly contrived shelves. A brass horn hung just below the cabin slide, and a painted flowered water-can stood on the little roof.

Tam marvelled at the ease with which the woman steered the boat round the many bends of the canal, never once asking her husband to help and guide her, or pretending to be helpless when a man approached as Miss Laker had taught. This was a woman working equally with a man and, indeed, giving him orders. Tam was thoughtful.

'Do you work for a company?' she asked.

'No, we're Number Ones,' replied the woman, and Tam turned to Juliet for translation.

'Number Ones are owners of their boats,' said Juliet.

'Have you been on the canal long?' asked Tam.

'Some years now. My man was a navvy up at Braunston Puddle, and we had enough put by to buy us own boat.' The woman steered effortlessly under a humpbacked bridge, and Tam wondered if she dare ask a more personal question.

'Is it,' she questioned tentatively, 'a good living?'

The woman shrugged. 'Can be. When we get us loads. We're empty now. We carry coal, but not from 'ere, 'e won't have that.'

Who was *he*? 'Why not?' asked Tam.

The woman pursed her lips but did not answer directly. Tam wondered if she was afraid, and if so of whom?

'An' loading at this wharf ain't easy, they charge high rates.'

'Do they? Who?' asked Tam.

'Them as owns it, old buggers,' said the woman.

'Did you know my father?' asked Tam. 'James Calder?'

'Aye.'

'And was he – having trouble recently?'

The woman looked at her and away. 'Mebbe,' she said.

Tam opened her mouth, but Juliet shook her head, and began to talk about more casual matters. And as the woman leaned forward to call to her children in the cabin Juliet whispered, 'Don't press her. She won't say much, not to outsiders.'

They were nearing the wharf now, and the sun was giving up the struggle and sinking into oblivion. Half a dozen boats were already moored, their horses being taken to the stables behind the inn. Women stood at their cabin doors exchanging gossip while they polished brasses or mopped paintwork. A delicious smell of hotpot rose in the air with the smoke from the tiny chimneys.

The 'Anchor' inn looked over the water, and from within came sounds of merriment and music. A girl stood outside, leaning over the rail, and

Tam gazed at her with interest. She was about the same age as herself, very slim, with a black close-fitting dress cut quite low. Around her neck was a necklace of beads, and in her ears huge gold rings. But it was to her face that Tam looked, for she was very beautiful. Black eyes flashed beneath black hair, plaited round her head, red lips curved in an oval, olive face.

Tam turned to Juliet. 'Surely she's a gipsy.'

'Yes, that's Car Boswell.'

'You sound as if you know her well.'

'I know most of the boatpeople. Anyway, everyone knows Car. She's very fond of the men, and men are very fond of her. Too much so, I warrant, she will be having a baby if she's not careful.'

'Juliet!' Tam was shocked. 'Do you *know* about such things?'

'Of course I know. Don't you?'

'Yes, but one should not speak of them, or so Miss Laker taught us.'

'I don't see why not if you know.' Juliet spoke with the genuine puzzlement of the true countrywoman, who thought the mysteries of life and death and procreation but a normal part of life. 'Look,' she said, pointing, 'our boat.'

Tam stared for a long time at the long packet boat, the windowed cabins, the open space at the rear end. She looked at the great mounted knife on the bow which meant that all must give way to the – she looked for the name, and it was there, in bright bold letters – the *Princess*.

She heard Juliet say they had better travel back while they had the chance and a boat was heading home, so they left the inn and the arrogant smiling girl on the wharf, and jumped aboard. Dusk was falling, a single star shone in the sky. Golden lamplight streamed from the open doors of the cabin. Tam thought how strange it was that until today she'd only known the world of the boats from the outside, she knew nothing of the inner workings of that world any more than she knew about men's world of business and finance. But she resolved to learn about both.

In the house, Juliet ran upstairs, but Tam lingered in the cool hall. It was a still evening. From the parlour, where she and Papa had stood so often to look at the flowers, came sounds of voices. Mama's clear tones, and a deeper, richer voice, a gentleman's voice.

'Come now, Miss Tamarisk.' Abby bustled in. 'Prepare yourself for supper. Your Mama has a visitor.'

'Who is it?' asked Tam, but Abby had already gone.

And that evening Annabel did not come to supper. To every question Abby shook her head mutely. 'Your Mama's resting,' she said. 'She won't be down tonight.'

When they arrived in London, they were all bone-weary. They had been up at dawn to board the fast coach. It was a twelve-hour journey, but Annabel had said they had no money to stay overnight at an inn. So they rode, uncomfortable in the hot, straw-strewn box, and the coach creaked and jolted on its way, stopping only to change the steaming horses, and to snatch a small repast at the posting inn. They arrived in London, cramped, tired and very hungry. 'We'll take a hackney coach to my friend, Mrs Sara,' said Annabel. 'She will help us in every way.'

Annabel might have dropped the use of her title when on the stage, but she still possessed the large-hearted, grandiloquent ideas of an aristocrat. The fact that she suddenly had no money, and that her furniture and house would have to be sold to pay the pressing debts did not worry her – yet. She had been astounded when the lawyer told her she was penniless, but she was not afraid. She merely put on her grandest air to talk to him, and although she could not persuade him to forget about the money owing, she did leave the impression that she was conferring a favour in having graced the old house with her presence, even without paying. Now she shrugged her shoulders. Poverty was one of those tiresome things, a temporary setback. Her theatrical friends would help her, as she had helped them in the past.

But when they sat in Mrs Sara's elegant drawing room with its yellow satin curtains, spindle-legged chairs, and wool-worked ottomans, and while Annabel poured out her story with many a laughing gesture, they gradually became aware of a strange tension in the atmosphere. Mrs Sara did not smile, did not even offer them food, much less a place to stay the night. At last Annabel stopped talking and waited, baffled.

'I'm sorry for you, Mrs Bel,' said her friend. 'And if only I were rich I would do all I could to help. But – your husband was improvident, wasn't he?'

That seemed to be all she had to say. Annabel rose to her feet and putting on her grand manner, she held out her hand. 'I do love to tease you, Mrs Sara,' she said. 'It is true that I shall leave London temporarily, and we shall live on a boat, I wondered which would be the best tale to tell to cover my, shall we say, eccentricity? I chose to pretend I was penniless, it seemed so – dramatic. Goodbye, dear Mrs Sara, would your servant kindly call us a hackney coach?' And they had swept out, leaving the actress puzzled as to which was the truth.

Annabel was thoughtful on the way to see her next friend. So was Tam. Both had learned a short, sharp lesson. But it was Abby who said, 'We'd better see Mr Waring first, Miss Bel, hadn't we? We can't spend all the night visiting your friends.'

Annabel looked more thoughtful than ever. 'Dear me,' she said, 'I am surprised at Mrs Sara. Why, when I gave her that piano last year we were the best of friends. It seems poverty is a disgrace then, Abby.'

'It is indeed, Miss Bel,' replied Abby, drily.

'We must find somewhere to stay, Abby. Faith, but I need a tidy-up.' She straightened her large, elegant hat. 'It seems that when one is poor, one has to hurry everywhere.' She paused, pondering. 'We will say no more about having no money,' she decided. 'It is now just an eccentric idea of mine to live on a boat.' And she directed the coachman to drive to the house of Mr Waring.

'Mrs Calder, Miss Tamarisk Calder,' announced the manservant, and withdrew.

The man in the handsome carpeted room jumped to his feet as the women were ushered in. He looked first at Annabel, as people always did, glanced at Abby, solid and firm in her best black bonnet, and then turned lingering eyes to Tamarisk, who dropped her own modestly, as Miss Laker had taught.

'Mr Waring,' said Annabel, giving him her hand, stylishly. 'Thank you, we will indeed sit down,' as he gestured towards the chairs. 'We have come on a matter of business.'

'I shall, of course, be happy to do anything I can to help,' said Mr Waring. 'And may I say how very sorry I was to hear of your husband's death?'

'Thank you. But to business. I own a packet boat. Now my husband is dead, we are planning to live on it, and I understand we have to obtain your permission.'

There was silence from Mr Waring, which went on for so long that Tamarisk, sitting quietly beside her mother, allowed herself to raise her eyes and covertly study the man. He did not look like a businessman, she thought, there was an outdoor look about the tanned face and the black springy hair and even the black eyes which looked out boldly from beneath the heavy brows. His shoulders were broad under his dark blue tail-coat, his legs were long in the light twill trousers, tightly strapped beneath his shoes. At last he spoke, and his tone was incredulous.

'Live on a boat?' he asked. 'Are you sure this is what you want to do?'

'If I wasn't, I wouldn't be here,' said Annabel, tartly.

'But – '

'Now don't tell me that it is no life for a lady, I beg,' Annabel smiled. 'A lady,' she said grandly, 'should be unafraid to move among the people, Mr Waring. You *are* Mr Geoffrey Waring, I assume.'

'I know little of ladies,' said Mr Waring, and Tam jerked her head up to see a mocking light in his black eyes. 'And no, I am Charles Waring, Agent of the Canal Company, which is the general manager. Geoffrey is my elder brother, and I think it is he you should see. But he is back in Chilverton. I am here on a matter of business.'

'Dear me, all this trouble for nothing. No matter,' Annabel tossed her head and tried to stifle a yawn. 'Please explain what is this permission we have to get, and why you cannot give it?'

Charles was tapping the table with his pencil. 'Are you sure you own a boat?' he asked.

'It is hardly the sort of thing one makes a mistake about,' said Annabel, her voice tart again. 'I might be uncertain as to how many brooches I own, but a boat is not quite the same thing.'

'And were you planning to run services?' he asked.

'No,' said Annabel, and Tam, suddenly bold, broke in, 'Is there any reason why we shouldn't?'

'I'm not sure I would advise it, at the moment.'

'But why not?'

Annabel interrupted. 'Hush, Tam. Mr Waring, it is a packet boat I own,

39

but no, I am not planning to run services, simply to live on it.'

'I see.' Charles rubbed his chin, and Tam watched him closely, wondering why he seemed so against the idea.

'Where will the boat be moored? Near your house?' he asked.

'I suppose so,' Annabel nodded.

'Then that should be all right.'

'Thank you.' Annabel was gracious. 'I must be away now to visit the jeweller before he closes.'

'You are staying in London overnight?' queried Mr Waring.

Annabel dropped her eyes. 'Yes, of course. Our carriage was otherwise engaged and we must travel by mailcoach, which leaves in the morning.'

'Madam, may I ask you to accept this house as your own – if there is no other you prefer,' he added hastily.

Tam looked unhappily at her mud-spattered gown. She didn't like Mama's pretence and she didn't like Mr Waring. She wished she were home at Cherry Trees. Then she remembered that Cherry Trees was no longer her home, and her eyes grew bleak.

But Annabel was already thanking Mr Waring, accepting his offer graciously, and Tam soon found herself in a most elegant bedroom, with Abby close behind her.

'Now just remember what your Mama told us,' said Abby. 'She is going to live on the boat for fun, and people are to think she's eccentric.'

'People think,' muttered Tam. 'Who cares what people think?'

'Just as long as you know they'll all be against you,' said Abby, and departed closing the door firmly.

Tam sniffed in a most unladylike manner, as she poured water from the flowered jug and washed her hands and face, then tried, unsuccessfully, to wipe the mud from her dress. Really, being poor was most undesirable, she thought, crossly. How could anyone live in one dress . . . ?

Clean again, she wondered what to do. The bed looked inviting, but she was too hungry to sleep; it was a long time since they'd eaten. She wondered if anyone would find her a cake if she went down. Cautiously she opened the door and walked slowly down the grand staircase. All the rooms seemed to be empty. Then she saw a large sitting room with a bowl of fruit on a table. She hastened inside, closed the door and ran to the fruit, cramming grapes and succulent peaches into her mouth with abandon.

Behind her the door opened.

She gulped, swallowed, and stood for a moment composing herself. But she was not her mother's daughter for nothing, and when she turned only her heightened colour gave her away. Charles Waring stood there, his hand on the bell-rope, and he stepped forward courteously.

'Pray sit down,' he said. And, as a servant entered, 'Would you care for some refreshment, cake and wine, or a dish of tea? I am sorry I did not offer before, you must think me an ignorant boor.'

'Indeed no,' said Tam, and somewhere inside her brain registered the delicacy of his wording. Then, quickly, lest he should mistake her meaning. 'I will take a little cake and tea, thank you.'

'I expect you are tired,' he said, as the servant entered with the food.

'We travelled since daybreak,' said Tam, cautiously.

He was silent for a moment, and the black eyes were serious. Then he said, 'Forgive me – but isn't there anything else you could do?'

Tam sought for an answer. 'Mama thinks it will be fun to live on a boat – ' She broke off at the look in his eyes. He knows, she thought. He knows we're poor, and that we have nowhere to go, and, humiliated, she looked down at her mud-spattered gown.

'I live in Chilverton most of the time,' he said. 'I knew Jamie Calder. I know – his circumstances. That's why I asked if there was nothing else you could do?'

'What kind of thing had you in mind?' asked Tam, hardily.

'Well.' The black eyes were dancing again now, and she was disconcerted at his change of mood which served to keep him in control of the conversation. 'For a handsome young lady I would suggest marriage.'

'That's my sister's opinion,' Tam murmured. 'That there's nothing for a girl to do but marry.'

'But you would have married. You would have gone through all the rigmarole of the marriage market, the knocking down of the prettiest girl to the highest bidder – '

'Mr Waring!'

'I beg your pardon. But it's true, isn't it?'

Tam looked thoughtfully into the London street. This man had a strange abrasive honesty which she could not help but admire, and tried to match in her own thoughts. She had intended to work with Papa, true, and she'd seen herself walking with him to the forbidden wharf, telling Mama grandly that now she was grown she would do as she pleased. But at no time had she envisaged working because she *had* to. She had fully intended to attend all the balls and parties Mama would provide for her coming-out, even a London season if necessary. It would have been fun, knowing that she could always come back to Cherry Trees. And if Mama had suggested marriage, she would have taken pleasure in turning her down, stating that she would stay with the boats and Papa.

'Why otherwise have you been taught to play the piano and sing prettily, and dance?' Mr Waring was continuing. 'But to enchant a prospective husband. And now you are going to bury yourselves on a boat, where you'll see no one, no county people that is. And among middle-class Chilverton society there is but one eligible man.'

'You are very conceited, Mr Waring.'

He roared with laughter. 'I did not mean myself, Mistress Tamarisk, but my brother, Geoffrey. Me, I'm no catch for any girl, I am a rogue and a radical.'

Tamarisk blinked. 'I don't know anything about your being a rogue, and I don't know much about radicals.'

'We believe in democracy, Miss Tamarisk. It is 1829, time that all men were equal.'

Tamarisk studied him. 'That's an uncommon fine thing to believe,' she

41

said. 'And those who talk most about it usually end by purchasing themselves a peerage.'

He gave a delighted laugh. 'A student of human nature, by heaven. Miss Tamarisk, you intrigue me. You didn't learn that at your young ladies' establishment, I'll be bound.'

No, Tam thought bleakly. My father taught me.

'My brother is the likely catch for a young lady,' Charles was saying. 'He is handsome, has money and position. What more could a girl want?'

Tamarisk pondered. 'She might want to fall in love.'

The black eyes danced again. 'Not on your life. Love will come after marriage, her mother will tell her, after a *successful* marriage, with money and position. That's why Geoffrey is the butt of all matchmaking mothers in Chilverton.'

'You *are* conceited, Mr Waring, like all men. You think all young ladies want is to capture a man – '

'Well, isn't it?'

'If it is,' she said hotly, 'it is because men put us in that position. What can a girl do but marry? If I wanted to become a lawyer, wouldn't you be the first to stop me?'

'It would be a waste to hide that pretty face in a dull courtroom.'

He was teasing her and she was angry that he wouldn't take her seriously. 'There you go,' she cried, stamping her foot. 'A pretty face and there's an end to it. I think, when you have finished getting equality for all men, Mr Waring, you might try obtaining it for women.'

His eyes danced again. 'I will think about it, Miss Tamarisk. And will you be wanting a vote, too?'

'Why not?' she countered. 'For I will tell you something, Mr Charles Waring, I am going to work on the boats. I always intended to help my father – ' her voice faltered. 'Now I have no choice. And before you tell me not, I saw the boatpeople yesterday, women working freely with men, seeming more free that those in our position. So I'm going to work, not marry.'

He sobered. 'Of course women work, poor women have to. Pah, what do you know of life in your exclusive ladies' academy?'

He stared at her so fiercely that she was taken aback. This man had the effect of a fresh strong wing blowing and beating around her, so that she felt buffeted.

She said, with as much dignity as she could muster, 'Mama worked. She was an actress.'

'Your Mama,' said this strange young man, 'is a law unto herself. She possesses a worldly naivety that would take her to the gates of hell unscathed.'

'I assure you that I am capable of working too, Mr Waring,' Tam said, with firm dignity.

'And ruin those lily-white hands? Or will you have a maid to clean the boat for you?'

She was amazed at his sudden anger, unable to understand the reason

42

for it, not knowing that he hardly understood himself why the thought of this girl being brought so low should upset him, why he should fear for her safety.

'I need no maid,' she said in a rage. 'And I will prove it to you.' And they stared hotly at each other, both bewildered by their own anger. He was the first to break the tension.

'I'm sorry, I should not speak to you so. I told you I was unused to ladies. But surely your mother could do something?'

'An actress?' asked Tam, remembering the words of the girls at Miss Laker's. She paused and added in a low voice, 'And your advice on marriage is all very well, but we have no dowry, no portion to bring to marriage, who would want us?'

And he was silent.

But she was disarmed by his apology, and was encouraged to ask about the canals and her father's strange statement about keeping the canal open. But there came the sound of a door opening and they both turned.

It was Annabel, and she looked tired. Her huge hat was askew, her hair untidy, her pelisse muddied. But there was a triumphant look in her eyes, and she held her reticule proudly. She had obviously sold her jewels. She eyed her daughter, noted her flushed cheeks.

'Come, Tamarisk,' she said. 'We will prepare for dinner.'

And Tam was not left alone with Charles Waring again. But she was thoughtful. So it was a masculine world, was it? And she had lived in a world of women. Miss Laker had ruled her academy without a man's help; at home, Papa had to give in to Annabel, and although running his own business, had failed. Poor Papa. The feeling of protectiveness returned. *Keep my canal open.* She would do that – more, she would find out about this masculine world of business, discover how and why Papa had been ruined, who had killed him. Her head jerked up as the thought entered her mind, yet admitted it had been there all along. She knew, somehow, that someone had deliberately ruined Papa, and in so doing, had killed him. She would find this man, this murderer, and be revenged.

Chapter Two

Chilverton was a small market town. The mill on the river ground flour as it had been doing for centuries, the church spire towered over the buildings, and there were new street lamps which made the inhabitants think they were extremely modern. Outside the town, collieries had been opened, there was a stone quarry, but the main employment was handloom weaving, spread from Coventry, and begun, it was said, with a number of Huguenot refugees who fled from France in 1689, leaving a legacy of French names scattered among the people. Silk ribbon weaving was largely a domestic industry. A small group of wealthy merchants imported and processed the raw silk. They then passed it to the middlemen, called undertakers, who handed out work to the cottage weavers.

The weaver worked on the loom in his cottage, producing the most complicated patterns. The whole family helped, doing the silk winding, filling the shuttles, picking up and preparing the warps. It had been their way of life for a hundred and fifty years, but now strange things were happening and the weavers were afraid.

The two men who faced each other in the small room were, by their dress, merchant and weaver. The former had an air of impatience and irritation which was borne out by his words.

'I haven't time to see you now.'

'I am Harry Earp – '

'Yes, I know you. You were a strike-leader, weren't you?'

'I was not.'

'H'm. So you say.'

'If I say it, then it is true, Geoffrey Waring. I go to the meetings, true. But the men are worried, and that is why I come to thee. Is there no work for us?'

The merchant's irritation grew. 'Damn it, man, is it my fault there are no orders? Since the Chancellor removed the import ban the market's been flooded with French ribbons.'

'I know all that, we all know it. So thee wants to drop our prices.'

'I have no choice.'

'But we have the List of Prices, agreed by both sides. We are paid by the piece – '

'You want to live too well, that's your trouble.'

'Geoffrey Waring, the List was agreed to prevent wages being forced down.'

'You're too damned proud, you weavers – '

'If we are proud, it is a just pride in that the fine gauze ribbons we weave are second to none. And our Guild is one of the oldest and most respected in the country.'

The merchant rubbed his nose thoughtfully as he surveyed the weaver. 'You're an intelligent fellow, Earp, you speak well. Maybe I could use you.' A look of something skin to cunning spread over his face. 'You know the men, you know the troublemakers. A few stray pieces of information from you, in confidence . . .'

'Then I would name myself first, Geoffrey Waring. For I am pledged to fight for our rightful price being paid.'

Merchant and weaver stared at each other and the merchant's eyes dropped first. 'Go,' he said. 'I have nothing for you.' And, as the man left the room, he turned to a waiting assistant. 'Damned canting hypocrite with his theeing and thouing. Dissenting troublemakers. What is it, Jenkins?'

'The carter, sir, he's not here, sir.'

'Not here? Is he ill?'

'He's dead, sir,'

'That's sudden.'

'Yes, sir, they say it's the cholera.'

The merchant frowned. 'And I've a load of ribbons here for London.' He ran out to the yard to the disappearing figure of Harry Earp. 'Here,' he called. 'You, Earp. Do you want work?'

The man turned.

'I've ribbons here for the boats. Load them in the cart and drive them to the canal, the *Mary Anne*'s to take them, she'll be waiting. I'll give you sixpence.'

And, as the man retraced his steps, he threw the sixpence on to the ground. Harry Earp picked it up, loaded the boxes on the cart, and drove to the wharf. He looked over the boats, searching for the *Mary Anne*, and saw with interest that there was a different boat in the lay-by, a packet boat called the *Princess*. He saw the girl standing on the deck and nodded a brief good morning. The girl nodded back. Neither guessed how closely their lives would be intertwined in the future.

The canal wharf stretched alongside the town and, as Tam nodded to the weaver she saw that, although early morning, it was already teeming with life, like an ant hill. Sacks of flour were being loaded into one of the boats, while farther along, a tramroad brought waggons of coal to other boats.

When they had arrived home from London, Tam had hurried the others into making the move to the boat, partly for fear they might change their minds, partly because none of them wished to stay to see the sale of their loved home. So they began to pack.

45

'We shall, of course, take our private belongings with us,' Annabel said briskly.

'We aren't supposed to touch anything, Miss Bel,' Abby said stolidly.

'Oh, pshaw, Abby, I know that. But just our very own possessions – '

Tam had watched her mother with disquiet, and the thought she'd so carefully stored away when she noticed her uncertainty returned in full force. Mama was little more than a delightful child in some ways, wilfully wanting her own way, yet always needing a strong person to lean on. Like Abby. Like Papa? Had Papa then been the strong one? And who now was to take charge? Juliet, with her naive innocence, was Annabel in miniature, while Celia, with her constant complaining, was hardly the type to take charge of anything. That left one person, Tam herself, and she wondered if she were capable of looking after six people and running a boat. Why hadn't she been brought up to do these things? What use would her fine needlework, her French conversation, her delicate paintings in water colours be to her now?

'Where shall we moor the boat once we live on her?' she asked.

'Not here. Not at the house. It would be too – ' Annabel broke off, but Tam understood. They did not want to be moored at the bottom of their former garden, staring every day at their beloved home being owned by strangers. 'It will have to be Chilverton Wharf,' Annabel ended.

'But, Mama, Mr Waring said we should moor it here – '

'Oh, pshaw,' said Annabel, and Celia asked, 'What was he like, Mr Waring?'

'Somewhat bad-tempered,' said Tam, shortly. Then, relenting, she added, 'He has a brother who is a most handsome fellow by all accounts.'

'Really?' Celia asked, brightening. 'Who are the Warings, Mama? We've been away so much, we know nothing of the society in Chilverton.'

'I don't know any Warings,' Annabel said. For Mama to "know" any-one meant members of the aristocracy only.

'The mother is one of those rich trade people,' Abby said. 'Determined to climb. They've built a big house, but they don't have any callers as yet. No gentry, anyway.'

Tam saw Celia registering this fact: We're gentry, or half-gentry, even if we have no money and our own relatives don't call.

'We must meet them,' Celia said determinedly. 'Are they married, the Mr Warings?'

'Neither of them is married,' Abby replied. 'I expect Mr Geoffrey is waiting for some high-born lady, while Mr Charles is a bit wild from all acounts and don't get on with his family very well.'

When Abby rose to clear the table, Tam helped take the dishes into the kitchen.

'You must teach us housework, Abby,' she said.

Abby set her to drying the dishes, and Tam studied her as they worked side by side. Abby, with her sturdy commonsense, her capability, was surely a most useful person, and she had been with Mama for years.

'What of Mama's family, Abby? Why did she quarrel with them?'

46

'I can't tell you about the quarrel, Miss Tam. Your Mama wouldn't like it.'

'But surely, if it was because she married Papa, they'd make it up now?'

Abby hesitated. 'It's more than that,' she said. 'And don't keep on, Miss Tam, because I'm saying no more.'

Tam thought of the visitor Mama had had when they first came home, the gentleman she never mentioned. Yes, there was much in Mama's life they did not know about.

'You've been a good friend to Mama, all these years you've looked after her.'

'Yes, Miss Tam.'

'We'll have to stick together you and me, won't we?'

Abby turned and looked at Tam. Not a word was spoken, but volumes were understood. Between them they would look after the family, and that included Annabel.

'We must make money,' Tam said. 'Then, in time, we could buy Cherry Trees back. And the only way we can make money is by running the boat. Not yet though, I don't know enough about these things. In the meantime we have to live on it, and Mama talks of making separate rooms inside. But it must only be temporary, we need to keep it as a packet boat.'

'Aye, well, you'd best see John about that,' said Abby.

So Tam took John to the boat the next day. And no one else had thought to ask him if he knew anything about horses.

'I worked wi' horses when I were a lad,' he replied.

'Good.' They walked out into the crisp autumn air, and Tam felt an overwhelming sense of freedom such as she had never known before. It enveloped her, blotting out her fears of the future. No more prison-like existence at Miss Laker's, no Belgium. Only Papa would never be forgotten.

She turned eagerly to John, and between them they worked out a solution for the boat.

The sun was shining the day they moved, the water sparkled invitingly. Tam turned to look again at Cherry Trees, mellow in the weak sunlight, and her heart almost misgave her. It looked so *right* standing there, its colours blending with the tawny browns of the leaves. Cherry Trees was something else she'd never forget.

They reached the boat, and Annabel and the girls stopped in surprise. The long interior, formerly rows of wooden benches on either side of the gangway, had been changed out of all recognition. The gangway had been moved to one side, seats joined together, while around every couple of benches, partitions of plain wood had been erected, making a number of tiny rooms. And only Tam knew that, by taking up the mattresses laid along the seats, the boat could still be used as a packet.

'Well, I really do congratulate you, John,' said Annabel. 'And these other men – '

'Boaters who helped me,' said John.

47

'Cupboards overhead. One large room here at this end we can use for a sitting room – '

'Saloon, ma'am,' said John.

'And the kitchen is already there – '

'We always call it the cabin, ma'am.'

'I see.' And they surveyed the small cabin, the black stove, the shining brass pans, the brass lamp hanging from the bulkhead, the folding doors which opened to reveal thick cups and plates.

'Why it's just like a doll's house,' exclaimed Annabel. 'But we must have our own crockery. Take these out, John. We have plenty in the house. The bailiff's men won't miss such a few. Now, how much do we owe these men for the wood?'

'Well now,' said one of the boatmen, 'we just happened to have this handy. It fell off one of the boats like.'

'Mebbe the boaters would like this old crockery,' said John, and they took it with gratitude.

Then they all trooped back to the house, with the men, and it was surprising the things they found that the bailiffs wouldn't miss: pretty china, curtains, linen, a small table that just fitted in the end cabin, and of course, all their bedding. The boaters also had many little gifts from the house, and somewhere along the way it was understood that this was in lieu of payment: a fine chest of drawers, a sideboard, a dresser – 'Mama, do you think we *should*?' Tam asked. 'Shouldn't these things be sold?'

'But they're mine,' Mama said. 'Bought with my dowry.'

Tam wasn't sure if that made any difference, but there was so much she didn't know about business. She found herself unable to penetrate further into the labyrinths of dealings which were not straightforward cash transactions. She felt it was all part of that secret masculine world kept hidden from them. But it seemed worth while when one of the boatmen said on leaving, 'We'll look out for you ladies when you're afloat, keep an eye on things like. If you have trouble anybody on the canal will help you, we'll pass word along.' And they loaded their furniture onto their own boats, and departed.

'Mama,' said Tam. 'I'd like to have a look in Papa's study before we leave, if you don't mind.' For there was something, somewhere, that didn't quite add up, even to one who knew nothing about business. In the study Tam halted beside the big roll-top desk.

'I'm puzzled, Mama, as to how Papa came to lose his money.'

'People do,' Annabel said vaguely. 'There have been many bankruptcies, so I've been told, due to the war. Why, there was a Chilverton man ran off to America leaving debts of over a thousand pounds.'

'But not Papa,' Tam said. 'He wasn't that type of man. He was careful and steady. He'd never gamble. He'd pay fair wages and charge fair prices. Mama, may I ask you a personal question? Were you very extravagant? Did you run up bills?'

'No, Tam. I would not do that to your Papa. And I did earn money when I was acting.'

'So you knew nothing till Papa died?'

'No. They sent for me when – it happened. I was with – friends. Then afterwards, Mr Benton, the lawyer, told me that Papa was ruined. That everything would have to be sold to pay his debts.'

'Did he show you any papers? Say to whom we owed money?'

'Why no. But it is true, Tam.'

'I'm not disputing it. What I cannot understand is . . . the boats are sold, are they not? The house is to be sold?'

'Yes. He said we had till the end of the month.'

'So, we've been talking about the bailiff's men. Where are they?'

'I don't know,' said Annabel.

'It seems as though,' Tam said thoughtfully, 'the creditors, whoever they are, mainly wanted the boats. They aren't so desperate for money that they wanted the contents of the house.'

Annabel stared at her, confused.

Tam said doggedly, 'It must be something to do with the boats. Are you sure there are no papers anywhere, Mama?' She picked up a heavy metal box lying on the desk. It was empty.

'The lawyer took the papers,' said Annabel.

Tam sighed. 'I'd like to keep the accounts in future, if I may,' she said.

'Accounts?' said Annabel, vaguely.

'Someone will have to,' said Tam. 'Had you not thought?'

'And are you skilled at keeping accounts?' Celia asked rudely, having followed to see what they were doing and catching the last part of their conversation.

'No,' said Tam, equably. 'But I aim to learn.' She picked up the metal box. 'This has a key, we need this,' she said. 'Now, if we go back to the boat, Mama, let's sort out the cabins. I would like the one at the end with the table.'

'That's the biggest,' expostulated Celia.

'Hush,' said Annabel, wearily. 'Let Tam have the one with the table, Celia. You have the next cabin, then me, then Juliet, and Abby and John at the other end.'

Celia looked sulky, but Abby came in to tell them that she'd prepared a meal on the boat, and they followed her back down to the canal.

They were all hot and dusty, so they sat on the small foredeck, open to the sky, where a pleasant breeze blew, and birds fluttered from the trees. Tam watched as another boat headed towards them, and got up to help the driver pass the line over their heads, smiled as the woman at the tiller nodded a greeting.

But they had to be practical. 'About clothes, Mama,' Tam said. 'We cannot use but one black dress.'

'I have sent some of your old ones to be dyed,' Annabel told her. 'They should be ready tomorrow.'

'Why do we need old clothes?' asked Celia.

'To work in,' Tam put in, quickly. 'Someone has to clean the boat.'

'But there's Abby and John – '

'We must apportion the work. John will see to the horses. He can do

49

the heavy cleaning, the deck and outside and so on. Abby can cook and see to the cabin and saloon. But I think we might clean our own cabins at the least.'

Celia looked sulky, but Annabel agreed. 'It is the best way. Are we ready to go then, John?'

John fetched the two horses, Darkie and Prince, and harnessed them in tandem to pull the long line. But the horses were restive, and another boat stopped while its driver went to John's assistance.

'One of you'll have to steer,' the boatman said to the girls. 'Has to be two people working the boats, that's the rules. One to drive, one to steer. You'd never manage them horses from the boat; they're used to fast travel.'

'But we can't – ' Celia began.

'I can steer,' Juliet offered. 'I've often taken a turn at the tiller on the boats.'

'You cannot stand for a long time, Juliet,' Annabel said.

'I'll do it if you show me how,' said Tam.

'I'll show you,' said the obliging boatman. 'Right, take 'em away, John!' he shouted. 'Hold out – ' and as the boat began to move, with John riding the second horse, he instructed Tam in the art of steering. 'Always remember the tiller moves the back end,' he advised. 'And remember it's a seventy footer. You'll be all right. My little 'uns can do it.'

Tam, somewhat gingerly, began to steer and with Juliet to give a helping hand she soon seemed to get the hang of it, so the man jumped off to return to his own boat. John kept the horses at a steady pace and the boat drifted along.

Reflections of trees and hedges were dark in the water. The westering sun was a red ball on the horizon. There was no sound but the clip-clop of the hooves and the occasional plop of a water vole. Tam thought it was uncommon pleasant to be a vagabond of a waterman instead of sitting inside meekly sewing a sampler, though she doubted if the respectable ladies of Chilverton would agree.

It was not far to Chilverton. But the canal wound through the meadows, in and out under humpbacked bridges, so that at times Tam felt the boat veering out of control, and there was almost a collision with the bank. She realised that seventy foot was indeed quite a length but gritted her teeth. If the boater's little 'uns could do it, then so should she – in time.

They were approaching the backs of a few houses now, saw a colliery winding shaft in the distance, and slowly approached the wharf. At its side was the 'Anchor Inn', and as they came alongside Tam could see a girl standing outside: the same girl who had stood there on the first occasion she'd been on a boat – Car Boswell, the gipsy. But this time there was a man standing beside her, and Tam drew a sharp breath as she saw it was Charles Waring.

She was immediately conscious of her untidy hair, her none too clean dress, her face, already reddened by the sun. She wondered how the gipsy always managed to look so immaculate. As the *Princess* passed, Tam averted her head, and began to talk animatedly to Juliet, sitting beside her.

Once at the wharf she was humiliated to realise that she had no idea how to tie the boat up, and stood helplessly while John struggled with the horses and the boat began to drift away from the side.

'Pull her in,' shouted someone, and she looked up to see Charles Waring on the wharfside. 'Throw me the line. Quickly.' She did so, face aflame, and he tied up. Then he came back to Tam. 'A minute, Miss Tamarisk.' He looked angry.

She stared down at him.

'I thought I told you to tie up down by Cherry Trees,' he said. 'You can't stay here.'

'Why not?' She looked around. There were a number of boats moored alongside, so that was the problem?

'These boats are here for loading, you'll block their way,' he said. 'Why didn't you stay where you were?'

The reminder of Cherry Trees coming on top of her struggles with the boat had unnerved her. Her eyes flashed green, and she strove for control, half wishing she could run to her cabin. But running was not in her nature, so she stood her ground, hearing Juliet speak.

'You must forgive us, we just couldn't bear to moor outside our home.'

And he stared then, and hesitated, before saying, 'Well, there's a lay-by yonder, where you can tie up.' And Tam turned to see the rows of boats, side by side with the stern ends ringed on to the path, while he went on, 'Go right down to the bottom end, can you manage it?'

She looked at the boat which would have to be backed out, then manoeuvred into the end corner of the lay-by, and shook her head mutely. He jumped aboard and took the tiller.

'Boats tie up here when they're waiting for orders or repairs or any other reason,' he explained, steering the boat expertly into the corner. 'Stay here for the present, but for God's sake keep out of sight.' Jumping ashore he ordered, 'Throw me the line.' He tied up, ran to the fore end and secured that too. Then he went with John to take the horses to the stables at the back of the inn while Annabel, Celia and Juliet went below. Tam was about to follow when Charles reappeared.

'You can keep your coal there,' he said. 'In that space next to those empty drums.' And he walked away.

Adjusting to life on a boat, in cramped conditions, with little money, hit them all hard. As the clear mornings changed into mist, and the only birds to be seen were crows flying over the fallow fields, the family watched Juliet anxiously, but she seemed to get no more colds than at Cherry Trees. Indeed, with the doors firmly closed, the boat was warmer than the old house which, even with big fires, had been draughty and cold. But coal would have to be bought, and day after day Tam would sit in her cabin, struggling with the accounts. When Annabel had sold her jewellery she had given Tam a hundred pounds, implying it was all she had. Tam suspected this was far from the truth, but felt she could hardly press the point. She did tell her mother that she would have to be responsible for

51

Abby's and John's wages, while she, Tam, bought the food. A hundred pounds seemed a large sum, but how long would it last, feeding six people and two horses?

John Dexter had instructed her in the art of simple book-keeping which he had learned as butler, and she studied her columns of figures. Potatoes, two shillings a pound, mutton, sixpence a pound. They seemed to be eating a lot of meat, together with items like quail. Quail? Tam called Abby.

'You want to see me, Miss Tam?'

'About the accounts, Abby. How do you pay for the food?'

'I haven't paid yet, Miss Tam. Miss Bel said we were to carry on as always.'

'Running up accounts?' Tam asked, incredulous. 'Not any longer, Abby, we *must* pay as we go along, or at least every week. Will you do that?'

'Certainly, Miss Tam.'

'And buy the cheapest meat. Not quail.'

'Miss Bel wanted – '

'I'm sure she did. But it's impossible in our present circumstances, Abby. Mama will have to learn to live within our means.'

'I've been wondering, Miss Tam, what you're going to do when your money runs out.'

'We'll have to start running a packet boat, Abby.'

'Will your Mama – ?'

'She'll have to. I don't suppose you've heard anything about how my father lost his money?' asked Tam.

'I don't talk to the boatpeople,' Abby said, affronted.

'Well, I do. But they won't tell me anything.' Tam looked through the window to where two women were shouting at each other at the tops of their voices. They did shout, some of them, and often swore; they'd go into the 'Anchor' with the men and sing and lift up their skirts and clog-dance, while the men played fiddles and melodeons. They seemed to enjoy life and its hardships with a gusto that cheered Tam, who often felt far from cheerful in these first few weeks. They were friendly, the boaters, they nodded and smiled, and came to their rescue if necessary, they would pass the time of day, but would never talk of private matters. Tam thought it was like being in trade and trying to penetrate the homes of the aristocracy: you could go so far but no farther.

She marvelled that her mother and sisters seemed not to realise yet that they could not go on living without income. She understood only too well what it would be like when the money ran out, and determined to start a packet boat service as soon as possible to supplement their meagre savings.

But first she must learn how to manage the boat. She set herself to mastering the art of steering. With John's help she took the boat away from the lay-by on to the pound as she soon learned to call the straight between locks. But when she wanted to go back she was puzzled. How to turn a seventy-foot boat round on a narrow canal?

'Take it to a winding hole,' advised Juliet. 'They're special places made to turn round. There's one, see?'

'How do you know all this?' Tam asked, surprised.

'Well, I used to go on the boats quite a lot,' said Juliet.

'Did Papa take you?' asked Tam, jealously.

'Oh no. They used to stop for me at the bottom of the garden, as that one did the first day you came back.'

'But, Juliet, what was your governess doing?'

'Oh, she used to sleep in the afternoon, so I went out.'

Tam glanced at her sister. She had always thought of her as baby Juliet, quiet, amenable. She realised now that she knew nothing about her, any more than she did about Mama, and wondered, a little apprehensively, what secrets she would uncover about each of them.

But with Juliet's help she learned the boater's language. There were no captains on canal boats, only steerers and drivers of horses. No port or starboard, just inside – near the tow-path – and outside: so you held in or out. You did not moor, you tied up. Perishable goods were 'sheeted up' as they called the covering up with large tarpaulins.

She looked constantly for signs of her father's packets, but saw nothing; the flyboats, of course would be indistinguishable. As the autumn mists shrouded the water, she felt that she, too, was trying to move through a mist, seeking boats that had mysteriously disappeared from the face of the earth, leaving no trace.

The girls cleaned their bedrooms, Celia with many complaints. Tam set about hers with a will, but had to admit that cleaning was not her favourite pastime. Coal dust flying round meant much dust in the cabins; the coal situation puzzled Tam, for though they kept a fire in the stove day and night, their stock in the little store never seemed to diminish, so she had no need to buy more coal. She went to the deck and scrubbed the paintwork on raw winter days till her hands were chapped and sore. Sometimes she would see Charles Waring on the wharf, where he had an office; he'd ride down on a black horse, tether the animal, then go inside. Sometimes he'd walk down to the wharf and talk to the boatpeople, and occasionally he'd even reach the lay-by. He would bid Tam good day and she would return his greeting, wishing she were wearing her best silk dress, for in some odd way Charles's look made her feel like a woman: she was aware of herself as she had never been before, and would drop her eyes and often escape below.

Christmas came and went. There were no presents, they decided it would be a waste of money. Nor did they go to church. Church seemed another luxury they could not afford, church needed clothes, and wearing clothes meant they had to be washed, and of all the work they learned to do Tam hated washing the most. Toilet facilities on the boat were limited, and water for the small tin bath had to be carried from the pump on the wharf, and though John kept them supplied with drinking water, Tam hesitated to ask for too much. Anyway, hadn't Miss Laker said that daily washing of the body was unnecessary? She knew the boatwomen washed their clothes in canal water, but as they emptied slops in it too, Tam couldn't face that. So there was nothing for it but to wash as seldom as possible. Tam, looking at the boaters' tiny cabins, overcrowded with children, carrying coal and bricks, wondered how they had the heart to keep their brasses so shining, their plates and ornaments so sparkling. But it gave *her* heart to carry on.

The days lengthened, John exercised the horses in the snow, the deepening frosts brought ice, and the Calders all marvelled at the boatpeople's sturdy acceptance of the weather conditions. They laughed and shouted as always and said this was a mild winter compared to some, only once did the ice-breaker have to grind its way through.

Yet winter had a beauty of its own. Tam watched the grey skies, saw a flock of geese feeding in the fields, and woke one morning to a hoarfrost, when every tree, every twig was painted white, and the world was a fairyland with the gaily coloured boats standing out in sharp relief.

She had decided to go with Abby into the town, eager to learn all there was to know about it. Down Gate Street, the main thoroughfare, with its quite large houses, its shops and small businesses, passing side roads.

'That's Temple Street,' Abby said. 'And that little hall is where they hold theatricals.'

Tam halted. 'All the time?'

'Oh no. Just when the companies come to town. Strolling players.'

They walked on, and now they were at the end of Gate Street, and stood at the entrance to a maze of narrow alleys leading to small cottages, and there was no shining frost here to brighten the drabness. The cottages clustered round a yard, with a pump in the centre of the yard next to the one privy, and near the cesspool. At the back was a field, and near the field an open, stagnant ditch.

'Come away, Miss Tam,' said Abby. 'This is the Patch, and it's here they get cholera.'

Tam looked curiously at the cottages, each with one extra large window.

'That's to let in the light,' Abby explained. 'They're weavers' cottages.'

And Tam was amazed. Was it from such unlikely surroundings came those beautiful delicate silks?

There were several men standing at the door of one of the cottages as if waiting for someone, and as Tam turned she saw a dark-haired man walking towards them. He nodded good day and Tam turned to Abby.

'I've seen him on the wharf.'

'Yes, that's Harry Earp. He's the weaver's spokesman. Come *on*, Miss Tam, we don't want to stand around here in the cold.'

Tam pulled her cloak tightly around her, and they walked over to the church, through the lych gate to where the small mound lay, darker now, the soil smoothed down, its raw newness gone.

'Oh, Abby, I never brought flowers,' said Tam, conscience-stricken.

'Well, there aren't any flowers in winter,' said Abby, practically, and Tam nodded her head sadly in agreement.

* * *

54

As the strong March winds brought daffodils under the trees Tam thought it was time to act. Annabel was bored and restless, Celia's complaints were longer and louder, their money was dwindling. She noted that a packet boat called at Chilverton twice a week en route to Coventry, and, talking to the passengers, discovered that a boat to Elsworth would be welcome.

'There's not enough boats since Jamie Calder stopped running,' said one aggrieved woman.

Elsworth was only five miles away, on the straight, and Tam felt quite capable of running the *Princess* there and back. She had taken the boat out daily for practice: at first she did not attempt a lock, for there were usually queues of busy boats waiting, but, as her confidence increased, she did learn to work the locks. John would unhitch the horses and lead them round, Juliet would take the tiller while she struggled with windlass and paddles, helped by the lock keeper. Her sense of achievement grew. Soon she would start running one packet boat, then she'd get more. Later on she would add flyboats, and become a fully fledged carrier.

There was still much to find out about the way she would have to pick up passengers, the departure points and so on, and there was only one man to ask, Charles Waring. She waited till she saw him ride into the wharf then, saying nothing to her mother, she tied on her bonnet and walked towards his office.

'Mr Waring,' she said.

'Miss Tamarisk. I pray you are well.'

'Very well.' She drew a breath. 'I wonder if I might speak to you.'

'Of course. Will you come into the office?' and she followed him into the dusty little room, its walls covered with maps. He pointed to a chair, but she remained standing.

'I want to run a packet boat,' she said.

'Ah.' He eyed her silently. 'But I thought you just wanted to live on the boat.'

'I told you I intended to work the boats. And there is need for another packet here – '

He said heavily, 'I cannot give permission.'

'What do you mean? Permission to what? It is our own boat.'

'You need permission to load at the wharf, whether goods or people. As to owning a boat, I asked you once before if the boat was yours, maybe the ownership might be disputed.'

She stared. 'But of course the boat's ours . . .' Her voice trailed away as she remembered her father's letter. *I gave this boat to your Mama . . . of course all property belongs to the husband . . .* Should this boat have gone then, with Cherry Trees, and the rest?

He said, as if reading her thoughts, 'I know how it happened. The *Princess* was in the boatyard for repair at the time. Somehow, the repairers hung on to it until – afterwards, when they returned it to your mother.'

'But – they never told us.'

'No. Some things are best kept quiet. Don't you see?' he asked. 'They were trying to help you. But you must be careful. That's why I told you to keep out of sight.'

She stared, dumbfounded. 'But we must run the boat to earn money.'

'I'm sorry,' he said.

'But they wouldn't take the boat now, would they? Papa's debts are paid . . . aren't they?'

'I cannot tell you about that.'

'Then tell me who took the boats.'

There was a long silence. 'I cannot tell you that, either.'

And she was angry again. 'You mean you won't,' she flamed. 'All right. But I'll find out, make no mistake. And I'll run the boats again, all of them.'

She flung herself out of the office but her anger cooled as she neared the boat. Now what would they do? The *Princess* didn't belong to them. At any time they might be turned off their only home, and her hopes of starting her father's business again would be gone. She needed money urgently now to buy another boat, and there was no way to earn money if they couldn't run. Frustrated, helpless, she paced around the deck.

It was Annabel who gave her the idea. 'Faith, I miss my acting,' she said, as an April breeze showed the first catkins. 'I shall die of boredom here, Tam.'

Tam looked at her mother. She was never quite sure of Annabel's motives for staying on the boat, nor did she feel that a woman who'd never lived with her family for very long would suddenly change now. Was the reason she did not take off for London simply that she had no offers of parts? Yet, almost from the start, Annabel had been going away, first for a day, then for weekends, saying vaguely she was visiting friends. She never told who the friends were, or where she went, and every time Tam wondered if she'd come back at all. And if Mama went, then Abby would go, and John, and they would not be able to manage. She had to keep Mama here.

'What a pity you cannot act here, Mama,' she said, and there was something niggling at the back of her mind that she couldn't quite remember . . . walking through the town with Abby . . . *This is where they hold theatricals* . . . 'Mama,' she said, suddenly inspired, 'why *don't* you act here?'

Annabel paused, struck. 'Why don't I get my own company of Players?' she asked. 'It won't be Drury Lane, but no matter.' She turned to her daughters, her face beaming. 'Travelling Players. We could move around the towns on our own boat, visit Stratford-on-Avon, Oxford . . .'

Celia said, faintly, 'But we cannot act, Mama. And we have no leading man.'

'Of course you can act, Celia, are you not my daughter? As for a leading man I shall go to London and find one of my friends. Juliet can move into that large cabin with Tam, then he can have the spare.'

'I'm not sure about moving the boat, Mama,' Tam said. 'Charles says the boat is not ours, it belonged to Papa and should have been sold, and if we moved it, they might decide to take it away.'

'Well, really.' Annabel had swung entirely to Tam's side now. 'I will go and see Charles myself.'

'No, Mama, don't you see? If we put a play on here, in Chilverton, we won't need permission to land, we're here. There is a little hall in Temple Street, I suppose we'll have to ask about playing there. Who owns it, Abby?'

'Mr Geoffrey, I should think,' said Abby.

'And where would he be?' Annabel demanded.

'I don't know where his office is – '

'Then we'll call at his house,' said Annabel. 'This evening.'

'Really, Mama, you can't do that,' Celia expostulated. 'Not without leaving cards. Not in the evening . . .'

'Nonsense,' said Annabel. 'This is not a social call. And I am not chasing Mr Geoffrey Waring all round the offices in Chilverton, I had enough of that in London. John, would you order a hackney coach for us. Six o'clock. You may all come with me, girls, if you wish.'

They prepared for their visit, Tam hurrying them along lest Annabel should change her mind. She put on her new black dress and wondered if Charles would be there.

Grange House was new, built in the fashionable Gothic style; well out of the town, it stood imposingly in its own grounds. Celia said, impressed, 'Obviously the Warings are people of wealth.'

The coach drove them to the door and they alighted. Annabel swept them past the butler, who, after receiving her card, and saying, 'I'm afraid Mr Waring isn't at home, madam,' was told imperiously, 'We will wait,' and they entered a large hall. 'I will inform Mrs Waring,' said the butler, and disappeared.

In a few moments they were shown into a drawing room, handsomely furnished, with none of Mama's exotic blue and gold brocades, but in more subtle, less fashionable shades. Mrs Waring stood to receive them. She was a tight-lipped woman in her fifties, whose mouth spoiled her comely features. Small, and inclined to thinness, she wore a grey silk gown, while around her neck hung a long rope of pearls. She held Annabel's card, and greeted her guests a little warily, as if she was not quite sure how they were to be classed, whether they were, as respectable merchant's relatives to be shown into the best rooms, or, being penniless, shown to the servants' quarters. Or, Tam thought mischievously, seeing the struggle on Mrs Waring's face, as strolling players, be shown the door. And she smiled ruefully at the ways of the world.

'My son is still working,' Mrs Waring said. 'He will be along presently.' She looked at the card. 'Mrs Calder . . .?'

'I am Annabel Calder – ' as if that explained it all. 'And these are my daughters, Tamarisk, Celia, and Juliet.'

'Ah.' Mrs Waring shook hands and motioned them to be seated, then waited, a little baffled.

Surprisingly, Celia took the initiative. 'We have not met as we have been away,' she said. 'Tam and I were at Miss Laker's Academy, and Tam spent a year in Belgium. Mama is often away too. She is the daughter of the

57

Earl of Sandford, and is really Lady Annabel Calder. Her family, alas, took umbrage at her marrying a mere merchant, and have no more to do with her.'

Tam gasped at this bald statement, yet, watching Mrs Waring, she saw it was entirely the correct thing to say. At one swoop, Celia had established Annabel as far above Mrs Waring in the social hierarchy, one who was demeaned by even mixing with merchants. Mrs Waring lapped it up, and smiled ingratiatingly towards Annabel.

'Your ladyship . . . and I was about to call you Mrs Calder.'

'It is my name,' Annabel shrugged. 'I seldom use my title. I dropped it years ago when I was on the stage.'

'On the stage?' Mrs Waring's face dropped too. 'You mean you were an *actress*? Did your family not object to that?'

'Oh no,' Annabel said airily. 'How could they, when one of my ancestors was related to Nell Gwynn?'

'Really?' Mrs Waring's face was an open book. She was saved by the opening door and the entrance of her sons. Introductions were made, and Tam looked at Geoffrey, the pride of all matchmaking mothers. She conceded that he was handsome: fair hair, fine-drawn features, blue eyes that had almost girlish lashes and which rested lingeringly on each of the sisters in turn, as though studying the opposite sex was a favourite pastime; his mouth was strange, seeming tight and sensual by turns, and when tight it had a cruel look. His clothes were impeccable: he wore one of the new frock-coats in green, with sloping shoulders and a trim, pinched-in waist, over close-fitting pantaloons. As he stood before Tam, she felt an instant dislike and knew the feeling was mutual. Behind him came Charles, and as he took her hand and bowed, his eyes glanced mischievously into hers, with no trace of his former hardness, and she was angry again, and wondered why this man had the power to rouse such strong feelings in her.

'We meet again, Miss Tam,' he said. 'I pray you are well.'

'Very well, I thank you, Mr Waring.'

She vaguely heard Mrs Waring saying, 'This is Jamie Calder's widow, Geoffrey, Lady Annabel Calder.'

Geoffrey stepped forward to greet them and Tam thought he looked ill at ease and wondered why. She saw Charles glance at his brother and there was a glint of amusement in his eyes. What had shaken Geoffrey so much?

'I am come,' Annabel said, 'simply to ask permission to use the hall in Temple Street for my theatrical company.'

Geoffrey stared, and Tam shot a glance of triumph at Charles from under her lashes. That would surprise him!

'But – are you living in Chilverton?' Geoffrey said.

'We live on my boat,' Annabel said. 'My packet boat.'

'Your packet boat?' echoed Geoffrey. 'I thought all the boats had been sold.'

'Oh no, Mr Waring. This boat belongs to me.'

There was a silence and Annabel said, 'You look surprised, Mr Waring.'

'I am indeed. Knowing – forgive me, Lady Annabel – that a wife's property belongs to her husband – '

58

'Ah,' said Annabel, enjoying herself hugely, 'but this boat was bought by my father, the Earl.'

Tam wondered how Mama could lie so blatantly. Did she think that putting word around that the Earl of Sandford was involved would mean that few would dare to oppose him? Even though they were estranged, blood was notoriously thicker than water. As long as no one asked for proof.

Geoffrey was saying, 'Allow me to take the boat off your hands. I would give you a good price.'

'Money means nothing to me,' said Annabel, grandly, and now Tam dare not meet Charles's eyes. 'I am living on the boat, I do not intend to sell it. I want to put on plays for the people. I am an actress, and all I need from you is permission to use the hall.'

There was a silence that seemed to go on and on. Tam looked at Geoffrey, who stood, the picture of indecision, and she wondered again, how this could be the prosperous merchant, the weaving manufacturer, the owner of canal shares?

It was Mrs Waring who intervened. 'Geoffrey,' she said, 'I wonder if I might have a word with you, if you will excuse us . . . ' and she led her son out of the room.

As Tam had surmised, Mrs Waring was greatly impressed by the nobility. She could not think how Lady Annabel had escaped her notice. She had no idea that she had been living so near. The fact that Annabel was always away and did not use her title had meant that she was all but anonymous in present-day Chilverton. Now that the Calders seemed to have dropped out of the sky like manna from heaven, Mrs Waring had no intention of letting them slip away. She whispered to her son, 'How is it that these people have been put in this position? Penniless, ruined?'

'I didn't know, Mama,' began Geoffrey.

'Didn't know she was Lady Annabel?'

'No, indeed, I knew nothing of the Calders.'

'But you knew they had been ruined?'

'Yes.'

'Her father is an earl, Geoffrey. A most important personage. It would not do to upset him. Such a man could be useful.'

'Yes.'

'Then – if they want to live on the boat I trust you will not oppose it?'

'No, Mama. But what if the boat is not theirs?'

'They are three pretty girls, Geoffrey. And soon you will be looking for a wife.'

'Yes, Mama, but there is more to it than that – '

'I know it, Geoffrey,' said Mrs Waring, who indeed had a far greater grasp of industrial affairs than her social conversation indicated. 'And I know we must tread warily. But an earl, Geoffrey – '

'We have no proof he owns the boat, Mama.'

'We have no proof that he does not,' retorted Mrs Waring. 'So in the meantime it would be wiser to assume that he does. We will discuss it all later. For the time being remember an earl is a powerful man, and an earl's daughter has precedence.'

'Yes, Mama.'

They returned to the surprised Calders and Geoffrey said smoothly, 'You could put on your plays at Temple Street Hall, as I do own that. It is where the Weston Band of Players come every six months or so. Though if you are using it I would stop them, of course. The fees are not high.'

'And the boat?' asked Annabel.

'Charles will tell you anything you need to know about tolls or whatever.'

'We do seem to be passed from one to another,' said Annabel, a little sharply. 'I take it that we now have the necessary permission?'

Geoffrey bowed his head. 'When,' he asked, 'will you require the hall?'

'Just as soon as I've fetched my leading man,' Annabel replied. 'We shall get down to rehearsals then – '

'But, Mama – ' objected Celia.

'Pray,' intercepted Mrs Waring, 'would you care to dine with us? There seems much to discuss. It will not mean waiting long, and we do dine late now, as I believe they do in London. The dear boys could take the young ladies into the gardens . . .'

'Very well,' said Annabel, languidly, and the five young people walked out into the pleasant evening, across the lawns surrounded by early spring flowers. As the path narrowed, Celia managed to walk in front with Geoffrey, and Tam smiled to herself as she noted her sister's smiles and nods, her kittenish ways, while Geoffrey appeared quite willing to flirt; he bent his head, smiling, and seemed quite taken with Celia. Tam wondered cynically if her being an earl's granddaughter had anything to do with his smiles.

Charles was talking to Juliet. 'I hope you take care, living on a boat,' he said. 'It can be cold and damp on the water.'

'Oh, we have the steam-pipe running from the stove,' Juliet answered. 'It makes it very warm and pleasant. Anyway, I've often been on the boats.'

'Yes, I thought I'd seen you around.'

'Have you?' Juliet dimpled. ' I don't think I've seen you, but then, I was never much on the wharf.'

They walked on slowly, and Charles said, 'I think you might be making a mistake.'

'What do you mean?' cried Tam.

'I think you would be better not to live on the boat.'

'Why?' asked Tam.

But Juliet was laughing. 'I do declare, Mr Waring, you are just being over-protective, are you not? You think we are too delicate to live on a rough boat. Confess now, that is what you meant.'

Charles looked at Tam, opened his mouth as though to deny it, then closed it again, saying nothing.

They started back. 'Life on the boats is not easy for a delicate girl.' His face was expressionless and he turned to Tam, 'You will take care of her?'

'Yes,' Tam said. Of course she would take care of Juliet, and it was good

60

of Charles to concern himself with her. Strange how gentle his voice was when speaking about Juliet, whereas with her he was angry and mocking.

The dinner was excellent, and Mrs Waring, Tam thought, was quite a pleasant person when she was not trying to be genteel. Indeed, Mrs Waring puzzled Tam; her house was furnished in a subdued fashion, quieter than Cherry Trees had been, for Mama's style was typical of the flamboyant Regency period, with much brio, but much vulgarity. Tam did not realise that Mrs Waring had spent her whole life matching and weaving silks, she knew much about design and quality. She also knew much about business and, given her head, could have run Waring's single-handed. But working women, above the lower classes, were rare fish indeed, and getting rarer as the new industrial men made money and pushed their wives and daughters away from helping them into a ladylike gentility. So Mrs Waring concealed her active brain and strove to be fashionable. And like many strong women, she obtained power by dominating her son.

Geoffrey Waring was not a bad man, but he was weak and unable to make decisions for himself, forced to rely on others. Thrust into the business by his mother – who overruled the misgivings of his father – Geoffrey spent much energy in trying to cover up his indecision and in appearing to be the successful businessman, and as masterful as his brother Charles, whom he secretly envied, though he would never have admitted it.

Charles was seated opposite Tam, and she glanced up to find his black eyes on her, and flushed.

'I was thinking,' he said, 'Chilverton is but a small town. There are a number of small tradespeople and farmers round about, but not too many. That leaves only the poorer people, mostly weavers with a few colliers and quarrymen and they haven't too much money to spend on entertainments.'

'I suppose not,' Tam said thoughtfully. 'Are the people very poor here?'

'Their incomes vary,' Charles said. 'When the weavers have work – '

'When they have work they have earned as much as a pound a week,' said Geoffrey.

'But not now,' said Charles.

'I hope you are not going to say that is my fault,' Geoffrey protested hotly. 'I can't help it if the people prefer French ribbons. I'm losing money too. That's why I had to cut prices.'

'Then you should have explained to them – '

'How can you explain to people who go on strike?'

'How else can they make their protest known? They have no vote. That is another thing they're agitating for.'

'Whyever should they have votes? That is ridiculous.'

'Please,' put in Mrs Waring, anxiously. 'Let us have no arguments.' She turned to Annabel. 'The dear boys are so high-spirited.'

'And my brother would ruin the business if he were in charge,' glowered Geoffrey. 'Anyway, I plan to build a weaving factory, that will put an end to this bickering over prices.'

'I wonder,' said Charles. 'When people are burning factories, breaking machines – '

61

'The factories must come, Charles. We're into a new age now.'

'Yes, I agree. But it means such a big change, the people are afraid,' Charles said sombrely. 'This has been their way of life for centuries, village craftsmen, the weaver, the blacksmith, the potter, the miller. They don't understand what is happening. We need men in government who *do* understand the people's fears, not like some of these we have in London now, who know nothing about the rest of the country.'

'You mean Parliament needs people like you,' put in Geoffrey, rudely. 'That's why you're agitating at your radical meetings. You're working against me, turning the weavers against me. Just because you wanted the business yourself – '

'Please,' Mrs Waring repeated, 'let us talk of happier things. Ladies do not wish to hear about these dreadful happenings in the world.'

'Why not?' asked Tam. 'When we live in the world too?'

Annabel tactfully changed the subject. 'How shall we let the people know about the plays?' she asked.

'You must put up posters,' said Charles. 'And if you'll give me the details I'll have them printed for you.'

'That would be most kind,' said Annabel. 'Now as to dates: every Saturday from June 1st. That will give us ample time to get a leading man and rehearse.'

'And the name by which you will be known?'

'Let me think . . . "Annabel Calder's Company of Players" doesn't sound very exciting.'

'Why not bring the boat into it?' Charles asked. 'How about "The Calder Boat Show"?'

'Yes, indeed,' said Tam, and Annabel nodded.

When they rose to go, Mrs Waring said, 'It has been a pleasure indeed, Lady Annabel.'

'And for us also,' said Annabel, absently. 'You must come to dine with us on the boat.'

'I think,' Mrs Waring said hastily, 'it might be better if you came here.'

'We would love that,' Celia put in quickly.

The coach dropped them on the wharf, and Annabel hurried ahead, the three girls tailing behind.

'Just think,' Celia said dreamily, 'we might marry the two Mr Warings and our futures would be secure.'

'There are three of us and only two of them,' said Juliet.

'I confess to liking Geoffrey,' said Celia. 'I would like to marry him more than anything in the world.'

'And you, Tam?' asked Juliet. 'Do you like Charles?'

'Indeed no,' Tam replied, a little too vehemently. 'Charles and I don't get on at all well. We argue the whole time.'

'I admit,' Juliet said, 'there is one of the Waring brothers I like full well.'

'I hope you are not going to say you like my Geoffrey,' said Celia.

'No,' Juliet answered, after a pause. 'I am not going to say that.'

Tam looked at her youngest sister. Juliet – in love with *Charles*? 'But you're only a baby,' she cried.

'I am sixteen,' Juliet said gravely. 'And many girls are married at my age.'

Tam stared ahead, a little put out. Geoffrey had seemed interested in Celia, it was true, and with their aristocratic connections, his mother would be satisfied. Celia had surely played her cards well. And Juliet . . .? Yes, Charles had talked to her and he'd been kind and smiling, quite unlike the abrasive self he showed to Tam.

So that leaves me, she thought blankly. Tamarisk, the oldest, and possibly the most attractive of the sisters, left out. Though she had said she wouldn't get married it was a little disconcerting, all the same, not to be asked.

Annabel went to London to find a leading man and stayed a week. Tam was not dismayed. She felt the worst was over with the grey winter; they had reached rock-bottom then and hopes had seemed to be buried under the snow. She'd struggled on because there was nothing else to do, but there had been times when her courage was all but vanquished. Now, with the spring, hope revived. It was still chilly, but the trees were heavy with May-blossom, and the geese had gone. With the prospect of money coming in she could turn her attention to finding out who had ruined her father. She decided to pay a visit to Mr Benton the lawyer in her mother's absence and before the shows started. She walked to the office in Gate Street and gave her name. After a short wait she was told that Mr Benton was away and no, they did not know when he would be back. And she knew with certainty that she was being put off, that Mr Benton did not choose to see her. She felt as though a heavy blanket of silence had been thrown over the whole business, and was determined to penetrate it.

She reached the boat to a welcoming smell of hotpot; Abby had given up all ideas of grand cooking and followed the boaters' recipes. Hotpot was ideal for cold winter days, with dumplings it was filling, easy to cook, and *cheap*.

Juliet was leaning over the rail talking to the woman on the next boat, and she turned as Tam joined her.

'Oh look,' she cried. 'Here's Mr Waring.'

Charles Waring was on his black horse, talking to one of the boatmen, and both men were looking at the girls. Then he rode towards them, reined in his horse, and dismounted.

'Good morning, ladies,' he said. 'I trust I see you well.'

'We thought you were discussing us with Josh Lawson,' said Juliet, dimpling.

'Merely asking him to look out for you,' Charles said, and Tam's eyes went thoughtfully to the pile of coal that never seemed to diminish. Could it be he . . .? She dismissed the thought as Charles went on. 'The boatmen are a good set on the whole, but there are one or two bad characters among them, as among all of us. I would not wish harm to come to you.'

'Why, Mr Waring,' Juliet laughed merrily, 'I know these people well.'

'And we've been here all winter,' said Tam, ungraciously.

'Won't you come on board?' asked Juliet, but he shook his head. 'Thank you, no. I am at work, as you see. But I do have a message for you. My mother sends her greetings, and would like you all to lunch with us on Sunday fortnight.'

'That would be lovely,' Juliet said. 'I'm sure Mama will be pleased. Celia too.'

'And I have had your posters printed.'

'Oh why didn't you take us with you?' Juliet asked.

'I wouldn't want you to tire yourself, Miss Juliet.'

'Oh, please call me Juliet,' the girl said. 'We are friends now, are we not?'

He smiled. 'I hope so.'

'And I shall call you Charles. And this is Tam.'

Charles nodded, and Tam returned his glance unsmiling.

Then he held up the posters which bore the words:

THE CALDER BOAT SHOW
Annabel Calder's Theatrical Company presents
ROMEO AND JULIET by Wm Shakespeare
at the Temple St Hall every Saturday from June 1st

'I'll take them round the town,' he said. 'And put one in the "Anchor".'

'How kind he is,' said Juliet, watching him ride away.

'I fear there is a streak of ruthlessness in the man,' Tam said. 'I sense it.'

'Oh no, Tam,' protested Juliet.

'His brother thinks so,' said Tam. 'He said he was a troublemaker.'

'Charles simply tries to help the poor,' said Juliet, and they went below, to where Abby was ladling out the hotpot and Celia watched her, a petulant droop to her mouth. But she brightened considerably as Juliet gave her the news of Mrs Waring's invitation.

'And we have the posters for the plays,' added Juliet. 'I wonder if Mama will be back today.'

'I wonder what the leading man will be like,' said Celia, who wasn't quite sure it would be proper to have a man living aboard.

But it was evening when Annabel did finally arrive; they were about to go to bed when they heard footsteps and rushed to the deck. Annabel looked tired and not a little put out. But she came in bravely, head high as she introduced her leading man: Tam stared in amazement; Abby, in the doorway, with disapproval; Celia's smile of welcome disappeared like snow in summer. Gilbert de Warrenne was a dessicated fop of about forty years of age. Looking at him, one could read his life story. As a young man he had been slim, fair and handsome. Now he had gone sadly to seed. He minced forward in the best Regency style and bowed over Tam's hand.

'Mr de Warrenne,' said Annabel, 'is a most experienced Shakespearean actor. We were lucky to get him.'

Or was he lucky to get us? wondered Tam.

Chapter Three

As the day of the performance dawned tensions mounted. All the girls felt nervous. It might be only a little show in a third-rate hall, but it was their first night, their acting debut. To Tam it was more than that. It was their only hope of survival, and she hoped the others realised it.

Rehearsals had been long and arduous. Annabel had decided on *Romeo and Juliet*, and when Tam – who had never been allowed to read such an indecorous play at Miss Laker's asked how five of them could take all the parts, Annabel had a ready answer.

'We'll have to double. First, the main character: I will be the nurse; Gilbert, of course, will be Romeo; Juliet won't have to be on stage too long or it will tire her, so she can be Lady Capulet. We shall have to play men's roles as well, but we'll leave the dressing for the time being. I brought a number of costumes with me. Now who is to be Juliet – Tam, I think . . .'

'Oh, of course,' muttered Celia.

'Tam is the prettier,' said Annabel, and missed the look of mortification on Celia's face. 'You, dear, shall have lots of parts: Capulet, Montague, and anyone who isn't on stage at the same time. Now, let us start.'

They read their parts. Gilbert said scornfully that he knew all of Romeo, and they were all a little surprised to find that not only did he know it but, once started, the seedy little man disappeared, and while nothing could make him young and handsome, he could at least act.

Tam soon learned Juliet's lines. Annabel was, naturally, quite perfect, while even Celia, buoyed up by the expectation of seeing Geoffrey again soon, entered into the spirit of the thing and was quite willing to play all the parts handed to her. Tam wondered if Mr Shakespeare would have recognised his play when Annabel had finished tailoring it to fit five people. All of them had to run off and change their clothes often but even so, large sections had to be cut out.

'It's a beginning,' said Annabel. 'We shall have to put on more plays, I'll sort more out.'

As the rehearsals progressed, so did the work. Annabel became a tyrant, berating them for being unable to act. Gilbert escaped her strictures, as did

65

Juliet, on account of her fragility, and the knowledge that she was so eager to please she would willingly have worked herself to death. Tam, who was a fair actress, endured some criticism, but it was, as always, Celia, who came in for the brunt of Annabel's censure.

'You are so wooden,' she screamed. 'A post. Bend, move, come alive.' And Celia, who was trying hard, was near to tears.

Gilbert said little on these – or indeed on any other – occasions. He spoke his lines then subsided on to the nearest chair. Tam watched him with disquiet: she stood nearest to him in the play, and often smelled the whisky on his breath, and guessed that his placidity was, in fact, due to the alcohol that seemed to send him into a near stupor. Nevertheless, he did seem to be able to act automatically, so perhaps it didn't matter, but she had qualms all the same. And the qualms were stronger than ever on the day of the performance as she joined her mother and sisters to wait for the hackney coach.

'Where is Gilbert?' she asked.

They looked round. Juliet ran to his cabin and knocked; there was no reply.

'When did we see him last?' asked Celia.

'We never do see much of him,' said Juliet. 'He's like a shadow.'

'He'll be here, he is a professional,' said Annabel, confidently.

They waited. And when the hackney coach arrived at the wharf Annabel insisted they set off.

'He'll be there on time,' she said. 'We're much too early.'

Tam stepped into the coach with the others. She stared through the window into the streets of Chilverton, wondering if anyone would be there to see the play. But as they neared the hall she was relieved to see that crowds were already walking along the uneven pavements. Their clothes were old, but their spirits were high, they laughed and shouted, and as the coach bowled past they raised a loud cheer. Later, dressed, she went on stage to peer through the curtains, and as she did so, Gilbert lurched through the door, definitely unsteady on his feet.

'Gilbert,' she hissed, 'are you all right?'

He drew himself up to his full height of five feet five inches. 'Of course I'm all right,' he said.

Tam forced her mind back to the play. She peeped through the curtains and saw to her astonishment that the hall was nearly full: bluff hearty farmers with their respectable-looking wives sitting on the best seats; men in caps and women in shawls – the weavers and boatmen – sat apart. As she watched, the Warings entered and swept down to the front row. A few small tradesmen followed, and the gaps were soon filled.

'Mama,' gasped Tam. 'The hall is full.'

'Well, what do you expect when I am appearing?' Annabel asked.

The curtains were drawn back, the play began. There was little in the way of scenery, certainly no balcony, but the time and setting of each scene was carefully described by Annabel at the commencement. The costumes were adequate, though some of them filled too tightly, and some, like

66

Gilbert's doublet, being too large for his small frame, had a number of tucks. But no one minded these failings.

Gilbert walked on to the stage, staggering a little, but word perfect. The audience clapped enthusiastically at every opportunity. If Celia forgot her lines, to be prompted by Annabel, no one noticed and, heartened by this acceptance, Tam went into the balcony scene.

'*Romeo, Romeo, wherefore art thou, Romeo?*' she said as Gilbert came weaving into view.

'*With love's light wings did I o'er perch these walls,*' he said, and fell down. As Tam gasped, horrified, he stood up shakily and proceeded as though nothing had happened. The audience seemed to think it was all part of the show.

'*Lady,*' began Gilbert, and Tam took hold of his arm to hold him steady. 'You should be ashamed of yourself,' she hissed, furiously.

'*If my heart's dear love,*' intoned Gilbert, swaying, and Tam carried on, mortified, glancing down at the first row of the audience, where Charles's black eyes were on her, amused. The scene ended without mishap, the curtains were drawn to loud applause.

'Mama, Gilbert is drunk,' Tam cried as she ran off stage.

'I know, Tam, I know. Abby, can you prepare something for him? We must get him through. It is going so well.'

The curtains stayed drawn for a long period while Gilbert was dosed with Abby's concoction. The audience grew restive, but at last the play went on.

Gilbert seemed sober now, the others entered, rushed off, changed, went on again. However much the play had been altered, the plot was clear to everyone. The star-crossed lovers, the tragedy. It was over. The women in the audience were weeping. But when the dead couple rose and bowed they cheered and clapped. Backstage, some of the audience came to congratulate the actors, and Annabel was in her element. But the Warings did not come.

The next morning Tam sat in her cabin. poring over the accounts. John Dexter stood beside her as she studied the figures.

'The takings are quite good,' she said. 'But there are also expenses. I'll lock the money in this box, John, and first thing in the morning you can take it to the bank.'

'Yes, Miss Tam.'

'Thank you. Will you ask Abby to come in now?'

He left, and Abby bustled in.

'I'll give you the money for last week's bills, Abby. Oh dear,' as she saw the balance sinking. 'We shan't make our fortune by one performance a week. Do you think we could put up the price of seats?'

Abby pursed her lips. 'Not now,' she said. 'Not with the way things are in Chilverton.'

'I thought not. Still, this was only meant as a stopgap, until I can get permission to run the boat, expand . . .'

67

'You need money to expand,' Abby pointed out.

'I know, Abby, I know. But I'll do it in time. The Calder Boats will run, as they did before. Packets, flyboats to carry freight – '

'And cost a fortune to run.'

'Yes.' Tam sighed as she thought of the relays of horses needed to be changed every six miles, the four men to each boat working shifts to ensure the flyboats never stopped.

Later, they all sat on the small deck, drinking tea, discussing the play.

'It went well,' said Annabel, proudly.

'Except for Gilbert,' said Tam, looking at the leading man sitting sullenly in a corner. 'You were drunk, Gilbert,' she accused.

Gilbert laughed. 'Did it matter in such a hall, before such an audience? When one is used to Drury Lane . . .'

'These people paid for their seats and have a right to their money's worth,' flashed Tam.

'Hark to the leading lady,' sniffed Celia.

'It was mortifying,' Tam said, 'wondering if we'd get through.'

'It was unpardonable, Gilbert,' said Annabel, and she continued sternly. 'It must not happen again.'

Since Gilbert's fall from grace on the opening night he had been behaving well. At first the family watched him with eagle eyes, but as the weeks went by and he showed no signs of being the worse for drink they relaxed their vigil, thinking he had learned his lesson.

As the anniversary of her father's death approached, Tam walked into the little churchyard. No stone had been erected on his grave, he was entirely anonymous, he could have been anyone, a nameless figure whose passing seemed only to be remembered by herself.

The shows continued but the audiences were dwindling, though Annabel put on another two plays. It was obvious that the locals had limited resources, the hand-looms had less and less work, and Tam fretted that she could not make money fast enough to buy another boat, and she was desperate to learn about running boats.

Ironically, the main stumbling block to this was the boatmen themselves, whose etiquette demanded she should not approach them as they stood talking on the wharf lest she be branded another Car Boswell. She learned this the hard way. A boat had drawn up on the wharf and there was an argument between the boatman and the wharfinger. The row grew fierce, and when lurid language began to fly Tam flushed, but stood her ground, biding her time. The boat pulled away, and Tam approached a group of boatmen standing nearby.

As she neared them they stopped talking.

'Excuse me,' she began, and immediately two of the men drew away. She stared in surprise as a third man, younger than his companions, gave her a bold stare and asked, 'Comin' for a walk, dearie?' and there was a loud guffaw.

Tam was so astonished that she stood stock still. Her head shot up. How dare he talk to her like that? She turned away as haughtily as she could, and one of the boatwomen cried, 'Why don't you smack 'is ear, cheeky young bugger?'

Tam stopped again, in gratitude, and the woman said, 'Come aboard.'

Once in safety on the little deck Tam said, 'I just wanted to know what was going on, Mrs – '

'I'm Liza Lawson.' She was a buxom wench of about thirty-five with three young children crawling round her skirts, and several older ones playing on the wharf. 'That man were refused permission to land. Why? Canal Company won't have it, see.'

'Why not?'

'Company likes to deliver its own coal hereabouts.'

'Can they stop anyone from landing then?'

'Oh, aye, it's the company's wharf.' She snorted. 'Even when you do land the charge is higher than most.'

'You mean canals have different charges for wharfage?'

'And warehousing. And Chilverton's is high. Then there's tolls.'

'Tell me about the tolls.' Echoes of her father's talk drifted back to her as she listened. High tolls. High charges. On the Chilverton Canal.

'Then we have to pass it all on to the customer. Ain't that right, Josh?' Liza Lawson belatedly acknowledged her husband's presence.

Josh looked at Tam consideringly. 'Now why would you be wanting to know all that?' he asked. 'You don't run flyboats nor yet carry freight.'

'Not yet,' Tam said. 'I want to, in future.'

'*You* do? Yourself?'

'Yes,' said Tam, equably.

'You ain't working for nobody?'

'No, I just want to get my father's boats running again.'

'Runnin' boats, a woman,' snorted Josh, but his wife turned on him, roundly.

'You heard tell of Widow Hipkiss, back in 1773? When her man died he was in debt, so she worked the boats for years to pay 'em off. Did well, an' all. On the Birmingham Canal, that were,' and Josh, suitably crushed, concentrated on filling his clay pipe.

Slowly the men began to respect her and, as Tam made it clear that she would stand no nonsense, they respected that too. They began to offer information: she learned that they worked from dawn till dusk; that they had to know every pit, every wharf on the canals; how to 'leg' through tunnels while the horse was led over the bridge, how to bowhaul a boat up and down locks and, when times were hard, more of the boatmen brought their families to live with them on the boat, and used the Tommy shops where goods were supplied on tick. She heard of strange tales and legends of ghosts, of 'Spring-heeled Jack' on the Grand Union Canal where boatmen feared to work a certain lock after dark because unaccountable things happened, lines mysteriously cut, paddles dropped shut of their own volition. Of the old lady said to haunt Crick Tunnel on the Leicester Section. 'If she likes you,' said one boatman, 'she'll come up and cook your breakfast.' Of a strange black creature with great white eyes alighting on a horse, back on the Birmingham Canal, which appeared ever since a man was drowned on that spot.

But it was romance that finally led to Tam's acceptance in the boating community. 'Courting' was difficult for people on boats that passed in the night – or day – only, and seemed to start when a young man caught sight of a girl who took his fancy. After smiling and nodding on innumerable journeys they might at last meet at a canalside inn, or even on the wharf. After that their strange courtship was carried on by letter.

'Aye,' said Mrs Lawson, 'Tom Wood, that's my nephew, wants to write to his girl, that's Rose, daughter of Bill Evans, a Number One, but he can't find nobody to write for him.'

'Well, I can write,' said Tam. 'But what's the point, if she can't read?'

'Oh, she'll find somebody to read it,' said Mrs Wood, comfortably, and so the nephew, all embarrassed blushes, presented himself to Tam, asking for a nice letter for Rosie, saying how he – he *liked* her, you know. And Tam wrote a passionate avowal of undying love, one of which Lord Byron might have been proud, and this was the first of many she was to write for lovesick swains. The letters were left with a lockkeeper, or similar trustworthy person, and in due course Tam was invited to her first boater's wedding. Boats assembled on the wharf, all resplendent for the occasion, the bridegroom's boat outshining them all, newly painted to receive the bride. After the ceremony they all went to the 'Anchor', where food was plentiful and ale flowed freely, and the painted water-cans were filled with beer. Fiddles and melodeons played merrily and couples danced and sang the night through.

And all the time Tam was learning about the system – or lack of it – on the canals: the high wharfage charges, the ridiculous tolls that varied from place to place, from freight to freight, and even had a dozen different charges on the same canal.

'What can we do?' asked the boaters. 'Send goods by packhorse again? There's no other way.'

'No,' said Tam, 'not yet,' and a little chill entered her heart. She remembered her father's misgivings, and felt that here was the key to his downfall. If only she could find the lock it fitted. But the strange thing was, however many different boaters she asked, none knew who had ruined her father. Or none would say.

'Really,' sniffed Celia, 'walking on the wharf as you do, Tam. It isn't seemly.'

'I know,' Tam replied. 'But it is interesting.'

'It's bad enough to mix with the boatmen, but when that Boswell girl is there too – '

Tam didn't answer. Car Boswell was a trial, she had to admit. When she was talking to the boaters, Car would often stand looking on, a smile of amusement on her face. Most of the older men took no notice of her, but the younger ones would often take her for a walk in the woods. And Tam tried not to blush, she knew what Car Boswell was, even though she wasn't quite sure what she did. And she sensed that Car recognised her lack of knowledge and it made her amusement all the more pronounced. Only once had she caused open trouble, when Mrs Smith, wife of a Number One boater, saw her husband talking to the gipsy. Then all hell broke loose. Mrs Smith screamed and swore, and ran after her errant husband, a cooking pot in her hand, which she broke smartly over his head. He turned in a rage, and soon the couple were fighting. When some of the boatmen tried to separate them, the Smiths joined forces and attacked them for their pains. Tam went back to the safety of the boat, Celia was appalled. But Car was there as usual the next day, when the Smiths had moved on, as though nothing had happened. Tam had no idea where Car lived, only that she was always hanging round the wharf.

There was a soft wind blowing when Tam walked towards Charles's office. Somewhere a boatwoman was singing, 'Once I had a dark-haired lover, and he thought the world of me . . .' The office was empty. She walked away, disappointed, when a voice asked, 'Lookin' for someone?' and only then did she see Car Boswell, standing beside a pile of wood, wearing a bright red dress, cut so low in the front it was almost without a bodice. 'Lookin' for someone?' she asked again, mockingly.

'No, thank you,' Tam said.

'Is it Charles you're after?' the gipsy asked, and Tam turned on her heel without deigning to answer.

'Aye, that's right, go back. I wouldn't think you'd want to run after him, considering what the Warings done to your father.'

Tam stood stockstill, and then turned. The gipsy had straightened up now, her mocking eyes resting boldly on Tam.

'What do you mean?' Tam asked.

'You're allus asking who ruined your father, ain't you? Well, I'll tell you, the Warings did.'

'How?' Tam's throat was dry.

'Run 'im off the canal, that's how.'

'What do you mean, run him off?'

'Put cheaper boats on his runs. Forced him out.'

Tam stared speechlessly at the gipsy, remembering her father's letters. *He's out to get me.* Remembering that Charles had tried to persuade her not to run the boat . . . Geoffrey's unease. John Waring had been her father's friend, but he hadn't been sure about Geoffrey. Remembering the blanket of silence.

'But the Warings don't own boats,' she said.

'They do. They put cheaper boats on your father's runs. It finished him.'

A packet boat passed in a whirl of colour, of people nodding and laughing, all seen through a haze. Maybe it was one of her father's boats . . .

'Ask 'em if you don't believe me,' the gipsy said.

'But how do *you* know?' Tam whispered.

'The boatmen know and what they know, I know. We saw it happen.'

71

Tam turned away in shocked amazement and walked back to the boat.

'Tam,' Celia said. 'You were talking to that Boswell woman.'

'Oh, be quiet,' snapped Tam.

'I won't be quiet. Mama, listen to Tam. Really, she doesn't have to talk to that – '

'I have to look for work,' said Tam. 'We have to earn money, don't we?'

'You're getting like the tradespeople, always reckoning up money. It's undignified.'

'Undignified it may be, but it has to be done,' cried Tam. 'I assume you want to eat as well as the rest of us, Celia.'

'Don't worry about me,' flashed Celia. 'I'm getting out of here just as soon as I can.'

'You mean if you can get Geoffrey to marry you,' retorted Tam, and she stormed out to the deck and stood looking over the water. Leave me alone, just leave me alone . . . It couldn't be true, could it, what Car Boswell said? And yet, Charles didn't want us to run the boat, neither of them did . . . *keep out of sight* . . . His words echoed again and again in her mind. The Warings own shares in the canal . . . A light touch on her arm.

'Come, Tam,' Juliet whispered. 'Abby has a meal ready. Come and eat. Don't mind Celia, Tam, you are working for all of us, you know you are.'

Healing words that dropped on to Tam's raw spirit like balm. She smiled, and allowed herself to be led back to the saloon.

Suddenly it was summer, the canal shimmered in a heat haze, Tam was on deck watching the boaters as they worked, when she saw Charles riding into the wharf. He had dismounted and was tying his horse to a post when she reached him. He turned and stood, handsome as ever, and she had to force herself to think of her father and summon her anger anew.

'Tam,' he said, his black eyes dancing. 'And what may I do for you, pray?'

'You may tell me something,' she said coldly.

At the tone of her voice he opened the door of the little office and motioned her inside. 'What is it?' he asked.

'I warned you I would find out who ruined my father,' she said, flatly. 'Now I have been told that he was run off the canal by the Warings.'

The smile left his face, and he asked expressionlessly, 'Who told you?'

'Car Boswell.'

'Ah.'

'Well,' she said, her ready temper rising, 'is it true?'

'Do sit down,' he said formally, and she sat on the edge of a chair. He perched opposite on a high stool. 'I had better explain,' he went on.

'Please do.' Her tone was icy.

'It is true that your father was run off the canal by someone putting cheaper boats on his runs. He lost money and tried to make up by mortgaging his house. He couldn't, and so his creditors took the boats and the house.'

'And who are the creditors?' she demanded.

'The Chilverton Canal Company.'

'But who are they? Is Geoffrey one of them? He owns shares in the Company, does he not?'

He was silent a moment as if thinking. Then he said, 'The canal is run by a company, and make no mistake, Tam, without the company putting up the money the canal would not have been possible. My father owned a number of shares and when he died they came to Geoffrey, yes, as the eldest son. But neither Geoffrey, nor my father, was the principal share-holder by any means.'

'Then who is?' She held her breath.

'Sir William Fargate. You've heard of him?'

She let her breath out slowly as if she had been running. Vaguely she heard Charles talking, 'The local squire, an unpleasant man, disliked by gentry and people alike . . . he owns a great deal of land, farms, coal-mines, the quarry; he is a Justice of the Peace, the church is under his jurisdiction . . .'

She stood up in her agitation, asking, 'What are you trying to tell me?'

'That Sir William is a powerful man.'

'And the canal?' she asked.

He too was standing now. 'He owns practically all the Canal Company shares. He owns boats, to carry his coal, but because canal companies are not allowed to act as carriers under the present law, he puts them all in Geoffrey's name. Do you understand?'

'Then the Warings do not own the boats?'

'Only on paper.'

'That's cheating.'

'That, my girl, is the business world you are so keen to enter.'

She was glad then that a knock came at the door, that Charles had to leave her. She sat down again but could not relax, she was wound tight as a coiled spring. The murmur of voices came from the other side of the door as she stood up again, paced restlessly round the little room. Sir William Fargate. It was odd how seldom her father had talked about him any more than the boaters did; he was never mentioned by name, yet all the time he had hovered over them like some dark presence, refusing to let them land at the wharf, overcharging . . . By the time Charles joined her again she had recovered some of her composure.

'So it was Sir William who ruined my father.'

'Yes.'

'Deliberately.'

'Yes. Fair competition is one thing, but this was unfair. He deliberately undercut your father in order to run him off the canal.'

'But why?' she asked.

'I truly don't know, Tam.'

'Was it fear of competition? My father's success?'

'Hardly. Sir William is not interested in running packets, or any boats except to deliver his coal. In fact he didn't even keep your father's boats.'

She looked through the window. Ducks were squabbling and squawking at the water's edge, waiting for pickings from the boats. 'I know why,' she said. She turned to face him. 'I've been talking to the boatmen recently. I learned about the whole sorry muddle. The high wharfage charges in Chilverton, the tolls. That's what my father talked about, what he wanted put right, to make one uniform waterway system all over the country.'

'He was right, Tam. I grant you that.'

'He was afraid of this new steam-engine.'

Charles stroked his chin. 'Ye-es. But many people think there is nothing to fear.'

'And do you?'

He prevaricated. 'There was a lot of speculation at first, then the bubble burst and people lost their money – '

'You haven't answered my question.'

'Do I think railways will be a threat? Yes, Tam. Sometimes the canal boats cannot deliver goods on time, and with perishable articles that's bad.'

'Yes.' She remembered the bad winters, the ice . . . but then nothing could run in bad weather surely? 'Did my father never talk about his plan to improve the canals?' she asked.

'Not to me, but I hadn't been working here long when he – '

'Maybe he spoke to your father?' She was remembering Papa's letter. *I am sorry John Waring is dead, I needed him in my fight.*

'My father was naturally interested in canal matters, but he was ill for some time, he couldn't do much. I believe there was some talk about getting the companies together to discuss these problems.'

'So my father would have approached Sir William about it?'

'I expect he would.'

'And that could be why Sir William was so anxious to get him out of the way. Changes like lowering charges would affect his profits.'

'Yes, indeed. But it would be very short-sighted of him. If these things were put right, the canals need not fear the railways.'

'And why,' her eyes sparkled dangerously, 'did you not tell me the truth? Because I am a woman? Yet Car Boswell knew about this business. Why didn't you tell me? Did you think I was just a delicate little lady who couldn't understand business, whose ideas of life came from novels?'

'No,' he said quietly.

'What then?'

'Because – I didn't want to upset you unduly about your father's ruin. I thought you would go elsewhere to live. I hoped you would.'

'Did you?' She could not hide the disappointment in her voice.

'Of course I did.' His own voice had risen now, as if in anger. 'I didn't want you to fall foul of Sir William. I could do nothing to help you; I own no shares in the canal. I have protested to him about the high charges, he laughs in my face. I wouldn't want you to make an enemy of him. I wouldn't want you to come to harm.'

And suddenly the air in the stuffy little office was high-charged, his dark eyes stared into hers, and she was forced to look away, at the dusty walls, the maps, the little window. Outside they could hear the noise and clamour of the wharf, but faintly, as if in another world. Here there was just Charles and herself, and her own thudding heart, in an oasis of silence where nothing else existed. It was he who broke the spell.

'Sir William could claim the boat, you know, if it was your Papa's,' he said.

'It was,' she said in a low voice.

Now he moved away, to the window, and she was left with her pounding heart.

'That's why I advised you to keep out of sight,' he said. 'Sir William seldom comes here, but I wasn't sure how far I could trust Geoffrey.'

'I suppose Geoffrey is really breaking the law, as well as Sir William?' Her voice was quite normal now.

'I suspect they have a similar little cheat going, where Geoffrey's canal shares are in Sir William's name.' Charles turned now, sighing. 'Geoffrey is Sir William's lackey. Getting on in the world by clinging to his coat-tails. But to be fair, fighting Sir William is a dangerous hazard, as your father discovered. You must understand that.'

'I do.'

'We must hope Geoffrey doesn't tell him about you. But as my mother seems to have taken to your family, she will influence Geoffrey.'

Another thought struck Tam, and she asked, horrified, 'Does Sir William own Cherry Trees?'

'I'm afraid so.'

'And – is anyone living there now?'

'Not that I am aware of.'

'I knew it,' she said hotly. 'I knew at the time that the person who ruined my father didn't really need the money he must have owed. I thought he just wanted the boats, but now I see he simply wanted my father out of the way.' She gazed unseeing out of the window, and a surge of pure hatred filled her whole being.

'Why don't you move away to another canal?' Charles suggested gently. 'Coventry, Warwick? Sir William doesn't own those canals, you'd be out of sight completely.'

She faced him, hazel eyes brilliant. 'No, Charles, I am not giving up. I said I'd fight the man who ruined my father and I will.'

'And how will you do that?'

'I don't know. But I will. I'll fight with every weapon I possess.'

He raised his eyebrows, seeking to lessen the tension. 'I take it from that you will not necessarily fight fair.'

'Fair?' She snorted. 'When did women ever fight fair? Against men? And men like Sir William who are so unfair.'

He laughed outright. 'Your honesty charms me,' he said, and she realised that he had it too, and she knew it had always been there, this recognition of some similarity in each of them.

She opened the door and swung away, back across the wharf. And did not see the admiration in Charles's eyes as he watched her.

* * *

The canal changed with the seasons. Autumn bringing blackberries and elderberries in the hedges, Michaelmas daisies and chrysanthemums in gardens, while house walls were crimson with Virginia creeper. The Statutes was held, crowds of men and girls stood in line hoping to be hired, Harvest Home signalled the end of summer. Winter and the canal ran dark, rooks cawed mournfully in the bare fields, sleet and snow covered the land, and the boats were ice-bound. Spring brought blue skies reflected in the water, the meadows were full of daisies and buttercups, ladysmocks and cowslips. Men in smocks sowed wheat and oats, in pasture land cows munched contentedly. The swallows returned from Africa and swooped over the water. Then it was full summer, orange tip butterflies danced over clover-fields, in the hedges pink roses bloomed. There was hay-making and poppies in the corn. The boatmen sang and the horse-brasses gleamed in the sun, the horses' heads adorned with little straw hats.

In July George IV died and William came to the throne. There was a proclamation in different parts of the town by the Sheriff, and a procession with the town band, when the weavers forgot their troubles and celebrated with gusto.

There was no performance on this holiday, and the Warings had invited the Calders to lunch. Tam was quite willing to go. Divided between putting on too many shows and thus exhausting her audience, and her eagerness to make money, she had, in the end, compromised with increasing to two shows a week, starting in the Spring. She had also taken to riding one of the horses round the outlying districts, telling the people of the shows. But she knew that something would have to be done, and soon, to improve their finances. Even with two shows they were only paying their way, no more. But just for today it would be good to leave all her worries and have a holiday . . . and to see Charles again.

'Are you ready, Mama?' called Juliet. 'The Warings' carriage is here.'

'I am not going to the Warings' today,' Annabel announced.

'What?' Celia cried. 'Mama, you said you would.'

'I have a headache,' Annabel replied. 'But you girls go, by all means.'

'But we can't go without you,' wailed Celia.

'Why not? The carriage is here,' said Annabel.

'It isn't proper,' said Celia.

'Oh, pshaw,' said Annabel. 'You walk up and down the wharf, at least Tam does. You are going, Tam, are you not?'

'I did want to,' replied Tam, and thought what a strange limbo they lived in, boldly running a theatrical company, living on a boat, yet still half-clinging to the gentility of chaperones and correct manners.

'Of course we must go,' put in Juliet, and at this show of strength from the baby, the girls looked relieved and went to the carriage.

As they drove through the gates of Grange House Tam found herself thinking of their old home. Cherry Trees had been so beautiful at this time of year. Blackbirds had nested in the ivy and filled the air with song, martins had swooped into the eaves; primroses and cowslips massed in the woods, with here and there a shy wind-flower, and when the orchard came

76

into bloom the whole world seemed a mass of pink and white blossom. She had not seen the house since they left: on her small trips on the boat she had always chosen to go in the opposite direction, she could not bear to see it standing empty, forlorn. To her, Cherry Trees was a living, breathing entity, in which they had lived and loved, and part of that love must surely still be there, waiting for them to return.

But she put these thoughts behind her when they entered Grange House and Charles took her hand, his eyes dancing merrily. To their former serious conversation he had never made any allusion, and she wondered about this now as he murmured about the weather.

'Dinner is served,' said the butler, entering.

'He means luncheon,' Mrs Waring said. 'Timson is not yet *au fait* with modern ways. Shall we go into the dining room?'

And now, led by Mrs Waring, who thought ladies should not discuss business affairs, and had ordered her sons not to dare mention politics at table, talk became casual indeed, and Tam found herself yawning into the soup. She looked up, confused, and indeed ashamed, to see Charles's black eyes on her. But he said nothing.

Mrs Waring asked archly, 'You've heard no word from your grand-father, the Earl?'

'No,' said Tam, shortly.

'Oh, but I'm sure we shall,' Celia said brightly. 'Mama will soon be tired of the boat, and then we shall all go to live with him at Trentham Hall, his country seat.'

Tam raised her eyebrows and said defiantly, 'We are doing well with the shows, so we have no need to live with relations,' and she glanced at Charles.

'Yes, indeed, I must congratulate you,' Charles said. 'And I have been thinking. You have two horses but no carriage. We have a carriage that needs horses.'

'What is that, Charles?' asked Mrs Waring.

'It is but an old one,' Charles said carelessly. 'I have ordered a carpenter to put it in order, then the Calders can take it off our hands, if they will be so kind. It is of no use to us. And Juliet is too delicate to walk far.'

'Why, that would be wonderful,' Juliet cried, clapping her hands. 'How kind you are.'

Tam thought Charles couldn't possibly have seen her riding Darkie round the villages. Couldn't have heard John telling her how the horses needed exercise, nor guessed how the repeated payments to hire the hack-ney coach every time they went to the Temple Street Hall emptied her slender purse. But she added her thanks, and they rose to leave.

'I've enjoyed it so much,' Celia said. 'You and I have so much in common, Mrs Waring.'

Mrs Waring smiled fondly at her. 'We have indeed. I have often wished I had a daughter. She would be able to help me with all the town junketings as the dear boys call them. I am now helping the Vicar with a social gathering to help church funds.'

'But I could help you,' Celia said. 'With a carriage I could come to you whenever you wish.'

And Mrs Waring said that would be wonderful indeed, and a date was fixed for Celia to go to Grange House. And glowing, Celia joined her sisters and Charles and Geoffrey who were to escort them back to the boat.

As they alighted from the carriage to the wharf Celia stopped. 'Geoffrey,' she said, 'you promised to show me the kingfisher along the canal.'

'It's quite a long walk,' Geoffrey objected.

'But a pleasant day for walking. Come.' And as Juliet took a step to accompany her, 'We shall not be long, Juliet. Wait for us here.'

Tam stood with Juliet and Charles, wishing she could be alone with him, and then blushed at her forward thinking.

'I'm going in,' she said. 'I must tell John about the carriage. He will be so pleased. Goodbye, Charles.' And she turned quickly towards the boat.

In the basin, several boatmen stood talking lazily, women in sunbonnets were holding babies as they sat on the small decks. The sun, westering now, glinted on the water, and as Tam walked the plank to the *Princess* she heard voices, Mama's contralto mingling with a deep rich tone. She knew she had heard that voice before. Then she remembered; it was when she first came home after Papa died, and Mama had a mysterious visitor.

She entered the boat. There was no sign of anyone. John would be with the horses, and no doubt Abby with him. The main room was empty. Then Annabel came from her cabin, and behind her strode a man. He was tall, middle-aged, with dark hair and eyes that had a vaguely familiar air to them.

'Oh, Tam,' said Annabel, flustered. 'Are you back? You haven't met my friend, have you? This is Lord Brooke. Brooke, this is Tamarisk.'

The man looked her up and down. 'So this is Tamarisk,' he said, 'I hope I see you well.'

'Very well,' said Tam.

'She's a fine girl, Annabel,' Lord Brooke said. 'I'll be going now. Goodbye, Tamarisk.'

Tam turned questioning eyes to her mother.

'A friend.' Annabel repeated. 'From the old days. I'm going to my cabin now, Tam, my head is much worse.' And she disappeared.

Celia had returned from her walk, and came aboard with Juliet. 'Who was that?' she asked.

'Hush,' Tam whispered. 'Mama is resting. It was Lord Brooke, a friend of Mama's.'

'What friend?' Celia pursued, suspiciously. 'What friend would visit Mama in this fashion?'

'What fashion do you mean, Celia?' Tam asked. 'This is her home.'

'But to visit her alone – a man. Tam, I warrant Mama knew he was coming, that's why she didn't go to the Warings'.' There was a pause as the three girls looked at each other, troubled.

'How long has she known him?' Celia hissed. 'Juliet, do you know anything of this?'

'No, Celia. I have never seen him before.'

'He must know her well. But to visit her alone . . . Say nothing of this, to anyone,' Celia said feverishly. 'Mrs Waring would be mortified to hear of any scandal.'

'But, Celia – ' protested Juliet.

'But nothing,' Celia replied savagely. 'What a good thing Geoffrey has gone. Pray do not mention this to him or to Mrs Waring, it is very indecorous.'

On the day Charles brought the promised carriage the girls were very excited; their own carriage, no more hired coaches. They were dressed early and assembled on the deck.

'We're ready to start,' said Celia. 'Where is Gilbert?'

They looked at each other in dismay. 'Oh no,' Tam muttered. 'Not again. He wouldn't . . .'

Celia wailed. 'We must go without him, Mama.'

'No, we cannot. We need him.'

They paced up and down impatiently, until at last Tam said, 'I'm going to look for him.'

'Not to the inn,' Celia said, horrified.

'Where else?' asked Tam.

She stepped onto the towpath and anger drove out apprehension. Even now people would be going to the hall, they had to put on the performance, it was their work, their livelihood. And just as they were getting back on their feet this fool of a man would ruin everything. She saw the boatpeople's pitying stares and this only fuelled her anger.

She hurried along the towpath till she reached the 'Anchor'. From within came shouts of merriment, of mirth, and, plucking up her courage, she entered the tiny passageway and stood, hesitant. To the left was the bar, its floor strewn with sawdust, and she heard the rumble of heavy voices, the clink of glasses from within. There were men everywhere, men in groups, talking, men at the bar counter, holding up money. She pushed her way inside and they all stopped talking to stare at her. She felt her face flame as she stared back, searching in vain each face to find that of Gilbert.

She pushed her way into the small parlour. It was quieter here, men were puffing pipes, sitting at tables playing cards. In a corner Charles Waring sat with Car Boswell. She took a step forward, trying to ignore him, but he pushed the gipsy aside, came to her. 'What do you want here?' he asked.

'Gilbert,' she said. 'We can't find him.'

Charles went to the innkeeper who pointed over his shoulder with his thumb. 'In there, dead drunk,' he said. And she followed Charles into a back room and saw Gilbert, stretched out on the floor. Charles slapped his face, splashed him with water, threw the rest of the water over him. Gilbert did not stir.

'He's dead to the world,' Charles said. 'You won't rouse him tonight.'

'Oh, Charles, what am I to do?' She was distraught. 'The play – '

He looked at her. 'This means a lot to you, doesn't it?'

'Of course it does. After all our work – '

'Well, there's only one thing I can suggest. Or perhaps two. Either you return all the money – '

'No – '

'Then you'll have to find another Romeo. It is *Romeo and Juliet* tonight? And I can but offer my services.'

'You? But can you act? Do you know the lines?'

'No to both questions. And I can't learn them in one hour or less, either. I could memorise some of it perhaps – '

'Come,' Tam said. 'Mama will know what to do.'

'You will have to read the part,' Annabel said. 'There is no other way. I will explain to the audience. Carry the manuscript with you, use your wits. If necessary improvise. We will help you.' She looked him up and down. 'You have the figure for it,' she said. 'The women, at least, won't be listening too closely to the words, I'll warrant.'

'We're going to be late,' despaired Celia.

At last they piled into the carriage, drove at a reckless pace through the streets.

'The costume,' Tam cried. 'It won't fit. Gilbert is so small.'

'Celia, let out the tucks, quickly,' said Annabel. 'Tam, you coach him. Come, girls, we are here.'

The hall was nearly full, and Annabel went immediately to the centre stage. 'Ladies and gentlemen,' she announced, 'I am sorry to tell you that Mr de Warrenne, our leading man, has had an accident and cannot appear tonight. We did not want to disappoint you – ' shouts of 'No' – 'so we have been lucky in obtaining the services of a man you all know, Charles Waring. He is not word-perfect, having to appear at such short notice, but I am sure you will forgive him, and help him in this most difficult task. And now, craving your indulgence for a few moments while we dress, we will present *Romeo and Juliet*.' The crowd stamped and cheered, and Annabel rushed backstage.

'Are you dressed, everyone? Charles, does the doublet fit? Yes, that will do, splendid. Now, let me dress.'

Tam watched from the wings as the new Romeo read out his speeches, and she wondered why he didn't seem to be nervous, when she was. She thought how well he looked in the doublet and hose, how black his hair shone in the glow of the lights. Then she was on stage, and she was Juliet.

He was talking of her beauty, and she lowered her eyes. '*Did my heart love till now?*' he asked, and he was before her. '*Thus from my lips by thine* . . .' He kissed her, a quick coming together of the lips, but both were startled, and Tam felt a sudden awareness of him, as a man, and she had to pause before carrying on. But she was shaken; in this man's presence her senses were heightened, she felt more alive, and she knew it had always been so. She responded to his fervour and spoke her lines with greater feeling.

As the Act ended, Tam waited breathlessly in the wings, and Charles came to stand beside her.

'How am I doing?' he asked. 'As good as Garrick?'

80

'You are wonderful,' Annabel said. 'You make a splendid Romeo. You should be an actor.'

Charles grinned. 'It's easy enough to read it from a paper, and when I have help – ' His black eyes rested on Tam. And then they were on again, and the play flowed onwards.

Soon the star-crossed lovers were saying their last farewells. '*One kiss?*' he whispered, and she was in his arms, and this was no quick pressing of lips such as Gilbert had bestowed, but a full-blooded kiss by an experienced lover, such as she had never imagined. He was holding her tight, pressing her body to his, and her arms crept round his neck. And the nearness of him set her heart pounding, so that when he released her she still watched him, feeling that he had invaded her, just by *being*. She said in a wailing voice, '*Oh, thinkst thou we shall ever meet again?*' A few more lines and he was gone and she was weeping. She knew she had spoken her lines with a depth of feeling not known previously, because she had never felt this way before.

The hall was still, the play wound on, and when the lovers finally died a great wail flowed through the hall. Then, as they rose to their feet, the people jumped up in a body, clapping and cheering.

'Splendid,' cried Annabel. 'The air was electric.'

They took curtain after curtain, and Tam knew that, whatever Charles had felt or not felt, nothing would ever be the same for her again.

Tam was surprised the next morning to find the world was just the same: boats swung slowly along the canal, women at the tillers; a packet boat raced by, the postillion sounding the horn, its decks full of travellers. In the saloon the family was assembled, so too was Gilbert, looking very sheepish.

'Well, Gilbert?' Annabel asked.

'I'm sorry,' Gilbert said.

'You were dead drunk,' Annabel said. 'You could not appear. Do you know what that might have meant, Gilbert? Paying back all the money to the audience and losing their goodwill. And that is unforgiveable. Absolutely unforgiveable.'

Gilbert did not speak, and Annabel went on. 'Luckily for all of us, we found another man, Charles Waring, who not only stepped into your shoes, but was exceptionally good. Frankly, I would prefer him to you any day.' She stopped. Annabel knew when to make silence speak.

'Are you dismissing me?' asked Gilbert, a little quaver in his voice.

'That depends,' Annabel said. 'On Charles Waring. He is to call on us this morning, and if he is willing to work for us I will gladly take him. If not, it won't be too difficult for us to find another man, we are an established company now, we are becoming popular.'

'It won't happen again,' Gilbert promised.

'And that,' Annabel said, 'is the most oft repeated statement of all drunkards.'

'Mama can be hard,' thought Tam, feeling a little sympathy for the luckless Gilbert who sat, head bent, the very picture of dejection. His actions had been unpardonable, true, but if it hadn't happened, then Charles would not have taken his place. And at the thought of his kiss her face flamed suddenly, and she muttered something about doing the accounts and fled to her cabin.

She thought again of being in his arms. Her body seemed to be holding strange new sensations that she could not understand. She remembered the girls' whispers and giggles, remembered Miss Laker's stern strictures, that these things were almost shameful, at least to nice young ladies, who did not talk about them. So why was kissing so uncommon pleasant?

She heard the clatter of hooves, peered through the tiny window and saw Charles dismounting. Her heart gave a funny little lurch as she saw him enter the boat. But she did not leave her cabin. She could hear the conversation. Annabel asking him to act with them regularly. His pleasant refusal.

'I cannot, Lady Annabel, however much I would wish to. My work often keeps me late. If there is something wrong then I have to deal with it immediately, you see. I sometimes work all night. I could try to be available if you need me, as last night when I was free, so please do not be afraid to ask. But on a permanent basis I could not promise . . .'

'I see,' sighed Annabel.

The talk went on, and then he asked, 'Is Tamarisk not here?' and her foolish heart was pounding again.

'Oh, she is in her cabin, wrestling with the accounts,' Annabel said. 'You may go along to see her if you wish.'

And he knocked, and stood in the doorway, and she hastily checked that there was no sign of the mattress, of beds, before sitting down again, pleased that she had on her best gown.

'I pray you are well,' he said, his eyes dancing.

'I am quite well. As Mama said, I am working on the accounts.'

And it seemed that they were talking on two levels, outwardly they talked of mundane things, but their eyes were saying something else. Or am I imagining it all, Tam thought wildly, as he said, 'You are still doing the man's work, then, Tamarisk?'

'I don't see why it should be man's work to add up,' she said. 'It has to be done by someone.'

'And how are things going?'

'Up and down. Like the lot of the weavers. Abby tell me they only earn about four shillings a week now.'

'Yes, there's been more trouble. Strikes and breaking of windows. In Coventry too. And I fear it will go on till the hand-looms are gone. Cheaper and faster, that is what this new world wants.'

'Nothing could go faster than packet and flyboats,' Tam said. 'Two horses at a gallop.'

'I wasn't thinking of boats, Tam, but of the new factories.'

'Don't you agree with them, Charles?'

'They'll have to come. It's the trouble during the changeover that I fear, that's why I attend all those meetings.'

'I know nothing about politics and care less.'

'Then you should. Big changes are coming.'

'Politics is just buying votes and buying seats in Parliament.'

He laughed. 'Of course it is. At present. The new bill aims to change all that. All men must have votes. That is the fair way to run a country.'

Men, men, men, she thought crossly. So every poor weaver wants a vote, but when I become an important carrier, I won't have any say in running the country. She looked round the cabin. She wondered if she should ask him to sit down, but there was only the bed . . . she wasn't scared of that, but of herself, that she might blush, and he would guess at her thoughts, he always seemed to know what she was thinking. So she dismissed the idea.

'How are you going to help?' she asked.

'When the bill is passed and we have a vacancy for a new Member here in Chilverton I shall stand for Parliament?'

'Will you?' She was impressed, in spite of herself. 'As a radical?'

'As an Independent. I hope to be an intermediary between the landed lords in Parliament and the new industrial people. That's if I am elected. My opponent will be Sir William.'

She raised her head. 'So you are fighting him too.'

'I am indeed.'

She was about to say how she applauded his action when another thought struck her. 'I doubt if it will help me and my boats,' she said.

And he laughed aloud. 'What a delightful feminine girl you are. I talk of world-shattering events, you think of your boat.'

'It won't help the world if we starve,' she said crossly. 'Truly, Charles, when you become a Member of Parliament can you not do something about his power with the canal?'

He smiled. 'Shall I send him to the Tower?'

'Don't joke about him,' she said in a low voice. 'He killed my father.'

He put out his hand as if to comfort her, and she was aware of him again, as a man, beside her. He was aware too, and he drew his hand away. But his voice was quite steady as if nothing had happened. 'Don't get too dramatic,' he said, and she turned away from him, wishing he had touched her.

'So it is true, you are working against your brother?' she said.

'In one sense. In another I am helping him, if he could but see it. But I admit it makes trouble between us, that's why I seldom go to Grange House nowadays. I stay at my house on the wharf yonder.'

'But why, if your father felt as you do, did he leave everything to Geoffrey?'

'He didn't. But at the start there wasn't enough in the weaving for both of us – still isn't. So he put me to the canals. Of course, things were easier then, trade was better. When he saw how things were going, he left the business to Geoffrey, but the bulk of the money to me. That way he knew

I'd stay and keep an eye on Geoffrey. Make no mistake, Tam, Geoffrey knows about weaving, he imports the silk and knows more about that side of it than I do. Father left the money to me in order that I might stand for Parliament, that was his wish.'

'I see.' She had the feeling that he was trying to tell her something, but she couldn't work it out.

'Don't see me as a Knight in Shining Armour, Tam, for few men are that. I must carry on working for the Canal Company – '

'Which is Sir William – '

'Which is Sir William, because I like the work well enough, and because I need the money it provides. Does that answer your questions?'

'I'm sorry,' she said, contritely. 'I am too curious.' But she still needed to ask him one more question before he left. 'You said once that if the canals were put right they would not fear the railways. How could I change the present system?'

He raised his eyebrows but he did not mock. 'The Canal Company makes the rules. To change the rules you must become a shareholder.'

'And to do that I need money?'

'You do indeed. And you'll also need to persuade Sir William to sell shares to you.'

'Yes,' she said. 'Thank you, Charles.'

He left, but her mind was busy, knowing now what she needed to do. Become a shareholder in the Chilverton Canal Company. And only then did the thought cross her mind that she and Charles might be fighting the same man, but they would be going in entirely different directions.

Celia determined the minute she set eyes on Geoffrey Waring that this was the man she would marry. She did not like living on the boat, and felt dreadfully ashamed of being among the common people; she could never, as Annabel did, pretend she had decided to take up an eccentric way of life, nor had she Tam's love of canals and her determination to succeed. Her dearest dream was to get away from her eccentric family, and live comfortably in a large house with a husband and children. She had no desire to fall passionately in love, though when Geoffrey came into view she firmly believed that she did love him. The problem was how to get him to love her. Though she would not ask for undying devotion, nor passionate avowals, merely a proposal of marriage.

She saw her chance was to play on her aristocratic grandfather, of whom, indeed, she was very proud. Geoffrey had money; he, and his mother, wished for a noble connection. She saw too, that his mother must be drawn in as an ally, nor was this difficult for her. Her own mother had never had much time for poor Celia, and she saw in Mrs Waring the mother she would have liked, the home-body who fussed over her children and so, presumably, loved them. Celia felt unloved.

So she flirted with Geoffrey, doing her best to attract him, knowing she was plain, but knowing also that plain girls get married too, and often happily, if only because they try that little extra to please their husbands.

She noticed Geoffrey's reliance on his mother, and strove to get to know her better. Now the gift of the carriage gave her the chance she so desired.

When the great day dawned Celia was up early, and though Annabel had wanted to rehearse a new play Celia would not hear of it.

'I am to visit Grange House,' she said, grandly. 'I must be prepared. Mama, is it not time we had new dresses?'

'You'll have to ask Tam, she keeps the purse,' said Annabel.

'And I know what Tam will say,' grumbled Celia. 'We cannot afford it.'

'As we cannot,' said Tam. 'Surely you don't need a new dress for daytime visiting, Celia. It is not a ball.'

'I am still wearing black,' said Celia. 'And it is time we moved to half-mourning at least. Mama, what possessed you to dye *all* our dresses?'

Annabel did not answer. Tam looked at her sister critically. She was right, of course, they did need new dresses, they all did. Even their blacks were out of fashion now. She said, to change the subject, 'Have you seen John about the carriage?'

'No,' said Celia, who thought that the event of her visit to Mrs Waring was so outstanding that the whole world must know of it.

'Well, you should have,' said Tam. 'Never mind, I'll see him.'

She stepped on to the towpath, realising as she did so she had forgotten her bonnet. The sun was already getting high, and she trembled to think what her skin would be like. And it was unthinkable to be out of doors without a bonnet, even the boatwomen would not be seen thus.

She reached the stables, hoping that John would be there, and had not moved to the 'Anchor'. John Dexter was a silent man, a good worker, and reliable, but when he'd finished work he liked to get away from his wife, who didn't want him under her feet, so he would sit on the bench outside the inn with a half pint of ale, watching the boats go by.

But this morning he was grooming the horses, and she said, smiling, 'You won't need to exercise them today, John. Celia wants you to take her to Grange House. I suppose you'll have to wait there, but no doubt the housekeeper will let you sit inside.'

'Oh, I'll be pleased to go,' John said. 'It'll give them a trot.' He patted Darkie and gave the brasses an extra rub.

'You're getting to be a regular boater, John, polishing the horse-brasses,' Tam said, smiling.

'Aye.' John rubbed the rosettes on the bridle, the crescent-shaped face-piece. 'Animals have always worn 'em, you know, Miss Tam. 'They're pagan charms really, said to bring good luck.'

'Are they? Well, let's hope they bring us some soon.'

'Pity you can't do a run to Birmingham,' John said as he made the finishing touches. 'You won't make much money in Chilverton now, the weavers are out.'

'Out? On strike?'

'Yes. Seems they took a petition to Parliament about these imports of French ribbons, but they wouldn't see 'em. So they're out.'

'Oh dear. So they won't have any money.'

She left him, wishing she'd listened to Charles when he was talking about the weavers. She'd have to do something, and soon.

She retraced her steps. It had rained in the night, and she breathed in the sweet scent of honeysuckle mingling with the other, riper smell of the soft earth. A cuckoo called monotonously, and there were flurries of wings over the water. It was all so pleasant that she did not go back to the boat but carried on walking towards the wharf. If Charles were there she could ask his advice.

There were two men standing outside the little office, both with their backs towards her. The nearer one turned, and she saw it was Geoffrey. She stopped in sheer surprise, Geoffrey never came to the wharf, and she wondered who the other man might be. Curiosity drove her onwards. She drew close to the men, and Geoffrey saw her. He looked discomfited, as if they might have been talking about her. The other man turned now, and Tam saw he was quite elderly. As tall as Geoffrey, he had the blotchy, mottled complexion of a drinker, and his face was hard.

'Did you want to see Charles?' Geoffrey was asking. 'I'm afraid he's not here.' He seemed to want her to go.

The man intervened. 'Aren't you going to introduce me?' he asked smoothly.

'Of course. This is Miss Tamarisk Calder, Sir William. Miss Calder, allow me to present Sir William Fargate.'

So very correctly, Tam thought coldly, are we presented to our enemies. Sir William was opening the office door and she entered, her heart thudding, her head held higher because of this, and she turned to face Sir William. The man who had ruined her father.

He closed the door, Geoffrey behind him, looking nervous. Sir William asked, 'Your name is Calder?'

'It is.' Tam stood her ground.

'Jamie Calder's daughter?'

'I am.'

'And you live on a boat?'

Tam's fear disappeared in anger. 'I'm not sure what business that is of yours,' she said.

'All canal business is my business,' he said. 'Is the boat your own?'

It had come then. Oh, to be able to lie like Mama. 'It was bought by Mama's father, the Earl of Sandford,' she said.

'Who disowned his daughter. Strange that he should buy boats for the man he never recognised.'

'For his daughter.' Tam knew her face was flaming, as she tried to extricate herself.

He raised his eyebrows, smiling a little. 'He bought a boat for his daughter to live on? It is hardly the life for a lady.'

And now Tam threw caution to the winds as her ready temper rose. 'We are living on the boat because we have no other home,' she burst out. 'My father had a thriving business on the canal, and someone ruined him – deliberately. I am going to find that man, Sir William.'

86

He was laughing now, but his face was not pleasant. His full lips were curved over decaying teeth, seeming to Tam almost like a grimace. 'And what will you do when you find him?' he asked, as though to a child.

'I will kill him,' she said clearly.

She saw Geoffrey's face, red, agitated, as he held out his hands as though in supplication. He was afraid. Sir William was a hard man, she knew that now, and she knew that she herself had a strength she had not realised she possessed, that gave weight to her words, that matched Sir William's own.

She looked at him, and he looked at her. And something in his eyes made her pause. She had seen that look before, in the eyes of the young boater who had asked her to walk with him. She had been angry with the boater, yet had half excused him for being young, and a man. This too was a man, an old man, and the lascivious look in his eyes seemed to Tam almost obscene. She wanted to run away, to hide from the expression of amusement on his face, that look in his eyes.

She walked towards the door. But he was before her, stepping back into the doorway, so she was obliged to squeeze past him, and as she tried to force her body sideways into as small a space as possible, he moved forward slightly, pressing himself to her. It was over in a flash, she doubted if Geoffrey had seen anything untoward, but she knew, had felt his body close to her thighs as she passed. Then she was outside in the cool, clear air, walking away, head high. I'll kill him, she thought, and was frightened of her own feelings.

Chapter Four

Tam wondered if her life would have been different if she had not met Sir William that morning, and knew somehow that it would not; it was as if the three families who had begun the Chilverton Canal were locked together in some destined struggle, as if the canal itself ordained it to be so; they had brought it into being, the three families, now it held them forever.

But she admitted that her confidence had been shaken, she was afraid of Sir William, and this fear only fuelled her hate. She realised how little she knew about men. Why had Charles's kiss seemed so delightful and Sir William's look so insulting? For the first time she missed the girls at Miss Laker's. Now she had no one in whom to confide. But for now, she knew she must concentrate her thoughts on the family's welfare, after the disturbing news of the weavers' strike.

'Mama, we are not doing very well here now. Even if we put on more plays people cannot afford to come. I wonder if we should move to another canal,' she said abruptly.

'No,' cried Celia.

Tam looked at her sister in surprise.

'Mama, don't let her take us away from here. Not now. I am sure Geoffrey will call on you soon, Mama,' Celia pleaded.

'But we can't stay here with no money,' Tam argued.

'Money, money, it's all you think about,' Celia sneered.

'Why, you're the one who likes to be a lady,' Tam retorted angrily.

'Because I am a lady. Mama is a lady. But you are not. You take after Papa, a tradesman, with your accounts – '

Tam was shaken, and angry too. Used as she was to Celia's complaints, she felt it hard that she should have to work and organise for all of them, only to find one of the family objecting to the very things that would bring them to prosperity again. And she was even more shaken when she told them about Sir William Fargate's threats and they refused flatly to believe her.

'I never heard such a stupid tale in my life,' Celia cried. 'Sir William is a most respected man, Geoffrey says.'

'He knows this is not our boat,' Tam pressed on. 'He told me so yesterday. That's why we'd be safer away from here.'

'You met him then?' asked Annabel.

'Yes, he came to the wharf with Geoffrey.'

'And did he say he'd take the boat away?'

'Well, no.' Tam shrank from telling her mother what had transpired.

'Of course he won't take it away,' said Celia. 'I'm sure Geoffrey wouldn't allow it.'

'Geoffrey couldn't stop him,' Tam cried in exasperation. 'How can you be so stupid, Celia?'

'And how can you be so bossy?' Celia was crying hysterically now. 'You act as if you were our mother and you have no right. I hate you, Tam, I hate you.' And she jumped up from her seat and ran to the door. In moments she was flying down the towpath, this act itself a cause for concern. Celia never went along the towpath alone.

'Go after her, Tam,' Annabel ordered. 'Tell her we'll stay here.'

'But, Mama – '

'Please,' Annabel said, firmly for once. 'Go to her. You too, Juliet. And don't hurry back. Go for a walk while I take a bath.'

As they walked along the towpath, Tam said, disturbed, 'Really, for Celia to say she hated me – '

'Don't you see, Tam, she's jealous?'

'Jealous? Of me?'

'Yes. She thinks you're Mama's favourite.'

Tam laughed shortly. 'Then she's mistaken.'

'Well, you know that when Mama brought us presents yours was always the biggest and best. I don't mind, Mama makes much of me because she thinks I am not strong, but she always says how pretty you are . . .'

'That doesn't mean she loves me,' said Tam. 'I don't think Mama loves anyone – except you, Juliet.'

'Then there was Papa. He was kind to all of us, but to you he was something special, wasn't he?'

Tam's face glowed, remembering. 'But Celia never cared much for Papa,' she said. 'She never took any interest in the canal, and complained that Papa was a tradesman.'

'But he talked with you, and favoured me a little because I was delicate. So Celia got left out.' They walked on. 'Look,' Juliet said, 'there she is,' and Tam saw Celia, standing by a fence, still sobbing.

'That is why she must have Geoffrey,' Juliet went on.

'*Must*?' asked Tam.

'Don't you see? It will be such a triumph for her.'

'Oh, Juliet.' Tam sighed. 'You are so *good*. I wish I were like you. But I'm not, I can't like Celia very much, she is so disagreeable.' She paused. 'But I didn't think she hated me.'

The girls caught up with Celia, and gave her Annabel's message.

'It's all right,' Juliet soothed. 'We will stay here.'

Celia threw a look of triumph towards Tam, who swallowed hard, but said nothing.

'Mama does not want us back yet, there is no hurry,' Juliet went on. 'So let us go for a walk.'

They carried on along the towpath, climbed a stile and sat on the edge of a grassy bank where Juliet started to thread a daisy chain. Celia's tears had dried now she was victorious, and Tam made an effort to be reconciled.

'I'm sorry if I offended you, Celia. But all I am trying to do is run the boats again.'

'If Papa couldn't do it, I don't see how you can,' Celia sniffed.

Tam sighed. There was no use arguing with Celia, they wouldn't get anywhere. She let her mind wander. Audiences were dwindling fast. Sir William knew they were here, so there was no point now in staying hidden. They had a packet boat, if he didn't succeed in taking it. They had two horses eating their heads off in the stables and needing exercise. Dare she do it?

'We could run a packet boat,' she said finally.

'How?' Celia demanded.

'Take up the mattresses, let people sit on the benches.'

'And where would we sit?'

'In the saloon. It's the only way, Celia, if you want to stay here.' And before she could start any more arguments Tam jumped up. 'I must go and tell Mama.'

She was walking back to the boat thinking about a route when the idea came to her. Of course, she almost skipped in her delight; they could not go to Birmingham to live, but they could fetch people from Birmingham to see the play in Chilverton. A special excursion. People liked travelling by boat, they'd be able to charge the fare and for the show as well. It was a capital idea. She began to run towards the boat in her excitement.

She stopped the minute she walked up the plank. From inside came the murmur of voices. She could not help but hear, there were no thick doors to close on the boat in summer.

'Come with me, Bel,' she heard Lord Brooke saying. 'You can't go on living here.'

'I can't come with you.' Annabel's voice was firm.

'Of course you can. It will be the same as before.'

'You are still married, Brooke.'

'I can get you a little house. You could bring Tam with you.'

Tam's head jerked up at the mention of her name.

'I have two other daughters. What of Celia?' Annabel asked.

'Celia will marry.'

'And Juliet?'

Silence.

'You're a hard man, Brooke,' Annabel said. 'But then you always were. Perhaps that's why I always loved you.'

'Yet you won't come with me now. A little house in the country. Later on we could go back to London, but I dare not show my face there for a time, I owe too much. But soon – '

90

'I couldn't leave the other girls, Brooke. Especially Juliet.'

'You left her times enough when your husband was alive,' Lord Brooke said.

'Naturally. He was her father. He looked after her.'

'Please, Annabel. This is no sort of life for us.'

'I'd be a kept woman, Brooke.'

Tam didn't stay to hear any more. She walked away blindly, along the towpath, past the 'Anchor'. She wondered if she were dreaming, that this was some nightmare she would wake from. That her mother . . . her *mother* . . . had been having some liaison with this man . . . while she was married . . . while Papa was alive. For this man she'd left Papa alone all those years . . .

When she returned to the boat later she gave her mother a cold hard look and then studiously ignored her, hiding her shock and anger.

She needed to see Charles, wanted to see him so much that even if she hadn't an excuse she would have invented one. So one morning, after breakfast, she tied on her bonnet and started along the wharf. It was, as always, a hive of activity. Sacks of flour were being lifted from the warehouse into one of the boats, in the distance a waggon, with sweating horses, was piled with more sacks. Tam stood outside Charles's office and wished for once, like Celia, that she didn't have to wear her black serviceable clothes; if only she could now be attired in sprigged muslin or silk. She drew a breath and knocked on the door. It opened, and he stood there.

'Well, Tamarisk,' he said, a warm smile on his face. 'And what might I do for you? Perhaps a business deal?' His black eyes were dancing wickedly, and she remembered the kiss, and the colour rose in her cheeks. She looked round the familiar little office, with its maps, its desk. Charles pulled a chair forward and motioned her to sit. 'I hope you didn't call before,' he said. 'I've been away for a few days.'

'Oh? Were you on canal business?'

'No, electioneering business,' he said.

She waited, but he didn't enlarge, so she told him briefly of the meeting with Sir William. 'So he knows we're here,' she said. 'I thought at first we'd be better to move away as you suggested, but the others don't want it. So I decided to run trips to Birmingham and back, to bring people to see the plays.'

'Well, that's an idea.' But he hesitated. 'You're going to dare Sir William?' he asked at last, and she nodded. In the mood she was in she no longer feared Sir William. If he took the boat away it would serve Mama right.

'You'd have to fetch the people, give the performance, take them back, return. It would mean a lot of work, and be very tiring.'

'It isn't terribly tiring to steer the boat.'

'There are locks on the Birmingham run.' He went towards the map. 'Ten miles,' he said. 'And the speed of a passenger boat is about six miles an hour. You'd go faster empty of course. But you'd still be mighty late getting home.'

91

'We have the horses,' she said. 'They need the exercise.'

He pulled his lip. 'Why won't your family consent to move to Birmingham?'

She stared blankly, unable to tell him that it was because Celia was hoping to capture his brother. She said at last, 'It is what we have decided.'

'Very well. And you would like me to get the posters printed?'

'If you would. I thought we'd go first on a Saturday, then if that were successful, we'd do Wednesdays as well. So – if you could get that done, and – and accompany us on the first trip to Birmingham, to show us the way?'

'I'll do all that,' he said, 'if you are determined. I'll get the posters, then we can go along and put them up. Let me see . . . would next Thursday suit?'

'That would be fine. About ten in the morning?'

'I'll be there.'

'Thank you very much.' She rose, moved to the door, to open it before he could forestall her. And then, as she stood, the words burst out of her mouth, and she was surprised at herself, for she hadn't intended to say them at all. 'What is a kept woman?' she asked.

He stood stockstill. But if he was surprised he didn't show it. 'Shouldn't you ask your mother?' he asked.

'No. Please tell me.' She was still turned away from him, facing the door.

'Has someone been saying things to you?' he asked. 'Some man?'

'Oh no. It was just something I overheard.' Now the words were out she was glad, but she couldn't look at him.

'Some information is normally reserved for married ladies,' he said. 'But maybe you should know, running around on your own as you do. A kept woman is one who is kept in a house by a man who is not her husband.'

'Is that all?'

'Except that they live as man and wife.' He was watching her now, she sensed it. 'A kept woman is a derogatory term,' he said. 'Because the man is usually married to someone else.'

Her face cleared. 'You mean like a mistress?'

He smiled. 'So you know that term.'

'Of course. Like the king had. All those little FitzClarences.' She faced him now, and her face was flushed with anger. 'They laugh at the husband. Why do they do it, these men? Why do they take a mistress?'

'Oh, there are several reasons. Maybe he is unhappily married. Maybe his wife is – er – cold to him. Maybe he marries for business and takes his pleasure elsewhere.'

'But could he not love the mistress?'

'Oh yes, of course.' He was still watching her intently, wondering if this was the answer she required. 'He might love her dearly. I believe the king loved Mrs Jordan, but he could not marry her. But Tam,' he grasped her wrist and forced her to look at him, 'Tam, if any man suggests that way of life to you, don't accept. Tell me first. Will you?'

'Why,' she was startled now, 'why yes, but it wasn't myself I was talking about. Truly, Charles.'

He relaxed his hold. 'Be careful, Tam,' he said. 'You are leading a strange life, and some man will jump to the obvious conclusions.' And now both his hands were on her shoulders. 'I wouldn't want you to throw yourself away,' he said. 'Not you, Tam.'

For a moment her eyes looked into his, and her heart beat at what she saw in them. But she wrenched herself away and didn't know why. 'Oh, pooh,' she said. 'How you do run on, Charles. Just because I asked you a question.'

'Yes, indeed,' he said, and his eyes were mocking again. 'I had forgot what an independent soul you are. And as hard to tame as a little wildcat. Well, Mistress Tam, I will see you next Thursday and we will sail to Birmingham.' He opened the door with a flourish, and she stepped out into the morning.

The boat set off in fine style, John riding as postillion; they swung away from the wharf, Tam at the tiller, forgetting her worries as they sped along at a cracking pace, the horses allowed to gallop, the slower boats giving way to them as they approached, and soon Chilverton was left behind.

The family had agreed to the plan without demur; even Celia had been surprisingly amenable, Annabel had seemed withdrawn, and Tam had felt she couldn't bear to speak to her. Not yet.

The country-side sped past: green fields, here and there a farmer working, his produce piled up on the small wooden staging, milk in churns, butter in crocks, and corn in bags, waiting to be picked up and taken to town. Houses were few, but they passed many boats, some heavily laden with coal or stone from the quarries, pulled by horses or mules, and with a man or woman at the tiller, and all, without exception, shouted friendly greetings as they passed. And Tam nodded back to the boaters, and smiled and called out, 'See you in Brum,' with the best of them. She saw Charles making his way towards her.

'Shall I take the tiller?' he asked.

'No need,' she replied. 'I enjoy it.'

'Hold,' he commanded suddenly. 'Pull in and let this boat pass.'

'But we're a packet – '

'This is a funeral,' he said. 'All the boats hold for her.' And he called for John to halt the horses.

The boat approached, and it was an impressive sight, as stately as if it were a monarch being accompanied by a funeral march. The coffin was placed 'back of the mast', and the relatives, black clad, stood around the tiller. They waited in silence as it passed, and then Tam asked, 'But where is he going to be buried, if he was born on a boat?'

'There's always one place they regard as their home,' Charles said. 'Probably the town nearest to where he was born. That's where he is returning to now. To the local churchyard.'

'I see.' Slowly John started the horses again, and they pulled away.

As they approached Birmingham there were many wharves: timber merchants, a stone depot, brickworks, a coal wharf, an iron-workers' foundry. And now there were houses, at first large ones then becoming smaller and poorer. Even quite a distance away they could hear the rumbling of wheels and the clang of hammers, and passed long rows of furnace fires where men hammered and swung large bars of metal. Flame and smoke belched from chimneys, and Tam asked, a little nervously, 'Are they the new factories?'

'Some of them. They make hardware in Birmingham.'

They were into the city now, passing church spires, and more houses, then they tied up in Gas Street Basin. They left John and Abby on the boat, and Charles showed them the offices. He paused at the notice board to put up their poster, and Tam stared at the public notice alongside.

'What is this?' she asked.

'A Pickford's poster,' Charles told her. 'Pickfords are important carriers on the canals.'

Tam was busy reading the notice, absorbing the information it contained.

'Messrs Pickfords beg leave to inform their Friends and the public in general, that they have established a Pair of FLY STAGE BOATS weekly from hence to Leicester and intermediate places, which load goods at Birmingham every Thursday afternoon, Warwick every Friday, Banbury and Oxford every Saturday, and discharge at Market Harborough and Leicester every Monday, discharge Warwick goods every Wednesday, and B'ham every Thursday morning.

Rates to Leicester: Light goods 2/6d per cwt.

Heavy goods 2/3d per cwt.'

'One day,' Tam said, 'I'll take over Pickford's business.'

'Tam,' he looked down at her, 'don't get too concerned with money. It seems to be a disease afflicting the whole country at the moment.'

'I know what it is to be without money, Charles. You don't,' she said sullenly.

'Has it been so very bad, Tam?'

She thought about how they were still walking along the knife-edge of poverty, even now their boat might be taken away . . . But it was something you could never explain to one who hadn't experienced it.

'Celia still talks of your mother's people taking you in,' he said.

'They would not,' she said flatly.

'Somehow I cannot think of your mother starving.'

'No.' She thought bleakly of Lord Brooke. He'd said she, Tam, could live with them. And what would she become then? She gave a snort of bitter laughter. 'Oh, Charles, there is so much you don't know.' And won't ever know. Men didn't. Not ever. They bragged around and talked a lot about politics and money, but it was women who knew the most about life, men had a sort of innocence, even when they spoke about wives and mistresses. As if there was a difference. At the thought of Charles being

94

innocent she wanted to laugh again. Then thought bleakly how much older she felt than even a year ago.

Then they turned back to Annabel, who was standing with Celia and Juliet looking around at the big buildings.

'Let's go for a drive round the city,' Charles suggested and called a hackney coach.

They went through the city, and saw that Birmingham was not all smoke and flame. They were driven through broad, well-paved streets with well-built houses. He took them to the goldsmiths' quarter, where skilled masters ran individual workshops. 'They used to sweep the waste gold dust out into the streets at the end of the day until someone discovered how to process it,' Charles told them. 'But there must be thousands of pounds' worth of gold dust buried beneath the pavements. In truth, streets paved with gold.'

He insisted on taking them to a hotel for lunch. And all the time Tam was pleased to be near him, knowing, admitting now, that she was in love with Charles Waring. Why didn't he speak, she wondered, when his eyes told her he felt the same way? And yet she hardly minded, this way was so pleasant, this sudden meeting of the eyes, this delicious sweet secret between them, so that Mama and the girls were entirely unaware.

On the return journey he insisted on taking the tiller. 'You'll be tired,' he said.

'But I'll have to do the return journey when we fetch the passengers,' she pointed out.

'Can't Gilbert help you?' he asked. 'Where is he?'

'Gilbert wouldn't lower himself to work on a boat. We can't expect it of him; after all, he is an actor.'

Charles made a strange sound, like a grunt of derision.

'I don't mind,' she said. 'I told you at the start I intended to work hard.'

'You did indeed.' He took one of her hands gently in his and looked at it. She glanced too, and saw it was red and, though though not calloused or blistered yet, it had a rough skin. Not a lady's hand. She wanted to pull away from him, to hide her hand, but he held it, not tightly, but just looking, and she felt the slow beating of her heart again, and wondered if he felt anything too, or if he were just studying her hand for blemishes.

'You must put some cream on your hands,' he said. 'Use elder-blossoms, they're out now,' he continued. 'Mix them with warm buttermilk and white honey.' And still he left her hand in his while she wondered jealously who'd taught him the secret of white hands.

They caught up with a coal boat and he let her go. The boat, seeing the carved knife-blade, gave way, and John pulled the line over the boat ahead. 'You need a boy to help,' Charles told her.

'But I've been running to Elsworth on my own.'

'This is farther. More locks. You'd never manage on your own. Anyway, it's the rules.'

'But we should have to pay him.'

'Yes, you would. I'll find a boy for you, one about twelve, ready to start work.'

She capitulated. 'Would one of Josh Lawson's boys be old enough?'

'Very likely. I'll see him.'

The boat sped on again, through the green fields. Charles stood beside her all the way, and Tam thought it was the most enjoyable experience of her whole life; the meadows sweet with new flowers, and she afire with young love.

Jim Lawson turned up for the run to Birmingham. He was a thin, under-sized boy, small for his twelve years. His parents were delighted he'd found work.

'But how will he manage when it's just for odd runs, not full-time work?' Tam asked, perplexed.

'Oh, don't you worry about young Jim, he'll be all right,' Josh Lawson answered her.

'But how will he find you when we get back? You'll be miles away.'

'Oh, I'll find 'em,' the boy said confidently. 'Anyway, I can sleep anywhere.'

'All right. I'll pay you fourpence to start. If you work well, and if things improve I'll increase it to sixpence.'

'Right,' Jim said.

They started off and Tam soon found she was glad of Jim's help. He knew it all, she thought admiringly, especially how to work the locks. And it was much easier with him to run ahead and prepare the lock, while she stood at the tiller.

They entered Gas Street Basin and Tam saw to her delight a queue of people waiting. They turned the boat and the passengers entered. They were a mixed crowd, she noticed, but not all workpeople. Curiously she asked one couple if they liked travelling by boats or if it was the play they came to see.

'Both,' replied the man. 'We like to travel by boat, it's so much more comfortable than coaches, and we're less likely to be robbed on the way. And when there's a play as well, it's a real good outing. It would be even better if we had a meal as well. Some boats provide them.'

'That would cost more,' Tam said, and the man nodded.

'Yes, but it would be worth it.'

The boat was soon full and still there were people left on the landing stage. 'We'll come again,' Tam called.

They returned, travelling in true packet boat style, the horses running, the big knife glistening in the bow. John entered into the spirit of it all, sounding the horn as they approached a slow, coal-carrying boat, and the line was swung over, and they raced on. It was exhilarating.

They disembarked the passengers, and found a waggonette waiting. 'Mr Waring's orders,' called the driver. 'To take them as wants to the hall.' So they set off again while John watered and rested the horses, rubbed them down and waited for their return.

Tam, knowing the audience was keen, put her best into the perfor-mance, but when the play ended and they returned to the boat she was glad of young Jim; she let him take the tiller, and the boat sailed through the soft darkness, the forelight spearing the water, the sound of owls calling as they flew overhead. Once, as they halted beside a lock, she heard a nightingale singing from the woods at the side. Her bones ached with tiredness, but as she sat breathing the warm evening air, she was delighted with the success of the venture.

On the return she spoke to Abby about food. 'Do you think we could prepare a meal for the passengers?' she asked. 'And if so, what would you suggest?'

Abby pursed her lips, thoughtfully. 'Why,' she said at last, 'we could give them a bun, or bread, but if we put a slice of cold meat on a plate it would look more like a meal. Pity you gave all them plates away.'

'Oh well, we can buy some more,' Tam said. 'It would be worth spending the money. We could buy cooked meat, and bread. What would we give them to drink?'

'Ale?' asked Abby.

'I suppose so. Tea would be too expensive. Anyway, the men would like ale best. But one glass only. And Abby – '

'Yes, Miss Tam, I know what you're going to say. And I will help you with it, and take the food round.'

'Oh, Abby, what would I do without you?'

Abby snorted. 'Well, I'm on the boat anyway, so it makes no difference, does it?'

'Thank you, Abby. I'll help too, now I've got Jim,' and she went to the boy and told him she would put his payment up to sixpence if he did most of the steering.

'I shall be helping with the meals,' she explained.

'That's all right,' said Jim. 'But why do you do all the work when there's them other wimmen doing nothing?'

But even that thought couldn't dampen her satisfaction. We're earning real money now, she said to herself. We're on our way. I'm a fully fledged carrier.

Autumn was dull, with mist and fog, making navigation far from easy, and on bad days Tam left the steering entirely to Jim, who seemed to be able to move along the murky waters by some sixth sense which told him when another boat approached and how near he could safely pass. He navigated the bends, the narrows under the humpbacked bridges with such ease that Tam wondered at what age he'd begun. He knew every inch of the route, indeed, he seemed to know every blade of grass in each field, not only in daylight but in the dark too.

There were always queues of people for the boat, so she started another run on Wednesdays and hoped to continue all through the winter. Now she was putting money by, and felt happier than at any time since her father's death. She did not see much of Charles, doubtless he was working on other stretches of the canal. She knew she was in love with him, that he felt the same way, and for the moment she was content to leave things as they were. It was pleasant just to know he was around, that somewhere in the world was this man who had, with his kisses, taught her the meaning of love.

December brought frost and snow, and some of the boatmen muttered uneasily that it looked like being a bad winter. As they returned from Birmingham ten days before Christmas in a flurry of snow and Tam's hands were nearly frozen to the tiller, Annabel asked, concerned, 'Can we carry on in this weather, Tam?'

'The boats work just the same,' Tam answered shortly. She tried to avoid her mother as much as possible, she didn't want to think about her and Lord Brooke, she hadn't time.

'The boats can't work if the ice gets too thick,' put in Jim. 'Sometimes they'm laid up for weeks on end.'

'That's bad,' said Tam. 'They can't get the cargoes through then.'

'No,' said Jim.

Tam pursed her lips, wondering if the railways would be able to run through frost and snow. But no, she comforted herself, nothing can work in bad weather, horse-waggons can't run when the roads are blocked with snow, and the railways would be just the same.

'It's only for a short period,' she said. 'Anyway, it might not happen this winter. We'll carry on for as long as we can.'

They carried on, but conditions were hard. When the towpath was slippery, the horses had difficulty in keeping up a fast pace, were reduced to walking. Tam had seen one horse, driven to speed in bad conditions, actually slip into the water. He was hauled out and seemed none the worse, but she did not want it to happen to Darkie or Prince. It was hard for John, too, out in the sleet and snow, and once Abby came up to the deck with a worried frown.

'I've made him a hot drink, can he come aboard for a minute, Miss Tam?' Abby asked. 'He isn't a young man, and this weather makes his rheumatics bad. It isn't easy for him.'

Tam frowned too, and she sent Jim to replace John, while she took the tiller. It wasn't easy for any of them, she reflected as they went below. She knew the family thought she was driving them too hard, but what was the alternative? What would they all do, sit and starve? Go hand in hand to the workhouse? She wished Celia would get married. She still visited the Warings regularly, but Geoffrey didn't seem in too much of a hurry, perhaps he needed a push. And of course there was Mama who was increasingly restless; now, as the bitter wind swept over the fields and the water, Tam allowed herself to think of Annabel, or rather, thoughts crowded in and would not be denied. Her old antagonism towards her mother and *that* man returned in full force. When John returned to drive the horses, and Jim came back to the tiller, Tam did not go below; she stood in the cold, wet, angry and mutinous, seeing the lights of Chilverton twinkling out of the dusk.

There were few lights in the Patch, and few fires in the grates. The night was quiet, and when the day dawned, still wet and cold, the looms were silent. The rain cleared by the afternoon but the stillness prevailed. Women stood in the street but they said little; an air of waiting hung over the area, even the children sensed something out of place and there was no running or shouting at play.

Harry Earp walked along the road, his step slow and heavy. His wife stood back to let him enter the house.

'Is it bad?' she asked anxiously.

'Tom Jacques has been sentenced to two years' hard labour,' he said.

'Oh no.'

'He was the strike leader. And he did break windows in Geoffrey Waring's warehouse. Enoch Randle has six months.'

'Poor Enoch.'

'Poor Enoch indeed. All those children – '

'They are sent by the Lord, Harry.'

'I know, Mirrie, I know, I meant no disrespect. I just wonder how they will fare. And is the new one arrived?'

'This morning. I've been with Lucy most of the night and day.'

'How is it, Mirrie? Is it living? Has she no fire?'

'It is a sickly thing, and yes, I gave them money for coal. It's Lucy who is suffering, Harry. I fear she is very poorly. She has the childbed fever.'

'Can we do nothing?'

'She needs a doctor, Harry. Or she will die.'

Harry was silent.

'I have seen this sickness many times. And Lucy is a poor thing at best. She must have a doctor, those children cannot be left motherless as well as fatherless.'

'No, Mirrie, she must have a doctor.'

'He wouldn't come without payment, Harry.'

'He might. There is much sympathy in the town for the weavers.'

'But we must be prepared – '

Harry went to the tin box that sat on the chest of drawers, opened it and took out the money within. 'It's the last of our savings, Mirrie.'

'The Lord will provide,' said Mirrie, and she pressed her husband's hand as he gave her the money.

Since Tam had started writing letters for the courting boaters the Calders never went short of food. Nearly every morning she would go on to the deck to find a rabbit wrapped in paper, sometimes even a pheasant. She knew well the strict poaching laws, but neither she nor anyone else ever saw who placed the articles there. She handed them to Abby without a word, and Abby sniffed, but cooked them in silence. Nor did their stock of coal diminish, in fact they never had to buy any at all. Tam realised ruefully how her attitude towards stealing was changing. In a comfortable home with plenty of money to buy all necessities, she'd agreed, if she'd thought about it at all, that rabbits were sacrosanct to the landowner. Standing in driving rain with little money in her purse, a rabbit meant a fine stew in a pot. Even more: she still burned with desire for revenge, and every mouthful of rabbit stew helped towards this end.

She was forced to take a few days' break at Christmas; Jim wanted to be with his family, and she herself looked forward to a time sitting in the cosy cabin, beside the stove. It might snow outside, but inside all was snug, indeed there was some satisfaction in sitting by the warm pipe in the cabin, looking out on a frozen world.

But the Warings asked them to dinner on Boxing Day, and Annabel, for once, did not wish to visit her 'friends', so they set out, Tam knowing she was excited at the thought of meeting Charles – if he were there.

They entered Grange House and Mrs Waring greeted them effusively. And he was there, coming forward with Geoffrey, taking her hand, smiling into her eyes, leading her into the drawing room. And suddenly the world was right again.

It was a pleasant evening. The table groaned with the amount of food placed upon it, the wines were superb. And afterwards they returned to the drawing room where the girls were asked to play and sing. Celia played first, while Geoffrey bent over her, turning the pages of music. Juliet sang in a sweet little treble, then it was Tam's turn. As she looked through the music she saw that Charles was beside her.

'Oh look,' she pointed to a sheet, 'my father liked this.'

'By Robert Burns?'

'Yes. He met him once, when Papa was a child.'

'Play then, Tam, and I'll do my best to sing.'

He began, and he had a fine voice. '*Oh my love is like a red, red rose, that's newly sprung in June . . .*'

All the while he was looking intently at her, and she knew that, for good or ill, her future lay with this man. She took her hands from the keys, wanting to end there, but he was continuing, '*And fare thee weel, my only love, and fare thee weel awhile, And I will come again, my love, though it were ten thousand mile.*'

She raised her eyes to his.

'Come,' he said. 'Let us sit over there.'

Geoffrey and Celia were already in one corner. Mrs Waring was boring Annabel with talk of servants, Juliet sat with them, quiet and withdrawn. Charles led Tam to the deep window-seat overlooking the garden as Mrs Waring asked Juliet to sing again. And Tam sat, waiting expectantly.

Yet Charles, when he spoke, said nothing of his feelings. He did not even look at her as he said, 'The soup kitchen is opening again.'

She closed her eyes in vexation. She was waiting for a declaration and he talked about soup kitchens! But aloud she said, 'I know there is much poverty around. I'm glad we go to Birmingham now.'

'There's been more trouble in Coventry, a factory set on fire,' Charles continued.

She sighed. 'Is that so?'

He pressed doggedly on. 'You remember I told you how my father left me his money in order that I might become a Member of Parliament?'

'Yes.'

'It is my wish,' he said. 'My life is dedicated to it.'

100

'To helping the poor,' she said, a little impatiently. 'You'd do better to open another soup kitchen.'

'And,' he went on as though she had not spoken, 'it will take all the money I have, plus the fact that at any time Sir William, knowing I am to oppose him, might dismiss me.'

She began to see the drift of his conversation. 'Yes?' she asked.

'I cannot,' he said, 'take on any other commitments.'

Tam realised she had been caught with her own petard, she had been saying she wanted to make money and he would not ask her to be a poor man's wife. Aloud she said, 'I have a dream too, to carry out my father's wishes.'

'If I got into Parliament I would have to move to London,' he said.

'And I,' she said equably, 'have to stay here. I hope the poor will repay you for your dedication.' And she walked away.

Charles watched her, brooding. He had told her not to see him as a knight in shining armour, and he was too innately honest not to know that his altruism was at times warring with an ambition for power. He knew that he was in love with Tamarisk Calder, but love and marriage were not always compatible, and in the meantime he could amuse himself with Car Boswell and any other doxy who took his fancy. Ironically, it was Tam's very indepedence that held him back. Had she shown any signs of weakness, instead of hiding it, that part of his nature which genuinely succoured the poor and helpless would have been overcome. So he watched Tam, but did not approach her again.

In January the weather worsened. For several days there had been ice on the canal. It was fairly thin and the boats were able to break it easily enough, but it made towing more difficult for the horses. However, Tam insisted on starting the Birmingham runs again, insisted on standing with Jim in the bitter cold, hardly knowing what drove her. They returned, tied up, and Abby brought hot drinks.

'Are you going tomorrow, Miss Tam?' Jim asked.

'I want to. Why?'

'It's freezing hard, don't reckon it'll be safe.'

Tam frowned. 'We'll see tommorrow, Jim.'

There was another sharp frost in the night, and when Tam looked out at dawn she saw a firm layer of ice on the water. But other boats were working, so she decided to go.

'It's getting worse,' young Jim said.

She looked up at the sky, it was a steely grey. Icicles glittered on every boat, on the waggons bringing the coal, on the horses' manes, but she was decided. 'We'll go. Maybe it won't be possible tomorrow. I don't want to stop without informing the people, they'll think we're unreliable.'

'But they know we can't work if the weather's too bad,' said Jim.

'No,' she insisted. 'The canals must be relied upon. We'll go today and put a notice on the wharf saying we might not be able to come tomorrow.'

John harnessed the horses and they set out, the wind whistling and ice cracking at the side of the boat. The horses were unable to gallop, the towpath was too slippery.

'We'll be late,' Jim said.

They reached the locks; lumps of ice were packed behind the gates, preventing them from opening flush with the walls. The lock keeper helped by scooping all the broken ice out of the empty lock before they could go in, so they would not jam. But it was slow work, and Tam's hands were soon frozen. Then they were on the pound again, and making steady progress through the cracking ice. They were two hours late at Birmingham, yet still people had waited, and Tam pointed out how right she'd been to insist on the canal's reliability. She pinned up a hastily written notice and they quickly started the journey back. The locks were worse now, with great lumps of ice piled up on each other, all having to be removed before the boat could get through. Jim produced a podger, a long pole with iron prongs on the end, which he thrust down into the ice, breaking it up and allowing some of the pieces underneath to go deeper and release themselves, then those on the surface could be floated away.

When they reached Chilverton, Tam was so weary she could hardly stand, but the waggons were waiting, as was Gilbert, and the show went on. It was far from her best performance she knew, and there was still the return journey.

Jim was waiting on the boat as they came back from the hall. 'It's bad,' he said. 'Tom Merrick says they'm iced up at Brum.'

'We must take these people back,' said Tam.

She marvelled at the lightheartedness of the passengers, who joked and laughed and seemed to be enjoying themselves hugely. And it was a fine night, clear and frosty, a half moon cradled in a deep blue sky, tiny stars pinpoints of light very far away. She watched a barn owl fly low over a field, heard a dog fox barking. Around them the ice whistled and cracked. At the locks all of them except Juliet worked to lift the ice lumps from the water, even some of the passengers. And finally they tied up in Birmingham, tears of exhaustion in Tam's eyes.

The passengers departed, clapping Tam on the back and thanking her for a grand adventure. She smiled weakly and turned to the others. 'Whatever is the time?' she asked.

'Twelve o'clock,' said Annabel. 'We can't go back in this, surely.'

'What do you think, Jim?' asked Tam.

'It's bad,' he said. 'But if we stop here we might be stuck for weeks.'

'And we don't want that,' said Celia, shivering.

'Are the horses all right?' Tam asked John.

'Yes, Miss Tam. They're strong.'

'I think we'll risk it,' Tam said. 'After all, we came here.'

'But it's freezing hard,' objected Jim.

'It's been freezing all day,' said Tam. 'Loose the lines.'

They set off through a world of ice, and it took all the efforts of the horses to get them along, the noise of breaking, crashing ice was tremendous. Tam was at the tiller, Jim at the fore end, leaning over the canal, breaking the ice with his podger, and they struggled on. There were no other boats around, it was as if they were alone in the world. Exhaustion drowned all thought, there was no Charles, no rejection, no Mama, no Sir William, there was nothing but heavy struggling work, aching limbs, and weariness.

They reached the locks, and the lock keeper came out of his cottage. 'They're frozen solid,' he said. 'You'll never do it.'

'We must,' Tam said in desperation.

They worked hard, all of them, even Annabel and Celia. They podged the ice, they lifted great lumps, ice scraped the sides of the boat and Tam, frightened, wondered what they would do if the boat was damaged, if they had a hole. They ground their way through, and were on the pound again. 'You'd be better to wait here,' the lock keeper advised.

'We're nearly home now,' said Tam.

They went another two miles and the going was rough. The horses were sweating, Jim could no longer break the ice. And suddenly there was a huge rending sound and Tam shouted, 'What is it, Jim? Is the boat damaged?'

'It's cut a bit, Miss Tam. But we can't get any farther, the ice is too thick.'

'But we can't stop here, Jim.'

'You'll cut the hull to ribbons, Miss Tam. We can't go on.'

They were stuck in the ice.

Tam had been looking forward to getting back to Chilverton, to sinking down in her cabin to sleep for hours. Now she had to decide what to do about the horses. 'Can we leave them out in the cold?' she asked. She looked round, there were no farms nearby, no villages. And it was two miles to the lock.

'There's a bit of shelter over there,' John pointed. 'Looks like an old barn. I'll take the horses there, give them a rub down; if you let me have two blankets they'll be all right.'

'And hurry,' Abby said. 'I've a hot meal waiting.'

John saw to the horses, taking the oats which they always carried.

The morning showed no signs of a thaw, and after breakfast Tam looked at Jim for advice.

'We'll have to wait for the ice-breaker,' he said. 'Have you got enough food, Miss Tam, cos there's a village about two miles away.'

'I can't see one,' Tam said.

'Over that way, it's in a hollow.'

'Well, that's a relief, though we've got enough food for a day or two, at least, haven't we, Abby? How long will the coal last?'

'Couple of days,' said John.

'Well, we're all right for today anyway.' And they sat in the warmth of the saloon, looking out over the frozen wastes. Jim went to find the village and came back saying there was a shop so they could get plenty of food, but there was no coal to spare, nor wood. Tam looked at their rapidly dwindling stocks. They had to keep warm. Without a fire they would simply freeze to death.

'How far are we from Chilverton?' she asked Jim.

'About four miles.'

She pondered. If the worst came to the worst they could take the horses to get some coal; but they had enough for the day.

It was late afternoon when she saw in the distance a man on horseback riding along the towpath. She went up on deck as he approached. It was Charles.

'Are you all right?' he asked.

'Oh, Charles.' Her relief was great. 'Yes. Can you get us out?'

'I'll get the ice-breaker through as soon as possible. Are there any more boats iced up behind you?'

'Not that I know of.' And as he made to ride on. 'How long will it be before the ice-breaker comes?'

'Days. We have the whole canal to get through. Are you all right for food?'

'Yes, there's a shop in the village.'

'How about coal?'

'We're running low. I wondered if we could take the horses to get some?'

'Yes, do that. Send Jim and John. There'll be something on the wharf you can load it into. You must have coal.'

He hesitated, looking down at her, and she asked, a glint of her old mischief returning, 'Aren't you going to scold me for being out in this?'

'No,' he said. 'You wanted to work the boats and you have to work in winter as well as summer. Take care of yourself.' And with that he rode away.

They remained in the ice for three days; sometimes they would walk in the fields for exercise, once they found a duck marooned on land and they scooped a hole in the ice for it to return, which it did, squawking indignantly. Other birds weren't so lucky, they were frozen in the snow. Tam, seeing this, put out food, and every morning a crowd of birds gathered round the boat.

It was on the third day that they heard the noise of thundering hooves and they ran out to the deck. Tam thought it sounded like a cavalry charge, and her startled eyes took in the sight of at least a dozen huge shire horses pulling an iron-sheathed breaker through the ice as fast as they could, half jog-trot, half slow-canter. The noise was tremendous, the thud of heavy hooves, the cracking of whips, and the shattered pack ice thrown up in all directions burst over the still air like a frozen firework display. It was the most spectacular event she had ever seen.

Chapter Five

Tam guessed that the bad winter kept Charles away from them, though even in spring he did not ride along the wharf so often. No doubt busy electioneering, she thought a little sourly; the Reform Bill that he'd been talking about for years had finally been passed, and she wished him joy of it. Living in the town she was kept abreast of events by the citizens of Chilverton, who took a lively interest in national affairs and celebrated each happening with gusto. When the Bill was thrown out of the Lords they turned the signboard of the King's head at the beerhouse upside down in protest, and when it was finally passed they celebrated in fine style. Tam wondered why they were so excited, not many of them would actually have votes after all, but Geoffrey told Celia that it was because they would be represented in Parliament for the first time, as would Birmingham. And Geoffrey wondered acidly where it would all end.

There were three days of celebrations, church bells were rung, there were processions in the streets with flags and banners led by brass bands. On the following day the poor of the town were given beef and ale and finally, on the Saturday, there was another grand procession, each person carrying a lighted candle, others in decorated wagons. Tables were placed in the streets and there was tea, followed by dancing.

The girls watched the jollifications with mixed feelings: Juliet clapped her hands with childlike pleasure; Celia, on hearing that the more important people of the town had been invited to a dinner party at the Town Hall, was mortified to think they had not been asked, though no doubt the Warings would be among the guests; Tam was concerned that they could not put on a play on the Saturday; while Annabel went to see Lord Brooke, making no secret of the fact now, and saying she would stay overnight with friends.

She not only stayed overnight, but for another week, and Tam was furious. They were able to put on a play, as by this time they all knew every part, and could double, but Tam was incensed that Annabel should ignore the fact that she was *working*, that she had a duty to be at her place. Tam was saving regularly now, hoping to expand, to buy another boat, and she

105

thought it might be easier to run a carrier business, or even an ordinary packet boat; this way there would be no trouble with erratic performers. Gilbert, fortunately, was no problem now, he was never drunk, never even went to the 'Anchor'; he had, it seemed, found another rendezvous in Chilverton or somewhere, which must be more congenial as he spent all his spare time there. But running carriers would put them in direct com-·· petition with Sir William, and Tam felt she was powerless against him at present. Later, when she had more money and boats, she would do it and glory in it, but for the present she had to stick to show-boats. Tam knew, too, that in the main her anger was directed towards her mother's compan-ion, the man Annabel had dared to put in her father's place, and she knew that before very much longer she would have to confront Annabel, her anger was choking her.

When Annabel finally stepped on the boat she was as light-hearted as ever. 'I'm so sorry I'm late,' she cried. 'But my friends begged me to stay on.'

'Had you forgotten that we had two performances?' asked Tam.

'Oh but, surely, just two – ' began Annabel.

'Is two too many,' said Tam. 'We're due in Birmingham this afternoon and we are going, Mama, so I hope you don't feel too tired.'

There was a curious silence. Celia and Juliet both stared. Abby, bringing in a glass of cider, stopped to listen. Tam went on, 'We must know, Mama. It's too bad of you stay away like this – '

'We'll talk later, Tam.' Annabel waved her aside. 'Now, what has been happening while I've been away?'

'Mrs Waring's Pick-Nick is at the end of July,' cried Celia, excitedly. 'That's only two weeks away.'

'Is that so?' asked Annabel, vaguely.

'Oh, Mama, I did tell you,' Celia said, vexed.

'You did,' said Tam. 'And we asked what a Pick-Nick was.'

'They're all the rage,' said Celia with an air of smug superiority. 'They can be held outside in gardens, and the Warings have large grounds, as you know.'

'Oh yes, I remember,' said Annabel. 'A garden party, I imagine.'

'We've been preparing for weeks,' Celia said. 'Sending out so many invitations. Absolutely everyone who is anyone has been invited.'

Tam said flatly, 'I shan't go.'

'You might wait for an invitation,' said Celia, spitefully. 'What makes you think you'd be welcome?'

'Why shan't you go?' asked Juliet.

'Because,' Tam said savagely, 'I have nothing to wear, and I am not going to anything, Pick-Nick or garden party, in a black dress that is the worse for wear.'

After all, Charles might be there, she thought. Since they had been iced up, hardly the place for a tête-à-tête, he had been present only once for luncheon when they were invited to the Warings', and then he had warned them how busy he was going to be in the future, for, once the Bill was passed, there would be an election, so his time would be taken up with meetings and general electioneering.

Celia interrupted her thoughts. 'I want a new dress,' she said. 'You must get one for me, Tam.'

'We can't afford it,' said Tam.

'Oh come, Celia's right,' Annabel said, sharply for her. 'She can't go in an old dress.'

'Not when she's hoping to bring Geoffrey up to scratch,' said Tam, and Celia flushed. She was more than a little worried that so far all Mrs Waring's and her own combined efforts had not resulted in a proposal. Tam saw her distress and was immediately contrite. 'I'm sorry,' she said. 'I'll get you a dress. And Juliet. I'm sure there is a good needlewoman in Chilverton who could make them. But I shan't go.'

'No one wants you to,' said Celia.

Tam walked on to the deck. What's the matter with me? she wondered. Why am I so bad-tempered? Juliet stepped up quietly behind her and sat down on the small seat.

'You will come to the Pick-Nick, won't you?' she asked gently.

'I don't know. Maybe I will.'

It was, oddly, Annabel who decided Tam. As they prepared to leave for Birmingham, John bringing round the horses, Annabel said, 'As we won't be able to put on a show on the Pick-Nick day, I shall see my friend Lord Brooke.'

'Why don't you bring him too?' Celia put in eagerly.

Tam opened her mouth in surprise. Celia, who had been so alarmed about scandal . . .

Later as they sped through the water, the *Princess* sending out white-edged ripples, and disturbing shoals of tiny minnows, she asked Jim to take the tiller while she went to speak with her mother.

'Mama, we have to think of the future. If Celia goes we shall need another girl. Where could we find one?'

'Oh, I don't know,' Annabel said vaguely.

'I don't understand you, Mama. You were so eager at the start.'

'Yes, but things are different now.'

'In what way? Mama, you're not thinking of leaving, are you?' Tam asked sharply.

Now Annabel's wandering attention was caught at last. 'What do you mean?' she asked.

'I mean Lord Brooke, Mama.'

There was a pause. 'Why do you say that?' Annabel asked.

'Because we could manage without Celia. I'm not sure we could manage without you.' And Abby and John, she added silently.

'Nonsense, Tam, of course you could manage without me. You seem very capable of managing everything. But the question won't arise, will it?'

'You see a lot of Lord Brooke.'

'Well, why not? Your father had been dead for a long time now.'

107

Tam's anger rose. 'From what I heard you had been seeing him long before that. When my father was alive.'

Annabel looked at her intently. 'When and where did you hear that?'

'I heard the two of you talking, on the boat.'

'Oh dear,' said Annabel, flatly. 'Oh dear, Tam.' She paced up and down, seeming on the verge of saying something, stopped. Tam watched her in silence.

'Well, there it is. Brooke has always loved me.'

'And wants you to be his mistress,' said Tam.

Annabel looked at her oddly. 'What else did you overhear?'

'I heard him say he has to keep away from London. Is that why you agreed so willingly to live on the boat, Mama? Because it would be easier for you to meet him? Than incur scandal elsewhere.'

Annabel shrugged. 'Scandal, pooh. I did not,' she added, with quiet dignity, 'leave you all to fend for yourselves.'

'To become his mistress, I should think not,' said Tam, hotly.

'Tam, it is a long story, and I don't feel I can tell you all. Not now, not yet . . . Someday you may know. But I promise you I shall not leave you to become his mistress.'

Tam breathed a sigh of relief.

'But,' Annabel went on firmly, 'I shall still see him. As I do now.'

'I think it's monstrous,' Tam burst out. 'Oh, I see it all now. The way you packed us off to school, would not have us home. Because you were never home, were you? You were on the stage. So you said. I expect you were with *that man*, while poor Papa was so alone – ' she stopped, choking.

'Don't you like him?' Annabel asked tentatively.

'Who? Lord Brooke? I detest him.'

'I'm sorry about that, Tam,' she said, and there was none of her usual vagueness in her voice. 'I had hoped you'd come to like him. For as I said, I shall not stop seeing him.'

'And you'll take him to the Pick-Nick?'

'Yes.'

'Then I shan't go.'

The Pick-Nick was the talk of the town, even the boatpeople knew about it, in great detail. A large wooden floor had been laid in the grounds of Grange House, upon which were set tables and chairs; huge amounts of food had been ordered, as well as an orchestra. Whether any of the invited gentry had attended no one knew for certain, but a number of carriages had driven through the town, containing elegant ladies in summer dresses with parasols, accompanied by well-groomed men. Celia and Juliet twittered around, each wearing a new dress of sprigged muslin, not of the latest mode perhaps, but pretty and new. Annabel was stylish as always in vivid blue, and Tam looked at her mother critically, thinking her outfit rather showy for a widow; she should still be wearing black or grey. And then another carriage drove up, stopping at the boat and Lord Brooke stepped out, bowing to Annabel, to the girls, to Tam, who was sitting sullenly on the well-deck.

'You're not going, Tamarisk?' he asked, looking at her work dress.

Tam studied him in silence. He was tall, taller than her father, with thick brown hair turning grey, and handsome features. Yet there was a dissolute air about him somehow, and she wondered if he spent much of his time in gaming-rooms and clubs in London, as well as the usual country pursuits of the aristocracy: hunting, shooting grouse in Scotland, salmon fishing in Ireland, then the attractions of Goodwood and Cowes, oh, she'd heard all about it all from Amanda Fotheringay. She wondered too if Mama accompanied him on any of these pursuits and realised that if she did then the world must know about their – *friendship* – and if so, what of his wife? And they were so *old*, Mama must be over forty now.

'It is a pity if you are not going,' he said, taking her silence to mean so.

'I don't wish to go,' Tam said.

He was beside her now. 'You like the boat so very much?' he asked.

'I do,' she replied. 'My father taught me all about boats, and I always intended to work with him. That wasn't to be, but I can still carry out his wishes.'

'Is it so important then?' Lord Brooke asked.

'What I plan to do, yes,' Tam said.

'But surely you can allow yourself a little enjoyment occasionally?'

'Not this time,' said Tam.

'Come, Brooke, she will not be dissuaded,' Annabel said. 'Girls, are we ready?' and the party stepped on to the towpath.

Tam watched them depart and wondered how to spend the time till they returned, wondered if Charles would be there, and wished she had not been so hasty. But she did hate Lord Brooke so. If Charles were there today . . . supposing he had changed his mind, had decided to give up his ambitions for love of her, and she wasn't there to accept . . . and a strange feeling of apprehension crept over her.

She wanted Charles. She wanted his arms around her, holding her tight, wanted to feel his lips on hers, wanted to see his black eyes resting on her, making her believe that she was beautiful.

She went to the tiny room used as a washroom and took off all her clothes. Before she started washing she looked critically at her body in the small mirror, or as much of it as she could see. There was a quality about it she had never seen before, a certain roundness, almost voluptuous, she thought and blushed. So was her body beautiful? She realised that she was seeing herself through his eyes, and found herself beautiful for his eyes told her so. Carefully she washed her limbs, her body, as though performing some solemn rite, then she went back to her cabin and lay on the bed, wishing he were with her. From time to time she touched her body, her breasts, her waist, her thighs. She felt restless and did not know why, felt a longing inside her but had no idea what she yearned for, except for Charles, of course, kissing her on the lips, his eyes telling her she was desirable.

109

And whatever would anyone think of me lying here with no clothes on? she thought guiltily and jumped up feeling slightly ashamed; she dressed hurriedly, went into the saloon, and sat down to watch the life on the canal as it went on all around her.

But she'd see him tomorrow. If he came to the wharf, she'd see him. They would work something out, it would all come right if she let it . . . She sat and dreamed.

The church clock struck the hour and she counted: nine. What time would they be back? She went out on to the deck, and sat watching the sun sink, the shadows fall over the boats, heard the first owl calling. Still they did not come.

It was nearly two hours later when she heard the sound of the carriage come to a standstill on the wharf, and the single lamp showed Lord Brooke escorting them all to the boat, before driving away. Annabel yawned dramatically and said she'd go to bed. Celia and Juliet were both strangely quiet.

'Did you enjoy it?' asked Tam.

'Oh yes, indeed,' said Celia, but her voice was oddly flat.

'It was very nice,' Juliet said dreamily. 'There was dancing, and they are dancing still, but Mama thought we should leave now.'

'We should have stayed,' said Celia, and Tam noted her despondent air. So Geoffrey still hadn't been brought up to scratch.

'Did you dance?' Tam asked Juliet.

'Oh yes,' answered Juliet, and there was an air of suppressed excitement about her. 'With Geoffrey. And Charles. It's the first time I've ever danced. Charles asked about you.'

'Did he?' Oh my love, I should have gone, Tam thought regretfully. 'You look flushed,' and she studied Juliet. 'Perhaps it was too much for you, the dancing.'

'Oh no,' Juliet said, her eyes shining. 'It was simply wonderful. I had no idea . . .' But she allowed Tam to lead her to the cabin, where she quickly undressed and lay silent. When Tam asked again about the dancing, Juliet said, 'Hush, Tam, let us sleep now, I'm tired.' And Tam was silent, as she thought of what she'd missed. Dancing with Charles, oh it would have been heavenly; she never had been to a real dance. She lay for a long time, still thinking, dreaming, about Charles. The moon shone fitfully between the drawn curtains, again she heard the owl. The water lapped softly at the side of the boat, and she wondered why she could not sleep. Yet she did not move, afraid of disturbing Juliet.

She heard the church clock strike twelve, and Juliet stirred. She was half asleep now, and did not open her eyes as her sister left the cabin. Doubtless she was going to the closet. But Juliet was a long time, and then Tam heard a strange sound. The sound of muffled footsteps on the deck. She sat up with a start, fully awake now. Juliet couldn't have gone out . . . she fumbled for the candle, and when it was lit, gazed round the cabin. Her sister's clothes were gone.

Where on earth was she going? A finger of fear touched at her heart.

110

Something was on Juliet's mind, she had suspected it for days, the way she walked around white-faced and deep in thought. Tam glanced through the window, she could see no one. She crept out of the cabin, silently to the deck: the moon came from behind a cloud, lighting up the canal and the wharf beyond, turning the piles of coal into silver. But of Juliet there was no sign.

To walk abroad at such a late hour, what could she be thinking of? Tam sat on the well-deck for a long time, she was tired now and wanted to sleep. She wondered if she should wake her mother, but some instinct caused her to wait.

As the clock struck two, she heard horses' hooves, and then a closed carriage came into view. She watched as it halted, and Juliet's figure was silhouetted against the shadows, talking to someone inside. At last the carriage drove away and Juliet came to the boat.

She saw Tam as she reached the rail and gasped, standing as if undecided whether to run away.

'Come inside,' hissed Tam. 'Before I wake Mama.'

Juliet stepped on the boat.

'Where have you been?' Tam whispered.

Juliet didn't answer.

'You were with a man,' Tam said tiredly.

'Yes.'

'At midnight? Who was he?'

'I can't tell you, Tam. I promised.'

'But, Juliet – ' Tam was perplexed.

Remembrance clutched at Tam, Juliet saying 'I like one of the Waring brothers' . . . So that was it. 'It's Charles, isn't it?' she said, her voice dull.

Juliet bowed her head.

'And you went back to the dance?' Tam was aghast.

'No. Not to dance. Just to see – him.'

'Did anyone else see you?'

'No. I don't think so.'

'You mean, he didn't *ask* you to go back?'

'No. It was not his fault at all, but mine. Let me go, Tam, please. Please.' Juliet looked deathly pale in the moonlight, as if she were about to faint.

'Why are you so upset?' Tam asked. 'What happened? Tell me, Juliet.'

'No. No, I can't. Please let me go.' And she wrenched away from her sister, and tiptoed to the cabin. Tam, fearful of waking the others, waited a moment then followed. When she reached the cabin Juliet was already in bed, and lay, eyes closed, head turned away, pretending to sleep.

Tam sighed and bent to pick up Juliet's underwear, left untidily on the floor, and stopped. What was that stain on her clothes? She blew out the candle. It would be her normal courses . . . but that had been last week. Sharing a tiny cabin, they could not but know all intimate details. So what was this? And then the diverse facts in her mind suddenly connected, and the things the girls at Miss Laker's had whispered made sense. She understood.

The full meaning of it all hit her. Charles, whom she thought was falling

111

in love with her, who had kissed her so feelingly in the play and held her hand on the boat, whose eyes said they admired her . . . but whose voice said not a word. Charles, who sat with Car Boswell at the inn. Who sympathised with the poor, yet who was a self-confessed rogue . . .

She had forgotten that Juliet liked him – or rather she'd been walking in such a cloud of love that nothing and no one else had existed for her. How could she not have remembered that he liked Juliet, too, had been so kind and thoughtful towards her . . . *Kind and thoughtful* . . . and she had thought he loved *her*.

She heard Juliet's muffled weeping in the night and said nothing. She wanted to weep too.

Saturday was always a busy day, with Abby out buying meat and ale, and Jim turning up to steer the boat, then the preparing of meals, the welcoming of the passengers in Birmingham, the play, the return. Juliet offered to help, but Tam refused, her sister looked so pale and wan she told her to rest. 'I'll see you later,' she said, but when she finally went to her cabin Juliet was asleep – or pretending. And when Tam awoke on Sunday morning Juliet was dressed and in the saloon with the others, and she took care she was never alone with Tam.

Tam counted the takings of the night before, and locked them away in her box until John could take them to the bank. They were doing well, she would have to think about getting another boat; if only their other affairs would come right. Mama and Lord Brooke . . . had Papa known? Had he been angry, hurt? Oh, that could wait, it paled into insignificance beside this business of Charles and Juliet.

And yet – Charles had never declared himself, indeed had seemed to warn her against too high expectations. As for that kiss, those admiring glances, the holding hands, that meant nothing to a man who obviously took any girl he fancied from Car Boswell to Juliet. *Juliet*.

She heard the sound of horses and looked up quickly, perhaps it was Charles. She saw, to her amazement, Mrs Waring and Geoffrey alighting from their carriage. She heard Celia shriek, 'Mama,' saw her rush into her own cabin to put on her best dress.

As Tam went to the deck, Mama was already there, welcoming her guests as if it were a royal garden party. She led them into the saloon, and Celia came in, trying to look as though she hadn't hurried, but her breathless excitement betrayed her.

'Well, I declare, it's quite cosy,' said Mrs Waring. She fanned her face. 'I am quite exhausted by the Pick-Nick. We had a great many guests.' Though none from the gentry, she forbore to add, and it was this, as much as her son's sudden and surprising pleading, that brought her so hurriedly to the Calders' boat to finally bring Celia into the family.

At last, after some small talk, Mrs Waring spoke to Annabel. 'My dear boy, Geoffrey, would like to ask for your daughter's hand.' She had the manner of one conferring a favour.

But Annabel was not to be outdone. 'Celia?' she asked. 'Indeed.' And pondered.

'You have no objections?' Mrs Waring asked, a little uncertain now.

'Well,' Annabel drawled, enjoying herself immensely, 'I had not thought of losing my daughters for a long time yet. And, of course, there will be no dowry.'

'Mama!' Celia cried in agony.

'However, we must leave it to the girl, I suppose. I would not want to stand in anyone's way.'

The happy couple looked into each other's eyes then, and Tam wondered ungraciously what they saw there. A safe home for Celia, children with aristocratic connections for Geoffrey? And was there a touch of envy in her uncharitable thoughts?

'Celia,' said Geoffrey, 'shall we go for a little walk?' And now Tam's uncharitable thoughts dissolved into a mad desire to giggle as she wondered where Geoffrey had taken Celia, whether he would propose on his knees on the towpath. She wondered also why the sudden haste, why he hadn't chosen to propose at the Pick-Nick?

Talk in their absence was desultory and all were relieved when Geoffrey and Celia returned.

'Mama,' cried Celia, 'we are to be married just as soon as we can get my trousseau together. We are out of mourning now. Do say yes, please, Mama. I suppose it must be a quiet affair?' she added, her voice tinged with regret.

'Very well,' said Annabel. 'I hope you will be very happy,' and she kissed her daughter.

'I would like, if I may, to give a small soirée for their betrothal,' said Mrs Waring graciously. 'Nothing elaborate, of course.'

It was Celia's moment of triumph. Tam kissed her and murmured her good wishes. Juliet, surprisingly, did not, but then, Tam realised, she had a lot on her mind; no doubt wishing she were getting married too.

And she will. Juliet will be the next to marry, Tam vowed.

There were no trips on Thursday, it was her free day, so after Tam had sent Wednesday's takings to the bank with John, she tied on her bonnet firmly and strode along the wharf. She had seen Charles ride along to his office and was determined to confront him. She could not stop seeing him, she needed his advice on business matters, but she realised with a sinking of the heart, as she neared the office, she also did not want to stop seeing him. For love didn't die all in a minute, it stayed there and turned to anguish.

After a pause to compose herself, she knocked on the little office door and he bade her enter. He turned to look at her, eyes dancing in the old remembered way, and for a moment her heart lifted. She had forgotten just how handsome he was. And now, in his tight-fitting breeches, his black boots, coat thrown off showing his light shirt, open at the neck . . . she gulped and took a deep breath.

'Your servant, Tam,' he said, with a mock bow, and then put on his coat.

'I've come to ask your advice on business matters,' she said coolly. 'If you would kindly spare me a minute of your time.'

'With pleasure.' He drew up a chair and she sat down.

'Shortly,' she said, 'I shall want to buy another boat. How much would it cost?'

'A new boat? Why, an ordinary boat would cost more than a hundred pounds. And a packet much more.'

'I see,' she said.

'And you'd need horses and two men.'

'Yes, I know.' But her heart sank a little. It was more than she'd expected.

'Are you doing so well on the Birmingham runs then?' he asked, and last week she would have talked enthusiastically about the trips, mentioned Sir William and her need to feel safe with another boat. Now she said only, 'Well enough.'

He waited for more.

She stood up. 'There's one more thing,' she said, and tried to avoid looking into his eyes.

'Yes?'

She fumbled with her bonnet strings. 'Juliet.'

'Juliet?' His voice was suddenly wary.

She turned to look at him now, her voice hardening. 'You *know*. She was a virgin, Charles, when you took her and – ' a word from a novel sprang into her mind – 'ravished her.'

'Who told you that?'

'Juliet did.'

'Juliet told you I ravished her?'

'Well, not exactly, but someone did, and she said she'd been with you. She is in love with you.'

He was silent and she stole a glance at him, wishing she knew what went on in his mind.

'Why is it you who has come to me?' he asked at last. 'What is your Mama doing?'

'Oh you know Mama . . . I didn't tell her. You must marry Juliet, Charles.'

He hesitated for a long time, and Tam knew a sick feeling of disappointment that he didn't deny her accusation, that he couldn't . . . finally, he said woodenly, 'If Juliet wishes me to marry her, then I will do so.'

Tam turned to the door. 'Thank you,' she said. 'I will convey your message.'

And that night when Juliet slipped away to her cabin, Tam followed. At last she was alone with her sister.

'It'll be all right,' she said.

'What will be all right?' Juliet asked.

'You and Charles. He is agreeable to marrying you.'

Juliet turned, her white face angry. 'What *can* you mean, Tam?'

Now Tam was angry in her turn. 'He is to marry you. He was with you that night, you admitted it. He made love to you.'

Juliet was still. 'How do you know that?'

'I – guessed.'

Juliet looked straight ahead. 'Whatever I did that night,' she said, 'was my fault entirely. I went to the house, deliberately – ' she broke off.

'But that's not the point, Juliet. He will marry you. I saw him about it.'

Juliet turned then, as if she had just grasped the purport of Tam's words, and Tam had never seen her sister so angry.

'You saw him?' she gasped. 'About me? How *dare* you?'

'I dare, because someone had to. Would you prefer Mama to find out?'

Juliet shrugged. 'What could Mama have said? She is hardly a fine example, is she?'

It was the first criticism Tam had heard her make of anyone. She stammered, 'Oh, Juliet.'

'You had no right, Tam. Celia said you are far too bossy, and you are. Since we came to the boat, you think you can order us all around.'

'But who else will?' Tam asked helplessly. 'Someone has to do it.'

'You had no right,' Juliet repeated tonelessly.

'But, Juliet, Charles is willing to marry you.'

'I shall not marry Charles Waring or anyone else,' Juliet said.

'But – '

'Don't interfere in my life, Tam, you know nothing about me. The soup kitchen has opened again, and I shall go to help. Leave me alone, I shall live here and help the poor, there are so many of them now. That is all.'

And Tam knew that Juliet, the baby, the delicate one, had a strength within her that none of them could surpass. Or – was it unreason more than strength? Tam was uneasy.

'I wish you'd confide in me,' she said.

Juliet looked at her, and her eyes were deep pools. 'Better not,' she said. 'I was wrong to do what I did, but I love him. I thought . . .' she broke off. 'Now I can make amends.'

'You mean by helping the poor? Oh, Juliet, you don't have to.'

'I have made up my mind, Tam.'

Tam looked at her sister and knew a sudden love. She wondered why she didn't feel jealous that Charles should have made love to her, but she didn't. Only a great pity.

'We must,' said Annabel, 'go to London, of course. Where else would we buy gowns?'

'But, Mama,' protested Tam, 'it will be most expensive.'

'Oh, pshaw, Tam, you have been saving for a long time.'

'I'm not going to my engagement party in an old black dress,' said Celia. 'Nor in one that has been run up by a Chilverton dressmaker.'

'We are out of mourning now,' said Annabel. 'And this will be a launching of you girls into society – society of a sort,' she amended. 'So I think lavender or pale grey would be fitting. I must have a new dress myself, I've stayed away from social gatherings for too long.'

It was very pleasant, reflected Celia, that the party was to be held at the Warings', who would, naturally, spare no expense. Celia and her mother-in-law-to-be were in perfect accord, each knew what the other wanted, though this was never mentioned. Celia knew that Mrs Waring would be proud to introduce her new daughter-in-law as a close relative of an earl, and that she would be even more pleased if they could meet. Celia pondered writing to her grandfather, without her mother's knowledge, of course; she knew his address, and surely he would be pleased to hear of his grand-daughter's happiness. Celia, a great reader of novels from the new circulating library in Chilverton, pictured a fond scene where a dear old man wept in her arms, and talked of the happiness future great-grandchildren would give him.

'How much will it all cost?' Tam persisted anxiously.

'Oh, we'll go to Madame Marie, we shan't have to pay yet,' Annabel said airily. 'Madame is an old friend of mine.'

'But – '

'Don't be *mean*,' Celia said, and Tam sighed.

They went to London, of course, and to Madame Marie's small establishment in Bond Street, where a bow window displayed one single gown. They entered the salon which was quite plain and a magnificent personage in sumptuous black velvet swam towards them. 'Mrs Annabel, I declare, I have not seen you in ages.'

'Dear Madame, we live in the country now, since the death of my dear husband, and would you believe it, we cannot stay for fittings.'

'You will not be coming again?' Madame looked wary.

'The journey is so tiring, Madame, and my youngest daughter is delicate. But we need new dresses in a hurry, and knew you would have the very thing for us.' Annabel put on her most charming and imperious air.

Madame looked at the girls in their dutiful black and clucked disparagingly. 'Skirts are fuller this year,' she said. 'And shorter too . . . One may show the ankle quite clearly.' And then she conjured beautiful dresses from her workrooms and the girls stood entranced. Celia, grasping her moment of glory, immediately chose the most expensive, a gown in lavender which really did make her look quite pretty. But it was too large. Madame called in girls with pins. 'The work of a moment to alter it,' she said.

But it was far more than the work of a moment. It took three hours for the dress to be pinned satisfactorily, and although Madame promised it would be done the very next day, it would not be in time for the early coach home. They would have to stay another day, but while they were here, why not be measured for the wedding dress? It could be sent on later . . .

Tam closed her eyes in horror.

Annabel's dress was also expensive. 'The very thing for you,' said Madame, presenting a dress à la Taglioni of tulle worked in lamé. Tam whispered, 'Do you have to, Mama? You have so many others.' But Annabel waved her away.

'I don't need a dress at all, Mama,' Juliet said, but Tam could not take this

116

self-sacrifice, and Juliet was persuaded into trying a very pale vilet de Parme, which suited her very well.

'And now, Mistress Tamarisk,' said Madame.

Tam stood, determined to choose a plain, inexpensive, serviceable dress, that could be worn every day. But Madame, who had been a sales-woman for longer than Tam had been refusing, cunningly placed before her a gown of pale blue, and she stood hesitant. It had been so long since she had a new gown, and she had never had a ball gown . . . She tried it on, and stood transfixed. The neckline was low to the shoulders where it met delightful puff sleeves. A plain bodice led to a heart-shaped waist, and below, the skirt was full with a band of tiny, intricate stitching just above the hem. She had forgotten just how wonderful it was to wear nice clothes, to look beautiful. As she knew she did, with her red-brown hair falling round her face, her hazel eyes sparkling.

'That is lovely, Tam,' Juliet said and Tam knew she was lost.

And then there were undergarments, shawls; 'printed satin, of course,' said Madame; black slippers, silk stockings, long gloves, fans . . . As Madame swept out Tam whispered, 'Ask how much they all cost, Mama.'

'Indeed I will not.' said Annabel, affronted. 'Ask the price of clothes indeed! Don't you dare, Tam. Such things are not done.'

Madame returned. 'You wish to take the parcels with you? she asked. 'The ones which don't need alterations.'

'Oh no, indeed, send them to the Piccadilly Hotel,' said Mama, lan-guidly. 'We shall stay there tonight.'

'And your home address now?' Madame asked delicately.

There was a pause before Annabel said, 'Send to the wharf, at Chilverton.'

'The *wharf*, Mrs Annabel?'

'That is what I said,' Annabel replied, her voice haughty, and they left the establishment.

'We should have sent the bill to Grange House,' fretted Celia. 'Did you see her look when we mentioned the wharf? But no, we couldn't, Mrs Waring might think we wanted her to pay.'

'And Mama, staying at the *Piccadilly*.' Tam was furious.

'I had to, dear, or she wouldn't have given me credit at all. Madame is a sly old fox, but the best in town.'

'But we cannot afford the Piccadilly, Mama.'

'Just this once,' said Annabel.

So they stayed, and Tam thought that however hard it was not to have money, it was harder still to pretend they had.

As the coach jolted them homewards, she said to Annabel, 'You haven't seen anyone who might be willing to take Celia's place in the play?'

'Not really.' Annabel was vague.

'But, Mama, we've just been in London – '

'Yes, well, I didn't have time. I'll have to go again with Celia, to fit her wedding gown.'

Tam said no more. Arguing with Annabel was like talking to the wind, your words were just blown away.

Grange House was resplendent with flowers and decorations, and Mrs Waring and Geoffrey stood to receive their guests.

'Dear child,' said Mrs Waring as Celia approached, 'you must stay here with us,' and Celia, pink with pleasure, moved to take her place at Geoffrey's side. 'Dear Lady Annabel,' cooed Mrs Waring, 'do let the maid take your wraps, then pass up the stairs, you will find friends there, I know. The Dowager Duchess of Carminster is here, such a dear lady . . .' and they walked up the fine staircase, bowls of flowers at the top, into a large salon, where groups of people were sitting, animatedly chatting. Tam's eyes sparkled; it was good to be at a party.

'Annabel. Come here.' The call came from one of the sofas where an elderly lady with hennaed hair and thickly powdered face sat. They moved towards her, and her purple gown was so awful Tam thought she could only be a Dowager Duchess, no one else would *dare*, and this was borne out as Annabel introduced them.

'Sit beside me,' the Duchess commanded. 'I only came because I heard you were to be here, Annabel. I have a country house in Leicestershire and this person is always sending invitations. This time she wrote that your daughter is being betrothed so I thought I'd come.' She surveyed Tam through her lorgnette. 'And so this is the girl. I'd have known her anywhere. How are you, Annabel? Still on the stage?'

Tam waited for her mother to explain that she wasn't the girl, but she did not. As Annabel sat chatting to the Duchess, Tam looked around the room wondering who else was there; She hadn't seen Charles yet. Then to her horror she saw Sir William Fargate, and he was approaching . . . oh, he wouldn't speak to them, surely.

'Your Grace.' He was before them now, and the Duchess looked up, none too pleased.

'Oh, Sir William Fargate, to be sure. We were just having a cosy chat, Annabel and I.'

'I merely wanted to point out that there is a cold collation in the dining room and then later we are to be entertained in the ballroom with music.'

'Well, I suppose we must go,' said the Duchess, scrambling to her feet. 'And what are you doing here, Sir William? You don't like socialising as a rule.' She was, Tam thought, exceedingly rude.

'I was over-persuaded this time,' Sir William said with a thin smile. 'It isn't my habit.'

'Can't tear yourself away from your money-making activities, eh? How are the coal-pits?'

'Doing well, thank you, your Grace.'

'Humph. Not so well for the poor little lads who work in 'em, I'll be bound.'

'I didn't know you were interested in the lower classes, your Grace,' Sir William's voice was barely audible.

and presses her ever tighter. The music ended, and his black eyes held to her hazel ones; they were quite serious but they said I love you.

He took her back to her seat and she wondered if she were dreaming. And now she wanted to sit and dream on, it was the second time he had held her in his arms, and it had been rapture. Don't think about Juliet tonight, just dream . . . A thin voice interrupted her reverie.

'May I have the pleasure of a dance?'

It was Sir William. She looked round, wanting to refuse, knowing she dare not, not before her mother and Mrs Waring and all the assembled company. But how could she bear his arms around her after Charles? She stood up, saying, 'I am a little tired.'

'Then we'll go into an ante-room, I wish to speak to you for a moment.' Her heart thudded, as he added, 'In private.'

They walked to a small side room, and she asked curtly, 'What is it?'

'Now,' he said facing her, 'what is it you wish me to do?'

'Do? About what?' she asked.

'Come, don't let's pretend. I'm not a fool. You make it clear where your sympathies lie, you threaten to kill me. I repeat, what is it you wish me to do?'

She pursed her lips. 'All the things I said before: lower the tolls on the canals, join with the other companies to make one uniform system so all boats can pass – '

'I don't own other companies.'

'You own the Chilverton, so must have some influence with the others.'

'And supposing I give you all these things? Will you pay the price I ask?'

'Price? What price?'

'I think you know.' He did not touch her, but there was that same lascivious look in his eyes, as before . . . Disgusted, she turned to go, but he caught hold of her arm.

'Be careful, Tamarisk. I could make things difficult for you.'

'How?' she demanded.

'Your boat,' he said, 'the *Princess*. It was bought by Jamie Calder in 1824 from Master's Boatyard. It belonged to him, and therefore, now to me.'

'My father's debts are paid.'

'No matter, the boat should have gone with the others. That is the law.' He stared down at her. 'Do you think for one moment that you could fight me in open court?'

'Not if you are the magistrate, I suppose.'

He laughed. 'Spirited, eh?'

'Sir William, just what do you want from me?'

'I want you. I have since I met you.'

'You've only seen me once.'

'More than once. I've watched you when you didn't know I was there.'

'What exactly are you suggesting?'

'I'm proposing a few visits to a little house I rent, a few hours in my company.'

She was outraged. 'How dare you talk to me like that? How dare you treat me as if I were a – a harlot?'

He laughed. 'All women are. All have something to sell, and most sell it for a wedding ring. You want the boats and the canal. I want you. It seems a fair exchange.'

'And if I don't agree, as I most definitely shall not?'

'You will agree. Because if you do not I shall recover the boat, the *Princess*. But don't be alarmed, I'll give you time to make up your mind. Shall we say three months?' Now, let us go back to your mother.' He bowed and, seething, she allowed herself to be led away as good manners decreed.

The date for Celia and Geoffrey's wedding was finally fixed for October, and as summer faded into a mellow autumn, each of the Calder women was wrapped in her own private thoughts. Annabel was away for much of the time now, Tam supposing she was with Lord Brooke, though he never came to the boat. Juliet walked around white-faced, and they all watched her with disquiet. Only Celia was happy, she took the carriage when the horses were not being used, and visited the Warings.

One morning after the Birmingham trip, Tam was sitting in her cabin, trying to keep her thoughts on the books. Sir William was, as always now, preying on her mind, and she wondered what she was going to do about him. When she heard the horse's hooves, she glanced through the window to see a carriage, and Geoffrey alighting, but did not move as he came to the boat and asked Annabel for permission to take Celia to Grange House, and Celia, all a-twitter, ran for her bonnet. After the two of them had driven away, Tam walked through to the saloon and found Annabel there alone.

'Where is Juliet?' asked Tam.

'She is gone to help at the soup kitchen,' Annabel replied.

'Oh, Mama, how could you let her go?'

'Because I could not stop her,' Annabel said, a trifle tartly. 'I have not noticed that any of my daughters do a thing I ask them to do. I begged Juliet not to go, I told her she was far too delicate to ladle out soup to such people. She merely put on her bonnet and walked out.'

'I'll fetch her back,' said Tam. 'Where is this kitchen?'

'As far as I can gather it's along Gate Street,' said Annabel.

Tam hurried back to her cabin to put away the precious box with the takings. She picked up her bonnet and stood for a moment before the mirror. Faith, she thought despondently, how dreadful my hair looks. I'm always too tired to brush it now when I go to bed, and there's never enough water to wash it as often as I'd like. Still at least we're making money now. But I'll have to get another boat next. My hair must wait. She stepped along the gateway to the towpath.

She noticed the soup kitchen before she came to it, saw the crowd of pallid men and women with babies in their arms waiting outside. There were so many people she did not try to push through them, but went round the back and entered the kitchen. Large urns bubbled on a stove, tended by several women.

'Have you come to help?' asked one of the woman. 'I'm Mrs Dawson.'

'I'm looking for my sister, Juliet Calder,' answered Tam.

'In there,' and Mrs Dawson nodded towards the other room.

Tam looked inside one of the urns, and saw a weak watery fluid. 'What is it?' she asked.

'Beef soup,' said Mrs Dawson.

'I don't see any beef,' said Tam.

'We put a pound of beef to a gallon of soup,' Mrs Dawson told her shortly.

'And I'll bet it's not best beef either,' said Tam, and all the women stopped working to stare at this intruder who dared to criticise, but she was already moving into the other room where the soup was being distributed, when she stopped, startled. Juliet was ladling out the soup and beside her, helping too, was Charles. And Tam's treacherous heart was lurching in the old remembered way, so that she had to stand a minute to recover her composure, before moving forward again.

'Juliet,' she said. 'You must come home.'

'That is what I've been trying to persuade her to do,' said Charles. 'But as she won't, you must get yourself a ladle, Tam; the more help we have, the sooner we'll be outside.'

'Juliet – ' Tam repeated.

'I am not going,' Juliet said. 'I told you, Tam, this was what I was going to do. These poor people – '

Tam's eyes went round the room. There was another smell here, mingling with that of the soup, the smell of unwashed bodies crowded together in one small room. Several of the children seemed to have colds, their noses were runny, they coughed incessantly. 'Juliet, you should not be here,' she said. But it was obvious that Juliet was not to be moved, so Tam rolled up her sleeves, picked up a ladle and set to work.

They worked for a long time, it seemed like hours: ladling soup; the women in the kitchen bringing more urns; handing out more. The room grew hotter, Tam felt her gown sticking to her back, and the smell grew more intolerable. Juliet's face grew whiter and whiter, and when at last she staggered against the table, Tam insisted on taking her into the kitchen and pushed her on to a chair. 'Stay there,' she commanded. 'I'll finish in there.'

And she did, with Charles, until she could hardly see, so weary was she, but the soup was running out, and to the few who were left, Charles said, 'Come back tomorrow.' They returned to Juliet.

'Shall I fetch the carriage?' asked Charles, but Juliet said, 'No, I am all right now. Come, I can walk.'

'She'll be better in the air,' said Tam. 'Let's get her to the boat.' And they walked on, supporting Juliet between them, saying nothing.

At the wharf, Juliet pulled away. 'Loose me, I'm better now,' she insisted. 'Let me walk alone, or Mama won't let me go again.'

'Juliet – ' began Tam, but her sister was gone.

She sighed and turned to Charles. 'I would like to talk to you,' she said.

123

'Then we'll go into my office,' and they fell into step.

'Did you speak to Juliet?' Tam asked.

'I did. She will not marry me, or anyone.'

'Then what are you going to do?'

'There is little I can do,' he said.

'If Mama finds out – '

'I think it better your mother does not find out,' he said smoothly.

'Well, you would say that, wouldn't you.' She paused, and as he looked down at her she was acutely aware of her old gown, her dishevelled appearance. As if that mattered now.

He opened the door of the little office and stood back to let her enter. It was quiet in here, and she looked round at the maps on the walls, thinking of the many times she had been here just to see Charles.

'It was good of you to come to help Juliet,' she said colourlessly.

'But I didn't come to help Juliet,' he said.

She stood by the door. 'Then why did you come?'

'Well, if you must know, I gave some money for the soup shop.' And at her look of surprise. 'Someone has to, did you think the meat comes out of the air? Many people in the town contribute, and we are promised help from a charitable society in London.'

'How much did you give? she asked expressionlessly.

'Twenty pounds.'

'And did you buy the beef?'

'Why, no. Why do you ask?'

'Because I saw the meat in the kitchen. One pound of beef to a gallon of soup, and poor quality beef at that.'

'I thought it looked a little watery,' Charles said ruefully: 'But then I don't know how soup is made.'

Neither did I until Papa died, Tam thought. 'Am I right in thinking Mrs Dawson is Dawson the butcher's wife?' she asked aloud.

'Yes.'

'Then you know where your money goes, Charles.'

He stared down at her, and she looked away. 'Here I go again,' she said in a small voice. 'Being bossy.'

'But you are right,' he said. 'I'll see Dawson, and make sure that the soup is better in future.' He picked up her hand. 'As you have so often said, someone has to do the hard things.' His voice held none of the old mockery, it was curiously gentle, and she stood for a moment, trembling. Don't be kind to me, Charles, please, I couldn't bear it. Not now . . . she thought and snatched her hand away.

'I must talk to you about buying a new boat,' she said, changing the subject to relieve the tension.

'Oh yes. You did mention it once before.'

She hesitated. 'Could Sir William take the *Princess* back?'

He was watching her closely. 'Did he say he would?'

'I just wondered if he had the right.'

'He could say the debts weren't paid.'

124

'But Mr Benton told Mama the sale of the house would pay off the debts.'

'H'm. But Mr Benton is Sir William's lawyer. Tam, there's little point in fighting Sir William; you saw what happened to your father. And you couldn't afford to go to law anyway. Oh, Tam, why don't you give up? Buy a little house somewhere.'

'Where?' she asked. 'What would we buy with the small amount we have? A weaver's cottage in the Patch? No, Charles, when I buy a house it will be Cherry Trees.'

'Very well. What kind of boat do you want to buy?'

'Which brings in the most money, packets or freight?'

'For one boat, a packet. For freight, you'd need several boats, horses, then you'd have to find your loads, it would all take time.'

'Very well then, I'll buy another packet.'

He sighed. 'You know, Tam, we talked about the railways. The Liverpool and Manchester Railway is working, and many people think it will be the transport of the future.'

'And many people think it will not.'

'True, opinion is divided. But trains can travel faster. If they should make a national network so that goods – and people – can go all around the country without hindrance, then believe me the canals will suffer.'

'And our only defence is a countryside network of canals with low tolls and a uniform policy.'

'Yes, if only the canal companies could see that.'

'Then we must make them. That's why I want to stay here. Too much is at stake. This canal is important, it is in the middle of the system. If Sir William keeps the canal just for his own boats, with his high charges for warehousing, it will affect the whole of the canal trade. He must be made to see reason, somehow or other.'

'You're right, of course. I believe already someone has said that a railroad would make the Trustees of his Grace of Bridgewater as anxious to let and sell warehouses and land, as they have been to grasp and retain them in the past. The same applies here. Well, I'll look out for you. Are you sure you have the money?'

'I'll manage.'

'I'd lend it to you, but at the moment I'm having to spend so much on the election – '

'Not buying votes, I hope,' she said, with a hint of her old mischief.

He laughed. 'All that will have to go. Though I suspect the old game of treating will go on.'

'Treating?'

'Buying men beer, getting them drunk, making trouble. Influencing the voters.'

'Sometimes,' Tam said, 'I have the feeling that men don't seem to have made much of a success of running the country.'

'Sometimes,' Charles said, 'I am inclined to agree with you. But we're improving, Tam, at least grant us that. So no, I shan't bribe anyone to vote for me, but there are expenses, and there is always the fear that Sir William might dismiss me for being so presumptuous as to oppose him. But Tam, be careful, and whatever you do, don't go to money-lenders.'

She was alert suddenly. 'I don't know anything about money-lenders.'

'Oh, there is one in Gate Street. That little office next to the printers. Their interest rate is so high that you spend all your life paying to them.'

'I see.' She went to the door, opened it. 'Goodbye, Charles,' she said, and walked away. Well, I have to see him, he's a sort of business partner, she told herself.

'Tamarisk.' Tam stood in the saloon, wondering if she had imagined the voice, but she went anyway on the deck, and found Charles standing outside, holding his horse.

'I came to tell you that I've just heard of a boat for sale if you are interested,' he said.

'So soon?' she was thrilled and excited.

'I went to Masters' boatyard yesterday, they're one of the best. They have a packet boat, it's one they built, but a little the worse for wear.'

'What happened to it?'

'It sank.'

'It must have been strong then,' she said sarcastically.

'It was an accident. Another boat rammed it, cutting its side.'

'Were there people on board?'

'No, it happened at night.'

She stared at him in perplexity, but he ignored her silent question.

'Masters can repair it, and they'll make a good job of it, if you want it.'

'And the price?'

'Round about a hundred pounds. It's a bargain, Tam.'

'All right. When can I see it?'

'I'll take you. When can you come?'

'Why – I can come now, but – ' she hesitated. The last thing she should be doing was to be alone with Charles. 'How far is it?' she asked. 'Can we take the boat?'

'It would take too long. Can you ride?'

'Of course.'

'Then we'll go on horseback. Across country, much quicker that way.'

'Yes.' Riding would be best. She had been alone with him in the office and didn't want to be alone again. Not with him too near . . . riding would be ideal. 'Wait a minute, I'll change into my riding habit.' She ran back inside and changed hurriedly. Then she mounted the horse John had prepared for her and they rode away, over the fields. And now Tam felt she could forget her troubles entirely, forget the odious old man, Sir William, forget that Charles was promised to Juliet, that Mama might become a kept woman. The wind sang in her ears and she let her worries slide away. This was happiness. It might be autumn, but she galloped over fields of pure gold, heard larks carolling over the common land for the joy of living. Chilverton was way behind them now, and she knew the same happiness

126

she'd experienced when she travelled on the boat with him, wild violets at her feet, the smell of honeysuckle on the hedges as they sped fast. And now he was slowing down. They were nearing the canal again, and the boatyard, and they came to a halt before a long covered dock, marked Masters Brothers, Boat Builders and Contractors. They tied up the steaming horses, leaving them in the care of a young boy, and walked towards the yard where she could see boats being made, men hammering.

Charles stopped before a partly finished boat.

'Tell me about what to look for,' she said. 'I must know what to buy.'

'I'll explain the process,' he said, and she was pleased that he no longer treated her as a silly child, but as a person on an equal footing. He led her around, showing her the wooden boats with riveted hull, the English oak keelson, the planking, the 'knee' which formed the shape of the boat, the curving of the stem and stern. She watched entranced as the final stages were explained, the inside of the hold sheathed with soft or hard wood, and the gap between the two layers filled with chalice, a mixture of tar, cowhair and horse-dung. Then the finishing off with the adze when the sides would be as smooth as if they had been planed.

'Then there is the making of the tiller and rudder,' Charles said. 'And the panelling of the small areas, the grooving. A blacksmith has to sheath the bow from ice with a thick iron strip down the stem. And lastly, the painting.'

'Can I see that?' she asked.

He led her over to the side where a man stood, working on the delicate picture of a castle.

'This is Joe Banner,' he said. 'His roses are famous.'

'You mean each painter's are different.'

'Oh yes. Some do long-stemmed daisies, some put marigolds in, but there are always roses.'

Tam went closer to inspect. 'Is it ordinary paint?'

'It's oil-based, then varnished over. It's always done that way.'

'I see.' She looked round, her mind now turning to the purpose of the visit. 'Now where is the boat for sale?'

'I'll take you to meet Mr Masters.'

Josiah Masters was working with his men, but he stopped and greeted Tam.

'Miss Calder thinks she might be interested in your packet boat,' said Charles, and Josiah led them to the boat, standing now in dry dock, a great hole in her side.

'Can it really be repaired?' asked Tam, her voice tinged with disbelief.

'Of course,' said Josiah Masters. 'We can make it as good as new.'

Tam looked at the hole dubiously. 'Then why doesn't the owner want it repaired?' she asked.

'Well now.' Josiah scratched his head.

'Who was the owner?' asked Tam, suspiciously.

'Sir William Fargate,' said Charles, grinning.

'And it was rammed?' The two men stared at her guilelessly. She

127

smiled. 'I see. I suppose Sir William wanted it repaired and was told it couldn't be done.'

'Oh no,' said Josiah Masters. 'It can be done. But we were too busy at the time, you see, and it would have cost a lot of money. As much as buying a new one.'

'I see,' she smiled again. 'How much is it now?'

'I reckon about a hundred, give or take a bit. We shan't know for sure till it's done.'

'I'll take it,' said Tam, decisively. 'When will it be ready?'

'I could put a man on it right away. Say two weeks?'

'Done,' said Tam. She walked round, looking at the name. 'The *Duchess*,' she read. 'Well, that goes with the one I have, doesn't it?' A thought struck her and she stopped dead. 'This was my father's once, wasn't it?'

There was a little silence. 'Aye,' said Josiah Masters.

A feeling of triumph welled over Tam, so strong that she felt almost faint. 'If you get any more boats like this,' she said, 'I'll buy them all.'

She said goodbye to Josiah Masters, and walked with Charles to the horses. 'You can't afford the whole fleet,' he said. 'And it might not be wise – '

'I don't want to be wise,' she replied. 'Oh, Charles, I can't thank you enough for getting this for me. It means I'm really on my way.'

They mounted their horses and rode back to Chilverton. Tam felt as if she were flying. At the wharf they dismounted.

'I shall be away next week. In London,' Charles said.

'On canal business?'

'No. To do with the election.'

'Oh dear. Sir William might not be best pleased.'

Charles shrugged. 'I know. But he can find no fault with my work, and if he did dismiss me it might go against him in the election. He's too astute not to know that.'

'Do you think you'll win, Charles? After all, he is very much hated. And if he's not allowed to buy beer now – '

'There are other factors.'

'Such as?'

'Many of the new voters are his tenants. So, if you live on a farm owned by Sir William, then you vote for Sir William. The poll isn't private.'

'I hope you win, Charles.'

'Thank you. Now about your boat. If I'm not back when it's delivered, well, you'll need two horses, and a man and a boy.'

'Where shall I get the horses from?'

'The boaters would help you. But I think – ' he pulled his lip. 'You ought to learn for yourself what to look for, and the best man to advise you would be Jake Boswell, one of the gipsy Boswells – '

'One of Car Boswell's relatives? I don't want favours from Car Boswell,' she said hotly.

He grinned. 'Don't worry. Her family don't have anything to do with her, they disowned her when she took up her present way of life. But I know

Jake, and he's the best judge of horse-flesh in the country. I'll ask him to take you to the Dirty Fair.'

'The what?'

'It's a horse fair in Shropshire. They call it that because the weather's usually bad. He'll see you're all right. You can't beat a gipsy when it comes to horses.'

'The Dirty Fair it is then. And, thank you Charles, for everything.'

'The pleasure is all mine,' and his eyes were dancing again as though the business with Juliet had never happened. And I, thought Tam, leading Prince to the stable, have forgot for the whole of the afternoon.

When Madame's bill for the dresses came Tam was appalled, but Annabel tossed it carelessly aside. 'Mama,' Tam said, horrified. 'I expected one hundred pounds, but not several . . . and this without Celia's wedding dress.'

'I confess I didn't expect she'd send it yet. But Madame will wait,' Annabel said.

'But this will take all our savings. I shan't have enough for another boat.'

'There will be the bridesmaids' dresses too,' Celia said.

'Who are to be bridesmaids?' asked Tam.

'Why, you, of course, and Juliet.'

'Oh no,' Tam protested, 'we cannot possibly. Anyway, Juliet isn't well.'

'You really are the most disagreeable girl I've ever known,' cried Celia. 'What would Mrs Waring say if I told her that my own sister is unwilling to be a bridesmaid?'

'I am quite willing, we just haven't the money for another new dress,' protested Tam. 'I thought you were going to have a quiet wedding.'

'It will be quiet. But there will be some people there, naturally. And we shall walk to church, as is customary.'

'Juliet isn't well,' repeated Tam, looking worriedly at her younger sister.

'Because you work her too hard, that's why. Rushing off to Birmingham, acting in plays, working in that stupid soup kitchen – '

'I don't want Juliet to work in soup kitchens,' cried Tam.

'Mama. Please speak to Tam. Tell her she must – '

'I think you should be bridesmaids,' Annabel agreed. 'You can order from Madame Marie, she has your measurements – '

'But, Mama, we haven't paid for the last dresses yet – '

'Madame will wait – '

'Wait till when?' Tam asked wildly. 'Really, I have so much expense at the moment, buying this boat – '

'Then you shouldn't buy boats,' said Celia. 'It's you who's extravagant. One thing I tell you, Tam, when you are ruined you shan't live with me, that I promise you. Juliet and Mama can, but not you, Tam.'

She really does hate me, Tam thought despondently. But she knew she'd have to give in. She wrote to Madame, and back came the reply. There could be no more dresses until something was paid on account.

'Well, I declare,' said Annabel, 'I will never patronise Madame's establishment again, never. Why, she knows – '

'She does know, that's the trouble,' said Abby, caustically.

Celia wept, Annabel stormed, and Tam fled to her cabin, checking over the accounts. But no amount of reckoning up could show enough to pay for the second boat, two horses, a man and a boy to steer, and to pay Madame. She sat deep in thought. She wished Juliet didn't look so white and ill. Her once sunny nature seemed lost now, she walked round in silence, insisting on going to the soup kitchen where, working in the stuffy crowded rooms, she twice had to be brought home by another of the helpers. Perhaps it would cheer her to be a bridesmaid. If only she could confide in Annabel . . . She wondered what would happen if she did not pay Madame. Whether Mama would be sent to a debtors' prison. She could not let that happen. But she had to get another boat before Sir William took this one back . . . Then it struck her. She might borrow the money. Just enough to get the new boat; then they'd have the earnings from two, they could pay it off quite soon, make enough to pay Sir William for the *Princess*. She made her mind up and, putting on her best bonnet, marched to Gate Street, straight to the money-lenders.

The man in the little room was officious. Tam put on her most haughty air and, with her best bonnet, tried to make a good impression and bolster her confidence. She intended to play every card she knew, her mother's father, the Earl, her sister's marriage to Geoffrey Waring . . .

She came out of the money-lenders triumphant with a loan of £150, the first instalment to be paid promptly on the first of the month, and each subsequent month. The boat was given as security. But she was surprised at how easy it had been.

Annabel took Celia to London and they returned with a beautiful wedding-gown of purest silk, and a long tulle veil. The bridesmaids' dresses, though pretty, were not expensive, Celia did not intend to be outshone. Tam was thankful that Mrs Waring was providing the wedding-breakfast . . . 'As it will be held at our home,' she said delicately. There had been another heated argument about who was to give the bride away. In the absence of relatives, Annabel suggested John Dexter, to be met with outraged cries from Celia. 'I will not be given away by a butler.' And Gilbert? 'That mountebank. Cannot you ask your father, Mama?'

'No,' said Annabel.

It was Celia who suggested Lord Brooke, who was asked, and agreed, to Tam's furious disapproval. It was utterly wrong that *this* man should take her father's place.

When he arrived at the boat on the wedding morning Tam felt it was but the beginning of a disastrous day and she was to be proved right. She refused to speak to him, more than bare civilities, heard him say to Annabel, 'It would be more fitting if it were Tamarisk, wouldn't it?', and she thought he meant that she as eldest should be getting married first, and was angry again.

They went to church on foot, as was the custom, walking two by two. Charles, as best man, walked with Tam, and as they stepped through the little lych-gate she remembered the old saw: 'Those who walk to church beforehand, will never walk as man and wife', and wondered why she was even surprised.

They came out of the church, where a number of people stood outside, watching in awe. And they all drove to Grange House, where among the crowds gathered to greet the happy couple, Tam saw Sir William and turned away in disgust. Juliet had stood up to the marriage service well, though Tam kept a watchful eye on her. Now they were ushered into the dining room where a splendid wedding breakfast awaited them. Meats of all kinds, fish, fruit and wine. Goose pie and boiled sole, turbot and lobster. Finally an exotic creation, shaped like a hedgehog, made from cream, eggs, sugar and orange-flower water, and stuck with almond quills.

After a few minutes, Juliet left the table hurriedly and Tam, following her, found her in the water closet, quite appallingly sick.

'It's been too much for you, Juliet,' she said. 'All this excitement and this rich food . . . Shall I fetch a doctor?'

'No. Please, Tam, no. I'll be well in a minute.'

'Then come, we'll find somewhere for you to lie down.'

Outside, a maid directed them to a guest room, where Juliet lay on the bed, and Tam sat with her, until she slept. Then she went to look for Annabel, who she saw dancing with Lord Brooke.

Not knowing what to do Tam looked around for help. And saw Charles making his way towards her.

'Oh Charles. Juliet has been quite ill, but she's sleeping now.'

'Shall I go and fetch a doctor?'

'She said not to.' And Tam found herself pouring out all her worries, confiding in him, as she always did. He was so easy to talk to, somehow. 'Juliet worries me,' she said. 'I've been worried for some time.'

'What's wrong with her?'

'You know she is not strong, and she's been so white and wan for weeks. She still insists on working in the soup kitchen, but yesterday she was quite ill before she left. I wanted to tell Mama, but she wouldn't hear of it.'

'What was wrong?' he asked expressionlessly.

'She was sick. Her – ' she swallowed. No, she could not say any more about Juliet's stomach upset, not to a *man*.

'How long has she had this sickness?' he asked.

'For several weeks now. But – ' she paused. How could she explain her fears? 'She hasn't been *normal* for – for two months now,' she blurted out, head averted. How could he possibly understand? Oh, she shouldn't be saying this. 'I'm afraid,' she stammered, 'she might be going into a decline, the consumption, you know. One of the girls at school suffered from it.' She closed her eyes.

'Where is she?' he asked.

'In the guest bedroom.'

'I'll go to see her.'

'But, Charles, you can't. Not in the *bedroom*.'

'I must, Tam.'

131

'Then I'll come with you.'

But he would not let her come in the bedroom. 'Wait outside,' he ordered. 'Please, Tam.'

She waited.

She never knew what Charles said to Juliet, but when they came out together Juliet said in a low voice, 'I shall marry Charles, Tam.'

Tam stared straight ahead as she digested this surprising development. 'We must tell Mama.'

'No,' Juliet was firm.

'But we must – '

'No, Tam. Not now, anyway. We can't upset Celia's wedding.'

'But, Juliet – '

'No, Tam.'

The sound of music came from the ballroom. Down there people were laughing and dancing. Tam stared at Charles and knew that somehow, despite everything, she'd hoped that it would come right, that he was in love with her, Tam, as he *was*, and so there would be the proverbial happy ending. So, as she looked into his eyes, with the music sounding below, she knew that this was the end of girlhood. This was when all hope died.

She didn't even remember walking down the stairs. Didn't even see Sir William until he stood before her, asking her to dance. *Dance*? When she never wanted to dance again. But then she saw Juliet, her white face, her slim body, walking with Charles to the door. And Tam danced.

'You are expanding your little business then, Miss Calder?' Sir William said.

Tam was silent. How did he know?

'You haven't forgotten my offer, I trust? Or would you like me to repeat it?'

'It would merely waste your time.'

'I can wait,' he said.

But even that wasn't the end of that dreadful day. The final blow was delivered by Celia. She came to Tam, Geoffrey with her, as she at last sat alone.

'Tam,' she sang.

Tam looked up dully.

'We never told you where we are going to live.'

'Aren't you going to live at Grange House?'

'Dear me, no. We want our own place. And we have it now.'

'Good,' said Tam.

'Aren't you going to ask me where it is?'

'In Chilverton, I assume.'

'Of course, though we shall often stay in London. But for our country house we are having Cherry Trees.'

There was triumph in Celia's eyes, triumph in her voice. All the slights, real or fancied, all the inadequacies of her childhood, were vindicated in this deliberate action. Celia had caught up with Tam at last.

Chapter Six

Tam had always met her troubles head on, and seldom stopped to worry about the whys and wherefores. But in the weeks following Celia's wedding her life became one big question mark, *why*? Why did this happen to me? She cried silently. Although she had mocked Miss Laker, some of childhood's teaching still lingered. Be good and you will win your reward. Well, she had tried to be good; she had worked for her father's memory, for all the family as well as herself, so why had Charles, whom she loved, and she thought had returned that love, taken Juliet? Why had Celia turned on her with such malice? Stunned by so many blows, Tam walked around in dazed bewilderment.

But life went on: boats still ran, people still wanted to see the shows, she had another boat ordered, horses to buy, men to hire, routes to work out. Madame's bill for Celia's wedding gown and the bridesmaids' dresses had arrived. Tam studied her accounts. Even with the money she borrowed, she had not enough, her only hope was that Madame would wait. She had decided, when the new boat was delivered, to make the new run to Warwick.

It was Gilbert who provided the new actor to replace Celia. He was a sixteen-year-old boy from Chilverton, whom, Gilbert said, he had met at the inn, and who was, surprisingly, able both to read and to act. A quiet, fair-haired lad, he had no objection to playing female roles. As it had not been many years since all parts were taken by males, neither Annabel nor Tam saw anything strange in this. Plays apart, they saw little of him; he lived in Chilverton and usually, he and Gilbert disappeared to some unknown rendezvous, and Tam had not time to wonder where, or indeed to think about them at all. Gilbert had always been a shadow, his companion seemed the same.

After a very quiet wedding, attended only by immediate family, Juliet and Charles disappeared to a house on the wharf, built by John Waring for his agent, and now owned by Charles. Tam went to visit Juliet after a short time. The house was larger than a lock-keeper's cottage, though small by Cherry Tree standards. The outside looked pleasant enough, built of local brick, the windows framed in climbing roses and clematis, and Tam knocked on the door, wondering why Juliet had not asked any of them to call.

The door was opened by a dark-haired middle-aged woman, who, when Tam announced her name, stood aside to let her enter. 'I'm Esther Winters, the housekeeper,' she said. 'Mrs Waring is in the parlour.'

Mrs Waring. How strange that sounded. Could she really mean little Juliet? And Esther Winters seemed part of that strangeness, though Tam couldn't have said why, except that she could have sworn she was not a local woman. The parlour though was a pleasant enough room, but sadly lacking much in the way of ornament. She greeted Juliet and asked with concern, 'How are you? You still look pale.'

'It's nothing,' Juliet said. 'I am quite well.'

'You like being here?'

'Yes. Very well.'

There was a pause and Tam looked at her sister. She wanted so much to ask if Juliet was happy, if Charles was good to her, but the words died in her throat. There was an aloofness about Juliet that seemed to forbid intimate questions. She asked instead, 'Is Charles working on the wharf?' knowing she had to talk about him.

'No, he is in London,' Juliet replied. 'Something to do with the election.'

'You mean – he's staying there?'

'He comes and goes.'

'But, Juliet . . . you must be lonely!' Tam cried. 'Come back to the boat for the time being.'

'No, Tam, I am quite all right here.'

'But you've always been with us – '

'I am busy now. I still go to help at the soup kitchen, in fact I have to go now.'

Nonplussed at this dismissal, Tam rose to her feet. Juliet rose too and waited for her departure. At the door, Tam turned. 'Juliet, what is it? Don't you want us any more?' Did Juliet's mouth quiver?

'Of course I do, Tam, I love you dearly. But as I am out so much I think it better you do not call very often.'

'But, Juliet . . . why?'

'It is better that way,' Juliet repeated.

Tam strode away, and was so disturbed that she put the facts before Annabel. Her mother looked troubled.

'I know,' she said. 'She worries me. But what can we do?'

'*Are* you worried? Really, Mama?'

'Yes,' Annabel replied shortly. 'I am worried about Juliet, I have worried about her all her life.'

'Because she is delicate?'

'Because she is delicate in body and – in mind.'

Tam looked up, startled at her usually vague mother. She had accepted Juliet for what she was, delicate, a little different perhaps, but no more.

Now Annabel had put into words something she knew had always been there in her mind. And she was shocked, and said in her dismay, 'You may have been worried, Mama, but you always left her alone.'

Annabel paused, looking through the saloon window at the grey water, the colourful boats. 'My life hasn't been easy, Tam, whatever you may think.'

'Why did you marry Papa?' Tam asked bluntly.

Annabel hesitated. 'I don't think I have to answer questions from you, Tam,' she said, a little sharply. 'There is much you don't know.'

'I know you were unfair to Papa. You went away, neglected him, neglected Juliet – '

'My staying at home would have made no difference,' Annabel said. 'I had a doctor from London to see her, one of the best.'

'And he said she could be left?'

'I couldn't have borne it,' Annabel cried, and Tam was surprised at the pain in her voice. 'Not to give up my whole life, my love, to sit here in Cherry Trees with your father. I couldn't have borne it, Tam.'

'Not with Juliet?'

'Especially with Juliet.'

'So you ran away?' Tam groped to understand this side of her mother she had never seen before, a side of hurt, of suffering, of fear of the abnormal. She'd always seen her mother as a fluttering, charming creature, but with no depth, no worries, never as an ordinary woman with a woman's fears and failings. Yet – running away, leaving her children . . . The moment of understanding was drowned by a rush of new anger and Tam knew she was no nearer to forgiveness.

'Juliet should not have married, Mama,' she said in a hard voice.

'Charles talked to me. He will take care of her,' Annabel said.

'But, Mama, his career. He aims to be a Member of Parliament. And if he is, he'll have to move to London, to entertain. How will Juliet manage that?'

'Oh.' And now Annabel moved back into her former languor. 'She will be all right, Charles will look after her. Now I must go,' and she turned away, her momentary revelations forgotten, relapsing into her vagueness. *Running away*, Tam thought bitterly.

'Oh Charles,' she thought, anguished. 'Why did you do it? Why did you take Juliet? You must have known . . .' Perhaps her mother was right, after all, to run away from facts; some things were too painful to be borne.

Jake Boswell was a typical gipsy; dark, swarthy, wearing a bright neckerchief, and gold rings in his ears. He was still a young man, but as his eyes rested on Tam they betrayed no awareness of her as a woman, which piqued her somewhat. But she dismissed the thought impatiently; they were on business. Jake had called to take her to the Dirty Fair. She mounted Darkie and they set off. Tam admired the way he rode, it seemed not, as with the English, an acquired skill, he rode as if he were part of the horse. And they seemed to understand one another well, the horse and

135

man, for with hardly a word from him the horse carried out his wishes impeccably.

It seemed the Dirty Fair would live up to its name, for it was a murky day, the skies were overcast; there had been rain in the night which had now reduced to mist and mizzle, and the roads were in a muddy state. But the gipsy did not keep to the road, he galloped over the fields, and she followed, trying hard to keep up with him.

At the fair there were horses everywhere, from ponies to heavy carthorses. There were unbroken colts from Wales, long-tailed steeds and donkeys and mules. There was shouting and whooping, neighing and braying, galloping and trotting, men running, holding horses by the halter, or even dragging them along. There was a riot of confusion, colour and movement at the Dirty Fair.

They rode slowly round the field then Jake, reining his horse in, said to her, 'Them two over there, with that groom, they're Fargate's horses.'

'*Fargate?* Sir William? But how do you know?'

'I sold 'em, as yearlings.'

'To him?'

'No, to your father.'

Tam felt as if something had hit her in the stomach knocking the breath clean from her body. 'Can we get them, Jake?'

'If you want 'em, yes.'

'I do. I want them more than anything in the world . . . If I can afford them.'

Jake said, 'Come on then. And be careful what you say. Watch me.'

They rode over, and the gipsy dismounted, looked critically at the horses. 'How much?' he asked.

'Forty pounds each.'

'Robbery,' said Jake. 'They're too wild for drawing boats.'

'Wild? They're good horses, steady as rocks,' said the groom confidently.

The gipsy muttered a word to the nearest horse, and immediately it reared up. Tam stepped back, startled, as the horse seemed to be in a frenzy, infecting its companion with its fear, till they were both prancing and dancing up and down. The groom held desperately to the reins, cursing and swearing at the horses.

'Told you they was too wild. Come, mistress, let's look for some better horseflesh.'

Tam followed, bewildered. 'What happened?' she asked.

'Leave 'em,' said the gipsy. 'We'll get 'em later.'

'But, Jake – '

'Trust me,' he said.

They rode back round the field, and Tam watched the scene with interest, the gaitered farmers, the labourers and carters, legs tied in sacking to keep out the wet, members of the country society seeking mounts, the Welsh with their soft, lilting voices, and above all, there were the gipsies.

They were easily recognisable, not from their dress, which was pretty

136

much the same as that of other men present, but for the coloured neckerchief, the gold ear-rings, the swarthy skin and jet-black hair. There were women too, black hair plaited round their heads, carrying babies in heavy shawls wrapped round their own bodies. As she watched, three gipsy men rode into the centre of the field on horses as black as themselves, and exhibited their horsemanship, riding, circling, jumping, standing in the saddle. Tam watched with pleasure, from time to time glancing back to the groom struggling with Sir William Fargate's horses, which were still rearing and bucking. No one wanted to buy such unmanageable mounts. It was not until late afternoon that Jake took her back.

'I'll give you fifteen pounds the pair, and that's too much for dogmeat,' Jake said to the groom.

'Thirty – ' said the the groom, sweating.

'Twenty, my last word,' said Jake. 'Otherwise you'll take 'em back to your master.'

The groom cursed him for a black-hearted villain, but he accepted the twenty pounds, and Jake and Tam rode away with the still excitable horses.

They came to a clear path and Tam said troubled, 'Are you sure, Jake? What's the matter with them?'

The gipsy laughed and spoke softly to the horses. Immediately they calmed down and walked docilely. Tam stared in astonishment.

'What did you do?' she asked.

The gipsy laughed. 'That's my secret,' he said. 'You've got what you wanted.'

'Well, thank you, Jake – ' she broke off as he gave a fierce exclamation. 'What is it?'

'Over there,' he said. 'Fargate himself.'

And she saw Sir William, on horseback, talking to the groom. They were standing by the path, and there were too many people around for it to be easy to avoid them, unless they made a detour all round the field.

'What do you want to do?' asked Jake.

Tam hesitated. 'Does he know you?' she asked.

Jake spat. 'We are old enemies. I've had more game from his woods than he has himself. And he knows it.'

'Aren't you afraid of him? If you're caught he'd transport you to Botany Bay.'

The gipsy shrugged. 'So? One country's pretty much the same as another. I'd survive.'

You would too, Tam thought, and so must I. 'Carry on, Jake,' she said.

They rode to where Sir William awaited them. He blocked the path, forcing them to halt.

'So – you have my horses,' he said.

'My father's,' said Tam.

Sir William looked angry. 'Don't try me too far, Mistress Calder,' he said. 'I've already made too many allowances for you.'

'Please let me pass, Sir William.'

'I'll get you in the end, you know that.'

She rode by, wondering in what context he meant that remark. And Jake said soberly, 'Be wary of him, Mistress Tam. He's a devious character, he sets his plans years ahead,' but she was too excited by her purchase to heed his warning.

They rode home with the horses. And later when Charles asked her what she had learned from Jake Boswell she replied simply, 'How to be a survivor.'

The second boat was delivered and Tam gazed at her with pride. The *Duchess* was indeed a glorious sight, newly painted, the hole completely repaired. The boaters came round to admire.

'Made a good job of it, Masters did. She'll hold more'n sixty people, that'll be good going. You'll be needing a lad now?'

'Yes,' Tam said to the boater who'd asked.

'I've got a lad, coming thirteen. Good little worker.'

Tam knew the boater by sight, she had seen him along the canal. 'Are you a Number One?' she asked.

'Nay, I'd keep the lad if I were. Nay, I work for 'Im.' The boaters never referred to Sir William by name, it was always ' 'Im'. A mark of displeasure.

'Why do you prefer the boy to work for me?' Tam asked. 'Sir William would no doubt find him work and pay as much.'

'We'd rather it were you,' said the boater, and Tam felt a warm glow of gratification. Her father had been respected, had been trampled down by Sir William, and now, through her, her father had come back and the fight had started again. The boaters knew it, and without a word they were pledging their support. They accepted her now as a boat-owner. 'Send him to me,' she said to the boater.

He came, his name was Jobey Rawlins, and she hired him. For the other staff she needed more thought. Young Jobey could work the boat, but the other man would have to take the money, and for this Tam wanted someone who could read and write, keep simple accounts. A man she could trust, preferably with a wife who could see to the food. She wanted written accounts, and none of the boaters she knew could provide this. It would be so easy when taking money for the trips, for some of it to be slipped into the pocket, so tempting. Tam wondered where on earth she could find such a paragon of trust. She wondered if any of the weavers were able to write, and one dull misty afternoon in November she made her way to the soup kitchen.

It was exactly the same as when she'd been in the last time: the smell of crowded humanity, the weary pallid faces. She walked along the line and called out loudly, 'Would anyone like a job?'

The women looked up – they were mostly women – and Tam went on. 'It is quite easy, preparing meals for passengers on the boat. And I'd need a man who can read and write.'

There was a silence. 'Did you say on a boat?' someone asked.

'Yes, that is so. I plan to run a packet boat to Warwick and bring people here to see the plays.'

The silence went on. At last someone said, 'We're weavers,' and there was

138

pride in the voice, dignity even in the poor clothes as the speaker drew herself up. 'My man's a weaver. Not a *boater*.'

Tam stared. 'You mean you wouldn't want this work?'

There was no reply, just a few shaken heads. Tam moved to the kitchen, wondering if Juliet was there. She was not.

'They are weavers,' Mrs Dawson, said nastily. Since Tam's remarks about the amount of beef in the soup, and Charles's subsequent inspection, she had not been best pleased with Tam, and did not see why she should pretend otherwise. So it was with some satisfaction that she explained. 'They think they're better than boaters, and they'd be right in most cases. Drunken lot, the boaters. And that Car Boswell – disgraceful.'

'Do you know what she does?' asked another helper. 'Those men who haven't got their families with them on board, take *her*. It's disgusting.'

'And her father whipped her till her back ran blood, and turned her out, but still she carries on.'

Tam moved back into the other room.

'If it pleases thee – ' A young woman of about thirty had detached herself from the others and stood before Tam. ' – I'll work for thee on the boat, Tamarisk Calder.'

'Who are you?' Tam asked.

'I am Miriam Earp. My husband is Harry Earp. He has no work, and he'd be willing to work for thee.'

'What does he do?'

'He's a weaver.'

'Can he read and write?'

'He can.'

'Does he know anything about boats?'

'No, but he can learn.'

'You'd be willing to leave your home?' asked Tam.

'We shall have no home after this week coming, and we have three children.'

'You are having to leave?'

'We cannot pay the rent,' Miriam said simply.

Tam stood, dubiously. True the weavers were out of work now, but was this a man who ran into debt? 'How much rent do you owe?' she asked.

'I'll tell you why they owe the rent,' said the next woman in the queue. ' 'Cos Harry and Mirrie gave all their money to help others. There's Enoch Randle now, his wife just had a baby, and she nearly died, she had to have food – '

'Hush,' said Mirrie.

'Take me to your husband,' said Tam.

They walked to the Patch, skirting the open gutter, and passed into the first cottage. Tam looked round with interest. The room was scrupulously clean, as Tam would have expected from someone so neat in her person as Miriam Earp. Three children sat on one of the small wooden stools looking at a book. There was no fire in the grate, but over by the window, a man sat at a loom.

'This is my husband, Harry Earp,' said Miriam. 'And this,' she now spoke to Harry, 'is Tamarisk Calder.'

'Don't let me hinder you if you have work to do,' Tam said hastily, but Harry Earp shook his head.

'No, I have no work. This is just something I had by, a little leftover. I do not like to be idle.'

Tam walked over to the loom and looked at the ribbon, marvelling at the fine, delicate threads of silk being woven into an intricate pattern. 'Why, it's beautiful,' she exclaimed.

'Aye. We are able to weave fine gauze ribbons on hand looms,' Harry said. 'Silk is a sensitive material to work with, so hand-looms are used for the more elaborate fancy patterns.'

He left the loom and they turned to the children, who stood up politely. 'This is Margery,' Miriam said of the eldest, a serious child of some ten years. 'Then Robin, he's eight. And this,' she smiled fondly at a pretty dark-eyed girl of three, 'this is Ruth.'

The children stood in line and said, 'Good day to thee, Tamarisk Calder.' They did not curtsey, but stood straight and still until Miriam bade them be seated. Then she turned to her husband and explained the purpose of Tam's visit.

Harry pondered, and Tam studied him. He looked reliable, intelligent.

'I need someone to take the money as well as steer, to keep accounts. You can read and write?' she asked.

'Oh yes, I had some schooling,' Harry said.

'And you are honest?'

'I am a Friend,' he said simply, as if that were enough. And then, seeing her bewilderment, 'They call us Quakers. Thou hast heard of us?'

'Oh – yes,' said Tam, hesitantly. 'At least I've heard of Dissenters. They say they are – ' she broke off, confused.

'Troublemakers?' Harry asked smiling. 'Because we have liberal ideas and refuse to keep to our station in life? Oh, I understand people's fears, they are afraid of what happened in France. We believe in bettering the conditions of the poor, but that is not our way.'

'Have you heard of Charles Waring?' Tam asked.

'I work with him,' said Harry, simply. 'He will speak for me, if thou needest more than my word.'

'I don't,' said Tam. 'But the boat is to fetch people from Warwick to see the plays – is not your religion against that? Though it is only a temporary measure. I want to earn money to buy another boat – ' and she found herself telling him all that had happened, her father, Sir William.

'Aye, I know Sir William and his ways,' Harry said. 'But I was not born a Quaker. I took the faith when I married Mirrie, and when I was already a weaver, else I should not perhaps have worked in a fashion trade. I try to follow the Friends' beliefs, but as for the plays, we shall not need to see them. And I cannot let my wife and children starve.'

'If you don't mind working for a woman,' Tam began.

'The Lord made male and female,' said Harry. 'In the Friends we do not

140

differentiate between the two, any more than between king and peasant. And the weavers, like other craft guilds, regard the wife as a trade partner, having the right to succeed and carry on the business after her husband's death.' He looked round the room. 'This cottage we would not miss,' he said. 'But this . . .' He walked back to the loom and put a hand on it affectionately. 'This has been a trusty friend. Aye, I'll be sorry to see this go.'

'It's not – your own?' asked Tam.

'Yes. We pay weekly subscriptions into a society, till we have paid for the loom. Yes, it is my own.'

'Then could you not sell it?' Tam asked hesitantly. 'Or store it maybe until work picks up again?'

'No one would buy it now,' Harry Earp answered. 'And there is no use storing it, these looms will never be needed again.'

'You wouldn't want to work in one of the new factories they talk about?' Tam asked.

Harry frowned. 'But is this work to be for men, or women? And what of the children? Here we all worked, true, but as and when we pleased. A factory would seem strange to me, and I would not want that for my children. No, Tamarisk Calder, thou hast decided me. If Mirrie is willing, and she is or she would not have brought thee here, I will take up thy offer, and thank thee for it.'

So it was decided, and Tam introduced them to the *Duchess* – their new home. 'We shan't be starting just yet,' she said. 'But move in when you like. We'll go together to Warwick to put up the posters, and you'll be able to learn your new trade.'

The boy Jobey proved his worth on the first trip to Warwick. He harnessed the two horses, showed Harry the intricacies of steering, and was rewarded by an extra sixpence from Tam for his trouble. It was decided that Harry should steer while Jobey drove the horses. When the boat tied up, then Harry would take the fares and see to the passengers, Mirrie meanwhile would have prepared the food.

It was a grey, perfectly still morning when they set out, with a slight mist that veiled the distant meadows and seemed to magnify the sound of the horses' hooves and shouts of boatmen. As they passed the junction of the Warwick and Napton canals the mist had cleared, a weak sun, low on the horizon, shone towards Napton Hill, and a light wind set the sails of the windmill revolving slowly. They tied up in Warwick, and the Earps accompanied Tam on her quest for places to put her posters: up the hill to Eastgate, Guy's Cliff. She was granted permission to embark passengers, and noted the wharf charges were not so high as in Chilverton. She felt quite happy as she reckoned up her total runs. Two extra trips to Warwick on the same days as her own would bring in more money for no extra outlay. If the hall became too full they'd have to put on more plays, but she did not want to push that as yet. And of course, not everyone would want to see the plays. They might try another excursion to Stratford. All in all she felt confident she would soon make enough money to pay off her debts.

The sun strengthened on their return, the trees were not yet bare, but yellow and brown leaves drifted down as they passed, and there were still small clusters of berries on the hedges. She tried to inject some of her own enthusiasm into Harry Earp, for she felt he was still sad at leaving his own trade. She talked of the romance of the boats, the important route from Birmingham to London, where the soldiers travelled – no, better not mention that, stick to freight, metal and glass. How they met other boats on the way with cotton from Manchester, cheese from Cheshire, earthenware and pottery from Staffordshire, woollens and cutlery from Yorkshire, lace from Derby and Nottingham. She said, eyes shining, 'It's like being at the centre of the world.' And went on passionately, 'We must keep the trade here, must be ready to face all competition.'

Harry looked over the side. Large flocks of starlings scoured the stubble fields, a flash of blue showed a kingfisher darting back to his bankside home. 'You mean the railways?' Harry asked, and Tam nodded. Then she talked of her father's plans. 'Yes,' Harry said soberly, at last. 'It will be up to us,' and she smiled, gratified. Harry understood.

She felt a strange reluctance to leave the Earps, they gave her a feeling of safety, such as she had not known since she was a child, when Papa held her hands and said all would be well.

The boat ran smoothly into Chilverton, and Tam parted from her new friends and jumped on to the towpath. And saw, to her surprise, two carriages waiting on the wharf, outside her own boat. She stopped. She was not fanciful, nor given to premonitions, but she knew these carriages meant bad news.

She walked towards the *Princess*, and though she wanted to hurry, her legs were wooden, as if in a nightmare, her limbs would not move fast enough, though she strove to force them. She saw a number of boaters' children standing, fingers in mouths, gaping at the carriages. And then she was on the boat and in the saloon, to find Lord Brooke there, with Annabel. Celia was seated opposite, Juliet near the window, and again it was part of a nightmare to see them all sitting there and not speaking, all turning to look at her as she entered.

'What is it?' she asked. 'Why are you all here?'

'I sent for Celia and Juliet,' said Annabel.

Tam sat down, as silence fell again on the assembled group.

'We waited for you,' said Annabel at last, and it seemed to Tam that her sisters' eyes held reproach.

'What is it?' Tam asked again.

Annabel put a hand to her hair in a dramatic gesture, but even she, the elegant and poised, seemed ill-at-ease.

It was Lord Brooke who spoke. 'I have news,' he said.

'News?' echoed Tam. What news might he have that could possibly interest her?

'It's Sophie, my wife. She died, last night.'

Tam's eyes, as they rested on him, seemed almost dull. 'Why are you here?' she asked. 'What do you want of us?'

'Why,' Lord Brooke replied, 'I am free now. Bel and I can be married.' He gazed, a little put out, at the blank faces of the three girls, realising that they did not know the first thing about him.

The Honourable Anthony Edward Percival Cavendish Carleton had the misfortune to be born a younger son of the Earl of Brooke. Thus he was brought up with the same extravagant tastes as those of his elder brother, Lord Cravenfield, with no hope of inheriting anything at all to pay for his pleasures. Not that there was a great deal to inherit. There were those who said that the earldom consisted of little more than a brook, and bestowing it had been a joke on the king's part. There were no rich coal deposits on the estate, no good farming land, nothing but heath and the river. And the Brooke men had always been reckless spenders, given to gambling and betting with the young bucks at White's and Watier's in St James's Street. By the time he was twenty, the Honourable Anthony had run through the money left him by his mother, and was in debt to the tune of some £50,000.

There was nothing for a poor young aristocrat to do but to look for a rich wife. In the meantime, war was declared on France, and as he possessed a certain reckless courage, Anthony begged his father to buy him a commission in the Army. He was with the 23rd Light Dragoons when they made a mad cavalry charge cutting deep into the enemy's flanks in July 1809. Half the regiment fell, and Anthony was wounded and shipped home. While he convalesced he spent more time at Watier's, notorious for its passion for betting and gambling. But he needed money more than ever, so when he met Sophie Garner, a great heiress of a good, though not aristocratic, family, he married her. Sophie's father and brothers were barristers at law, canny men; they did not mention that Sophie was in poor health, and although they could not prevent Anthony from spending her money, once married, they did tie it up in trusts so that he would have none on her death. She provided him with a heir after twelve months, then the doctor pronounced that her heart was weak, there could be no more children, and Sophie retired to an invalid's couch.

Anthony returned to the London of raffish high society, of gaming clubs and prize-fights, of theatres and opera and Vauxhall Gardens. He met Lady Annabel Wayne, herself just come out, but already offending her strict father by dabbling on the stage, already a member of Almacks, that exclusive ladies' club controlled by such important beings as the Ladies Castlereagh and Jersey and the Princess Esterhazy. They fell in love and carried on a notorious and passionate affair. He was recalled to his regiment in 1811, and sent to Spain, and was with the Allied Armies when they entered Paris in 1814. He did not see Annabel again until 1816, and by this time his fortunes had changed. His brother, Lord Cravenfield, also in the Army, was killed in action, and as soon as Anthony had taken his title his father died, and Anthony became the Earl of Brooke.

Sophie was still on her invalid couch, and had little to offer a red-blooded male, so again he returned to London and saw Annabel on the stage at Drury Lane. He was astonished to find that he was still in love with

143

her. But she was married now and had three little girls, though she told him her marriage had been contrived and arranged by herself. 'My father is strict,' she said. 'He thought me too wild, and disowned me once he saw me married. But I knew you'd come back, Brooke.'

But he still had no money, he gambled away the little he had from the estate, his wife's money too. Divorce was impossible, nor would it have occurred to either of them to take up this option. Annabel felt she had made a bargain with her husband, he had given her his name to placate her father, she did not feel she owed him the loyalty of her body, but she would not have dreamed of leaving him. She and Anthony belonged to the same set, where affairs and liaisons were common among married people, they carried on where they had left off.

The years passed and their love did not diminish. Lord Brooke intended to marry Annabel as soon as his invalid wife died, so when the event finally happened, it did not seem strange to him that he should come immediately to claim the woman he had loved for twenty years. Now, looking at Annabel's daughters, he realised how little they knew of him and his story.

The silence could be felt. Tam watched a boat, loaded with coal, glide by, a woman at the tiller, squat, dumpy, wearing a black alpaca dress and a white apron, two children beside her. Annabel now spoke.

'You know Lord Brooke, and that we have known each other for many years.' She went to him and put her arms around him. 'Anthony, dear Tony,' she said. She sat beside him, and her daughters sat opposite in a row, three disapproving judges.

'Marry? So soon? What of the proprieties?' Celia asked, horrified.

'I am sorry. I perhaps came in too much haste – ' Lord Brooke said.

'I think you did,' said Celia. 'If your wife died last night and you propose marriage the very next day, it is most indecorous.'

'I know you must think me unfeeling,' Lord Brooke said. 'But there was never any love between Sophie and myself – '

'Yet you married?' Celia asked.

'I confess it was done without love and without much thought,' Lord Brooke told them. 'I was young, my parents wished it . . . Almost immediately afterwards I met Annabel and we fell deeply in love. We have loved ever since.'

'While you were both married to other people.' Tam's voice was heavily censorious.

'I'm afraid so.'

'But all that will be well now,' Annabel put in quickly.

'We shall not marry immediately,' Lord Brooke assured them. 'But we are not young, we do not feel it necessary to wait a year, or even six months – '

'You will, at least, let the poor lady be buried first, I trust?' said Tam.

'A few weeks perhaps,' Lord Brooke carried on imperturbably. 'Then we can marry from Greytowers – my home.'

Celia blinked. Marry from Greytowers, ancestral home of the Earls of

144

Brooke. Conflicting emotions chased over her face. If she and Geoffrey were invited to Greytowers they would meet interesting people, the sort of people they badly wanted to know. 'We – ell,' she said. 'I suppose it is all right.'

'Juliet?' asked Annabel.

'I have nothing against it,' Juliet said colourlessly. 'I hope you will be very happy, Mama.'

Annabel drew a breath. 'Tam?'

'Obviously I cannot stop you, Mama,' Tam said. 'But I do not approve of what you are doing. I shall never approve.'

'But Tam, you must. You will come to live with us.'

'Oh no,' Tam shook her head. 'Never.'

'But what will you do?' asked Annabel.

'Do? What I am doing now. Stay on the boat. Oh – ' her rage boiled over. 'Have you no feeling for Papa, Mama? You might have deceived him in your lifetime with your – with *him* – but surely you have some sympathy for Papa's work. This was Papa's boat, I have bought back another of his boats, I intend to carry on.'

'But, Tam, what is the point?' Annabel asked. 'Nothing can bring poor Jamie back.'

'I can carry out his wishes. Fight the railways, if they come, keep the boats running . . .'

'You can't change things, Tam,' Annabel said.

'I can and I will. And for that I must stay on the boat.'

Now Annabel was angry too. 'This is really very funny,' she said, rising to her feet and put a hand to her head in the old remembered way, 'that you, Tam, you above all, should go on so about your Papa . . .'

'Bel,' said Lord Brooke, warningly.

But Annabel was roused now. And Tam, her own temper flaring, stood up too and faced her mother. 'What's funny about it?' she asked.

'Because,' Annabel shouted, 'he was not your Papa at all!'

'*What?*' Tam stared incredulously. 'What *do* you mean? Of course he was my Papa. He was your husband . . .' her voice trailed away and she stepped back as she stared at Annabel in dismay. *Don't tell me*, her eyes begged.

'I hadn't meant to tell you, but you should know,' Annabel said. 'You are Brooke's daughter.'

'I'm what?' Tam was whispering now. Her voice had gone, her whole body felt weak.

'That is why my parents quarrelled with me, that is how I came to marry Jamie in the first place . . .' Annabel's voice faltered at the shocked outrage on her daughters' faces.

'Mama,' squealed Celia.

Tam strove to understand. She asked, 'How could this be?'

Now it was Lord Brooke who answered, for Annabel had turned away. 'I told you we were deeply in love. I had to go away, fighting in the wars. When I returned your mother was already married to Jamie Calder.'

145

'And did he know – about me?' asked Tam, faintly.

'He knew,' said Annabel. 'We didn't meet socially. He wanted to get his canal built, so he pestered everyone with money he could think of. He approached my father, who also turned him down. But that's where I saw him, at my home, and I saw his eyes following me around with dog-like devotion. I remembered that, and though Sir William did finance the canal in the end, Jamie needed money to start his business, buy a house. I approached him, told him that if he would marry me I would give him the money he required, or rather my father would. My father agreed, then washed his hands of me. It was a bargain.'

Tam recalled her father, the man who had always been so kind to her, loved her. She said choking, 'He was so good to me, he was my Papa, I want no other.' She looked desolately through the window at the water. She had thought there was nothing more she could lose, but there was, they wanted to take her father away from her. In the distance she heard Lord Brooke say, 'I'm sorry, I think I'd better go now.' She was hardly aware of his leaving, she was grieving, perhaps now more than ever, for the only father she had ever known.

Celia was looking at her angrily. 'It would be Tam,' she said. 'It was bound to be. So that's why you favoured her, Mama.'

Tam turned then. Poor Celia, she thought clearly. That even in her hour of triumph she should be outclassed by herself. And outclassed was the right word, Celia set such store by her aristocratic connections. It had been Celia who had mocked at Tam for her working with figures, telling her she took after Papa, the tradesman . . . Tam felt hysterical laughter rising to her throat. And then it came out, peal after peal of laughter, and she was screaming and sobbing, and she saw their faces looming around her through a mist, shocked, distressed, then someone slapped her face hard, and she was taken to her cabin, where she wept through the rest of the day and night. When she emerged there was a hardness in her face that had not been there before, the final gentle contours of girlhood had gone, had been moulded into the stronger cast of womanhood.

For two weeks Tam drove everyone hard. The boats ran as planned, she counted the takings every morning. Her payment to the money-lenders was due on the first of December, then there was Madame's bill to pay . . . She was absorbed with her figures to the exclusion of all else, perhaps deliberately, so that she need not think of her mother's revelations. Tam told herself she was too busy to think, as she took the tiller on the boat, helped Abby with the food, avoided her mother, and visited the Earps on the occasions when they were all free.

She found a strange solace with the Earps. Already the cabin was a cosy little home, doors shut with the inner panels painted with castles and roses, the big kettle singing on the hob of the black stove, the brass lamp swinging above, the lace-edged plates hanging on the walls. Here Mirrie would sit in the evenings, working on her sewing, her fingers never idle. And on the mornings when the boat didn't run Harry would sit with the children, teaching the older ones their letters. But it was the sense of peace that Tam found so soothing, an indefinable something that enveloped the family and the small cabin, and which was in some way to do with their religion, although they never talked about it, unless Tam brought up the subject. She grew very fond of Mirrie, and marvelled at the different types of people she had as friends. Perhaps, Tam thought, we take as friends those who fill our needs at any given time. She heard about the coming election from Harry, he went to help when he was free. Tam gathered he spoke at meetings, together with Charles.

Charles was something – or someone – else Tam pushed to the back of her mind. She had been so used to asking his advice, it was difficult not to carry on doing so. Yet, remembering Juliet's coolness – was not that what it was all about? – she knew she must. She pushed herself to the limit, working and concentrating, the emotional happenings tightly corked in the back of her mind. So when she listened to Harry on the election, heard him talk of William Fargate, she refused her mind to listen to anything about Charles.

And the electioneering wasn't going too smoothly. The old system of 'treating' still went on, when Sir William's agent, a fox-faced individual named Harper, bought beer for the colliers who lived on the outskirts of the town.

'But what can they do? What is Harper's plan?' asked Tam.

'Oh, it's just to make trouble. Going to the polling booths on election day, shouting and jeering to make others vote against Charles. Making trouble at the meetings.'

'Why do the colliers let themselves be used in this way?' Tam asked. 'Surely they should side with Charles? And they have no vote.'

'Aye, that's the problem,' Harry said. 'They have no vote. Some of them thought they would get it when the Bill was passed, they've all been working for it, colliers and weavers alike. They feel they've been wronged. They are resentful, and when men are resentful they act without reason. Or they see unreason as reason. They are resentful about loss of earnings and somehow they take William Fargate's treats as part of their settlement.'

'I fear there is trouble brewing in the town,' said Mirrie.

'And not helped by the gangs of rough strangers I see everywhere,' said Harry. 'I feel thou wouldst be better to stay here, Mirrie. And thee, Tamarisk.'

'Perhaps they should have the vote,' said Tam, doubtfully.

'Every man should have a vote,' said Mirrie. 'And every woman too.'

'Why, Mirrie, I didn't know you were such a radical reformer,' cried Tam.

'Oh, the Friends were ever regarded as rebels,' said Mirrie, proudly. 'Christ is our only Master, and before him all men are equal, and women too.'

'Well now,' said Tam, astonished at this view, 'I cannot see women ever getting the vote. Though I sometimes think we should. But these rough

147

crowds, Harry, are they all Quakers and Methodeys?'

'Alas, no,' said Harry, who was facing his own private fears of sowing a wind and reaping a whirlwind. 'I would feel easier in my mind if they would all go to a prayer meeting and pray that God's guidance to be directed to Sir William.'

Tam snorted. 'I can't see Sir William being guided by God or anybody.'

Mirrie soothed. 'It was bound to happen, Harry. The trouble here has been brewing for a long time and will go on for longer, I fear.'

Tam looked at Mirrie's quiet exterior, her gentle calm, and was astonished anew. Yet she found some measure of calm herself in that peaceful cabin, and would go back to her work refreshed, so that, on a day two weeks after the death of Lady Brooke, as the boat swung towards Birmingham, brown earth and green fields on either side, she was ready to examine her feelings regarding Mama and her own dubious parentage.

She found them strangely indefinite in some respects, Lord Brooke meant nothing to her. Jamie Calder was her father, he was the one who had picked her up when she fell as a child, who soothed her tears, who had joked with her as she grew older. 'My, what a beautiful lady we're becoming,' when, at twelve, she'd daringly curled her hair into a bunch of curls over her forehead in the modern style. To be presented with a perfect stranger and told this was her father meant no more than if he'd been a fifth cousin twice removed.

Her feelings towards her mother were not so obscure. There was anger first and foremost, that she should do such a thing, that she should marry another man while in that condition – though Annabel had said he'd known – but worst of all that she should go on meeting her lover throughout her marriage. Now she knew why they had been sent off to Miss Laker's and made to stay during the holidays, it was so that Mama could meet him. The fact that she might have been illegitimate did not register yet, she hardly grasped the fact. But the worst thing of all was that it was her mother. Other women might be mistresses, kept women, Car Boswells, might have lovers and fancy men. *Mothers* were pure. And that is what Tam could not forgive.

And nothing, she vowed, would make her go and live with them. Nothing. She would stay on the boat, and work for her father's ideals just as she had always planned.

Annabel announced that she would stay till Christmas. She did not try to persuade Tam to come with her, merely let it be known that she would be welcome. Tam pursed her lips and said nothing. She paid the instalment on the new boat on the first of December, and was daring to hope that things would work out when, barely a week later she saw Annabel poring over a letter.

'Is anything wrong, Mama?' she asked, and Annabel handed it to her. It was another reminder from Madame, couched in very strong terms, saying, in fact, that unless the bill was paid immediately, Madame would take action. As non-payment of debt meant prison, Tam was momentarily scared. 'Mama!' she cried out in horror.

'Really, the woman is insufferable,' Annabel said angrily.

'Have you no money left from your jewels?' asked Tam.

'You know I gave you all that money, Tam,' said Annabel. 'You said you would see to the accounts. I shall write and let her know that I am marrying Lord Brooke,' Annabel went on airily. 'That will quiet her.'

'Except,' Abby put in, 'Lord Brooke is quite impoverished, as everyone in London knows, Miss Bel.'

Tam looked up sharply. 'Impoverished, Mama?'

Annabel shrugged.

'I thought he was an earl, with a country seat,' pursued Tam.

'I'm glad you show a little interest,' said Annabel, a little waspishly. 'Though I note it is in money matters you show interest, nothing more. Typical of you, Tam.'

'If more people showed interest in money matters we might be in a better position,' retorted Tam. 'But what is this about Lord Brooke?'

'He gambles,' said Abby, as Annabel did not answer. 'Always has and always will. His wife had money but it died with her. He will have nothing but a load of debts. Maybe Madame knows about all this, Miss Bel, maybe that's the reason for her sending this letter now.'

Still Annabel was silent, and Tam asked incredulously, 'Is this really true, Mama?'

'I fear he is a little over-fond of the cards. But he has been unhappy in his life.'

Tam snorted. 'So how will he be support you, Mama? And what of this plan to take me with you? What would I live on?'

'Oh hush,' Annabel said pettishly. 'Plenty of people live without money.'

Tam thought of the life her mother would have. Balls and parties and gaming tables, hunting and shooting, fine clothes and dancing, forever in debt. Though she disapproved of so much frivolity, she could not quite relinquish the whole idea of balls and parties, she was too fond of them herself, to take up such a self-sacrificing way of life as that of Mirrie and Harry. Such faith required much discipline, and Tam knew it was not for her. Surely there was a middle way . . .

But she was worried. Annabel had ordered the dresses, now did not seem to care if she paid for them or not. It seemed a dreadfully dishonest way to live. She wondered if Celia would be willing to pay her own share of the bill now she had money, but thought not. If it should come to a court case, Celia would no doubt pay her own share and leave the others to take the consequences. There seemed no immediate solution.

The second week in December brought sharp frosts, and Tam was reminded of the previous year when they were iced up. The Earps took the boat to Warwick, returning with but twenty people.

'It's the weather,' Harry Earp warned. 'Bitter cold. I fear the numbers will dwindle now, Tamarisk.'

The same thing happened at Birmingham. Cold, with a flurry of snow; winter was settling in early, there was much sickness about, people did not want to travel. Tam hoped Juliet was not going still to the soup kitchen, but just had not the time to worry about anything else. And she had studiously kept away from Charles who was busy with pre-election meetings, which were, to all accounts, growing more uproarious every day. On the nomination day, Harry told her, five hundred people had been conveyed by waggons lent by farmers into Chilverton where they were treated to bread and cheese and ale. Yet she felt she needed Charles more than ever before. She needed his advice, for unless passengers increased she would not have enough to pay the next instalment to the money-lenders, let alone Madame. She longed for someone to confide in, but hesitated to talk to the Earps, for apart from worrying them over a private matter, they would, she knew, merely offer to work without payment, and this hardly seemed fair. So she paid them, paid the two boys, Gilbert and Richard, bought food for all, and fed the horses.

They sailed to Birmingham on the 19th of December. Tam took a turn at the tiller and never had there been a drearier day. Rain pelted down, and she wore an oilskin covering over her dress and cloak; her hands, covered with mittens, were chapped and sore. They pulled up at the Birmingham wharf in hard, sleety rain, to find few people waiting there. Well, they'd been doing this run for a year, doubtless they'd have to find another town after Christmas. Together with another actress, instead of Annabel.

She handed over to Jim, and went below to where Abby was slicing meat. Tam warmed her hands at the stove, then turned to watch as Abby picked up a large loaf. 'Abby,' she said, 'when Mama leaves . . . will you go too? You and John?'

'Are you set on staying then?' Abby asked.

'Yes,' said Tam.

'Well now.' Abby stood for a moment. 'I didn't say anything before, I didn't know if you'd change your mind. And even if you hadn't, I wasn't sure myself what I'd do.' She took a breath. 'I've watched you struggle with everything since your Papa died, doing more than anyone. And though my loyalty has always been to your Mama, yet I might have stayed with you if I just had myself to consider. But I don't, Miss Tam, it's John, you see.'

'John?'

'Aye, Miss Tam, it's too much for him, out in all weathers. Look at him now,' and they peered through the window to see John, guiding the horses, head bent against the driving rain. 'He's sixty, Miss Tam, and it's too much for him now he has the rheumatics something terrible. I'm sorry, Miss Tam, I really am, but Lord Brooke's offered us a home with him, and though I don't approve of all his doings, for John's sake I'll have to go.'

'I see, Abby.' Oh dear heaven, what would she do without them?

'Don't blame your Mama too much,' Abby said. 'She really loves him, you know, she always has. More than anything – '

'Or anyone,' said Tam.

'Your father, Mr Calder,' said Abby. 'He was willing, you know.'

'Yes, I believe they struck a sort of bargain,' Tam said.

150

'Nay,' Abby chided her. 'He loved her too.'

'Did he, Abby?'

'Oh yes. He didn't marry her just for the money. He loved her and he loved you, Miss Tam.'

'Did he? I loved him. Oh, Abby – '

'There, there.' Abby held out her arms. And Tam was crying now, for the father they had taken away from her. 'Nothing's changed,' Abby said. 'He was your Papa, you know.'

'He *was* my father, he was,' she said.

Abby held the girl to her ample bosom, and she wept healing tears.

They put on the play, and it all seemed lacklustre, there was little applause. They took the people back and returned from Birmingham. And as they tied up on the lay-by Tam saw the burly constable waiting for them.

'Miss Calder?' he asked.

Tam's heart jerked. It had come then, Madame's summons for repayment of debt.

'What is it?' she asked.

'It's a letter for you, Miss Tamarisk Calder.'

'From whom?'

The constable looked uncomfortable. 'I don't know, Miss Calder, I was just asked to bring it. I'm sorry.'

He walked away and Tam took the letter, went below to her cabin. She sat by the little table and opened it. It was from Mr Benton, the lawyer, and was couched in such legal language that she found it difficult to understand. After re-reading it, she began to grasp the sense, and it was nothing to do with Madame at all.

'The boat, named the *Princess*, bought by James Calder, belonged to his creditors, the Chilverton Canal Company . . . The boat must be handed over on the 31st December, or proceedings would be taken.'

Tam stared ahead, seeing nothing. There was nothing she could do. She could not even afford to pay a lawyer to contest the case. Even if she had a case . . .

She sat for a long time, hearing the splash of the water outside. Later, after a very subdued supper, during which she tried desperately to act as if everything was normal, she excused herself, saying she had the accounts to do. She lay on her bed, listening to the rain on the roof. She slept little, and made herself a cup of strong tea long before the murky dawn spread over the canal and the usual boaters' cries began. Annabel swept in to announce that she was going out, and when Lord Brooke's carriage arrived she left without another word. There was no sign of Gilbert and Richard.

Abby bustled in. 'Are you all right, Miss Tam?'

'Yes, of course, Abby. I'm just going to go over the books.' She counted the takings and took the money to John. Outside the boat she could hear a continuous noise from the town, yells and shouts. This must be the election fever they talked about. Later she heard Annabel come in. She was talking to Lord Brooke, saying, 'Yes, I'll be all right now.' Lord Brooke's

151

low tones, then his departure, and Annabel's peremptory call, 'Tam, Tam.'

She walked out, stone-faced. Annabel cried, 'Such a thing has happened to us. We were driving through the town, and all those rough men – ' Tam stared. Annabel's elegant dress was spattered with mud, her cloak covered with smelly vegetable matter.

'Why, what happened, Mama?' Tam asked, but she could not seem to summon up enough concern, she just could not worry about anything else; not now, her mind was too swollen with shock to take in anything else.

'It's that man,' cried Annabel.

'What man?' asked Tam. 'What are you talking about, Mama?'

'Gilbert. That man I befriended. They've run him out of town. Him and the boy.'

'Whatever for? What has he done?'

Annabel sniffed in answer. If she knew she did not say. Abby helped her undress, put her to bed, gave her a hot drink.

In the morning Tam found out why Annabel had been attacked. She went on to the towpath and found a crudely written note pinned to the boat . . .

'*Friends and neighbours beware of the man who lived here* – ' There were a few more words, then a blank, and another line which Tam found not only offensive, but extremely puzzling. She stared in bewildered astonishment, as a hand reached out and pulled the note off. She swung round. It was Charles.

'Who – ?' she began to ask.

'I can't stop, Tam, it's the election. But I heard about this in the town, and that some wag had written the thing you see here. It's a habit of some people to make little verses about scandals. Take no notice. I must go.' He wheeled his horse. 'It's getting rough in the town,' he called over his shoulder.

Tam went aboard to find Annabel coming out from her cabin, dressed, carrying a large hold-all. 'This is the end,' she said dramatically. 'I'm going, Tam.'

'Now, Mama?'

'Now. After this – this outrage, I can't stay here. Nor can you. You must come with me.'

'No, Mama.' It was easier to let them all go. Only she would stay and then maybe find a solution, when her head cleared, when she could think more lucidly . . . she wondered vaguely why Gilbert and Mama should be attacked now, maybe Sir William was behind this too – getting them all out of the way.

'You can't live alone, Tam,' Annabel protested.

'No, Mama.'

'Then what?'

'I can live with the Earps. They are most respectable people.'

'It's no use, Tam. It's all finished. Now Gilbert's gone and the boy with him – '

152

And the boat, Tam added silently, knowing her mother was right.

'I told you I would go, Tam. I haven't deceived you.'

'No.'

'There's no point in continuing, you won't find any more actors, not for the money we pay. I'll tell you. When I went to London to find an actor for the boat no one would come except Gilbert, and that was because he couldn't find employment any longer, for he is a drunk. I didn't know about the other then.'

'What other, Mama? Gilbert made no trouble.'

'That dreadful mob in the town,' Annabel said. 'They were even screaming terrible names at me. Strumpet, they said. I cannot stay a moment longer, to be so abused.'

'No, Mama.'

'Lord Brooke wants you to come, Tam. He would welcome you.'

'I shall never live with Lord Brooke,' Tam said, and while Annabel stood, fuming, she went on. 'What about Madame's bill, Mama?'

'Oh that. I'll pay later.'

But Tam knew she would not. She turned to Abby. 'And you, Abby? Are you going now?'

'Not until you find someone to replace us, Miss Tam.'

Tam looked at the woman, noted the grey in her hair that hadn't used to be there. Thought of John. It's too much for him, out in all weathers . . .

'You might as well go, Abby,' she said. 'I shan't run any more trips this week.' *If ever.*

'Miss Tam,' said Abby. 'Will you go to the Earps? Promise me, else I won't leave.'

'I promise I won't stay on the boat alone,' Tam said. 'Though heaven knows the boaters won't hurt me. It's people like Mama who hurt me: friends and relations.'

'Shall I send for Celia? Juliet?'

'No. I'll be all right.'

She didn't even watch Annabel go, taking Abby and John with her. Instead she stayed in her cabin. Finally she went to the Earps, and told them there'd be no more runs before Christmas.

Mirrie said troubled, 'Art thou all right, Tamarisk?'

'Yes,' she said. 'Of course.' You'll know soon enough, she thought. 'I'll see you later to tell you what we shall do.'

She returned to the boat. Abby had left a meal, but she did not want to eat. She paced up and down, hearing the patter of rain on the roof, the water lapping carelessly against the side of the boat. Her boat. Papa's boat . . .

What could she do? Settle for a hateful life of debts and gambling with a mother she did not like and a man she despised? Find some young man to marry her? How could she live with another man when she loved Charles?

Charles. It had been so long since she'd really talked with him. She needed his help and advice now, needed him as she'd always needed him. He wasn't her lover, he was brother, father, friend, the one person she could confide in, the one who understood. She had to see him. It was a driving need that couldn't be denied: to talk to him. Just to sit near him would soothe, to be beside him was all she wanted. But where would she find him? It was election day, but no doubt he'd be in the town somewhere, at the polling booths perhaps. It was early afternoon when she put on her bonnet and went to find Charles.

She had heard shouting as she left the wharf, but thought it all part of the election. Now, as she approached Gate Street, and made her way towards the market square, she saw it was full of people. Thinking they must be polling there, she carried on, and soon she realised that what she thought to be a demonstration in favour of one or other of the candidates, was, in fact, something far more serious. Cheering had turned to jeering, or perhaps it had been that all along, missiles were being thrown, and she was scared that Charles might be the person at whom the crowd's anger was directed. So she hurried on.

'What is it?' she asked a man on the edge of the crowd. 'What's going on?'

'It's Harper, Fargate's man,' she was told. 'For days he's been bringing his colliers in to demonstrate and make trouble for Charles Waring. He's treated 'em all to beer, made 'em drunk, now they're all here and a'going for anybody. An' we was fighting back, like.' But it was obvious no one really knew who was fighting who, or why.

She could see the Court house, where the polling booths were. She couldn't see Charles, but there was a man she guessed was Harper, and a stone hurled through the air, then another. The roads were filled with horsemen and foot-passengers. Special constables had been sworn in, and some of them now rode into the crowd on horseback, and seemed at first to have some effect, that the crowds would go quietly. Tam pushed her way towards the booths, but there was still no sign of Charles, and she realised her madness in trying to see him on election day. But she had no knowledge of elections or voting. She had heard all the talk of 'treating', of men making trouble, but had never understood – now she saw the outcome. These crowds of drunken men were supposed to bully serious voters into voting for the man who had 'treated' them, Sir William. But something seemed to have gone wrong. They were getting out of hand and moreover were turning against the man who had brought them there. Perhaps they intended that all along. But the crowd, once seeming on the verge of dispersing, now surged back, more stones were thrown.

Someone shouted out that no more voting could be done, and the poll had been adjourned. And now the magistrate could be seen at the window of the 'King William Inn'; he opened the window and in a ringing voice read the Riot Act. His voice was penetrating, and for a few minutes the noise was hushed. But only for a few minutes.

Tam turned to go back, but found to her dismay that she was hemmed in by the crowd. She turned and saw that Charles had come onto the platform, and had he been allowed to speak he might have been able to soothe the crowd. But he was elbowed aside by Mr Jennings, the High Constable,

154

who ordered the crowd to go away in a high hectoring voice which enraged rather than quieted. Someone threw a potato at Mr Jennings, and immediately more vegetables from a luckless greengrocer's were thrown. Windows were smashed, and men shouted that the military had been sent for. It was enough. The tradesmen hastened to barricade their shops as the crowd pushed its way along Gate Street, and Tam was pushed with them, unable to get free.

She could see constables, armed with carbines and sabres, riding on horseback bearing towards the crowd, but they stayed on the edge, forcing the mobs back again. Tam could see nothing now but the fierce movements around her as she fought to stay on her feet. They were shouting, 'Let's get Harper, he's the villain! He's in the inn. Let's break the door down.'

She looked back once towards the election platform and thought she saw Charles making his way towards the crowd. But she had no time to look again, as she was pushed along with the crowd, this way and that, desperately trying to stay on her feet.

It was beginning to get dark. And now there was a loud, frightened cry, 'The military. The soldiers.' And she saw clearly horse soldiers with drawn swords riding towards them. Terrified, the crowds tried to move back, then swept right to the platform, Tam with them. Some were able to scatter into a narrow alley-way behind the houses, others pushed on. Tam, swept backwards now, thought if she could gain the safety of the platform she might scramble up on it. She saw soldiers riding through the crowd towards her, felt a push as the crowd, maddened now with fear, heaved back, and, unable to hold her balance, she fell . . . She saw a soldier way above her, saw the horse's legs as it reared, saw the giant hooves almost above her and she screamed with terror.

And then two strong arms reached from beneath the platform and pulled her through to the other side, and held her for a long moment as she gasped and shuddered as though drowning. The arms held her tightly, and she whispered, 'Charles.'

For a moment they stood, in the comparative quiet of the tiny yard at the back of the platform. Both were shaking. He asked urgently, 'Are you all right? I saw you there, and tried to reach you . . .'

'I'm all right.' But her heart was still thumping, and he still held her. He drew her closer, and was covering her face with kisses, as though he had waited for so long that he could wait no longer. Then his mouth was on hers, he was kissing her, pressing her close to him, she felt his hardness against her body, and responded, knowing that this was what she had always wanted, to hold him, to be one with him, never to let him go.

He drew her into a tiny room, pulled her towards him without loosing his hold and, both their senses heightened by fear, they clung together, forgetting everything but each other, clinging mouth to mouth, arms entwined.

And he laid her gently on the floor, and she helped him remove her skirts, felt his hands caress her limbs, carefully, knowingly, as a musician

155

knows a delicate instrument, until she was roused fully, and he taught her the meaning of love. If he was not now gentle, she did not care, if at times his kisses burned too fiercely, some wildness within her rose and matched his ardour with her own, and she slid her hands round the back of his neck, pulling his lips to hers as her body awoke to passion.

At last she lay back, his head resting lightly on her breast, and her fingers softly stroked his hair.

'You love me,' she said then.

'Yes.' His voice was quiet. 'I love you.'

'Then why did you marry Juliet?' she cried.

'Juliet had to be taken care of.'

'Then you should have thought of that before you – '

'I didn't. Not with Juliet. Damn it, Tam, I've been with women if they're willing, but I wouldn't take a girl like Juliet.'

'She was willing. She said it was you.'

'Did she? Are you sure?'

Tam tried to think back, but she was too confused. She said, 'Then who – ?'

'Leave it now, Tam. It's Juliet's secret.'

'But you know?'

'Of course.'

Memory returned. 'I like one of the Waring brothers,' and Celia saying, 'Don't say it is my Geoffrey . . . ' No, Juliet had never said who it was.

'It was Geoffrey,' she said flatly.

He didn't speak.

'Oh, Charles, why . . .?'

'Somebody had to. You see, on the night of the Pick-Nick, I saw Juliet come to the edge of the garden, saw her approach Geoffrey, they went into the summer house. I – guessed what had happened. I asked Geoffrey about it, told him he must marry her. He denied it – '

'And then came rushing down to ask Celia to marry him. I suppose he thought Juliet could make the wrong sort of wife for a man with his ambitions.' She turned away from Charles. 'Poor Juliet. You – don't love her?'

'I do, in a way. She is so sweet.'

'Your habit of protecting the weak . . .' she said.

'She is having a child.'

Tam stood up startled. 'Is she? Oh God. Oh God, Charles. Then that explains it all . . . her aloofness, not wanting to see us. Oh, I should have guessed. Will she be all right?'

'Esther Winters will take care of her,' Charles soothed. 'She's had experience of nursing, and she's a cut above the usual run of sluttish nurses available. And I'm trying to get a new young doctor, Dr Phillips, to come to the town.'

Tam said despairing, 'Oh, Charles, what are we going to do?' and they stared at each other, bewildered.

'I shouldn't have – ' he started.

'Shouldn't have what?'

'I shouldn't have married Juliet, loving you. I didn't declare my love, Tam, I had nothing to offer as yet. I wanted to wait, but I felt I had to help Juliet, money or no. What would she have done? I wasn't protecting Geoffrey, but I couldn't force him to marry her . . . So *I* did. And so, I should not have made love to you.'

'It was my fault as much as yours,' she said, her honesty surfacing. 'I came to see you, I'm always coming to see you. Because I can't – ' she broke off. Can't live without you. Don't say it, don't tell him that. Or he might want you to stay with him. There's his career, and Juliet. Always look after Juliet, Mama had said so many years ago. Even if Mama didn't herself, Tam had to look after Juliet. Juliet was Charles's wife, and now she, Tam, could never be, because a man can never marry his wife's sister, nor his deceased wife's sister.

'And there's Parliament, the election.'

'Damn the election.'

'You want it, Charles. It's your dream.' She thought of the ugly scribbled note on the boat about Gilbert. What would be scribbled about them if anyone found out, when he was a Member of Parliament? And she knew she must live without him, that she must, however hard, find a way.

'I'll go now. The crowds seem to have gone. I'll go. It's better, Charles. You must take care of Juliet.'

'But, Tam – '

'It's better this way. I'm glad you love me, knowing that will help . . . But I'm going now. Alone.'

She was away now, running. The crowds had dispersed, the soldiers were gone. She was crying, deep, tearing sobs that shook her as she ran. Back to the boat, the empty boat.

She sat in her cabin, and remained there all night. Her mind was clear now, as everything she had pushed away re-surfaced. I cannot carry on, she realised. She could not put on any more plays, could not find actors or rehearse them in time. Maybe she could carry on running one packet boat, but they'd have few passengers in the middle of winter, and without the plays the takings would be down. Not enough to pay Madame, or make the repayments to the money-lenders; she hadn't realised just how much she had to pay to the latter, hadn't quite understood when they talked about interest, still did not, but she reckoned she'd be paying the loan four or five times over . . . Time, she needed time . . . The boys would find work elsewhere, she could sell the horses, but what of the Earps, who had let their loom go, lost their home, were so happily settled in their new way of life, dependent on her? Would it all have to go . . .? Just as all those she had loved were gone: Papa, Mama, Celia and Juliet. And Charles who could never be hers, could never be free to love her. She didn't regret what had happened with Charles. He would be with her now, always, belong to her always. She was comforted by knowing the truth, that he'd married Juliet because Geoffrey had left her, because she was having his baby . . .

Baby! Tam sat up suddenly. Juliet was having a baby. And the same

157

thing might happen to her . . . I have been betrayed by my womanhood, she thought.

And then the longing started, the longing to see Charles, to be with him again, to hold him, to have him near her, within her . . . and she knew that she could not stay here like this, or she'd run to him, as she had run so many times, she couldn't keep away. She'd been running to him yesterday . . .

She had to find some way of keeping away from him.

She sat for a long time, then at last slowly rose and carefully put on her new dress, the dress she'd worn for Celia's wedding, put on a cloak and went to the Earps. She knocked on the side of the boat as all boaters did, for no one ever looked inside another's boat, even when crossing its deck to get to the towpath, one always knocked. When Mirrie answered Tam said she must talk to them, and later, might she borrow Jobey to drive the carriage?

In a moment she stood in the Earps' cabin, her mind clear and cool, her heart dead. 'I want to give the *Duchess* to you,' she said.

There was a silence, she could hear rain pattering on the roof. 'What dost thou mean?' Harry asked.

'I shall be going away, and so I want to give the boat to you, to run as a packet.'

'But – ' Harry was nonplussed, 'Where art thou going?'

'I cannot tell you now,' Tam said, 'but you will know in time. Please accept the boat, it will make me happy.

'But the *Duchess* is worth a lot of money – ' Harry said.

'Money will be no problem where I am going,' said Tam.

Mirrie noticed the strain on her face and put an arm around her shoulders. 'If it makes thee happy,' she said, and looked at her husband.

'Well.' Harry blinked. 'In truth we like the boat, Tamarisk. It gives us freedom to work for ourselves . . . and if it were mine . . . yes, I would welcome that. But to take it for nothing.' His face creased in worried lines.

'Oh, Harry,' Tam said, half vexed. 'I understand now why Quakers are said to do well in business because they are honest in a dishonest world. Most people would jump at the chance of something for nothing.'

'I will tell thee what I will do,' Harry said. 'I will, if thou agreest, pay thee so much every week, as I paid for my loom, and then in the end I shall have paid for the boat.'

'Very well,' said Tam.

'Tamarisk,' Mirrie said, 'please think over what thou be going to do. I am worried about thee.'

'Oh, Mirrie, you don't know the story . . . there's so much you don't know.'

And I could never tell, she thought as she left them. To Mirrie life is so simple, good and bad. What would she think of me if she knew the truth? About me and Charles? About our love? And what I am going to do.

Jobey drove her to the Manor, and she sat, cold and still. She had burned her bridges now, she must go on . . .

158

And then she was asking for Sir William Fargate, and he came towards her, this man she hated.

'Ah, Tamarisk,' he said. 'Have you come to gloat over my downfall?'

'What?' she asked bewildered, still living in her own world.

'I lost the election.'

Then Charles had won. Her heart leapt. 'I did not know,' she said. 'No, I came for another reason.'

He took her into a large room with wide windows overlooking the gardens and asked her to sit down.

'Do you remember your proposition?' she said quietly.

'Of course. You wish to take it up?'

'No, Sir William. Hear me out. You made it clear what you wanted from me. Now I have a proposition for you.'

'Yes?'

'I agree to what you want. But you must marry me.'

'Marry you?'

'Yes.' She stood firm. 'My family is as good, indeed better, than your own. On both sides.'

'Brooke, by God.'

'Oh yes,' she said bitterly, 'I am not the daughter of an impoverished tradesman who might be taken lightly. I do not love you, I never shall.'

'Then why the marriage. Money?'

'I want the canal. I should want your shares, made over to me. I know a wife's property belongs to her husband, but it must be made legal, that I am to have sole ownership of the Chilverton Canal Company, to run it as I see fit, and on your death it would come entirely to me. I think this can be arranged, as it is not part of the entailed property. That, Sir William, is what I am marrying you for. Not *why* I am marrying you.'

'A bargain.'

'Yes. My mother made such a bargain too.'

'I fail to see what you'd gain from marriage,' he said.

Married to you I could not fly free. I shall be caged, she thought, but instead said aloud, her voice icy, 'I'd gain on your death.'

He winced. 'By God, you're a hard little nut, Tamarisk.'

She bowed her head. 'I believe I am.'

'Very well,' he said. 'We will be married.'

PART THREE

1837–1855

No Spring, nor Summer beauty hath such grace
As I have seen in one Autumnal face.

John Donne

Chapter One

Tam did not like Chilverton Manor, she thought the huge grey exterior was as forbidding as a prison, and just as isolated. The first William Fargate became Lord of the Manor after sailing with the king's son on a crusade in the thirteenth century. His power was absolute, and included the execution of criminals, for which purpose a gallows had stood waiting in the neighbourhood, though it was now happily removed. Inside the house there was a fine staircase, and large drawing rooms overlooking the gardens; there were portraits, and ornaments of great value placed carefully and formally around, but it was a masculine house, as though neither the late Lady Fargate nor any of her forebears had been able to stamp their personalities on the Manor. It was a squire's house, a drinking, shooting, man's house. Sir William, like most country squires of the time, was a dedicated hunting and shooting man, not given to much entertaining, though he liked to have his hunting friends round him occasionally and, during the season, they would stump in to breakfast talking in loud voices of the foxes they had killed. For the rest of the time the Manor echoed with emptiness, one could wander around the large rooms for hours – and be bored to tears. There was an excellent housekeeper, Mrs Sanders, and Tam left the running of the Manor to her while she spent as much time as possible outdoors with her beloved canal.

The canal was now hers: signed and sealed, with a further rider that it would remain hers on Sir William's death. It was, she knew, a legal contract between themselves. A married woman was treated in law as an idiot, unable to contract on her own and her husband was liable for her debts. It was, in effect, a bond of honour while he was alive, she would gain only on his death.

There were still two very small shareholders, but no mention of Geoffrey, which surprised and pleased her; he had evidently pulled out. She was in charge, and had, with ownership, put the accrued dividends into a reserve fund, which amounted to a tidy sum, until one remembered the amount which had to be spent on maintenance. But dividends had been high, as much as forty-eight per cent in the good years, and Sir William had been careful.

He was equally careful now. He spelt out her dependence on him, her duties. When he required her company at an occasional visit, or when he entertained his hunting friends, she was to act as hostess, and for this she must be well dressed; he would pay for her clothing, but all bills must be sent to him for she would have no ready money. For spending money he told her she had the canal dividends, and so she was able to pay her debts. 'For the rest,' he said, 'you'll have to wait until I'm dead,' his meanness immediately taking away any gratitude Tam may have felt towards him for the canal.

It was a dreary life. She started making herself available for afternoon teas on the advice of the Duchess, who sympathised with the girl and who liked to visit her when in the area. So at five o'clock on Wednesdays, the ladies of the neighbourhood might drop in as they pleased.

Celia glanced round the drawing room on this fine August day of 1837, and the old envy reasserted itself. She had been married first, but Tam was her ladyship, not that she would change her dear Geoffrey for a title of course, but it did seem hard that Tam, who always seemed to have the best of everything, was now the chatelaine of the Manor. Still, it was nice to be able to visit with Lady Cortain from the hunting fraternity in nearby Leicestershire, Lady Marning and Lady Carruthers, both wives of local squires. And, of course, the Duchess, who came often because, she said, she was fond of Tam. Celia sniffed, then began to listen as the conversation turned to the recent coronation.

'What will she be like, one wonders?' asked Lady Marning, who was, at twenty-two, quite beautiful in a glacial way. 'She is so young, we know so little about her.'

'They say her mother was very strict,' put in Lady Cortain, who wasn't really interested in anything but horses and hounds. 'Kept her secluded.'

'Because she was shocked with the language and habits of her royal uncles,' said Lady Carruthers, who at forty, had a weatherbeaten face and was shocked at nothing. 'What do you think, Duchess?' and they turned to the only one among them who had intimate knowledge of court circles.

The Dowager laughed. 'Who can tell how a girl of eighteen will turn out?' she asked. 'No one knows much about the Queen, though she seems to have character.'

'At least she can't be worse than the late king,' said Lady Marning.

'Oh, William wasn't so bad.' said the Dowager. 'I think he tried. He wasn't cut out to be a king, he was happier as a sailor. But he was determined not to die till Victoria was eighteen, or her mother would have been Regent.'

'Who will guide her now?' asked Lady Cortain.

'She has her Uncle Leopold of Belgium,' said Lady Carruthers. 'And Lord Melbourne, her Prime Minister.'

'They say *he* sees quite a lot of her, six hours a day or more, and that an apartment is permanently kept for him at Windsor,' said Lady Marning.

'He's acting as her private secretary,' said the Duchess.

162

'Is that what they call it?' asked Lady Marning.

'Oh, really, all this gossip.' Tam spoke for the first time. It was known that she detested gossip.

'But my dear,' said Lady Marning. 'There was a piece in *The Times* this morning. "Is it for the Queen's service – is it for the Queen's dignity – is it becoming, is it commonly decent?" Some say she will marry him.'

'I should think he's had enough of marriage with Lady Caroline Lamb,' said Lady Carruthers, caustically. 'She had that scandalous affair with Byron, if you remember . . .'

'And only last year he was served with a writ because of his liaison with Mrs Caroline Norton,' put in Lady Marning. 'And cited by Lady Brandon's husband – '

'And it is rumoured that his real father was Lord Egremont – '

Tam rang for the maid to bring more cakes and wine, and only the Duchess guessed that the subject of real fathers was distasteful to her. Celia, who enjoyed listening to gossip about the upper echelons of society, it proved that though they might be above her in station they were less righteous, smiled as Lady Cortain leaned towards her.

'Will you be hunting this season?' asked Lady Cortain.

'I'm not sure,' Celia replied. 'I have the children, you see . . .'

'Really?' Lady Cortain looked faintly puzzled. 'Is it two girls you have or a girl and a boy?'

'Two girls,' Celia replied.

'Oh yes, of course, it's Tam who has the boy.' And Celia felt again the familiar stirrings of jealousy. Geoffrey did so long for a son . . .

'I have boys too, but I can't see how they'd interfere with hunting,' Lady Cortain went on. 'Don't you have a good nanny?'

'Yes, naturally, but I like to be with the children,' Celia replied. 'And besides,' she hesitated, 'there will be another one soon,' and she flushed.

'Really? How jolly. I rode to hounds for six months while I was expecting both my boys, and they were none the worse, I assure you. John says he's surprised they weren't born on horseback.' Lady Cortain gave a loud laugh, and Celia flushed again. She thought Lady Cortain most indelicate, her own mother-in-law would never talk that way. She took another dish of tea and a small cake, knowing she was getting quite plump, and it was not altogether due to the coming baby. But Geoffrey didn't seem to notice. Celia sat back, a self-satisfied smirk on her face, her envy forgotten. She was perfectly happy with Geoffrey. She didn't mind that when he went to London he always stayed overnight, and that it had been whispered he went to those shows and even took out dancing girls. Celia didn't object, gentlemen did these things. She was his wife, and he had taken them to see the coronation – staying at their town house – so life had turned out pretty well after all. It was so enjoyable to mix with these people, to see Mama and her husband occasionally, to have them stay with her – as Tam never did – and to introduce them: 'My parents, the Earl and Countess of Brooke,' for one couldn't keep calling him Step-Papa, it was too silly. Celia would have given anything to have been the real daughter of Lord Brooke, scandalous or no.

'We'll be having an election soon,' said Lady Cortain. 'Tell me, Lady Fargate, will your husband be a candidate this time?'

'I really don't know,' Tam replied. 'Sir William never tells me about his affairs.'

'We have a lively young member of Parliament now,' said Lady Marning. 'A radical he might be, but he is most handsome.'

'He is enlivening the town,' said Lady Cortain. 'We hear about it even in Leicestershire: how he roars around, castigating people for owning slum property, even getting a new doctor to help his cause.'

'We needed a new doctor,' said Lady Carruthers. 'The old one was a fool, I wouldn't have him to my servants.'

'Nevertheless, it is not for a physician to interfere in the running of the town,' Lady Marning reproved. 'One wonders where this giving of votes to the people will all end.'

Celia stopped listening. It was no joke having a radical for a brother-in-law, especially when it was Geoffrey who owned the property in the Patch. Talk petered out, and she watched as the ladies rose to go, and waited. She had news for Tam.

Her sister re-entered, and with her was a small boy tugging at her hand. 'Really,' Celia said, 'you do spoil that child, Tam. Why doesn't he stay upstairs?'

'Because I like to see him,' said Tam. 'Our mother didn't have much time for us, or have you forgotten?'

'Mama was an actress,' Celia said as if this explained it.

'And I am in charge of the canal, but I intend to spend time with my son.'

'I'm surprised Sir William allows you to go riding down to the wharf every day,' Celia said disapprovingly. 'It's unfeminine.'

'You always said I was unfeminine,' Tam retorted. 'Maybe you're right. But I'm doing what I want to do.'

'Well, I suppose,' Celia said, 'it won't be for long.'

'And what do you mean by that?'

'I did hear,' Celia said, 'that there was a surveyor looking over the land hereabouts last week.'

'Indeed?'

'A surveyor from the railways.' Celia waited hopefully for some signs of shock, but none came. 'Maybe Sir William told you,' she ended.

Tam shrugged. 'Maybe. But he can't do anything till a company is formed, and that's far away.'

The little boy ran around the room and she made no effort to stop him. Celia, foiled of any triumph, eyed the child in disapproval as she rose to go. 'I expect,' she said, 'you will have to make the most of him, I don't suppose you'll have any more children. I mean Sir William is – ' she paused delicately.

'Yes, indeed,' Tam said as she rang for the maid. 'So nice to see you, Celia. Goodbye.' And, as she left, Tam walked to the heavy ornate mirror over the mantelpiece, letting out her breath in a sigh of relief, unclenching her hands. She stared at her reflection. At twenty-six she wore her hair parted in the middle, then brushed into a knot on the top of her head; but her unruly hair never would lie smooth, wisps and tendrils escaped and fell around her face. Like her nature perhaps; however hard she strove to appear indifferent some tempestuous feelings always escaped, showing themselves in her heightened colour, her clenched hands. The last years' efforts at self-control had altered her expression, there was a hardness around the lips which did not smile so often. Only the eyes had not changed, they were still smoky in repose, still flashed green fire when she was angry, when her husband spoke to her. Her dress, with its low draped bodice and Donna Maria sleeves, was of the latest fashion; she always dressed stylishly, as though this too might provide an armour beneath which she could hide.

She turned and walked to the window. She knew what Celia had meant: Sir William was too old to father children. If only she knew . . .

Tam remembered her wedding night. Sir William, fat and paunchy under his nightrobe, looking down at her.

'Take off your clothes,' he ordered harshly.

'Oh no, surely not – ' she jumped up from the bed.

'Take them off. You got your bargain, mistress, I get mine. I married you, but this is what I wanted. Take off your clothes.'

Slowly she disrobed, not knowing that her very slowness added to her desirability. At last she stood naked and vulnerable. He looked her over, his eyes greedy, and then his hands were on her, tubby hands, with thick fingers, pressing her breasts, her body, down to her thighs and beyond, pulling her to the bed. And then the gropings . . . the efforts, the pushings, and his fury as he muttered, 'Dammit, I can't,' and when she cried out, he spat out, 'This is what I married you for.' And again he sought to enter her and could not, and Tam remembered the night with Charles, the love, the desire, the winged happiness. And now love and desire were crumpled in a rich bed with this loathsome man.

And night after night he demanded it of her. That she strip naked, that she lie there while he made these efforts. Occasionally he was successful, after a fashion, and when this happened he immediately turned away from her and slept. And Tam hated him.

She hated him so much that she wanted to hurt him as much as possible. Two weeks after her wedding she faced him in the breakfast room.

'I am with child,' she said.

He looked up, startled.

She said cruelly, 'It is not yours. It couldn't be, could it?'

He stood up, purple veins standing out on his forehead, while she watched him, unmoved. 'Damn you,' he shouted. 'You dare to tell me you've been with another man?'

'Before our marriage,' she said.

'And you were with child? So that's why you were so eager to marry – '

'No,' she said coldly. 'I married you for the canal. I have it now, so you can do as you please. Turn me into the street, do what you will.'

165

He came towards her, grasping her wrist. 'You'd like that, wouldn't you? You'd get out of your duties then. Oh no, mistress, I married you because I wanted you and I shall keep you. So have your child, Lady Fargate, the world will think it's mine.'

She stared up at him amazed. 'You'd do that? Bring the child up as your own?'

He shrugged. 'Why not? I shall appear a fine fellow to father a child, and your lover will never be able to claim him.'

She felt a finger of fear then, knowing she had given him a hold over her that was dangerous. Did he guess who her lover had been? There wasn't much he didn't know about the happenings in Chilverton, he had spies everywhere. She half wished she'd let him think the child was his, yet knew she could not have borne the lie, nor given him the joy of fatherhood when she might withhold it from him. She learned then how women, placed in a subordinate position, can be cruel too.

She learned much from the marriage. Knowing so little of men she had half thought, in her innocence, that his desire for her had indeed contained a little love, even a little tenderness, that the hate was all on her side. But there was no love, no tenderness, she felt now that he merely wanted a whore, that he treated her as a whore, so with him she became a whore, taking all she could from him.

Not that, clothes apart, there was any chance of taking anything from him. He informed her exactly what she might expect from him for the child. He would pay for the baby's upbringing and education; all bills, as with her clothes, must be sent to him, and all bills must be itemised, he added cruelly. Every baby's toy had to be accounted for. But, Tam thought, I have the canal, and I have my son.

He had been born on a wind-swept morning, five years ago, after a long, protracted labour, which was usual, the physician attending her had said, for a first child. She had told no one of the coming birth, not even her mother and sisters, had concealed her figure with long cloaks when she went out of doors, and she was able to put the canal into its new working order before she was forced to stay indoors. Only Mirrie knew, as the time approached, and she had naturally assumed the child was Sir William's. Mirrie knew nothing of Tam's love for Charles, and Tam dare not speak, for his sake. That was why she objected to gossip: no one, she thought fiercely, must talk about Charles as they talked of Lord Melbourne, not when he was just embarking on his career . . . Charles didn't know about the child, either.

Tam was astonished that no one had suspected. Her love had been so all-embracing, it seemed to encompass the whole world, the very house-tops seemed to shout a paean of love to everyone who cared to listen. How could they not know, when he was the finest man who had ever breathed?

The baby's face, at birth, had been Charles's in miniature, and he grew to have the same dark hair, the same shaped face, only the eyes were different, being a bright clear blue. Tam named the boy James after her father.

166

She watched him now as he ran around the room. Not for young Jamie the confines of his room and Nanny while Mama was away. When she went to the canal she took the boy with her, even in bad weather, when they took the carriage, other times he rode beside her on a small pony.

He stopped his running and turned to her. 'Mama, are we going to the canal?'

'Yes, Jamie, we'll get ready now.'

She took his hand and they walked up the fine staircase. 'Mama,' Jamie said. 'It is my birthday soon. Will I have a birthday party?'

'Of course, my love.'

'And who will I ask?'

'Oh, everyone you know, of course. Your cousins, the Cortain boys, the Marning girl, the Earps.'

They entered Jamie's room. The day nursery was a sunny room on the second floor where a governess, Miss Booth, was in charge. She taught her small pupil the rudiments of reading and writing and looked after his needs when his mother was occupied. But it had been made clear to her from the start, just as it had to Nanny, that he was to accompany his mother whenever she so decided, and Lady Fargate's word was law. So now, when Tam came in and said, 'I shall be taking Jamie riding, Miss Booth, will you see to it?' Miss Booth merely replied, 'Yes, milady,' and turned her small charge over to the nursery maid to dress him in his riding habit.

Tam attired herself in a dust-coloured habit, its corsage a little pointed, buttoned up to the throat, a ribbon cravat attached by a gold brooch, and top hat trimmed with lace, and set off for the stables, Jamie trotting beside her.

'Will Grandmama be coming to my birthday party?' he asked. 'And Grandpapa?'

'If you wish,' she said.

'I do. I love Grandmama. And Grandpapa.'

He did, too. And of course, Lord Brooke was his real grandfather, although he didn't know that. Tam, uncertain as to what to tell him, merely explained that Grandmama had been married twice and left it at that. Whether she would ever tell him about her real parentage she had no idea, for it would bring up the thorny question of his own. She felt no more affection now for her real father than she had when her mother told her, nor had her animosity towards her mother lessened. She wondered what she should do about Jamie. Would he, in the future, turn to her with shocked eyes as she had with her own mother? No, the circumstances were entirely different, she reassured herself. Yet it was a dark cloud hanging over her, always there, a fear that would not be dispelled, often lying dormant, but sometimes, as now, spreading its darkness over her till she was filled with fear. Would he turn from her one day, her laughing Jamie, as Papa had always turned from her when Mama beckoned?

The groom was helping Jamie to mount, and she said; 'Yes, we will ask Grandmama and Grandpapa to your party. And – Papa?'

'I don't like Papa very much,' Jamie admitted, and then added reasonably.

167

'But I don't see very much of him. Still, I shall invite him to my party. He did give me this pony.'

It was true he didn't see much of Sir William. At his birth there had been some ribald comments tinged with admiration, from visiting squires, at the birth of a son exactly nine months after marriage; Jamie had been very accommodating, arriving two weeks late. After that, Sir William left the boy alone. Jamie stayed in the nursery except when Sir William was out, when Tam brought him down to be with her. On the odd occasions when the two did come face to face, Sir William spoke to the child only if necessary. He was strict, and Jamie learned early to keep out of his way. As soon as he could walk he had made his way to the stables, and Tam encouraged him in this knowing he was happy there.

Together the handsome woman and the dark-haired boy rode now to the canal, and Tam's heart lifted as she saw it, the coloured boats and the laughing dark faces of the men. It was a warm day, the trees were in the fullness of their summer green, a light breeze rippled the water. The *Princess* was moored in the lay-by. Tam had, as she said, kept it for her own use, leaving Jim in charge, to exercise the horses, to be ready for when she should wish to use it. And she had cause to be thankful for the *Princess*. On the many times when she had fled from Sir William in the beginning, when she hadn't wanted to face even Mirrie, then she'd ask Jim to take it away, or she'd steer herself, away from the noisy wharf and the coal and the dust, into the countryside, to the trees and the placid water that brought healing to her ragged nerves. There was no view of the canal from the Manor, and she missed the lapping water, the cries of the birds. She never mentioned her sense of loss to anyone, Tam kept her thoughts to herself these days. If people thought she was hard and uncaring, let them.

She rode on the wharf, which was as busy as always, and dismounted. Jamie slid from his pony and ran eagerly towards the boats. Tam never stopped him from playing with the boatchildren, she remembered her own childhood too well. Anyway, Jamie was to be brought up to manage the canal.

She entered the little office and greeted the Deputy Agent. She always called him that, had carefully pointed out, on his elevation from wharfinger, that though Mr Charles Waring might now be a Member of Parliament he was still Agent. As Charles was away so often he, Jerome Randall, would deputise on full pay, but when Charles was here then Jerome was to move downwards, again with no loss of pay. She liked Jerome. Small, wiry, energetic, he had a go-getting quality which she recognised instantly, and which was the reason she promoted him. Charles had the same quality. Jerome was also attractive to women, and she recognised this too, and it also appealed to her. He never said a word out of place, and never would, but there was always that faint look in his eyes which told her she was an attractive woman, and which pleased her. He was in the mould of Charles, without Charles's handsomeness or education; she would never fall in love with Jerome, but she found him pleasing. And there was, underneath, a masculine quality of strength which sustained her.

168

'The *Duchess* is not back yet?' she asked him now.

'Not till this evening, milady. It started the run to Coventry today.'

'Yes, I know. Were there enough passengers to justify the run?'

'Yes, indeed, it was nearly full.'

Jerome showed her the latest figures of tolls taken, warehousing prices, maintenance work carried out. There was no need for Lady Fargate to come down every day and see these things he knew, but she was his employer now. And it was due to her that conditions on the Chilverton Canal had improved, tolls and warehouse charges had been lowered, there were no refusals now to let any boatman load at the wharf. And she grasped business matters well, considering she was a woman, in fact there were times when she was ahead of him which puzzled him greatly, seeming to arrive at her judgements by some sort of women's intuition which Jerome, following more slowly by masculine logic, found amazing. Especially as they always reached the same conclusion.

'Everything seems to be going well, Jerome.'

He hesitated. 'I think you should see this, milady.'

'Yes, what is it?'

'A letter from the Staffordshire and Worcester Canal Company – '

She took it and looked at it. 'Why, it's to their shareholders. However did you get this?'

'I got it from their agent, milady,' Jerome said smoothly.

Tam laughed. 'Good work, Jerome. You're a man after my own heart,' and he flushed pink at her praise. She puzzled over the letter, couched in long-winded prose, and said impatiently, 'Oh, the way men write papers, they must spend hours on this sort of thing. What are they rambling about, Jerome? I haven't time for all this.'

'They are worried about the railways, milady.'

'And it takes two pages to say that? Why are they worried?'

'I think it's well to be wary, milady. Some canals have already turned themselves into railways, or sold themselves to railway companies.'

'Stupid fools. They're just panicking. They can't see farther than the end of their collective noses. Just interested in their own little profits.'

'Profits of the moment, milady.'

'Exactly. We ought to get together, all of us, and discuss these matters. Stand firm, have no sell-outs.' She wondered how best to set about it. If only she could talk to Charles . . . Then she said, 'But we don't have to worry just yet, here in Chilverton, do we?'

'There has been talk of a railway coming here.'

'I know. I've heard. But it's only a rumour as yet.'

'True, milady. But all it needs is someone to float a company, get an act through Parliament – '

Float a company. Where had she heard those words before? She realised that Jerome was worried. 'You think it will happen, don't you?'

'It's extremely likely, milady. And I've heard that Pickfords are pulling out.'

'Pickfords? The carriers?'

'Perhaps next year.'

She paced up and down in angry frustration. 'If they pull out it would mean a chance for someone else to take over their business. Oh, if only we could run as carriers – '

He stared at her, saying nothing, for he was more than a little perplexed at the way Sir William and his wife ran the canal. She owned the company, he still owned boats, still delivered his own coal, paying the tolls due to his wife. It was an intriguing situation, the like of which Jerome had never heard. A woman running a business, and seemingly with the approval of her husband. Was he perhaps, indulging her, an old man with a beautiful young wife? Jerome hastily turned his thoughts away from Lady Fargate's beauty which at times troubled him greatly.

Tam herself was uneasy as she left the office and looked for Jamie. Jerome had seemed so pessimistic, almost as though there was something he knew that she didn't. She walked to the water's edge and saw Jamie on one of the boats.

'Mama,' he called. 'Josh is going to the Dirty Fair next month. Can I go with him, Mama?'

She looked down at her old friend Josh Lawson, and thought of the time she'd ridden to the fair with the gipsy. A sudden longing came over her. 'I'll take you,' she said. 'We'll start early, ride there.'

'Oh, Mama.' His eyes were dancing with eager anticipation.

'Come along then.'

He came willingly, and the Lawsons watched them, smiling. And Eliza Lawson bent to whisper to her husband, 'She don't change, does she? Since she lived on the boats. Just as wild as ever.'

Tam and Jamie were walking away.

'Are we going to Auntie Juliet's?' he asked.

'Yes,' Tam replied. 'As usual.'

Tam knocked at the door of the house on the wharf, and Esther Winters entered and showed her into the parlour.

A cheerful fire burned in the parlour grate, and before it, on the large oak settle, Juliet sat, one arm around Roderick, reading to him from a book. He was a pleasant little boy, Tam thought, normal and intelligent, perhaps a mite too quiet, probably because Juliet kept him with her almost all of the time. Tam had offered, in the beginning, to take Roderick to the Manor to play with Jamie, but Juliet had refused. She loved him dearly, that was obvious, and she could not bear him to be out of her sight. Though now, as Jamie entered, running straight to Roderick, saying, 'Come out to the wharf,' and Roderick stood up and looked at his mother, Juliet nodded, and the two boys ran outside.

'Juliet, dear.' Tam went to her sister and kissed her cheek. 'How are you?'

'I'm very well.'

She looked well, Tam thought. She seemed to have lost the almost childish art of prattle which had been such an endearing part of her, and in its place was a quiet air of happiness that had been there since Roderick was born. Tam shuddered as she remembered the time of his birth. Juliet had been very ill, they had feared she might not recover. Yet, when the baby had been handed to her, she had clasped him to her with surprising strength, had, Dr Phillips said, willed herself to get better. She was still not strong, but Esther helped with the housework and with the child, and Juliet was content.

'How is Charles?' Tam asked. 'Do you hear from him when he's in London?'

'Oh yes, he writes. He is very kind to me.'

'You should go to London occasionally, Juliet, and stay with him. You are so much alone here.'

Juliet seemed to shrink into herself. 'Oh, I wouldn't want to go to London. And I am not alone, I have Roddy.'

'Yes, well, I suppose you're better here in the country.'

'I am quite well,' Juliet said with dignity. 'Charles is very kind to me, as I said. But he only married me out of kindness, he does not require me to live with him in London.'

Tam looked at her in surprise, and then decided it would be best to talk of other things. They chatted for a short while, then Juliet stood up. 'If you'll excuse me,' she said. 'I am going to the Patch.'

Tam sighed. She knew from past experience that nothing she said – nothing anyone said – would deter Juliet from her self-imposed mission. When the soup kitchens were opened, Juliet would go to assist; when work improved she simply went down to the Patch, saying she was going to help with the children, taking Roddy with her. What she did no one really knew, but the people were used to seeing her among them, and she was never molested. At first Tam worried, had followed her into the narrow courts and alleys that were the Patch. She watched her walk along the court, saw her approach the children, talk to them, give them sweetmeats from her bag. The weavers accepted her, let her into their homes where she looked after the babies and tiny children who were too small to help with the ancillary tasks, filling the shuttles, and so on. To those who were left Juliet would painstakingly teach the alphabet, which few of them wanted to remember, or had much use for.

Tam sometimes wondered just what went on in Juliet's mind. But there was no one to talk to about her, no one but Charles, and Tam was careful never to be alone with him, so there was little opportunity for a tête-à-tête. And she couldn't bring herself to confide in Esther Winters: she wasn't sure why, she seemed competent enough, but there was a grim, watchful air about the woman that Tam didn't like, and though she shrank from discussing private family affairs with her, she often wondered just how much Esther knew – or guessed.

But the worry was there, and once, after much consideration, Tam did begin to talk things over with Mirrie, even going so far as to tell her the truth about Juliet's child. She knew Mirrie wouldn't talk. 'It's as though she's imposed this severe penance on herself,' Tam said. 'For her sin, as she sees it.'

'She is too hard on herself,' agreed Mirrie. 'I tried to talk to her once, but it was no use. Her mind seemed closed. Rigid.'

171

'I know,' Tam sighed. She had even, herself, tried to bring up the subject of the baby, of Geoffrey, thinking Juliet might be eased to talk about it, but it was useless. Juliet simply turned a blank face to her, as if she hadn't the faintest idea what she was talking about.

'I think it best to leave her, let her do what she will,' Mirrie advised. 'After all, she seems happy.'

'Yes, I suppose so.' So she said no more to Juliet, said nothing now as her sister put on her cloak and called for Roddy as she left.

Tam turned to Esther. 'How is Juliet?' she asked.

'I get worried about her sometimes, milady.'

'Is she ill?' Why do we keep up this pretence that Juliet is normal? Tam wondered. And when did I first realise that she wasn't? When Mama said how worried she was about her? I had always accepted Juliet. . . You do, when you live with a person, it's the others who think they're odd . . .

'She goes out in the evenings. Alone,' said Esther.

'Where does she go?'

'I don't know.'

'Couldn't you go with her?'

'She won't let me. Anyway, I have to stay with Roddy. She don't take him.'

'She's always liked to walk along the wharf.'

'Yes, she always did,' Esther agreed grudgingly. 'But she seems to go more now.'

'Maybe she goes into the town, sometimes they have Players at Temple Street Hall. Or maybe she goes to church, or some meeting there.'

'No, milady, she don't ever go to church.'

'Then what is it, Esther? What are you worried about?'

'It don't seem right, a lady walking around on her own.'

'She will not come to any harm,' Tam said firmly. 'All the boat people know her, we used to live on a boat once, so we all got used to walking around here.'

'Yes, milady. But I thought you ought to know.'

'Have you told Mr Waring?'

'No, milady, I thought he had enough to do.'

'Well, I'll talk to him. When is he expected?'

'He'll be here in a few days. Parliament's finished, there's going to be an election. So he'll be coming home, and staying while all the electioneering goes on.'

And it was there again, as it was always there, the thudding of the heart, the excitement, so that even Juliet was forgotten. After five years. Five years of carefully keeping away, right from the start, when she'd stayed with Mirrie and Harry and he'd come down to find her and she had refused to see him. Not till after she was married, when she was careful to see him only in his house, with Juliet present. She'd been there when the baby was born, wrapped in her own voluminous cloak; she'd heard the doctor say, 'There must be no more children,' saw the reproving look he gave Charles . . . Later, she'd said woodenly, 'Your job at the Canal Company

172

will be yours whether you are here or not,' and he'd replied, 'I can't accept that.'

'You have no choice,' she'd said coldly. 'I shall pay the money over to Juliet, she needs it and she is my sister.'

That was the pattern. When she knew he was coming she stayed away from the wharf, avoiding him, never once running the risk of being alone with him. She dare not. She knew she would throw herself into his arms, cry out . . . Take me away. I'm not the strong hard person everyone thinks I am, inside I'm as lost as Juliet . . .

And the loss never went away. She thought it would; that once he was away she'd forget. But she didn't. Every time she entered into the little office he was there, his black eyes dancing, every time she walked along the wharf he was beside her. At night she was only able to endure the degrading experiences with her husband by thinking of him.

And now he was coming home. Again she would have to put on her armour of self-discipline, stay away from the wharf, away from him. Maybe he didn't even want her now. After all, he never called at the Manor, he never had. She'd given instructions that he was not to be received, but even so, he never made the attempt.

She said goodbye to Esther, called Jamie, and together they returned to the Manor.

Sir William was standing near the stables, a gun underneath his arm, and she wondered what luckless creature had lost its life this afternoon, the pheasant shoot didn't start till the beginning of October. But Sir William, she knew, would shoot anything on sight, any bird: lark, thrush or owl; especially owls, he feared they might take his young pheasants, and their deaths were to be reserved for his pleasure, not to appease an owl's hunger. Tam, who loved to see birds flying free, who envied them their freedom, was sickened by the slaughter on the days of the pheasant shoot, but, when the men came in and piles of birds were sent to the kitchens, she always managed to fill a bag and take them to the boats which happened to be at the wharf. If the birds had to be eaten, let it be by someone who needed a meal. She had not forgotten how the boaters had kept her supplied with food during the hard times. And they grinned and accepted, keeping the pheasants out of sight, for if Sir William found out, they'd be up before the Bench and likely transported. And me with them, Tam thought with a sardonic smile.

She did not speak, but he said abruptly, 'I wish to see you, at once.'

How formal they were. What would it be like to be married to a man who wanted to see you because he loved you? 'I will change first,' she replied.

'I shall be in the drawing room.'

'Very well.'

She put on her plainest dress, as she always did when facing him, never wanting to bring that lascivious gleam to his eyes. Not that he needed clothes for titillation; she wondered sourly what he had done before he

173

married her. She knew the answer, he'd taken any little girl on the estate who tickled his fancy, and none dare deny him, he was the squire.

She entered the drawing room and as he rose, she surveyed him coldly, this hard-faced man with the red face, the bald head, the paunch, the signs of his seventy-two years.

'Now the election is coming I shall expect you to entertain my friends,' he said.

'I always entertain your friends when you ask.'

'He nodded almost imperceptibly. 'Elections mean work.'

She looked up at him. 'You mean you want me to go out electioneering?'

'Don't be foolish. There are many duties: talking to people, getting them on our side, one way or another. Politics is all about scheming.'

'I have no politics.'

'Naturally. You are a woman. And no doubt pleased to be of help to your husband. For make no mistake, this time I intend to win. The town has had enough of that seditious radical.'

She bit her lip, wondering if he knew, if this was a refined piece of torture. She would have to be very careful. So she was silent; she had learned to curb her ready temper in his presence – as far as she could. Temper only goaded him to physical cruelty at worst, at the least to spiteful remarks. She learned slowly, for she had no knowledge of such matters, that there were some people who took pleasure in inflicting pain, and he was one of them.

He noted her silence and his lips stretched into a thin sharp line. 'There is one other matter,' he said. ' There was a surveyor over my land, from the railways.'

Her heart began a slow, painful thudding of dread. But she kept her voice steady. 'I heard,' she said.

'You know, I presume, that there is already a line planned to run from London to Stafford. We plan another branch line to connect with this.'

She said, pale now with shock, 'You – allowed it?'

A faint smile spread over his face. 'Allowed it? I instigated it.'

Not a muscle of her face moved. She knew he would love to see her cringe, and knew she never would. 'When?' she asked.

'I've been planning it for years.'

'So that's why you let me have the canal so easily.'

'Of course. I always intended to have a railway line run through here. Railways are the coming thing, they will be fast, and carry my coal all over the country.'

'And would you have closed the canal?'

He shrugged. 'Of course. Just left it to decay, as it will soon enough. In ten years' time canals will be as forgotten as stage-coaches.'

'Why do you hate me so?' she asked quietly.

'Why?' He took a step towards her. 'Why? What have you ever shown me but hate?'

'You know why. You ruined my father.'

'He wasn't your father – '

'Don't,' she whispered. Don't open these wounds. I loved him.

He was close to her now, his wrist holding her arm. 'And you stand there,' he said thickly. 'Like a marble statue, so unattainable – '

'Unattainable? Why, every night – '

'Every night you turn your aristocratic nose up in disgust, don't you? Every night you pull yourself away from me, you never let me approach you – '

She repeated, genuinely puzzled, 'You take me, every night.'

'And you think that's enough, my beauty? Even a common whore puts on a bit of a show. Even the coldest of wives at least appears anxious to please her husband. Not you.'

'Why should I try to please you? I didn't love you, you knew that.'

'Why? Because I gave you the canal instead of leaving it to rot the sooner. I give you clothes, support you, and your son, your bastard. And you? You lie thinking of your lover. Someday I'll catch you out.'

'And then?'

'I'll ruin him.'

'And you think that would make me love you? Why, you fool, I hate you, I have always hated you. I wish you were dead.' And, wrenching her arm from his, she ran from the room.

In her bedroom she wondered drearily whether if she had pretended affection, thrown her arms around him as a true whore did, he would not then have started the railway. And knew she could not do it, not even for the canal . . . she could lie passive and let him do unspeakable things to her, learning to shut her mind to him, but she could never pretend to love him. He was physically stronger than she, he could force her into doing many things, as all men could all women. But none of them could force what they seemed to want most – affection. So we win in the end, she thought.

But what to do now? She'd worked so hard to improve the canal. She remembered Geoffrey; so that's why he'd pulled out. He would be going into railways, with his master. Why hadn't she known that Sir William wouldn't have just *given* her anything of value?

And now, what? She clenched her hands. 'I'll fight him,' she muttered. 'I won't let him put us out of business. I won't . . .'

But how? She realised with a sinking heart that she knew so little of these matters. All these acts of Parliament, the lobbying of MPs . . . There was only one person who could help her now who would know all about it, what to do. She would have to see Charles, talk with him. He was coming home, he'd be down on the wharf. She'd *have* to see him again . . .

And part of her was rejoicing.

Chapter Two

Tam spent two hours getting ready to meet Charles. She brushed and re-brushed her hair, and studied her face in the mirror: never had it seemed so unlovely. She ransacked her riding habits, discarding one after the other until she was satisfied. At last, dressed, she took one final look in the mirror. The habit was of dark green zephyr cloth, the corsage decorated with buttons, and with the fashionable gigot sleeves. The petticoat, collar and cuffs were of cambric and trimmed with Valenciennes lace. She pulled on a black beaver hat trimmed with ostrich feathers and a green gauze veil, while her maid helped with the black half-boots.

'You look lovely, milady,' said the maid.

She walked to the stables and chose her mount with the same care. Not the steady plodder she used when Jamie accompanied her, nor the chestnut, who wasn't always reliable, but Rajah, the black thoroughbred, pride of the stable. The groom helped her mount, and she was away.

She saw him go into the little office as she rode into the wharf. She gazed out over the water and saw nothing, heard the cries of the boatmen only faintly, as if they were in another world. Finally, composed, she dismounted and with trembling fingers tied the horse and knocked. He called, 'Come in,' and she entered.

He turned and saw her, and he was just the same. Perhaps there were little lines on his face that hadn't been there before, but it didn't matter. He stood, staring at her incredulously, and she whispered, 'I had to see you.'

He took a step towards her, she put out her hands, intending to ward him off. But somehow she was in his arms, he was holding her close. And the hardness round her heart, that showed on her face, melted away and she was a girl again, young and in love.

He released her. 'Come,' he said. 'Sit down,' and they both sat, staring at each other as though they could never see enough.

'I had to keep away . . .' she said at last.

'Why did you do it, Tam?'

'Do what?'

'Marry him. That old man. Have his child.'

'I was alone,' she said with dignity. 'I had no one to turn to. I couldn't come to you, not with Juliet . . . My mother had gone to Lord Brooke. Celia , even Gilbert had left. I had nobody.'

'But to go straight from me to him. To have his child . . . Oh Tam, these last years when you wouldn't come near me, when you avoided me, I thought, maybe you were happy with him, with the child . . .' and she saw his eyes were hurt, puzzled. Knew she couldn't keep it from him, it wouldn't be right.

'Jamie is not his child.'

He did not speak for a full minute. Then, 'Oh, Tam . . . why didn't you come to me?'

'How could I? You had just been elected. You are a Member of Parliament.'

'Yes, but – ' He was pacing around now, and she had the impression of a tremendous force being held on a leash. She sat, passive, and it was as though he possessed her just by being there.

She said in a low voice, 'Last week I had friends visiting, Lady Cortain, Lady Carruthers. If you heard how they talk, about Lord Melbourne, the scandals in his life . . . even about his visiting the Queen.'

He halted his restless pacing. 'I thought ladies didn't know about such things,' he said. 'I might have expected it from the boatwomen – '

'Don't be foolish,' she said impatiently. 'Women are the same everywhere, they love scandal and gossip. I couldn't have them talking about us like that, Charles. It would ruin everything, wouldn't it?'

'Oh Tam,' he said ruefully, half laughing. 'I swear I shall never understand women. You'd marry that man just to prevent people talking? You who were so bold.'

'No,' she said. How to explain that somehow it would cheapen their love, besmirch it? 'Anyway, I'm tired of gossip, there's been enough about my own family. And besides, it wasn't just that . . . I have the canal.'

'Yes.' He smiled suddenly. 'And now you come to me again, so I presume that you want something from me? Or are we destined to meet only at elections?'

'I do not want something,' she said, smiling now with relief. 'Charles, Sir William told me that he is planning to bring a railway branch line here. You must stop him.'

He noted that she called her husband Sir William, formally, and asked, 'What can I do?'

'Oh, *Charles*.' A hint of the old impatience was back, and he smiled, loving her. 'You are a Member of Parliament, Sir William will have to get an act passed first. You can stop it.'

He laughed aloud. 'If only it were so simple. I am just one of many. I can't stop a bill being passed on my own.'

'But you could try – '

His face sobered. 'If I did I'd have to believe in what I was doing. I'm not sure that I do believe in this.'

'Charles. Lots of people disagree with the railways. Why, there was a

177

meeting of people protesting against it recently. More than two hundred were there.'

'Who were they?'

'Owners of houses along the proposed line, farmers mostly. They fear the noise will kill the animals – '

'How will it do that?'

'From fright mainly. Especially when the cows are – '

'In calf. And are these bold farmers tenants of Sir William?'

'I don't know. I suppose some of them might be.'

'Then their protests will soon die, won't they? Tam, we have to consider whether it will benefit the town as a whole – '

'It won't. Of course it won't.'

'It will,' he contradicted her gently. 'It's a matter of speed. It worries me now that I can't get to Chilverton often enough. With a railway line from London I could get here in a few hours.'

'But this is just a branch line. Sir William means it to carry goods.'

'Then it might not make the difference you fear. It all depends on the canals themselves, whether they are competitive. But you won't stop the railway, Tam. And no doubt if it succeeds it will carry passengers too.'

'You are assuming you'll win the election,' she said, a little maliciously.

'I think I will. Times are changing, Tam. There's a restlessness abroad those in power would do well to heed.'

'And you warn those in power, I suppose?'

'I do my best. So far they take little heed. But they will. You must come to one of my meetings,' he ended, eyes dancing, with the sudden change of mood so characteristic of him.

'I will be too busy. Sir William expects to do a lot of entertaining,' she said.

'Yes, I suppose you must be. Do you like living at the Manor?'

She grimaced. 'It's like living in a museum,' and he laughed.

'And do you visit your tenants in their cottages?'

She paused. 'No.'

'You should. Some of those old thatched buildings are in a very dilapidated state – '

'I can't do everything,' she cried. 'I have my hands full with the canal. Anyway, I'm not a reformer.'

'I think you are,' he said. 'And if I offered you votes for women you'd be at all the Chartist meetings. Well, I can't promise to stop the railway, Tam, but I'll keep my eyes open for any trickery.'

'Oh, there'll be plenty of that, I'll be bound.'

'When is your next Canal Company meeting of shareholders?' he asked.

'The what?'

He gave a shout of laughter. 'Oh Tam, don't tell me you don't hold any such meetings.'

'There's not much point since I own nearly all the shares.'

'You should hold annual meetings, to let the shareholders, even if there are only two, know how things are going, the dividends you are paying, and so on. I assume you are paying dividends?'

'Oh yes, the books are all correct.'

'So, if you hold your meeting, you can register your protest, get in touch with other companies, and so on.'

'I see. Yes, I'll do that. Will you be at the meeting?'

'I'm not a shareholder.'

'But you are Agent of the company, I want you to be there.'

He looked at her, smiling impishly. 'If you so order me, my lady.'

She touched his arm. 'Charles. You don't mind working for a woman, do you?'

'Not when the woman is you, no.'

'But supposing it weren't me?'

'That doesn't come into it, does it? It is you. And yes, I will attend the meeting, and bring the books.'

'Thank you, Charles.' A little silence fell, and it was pregnant with meaning, of things waiting to be said, of memories of the night they made love. She turned away from her thoughts. 'Juliet,' she said. 'She is – strange.'

'I know. Esther keeps me informed.' A frown furrowed his brow. 'I asked her if she wanted to come to London, but she refused point-blank. And the doctor said it would not be good for her health. London stinks in the summer, the streets full of dung, the poorer parts have heaps of rotting garbage, the river smells – '

'The Patch is none too sweet either, and she spends all her time there.'

'I know. Is she much changed, Tam?'

Tam hesitated. 'I'm not sure. Maybe she was always like this and we never noticed. She seemed so eager to please, yet she always did what she wanted. Now she's lost that desire to please.'

'But she loves the boy?'

'Oh, she worships him. And she cares for you, Charles, she often talks about you.'

'And Geoffrey?'

'I don't know. She never speaks of him.'

'Does she see him?'

'When we're invited to the house. . . you mean alone? Oh, I don't know, surely not.'

'But we don't know, do we? We didn't know how often she'd seen him – before.'

'Oh she wouldn't, Charles, not now. Not while she carries such a burden of guilt – '

'I thought maybe that was why – '

'But surely Geoffrey wouldn't . . . Can you not ask him?'

'Much good that would do. Geoffrey always was a ladies' man, far more than I was. I hear about his amours in London from time to time.'

'And you?' she asked. 'Do you never go with women?'

'If I do,' he said, suddenly intense, 'it's been to blot out the memory of you. And I didn't succeed even so. I kiss another woman and your face is there . . . and I damn you to hell for marrying that man you hated.'

'What else could I do?' she said wildly. 'You shouldn't have married Juliet.'

'I didn't know I'd go on loving you so much. And I seem to remember that it was you who persuaded me . . .'

She turned away from him then. And he came to her and his voice was gentle. 'I'm sorry, I shouldn't have said that. At the time there seemed no other way. Juliet had to be taken care of . . .'

'Yes.'

'I spoke to Juliet that night. I asked her if she wanted to have the child adopted. She said she couldn't bear to part with it, it would break her heart. Of course she didn't know about me and you, that you – '

'No. She didn't know that I loved you,' Tam said.

'She had to be protected, Tam, and the child have a name. This was before Lord Brooke's wife died, remember, and even after your Mama married him – would he have taken Juliet and a baby?'

Tam remembered suddenly that long-ago conversation she'd overheard, and knew that Lord Brooke would never have taken Juliet, with or without a baby.

'But I wish you had told me, about yourself,' he said.

'And what would you have done? No, Charles, it's better this way.'

He said slowly, 'I'd like to see your boy. Strange, I am called Father by Roddy, yet this one – what is his name?'

'Jamie.'

'I cannot own. May I see him one day?'

'Of course. I'll bring him to you.'

'Do that.' He stepped even closer to her and again she was in his arms. 'When shall I see you again?' he asked.

Her body seemed to be melting. Heaven was back, and for a moment it was enough to rest there, holding his dear body close to her own . . . But only for a moment, then her treacherous awakened body was clamouring for more . . . she stepped back. 'No,' she cried. 'No, we can't.'

'Can't ever meet?' They were apart now, both flushed, panting.

'Yes, oh yes. But not – anything else.'

'But we love each other?'

Sanity returned. 'Yes, and I'll be having a child every time,' she said. 'And what would Sir William say about that?'

He clutched her arm. 'He doesn't – live with you in that way? Tell me he doesn't, Tam.'

She closed her eyes, remembering. 'No,' she said, with a shaky laugh. 'Not in that way. But, Charles, we can do nothing, cannot meet as more than friends. We must be content with that.'

And she turned from him and walked to the door, striving to compose herself, to keep herself walking steadily when she wanted to fly, felt she could fly, just because she'd seen him again.

* * *

180

The postillion's horn clamoured, the horses came in at a gallop, narrow boats gave way. The *Princess* was approaching the wharf, and Tam's heart lifted as it always had since she was a child and saw her first packet boat. She watched until the passengers had all alighted, then jumped aboard to the small cosy cabin.

'I'm glad to see thee, Tamarisk,' Harry Earp said. 'I wanted to have a word with thee.'

'There's nothing wrong is there, Harry?'

'Nothing.'

She sat on the nearest seat, watching the bustle of the wharf through the open door. Mirrie handed her a dish of tea and she took it smiling.

'It's about my boy, Robin,' Harry went on. 'I have paid off what I owe to thee for the boat and, as thou knows, Robin is at school at Coventry – '

Tam did know, and that the girls too attended this school, for the Friends believed in education for girls as well as boys. 'You must miss your children,' she said, thinking of Jamie.

'We know they are well cared for, they board with Friends of my acquaintance, and they come home often. But Robin is thirteen now, and I asked him what he wanted to do in life. He said he wanted to work for the canals.'

'Did he?' Tam's heart warmed to the boy who showed such good sense.

'I would like something better than a boatman's life for him,' Harry went on. 'Meaning no disrespect, Tamarisk, for I am satisfied. But thee must understand, having a boy thyself, a parent's feelings. I wondered if an opening might be found for him, with a view to working his way up, perhaps as Agent in time. He is a bright lad, and willing.'

'I am sure something could be found,' Tam said, 'I will have a word with Charles about his training.'

'I thank thee, Tamarisk.'

'I'm glad the boy would like to work for us,' said Tam. 'We need helpers, Harry. You have heard about Sir William's proposals for a railway?'

'I have. What dost thou think to do?'

'Fight him,' said Tam.

Harry was thoughtful, and Tam guessed his dilemma. He disliked Sir William, but he was her husband. She said, 'Sir William and I do not see eye to eye about the canals, but he does not interfere in the running. And I know you are against all he stands for, so you need have no fear of distressing me if you fight him too.'

'I do not think thou wilt stop the railway, Tamarisk. On the other hand, I would not like to see all these boatmen put out of work, and I am not thinking solely of myself. What is it thou wants me to do?'

'First of all I plan to hold a meeting of shareholders where we can decide our course of action.'

'But I am not a shareholder.'

'No, I wondered if you would like to become one. Even a small portion would entitle you to attend. I have already asked Jerome, he is coming in with us.'

Harry turned away to ponder on the idea, and Tam watched the boats come and go. Harry would not be hurried, she knew; reformer he might be, but his actions were careful and reasoned.

'What thinkest thou?' he asked his wife at last.

'I think it would be a good plan,' she replied.

So it was settled, and Tam fixed the date of the meeting.

They gathered in a room in the town: Jerome and Harry, and the other two small holders; Mr Davison, a tenant farmer with a quiet demeanour, and Mr Snell, the auctioneer, a sharp-featured individual with a long nose and lugubrious manner.

Being the major shareholder, Tam took the chair and asked Charles to read the reports of finance. Both takings and dividends were down, due to the lowering of tolls and wharf charges, and Mr Snell frowned. And the maintenance charges were up: the stopping of leaks, planting hedges, fettling up the track, wear and tear on locks, the cost of men employed, lock keepers, carpenters, navvies.

Tam knew nothing of shareholders' meetings, she simply proposed all the motions herself, but no one seemed to mind. She proposed that more be ploughed back into repairs and improvements in the coming year. 'This might lower the dividends even further,' she warned. 'But it will ensure our prosperity in the long run.' And this was agreed, only Mr Snell disapproving.

'Now,' Tam said, 'we come to the main purpose of the meeting. The proposed railway line, which will run in competition with the canal. That these railways are not generally wanted is borne out by this writer in the magazine *John Bull*, which I will read out to you.' She stood up.' "We denounce the mania as destructive of the country," ' she read. ' "The whole face of the kingdom is to be tattooed with these odious deformities, huge mounds are to destroy our beautiful valleys, the noise and stench of locomotive steam engines are to disturb the quietude of the peasant and farmer, the animals will keep up one continued uproar through the night along the lines of these most dangerous and disfiguring abominations – " '

'Hear, hear,' said Mr Davison.

'I must confess I shall not like to see our pleasant market town's buildings blackened by smoke,' added Mr Snell.

'Carry on, Lady Fargate,' said Charles, his eyes twinkling.

'There is quite a lot more,' Tam said. 'And I don't propose to read it all. But the article does end by talking of those – ' she bowed to Mr Snell and Mr Davison – 'who have sense to appreciate, and prudence to preserve, the order of things as it exists, in perhaps the highest state of civilisation England has yet known.'

'Hear, hear,' said Mr Davison again, gratified at the flattery.

'Those are my sentiments, said Tam. 'So what are we to do, gentlemen? I have looked to see what other canal companies have done to protect their interests and I understand they oppose the railways in certain standard ways. They issue pamphlets, hold meetings, send petitions to Parliament,' and she glanced sideways at Charles, who grinned. 'But above all,' she ended, 'we must press for uniformity – for the whole network of canals working together instead of against each other. And I propose we get together with the other companies to put this view.'

'I think this is sound advice,' said Jerome. 'And I propose that we send a representative to meet and talk with other canal companies.'

This motion was seconded and carried, and they pondered on who the representative should be.

'Who else but Tamarisk Fargate?' asked Harry.

'A woman?' Mr Snell's voice was disapproving.

'Tamarisk is the one who has worked hardest for the company,' said Harry.

'I second that,' said Jerome. And again the motion was carried. Tam was the representative of the Chilverton Canal Company, pledged to meet the other companies and work for their combined success.

The meeting closed, and the group dispersed. Tam, putting her papers together, was left alone with Charles.

'I must congratulate you,' he said.

'On what? My successfully holding a meeting? Did you think I couldn't do it?'

'You did well. You not only carried the meeting your way, but you enrolled two members who were willing to vote with you, suitably encouraged beforehand, no doubt.'

'Harry and Jerome are friends of mine, they want to help – '

'Exactly. You're learning business methods fast, Tam.'

He was grinning, and she said, 'I don't know what you mean. It just seemed the most sensible thing to do.' He was close to her now, and the familiar heart-thudding began. She strove to be casual. 'Thank you for coming. I am sorry to take you away from your electioneering.'

'One night cannot hurt.'

They had reached the street. 'Your carriage is waiting?' he asked.

'Yes. Over there.'

'I thought you might like to walk with me to the wharf.'

She stopped. 'I don't know . . . the coachman might report to Sir William.'

'What? That you want to see the books in the office?'

'Well . . . just for a moment.'

She walked briskly to the carriage, asked the coachman to wait another ten minutes while she went to the office. Then, accompanied by Charles, they set off. But they did not go to the office, nor to the wharf, but entered a narrow lane with tall blackthorn hedges on either side.

For so long she had wanted to talk to him, had wanted to know every detail of his life since birth. She did not dare attend his meetings, but she talked with Harry, she kept her ears and eyes open as she walked on the wharf, in the town. And she knew that the people loved him. There was a warmth, a compassion about him that they needed and responded to, just as she did. She felt at times that she lacked these qualities herself, or rather that they were submerged, and being more so by the life she lived now, among cold hard people. She needed his warmth in order to become whole, and she even felt jealous of the many ordinary people who called on him, taking away the warmth that she required. And was immediately ashamed of her feelings. Yet now, as they walked, she could find nothing to say. He put his arm around her, and they walked slowly through the summer dusk, between the tall hedges with their ripening berries, small moths floating before them. Somewhere a vixen screamed.

He stopped, and kissed her gently. 'I love you,' he said, and they were the sweetest words she had ever heard.

'When I was a child,' she said, 'I used to come to the wharf sometimes with my father. And I wished that I could live on a boat, just sail away forever. I still wish that, Charles, only with you . . .'

They stood in the scented darkness, he kissed her eyes, her neck, then held her gently. As they walked back, arms linked, among the scattering moths, they could hear horses cropping the grass on the other side of the hedge. And then they were back in the street, and he escorted her to the carriage. She knew, they both knew, that they were playing with fire.

'Come, Amanda,' said Celia. 'Say goodnight to Papa. Amanda, do you hear? That's right, Becky . . . See, Amanda, little Becky is coming forward, and she only one year old . . . *Amanda*!' Celia turned, appealing to Geoffrey.

'Goodnight, Becky, my love,' he said. 'Go with Rose now, back to Nanny. Come, Amanda, don't toss your head like that. Now, say goodnight.'

The child came mutinously to her father, held up her cheek to be kissed and marched back to the nursery maid.

'Really,' said Geoffrey, a little displeased. 'That child is beginning to act like Tam.'

'Oh dear, I hope not.' said Celia, anxiously. 'No, Geoffrey, I'm sure you are wrong. It's just a little childish tantrum, nothing more.'

'She's a wilful little madam,' said Geoffrey. 'Just as Tam has always been.'

'You don't like Tam, do you?' asked Celia.

'No, she is most unfeminine,' replied Geoffrey, who, not being very masculine himself, required a woman to be entirely docile, without a mind of her own, to be called feminine. Celia, who thought Geoffrey a god among men, managed this very well, while his mother, who had a very able mind, succeeded with a lot of play-acting.

'Little Becky is so sweet,' Celia said.

'Yes, indeed, she is like you, Celia.' Geoffrey permitted himself to grant a compliment, and Celia beamed. 'I only hope the next child will be a boy.'

'Oh, so do I,' breathed Celia. 'I pray every night that it will be so.'

'Trouble with feminine women they do seem to produce girls,' Geoffrey muttered to himself. 'I've noticed it many times. Girls like Tam have boys.' He thought it most unfair.

'Come, dearest, we must prepare for the dinner party,' Celia coaxed him into a good humour. 'I confess I'm looking forward to it, Tam doesn't entertain very often, but when she does it's worth going to. Everyone will be there.'

'It was supposed to be an election victory dinner,' said Geoffrey morosely. 'And now Sir William's lost again.'

'I know. It's so sad. You don't think his tenants dared to vote against him, do you?'

'No, but Chilverton's only part of the constituency,' Geoffrey explained. 'There's Cresby and Maxbyton, and they're entirely separate from him.'

'The election was quiet, that's one good thing. None of the trouble of last time. Well, I'm going to ring for my maid,' and she disappeared.

She hummed a little as she dressed. 'Is Mrs Waring ready?' she asked, for they shared the maid.

'Yes, Madam.'

'Good.' Celia and Geoffrey had only stayed at Cherry Trees until the birth of their first child, when they moved back to Grange House. It was, Celia explained, too small for a growing family, and dear Mrs Waring was lonely in the big house. Both facts were perfectly true, and both Celia and Geoffrey, with their habit of self-deception, firmly believed them to be the sole reasons for the move. Celia wouldn't admit that she had never cared much for Cherry Trees, that she'd only bought it to spite Tam. Geoffrey wouldn't admit that he needed his mother's sound business advice, though neither called it that, it was referred to as 'telling Mother about the weaving'. So Celia had said to Geoffrey, 'Cherry Trees is rather small for an important business man like yourself, Geoffrey. We need a better place to entertain.' Geoffrey agreed, and Cherry Trees was left tenantless, with just a caretaker. They didn't intend to sell, Celia told enquirers, it was nice to have a country cottage to retire to if pressures of business grew too much . . .

Geoffrey would have liked to sell it. He was rather concerned about his present financial affairs. When he'd held Sir William's boats in his name, he had, though the profits went to Sir William, been paid handsomely for his services, and had also received the canal dividends due to him. Now that had changed. Sir William had given the canal to Tam and exchanged Geoffrey's shares for the promise of railway shares, and though Sir William had explained that his coming railway would more than double the investment in time, the railway wasn't even built yet, and Geoffrey was feeling the pinch, feeling too that somehow Sir William had cheated him, though he was powerless to complain.

Apart from his property rents Geoffrey had only his factory now. He'd started in a small way, and gradually expanded, employing women where he could at half the normal wages. The women brought the children with them, and they acted as helpers. He still gave out work to the hand-loom weavers, paying them below the List Price, and he had dismissed the undertaker, giving out the work and supervising himself, which action did not please the weavers. He bought silk in the cheapest market and sold in the dearest, insisting on the most elaborate and delicate patterns, for this was the work the hand-looms did best. Yet still he had to face competition from the French with their highly developed silk industry, and the only way forward, as far as he could see, was to pay lower wages still.

He joined his wife and mother, and they went down to the waiting carriage.

'I wonder if Charles will be there,' speculated Celia. 'He is the rival.'

'He is also my brother,' said Geoffrey. 'And in the family – ' for though he'd never admit it, Geoffrey had a sneaking regard for Charles. 'Sir William could hardly not invite him.'

Tam had put the same argument to Sir William, when discussing the guest list. He had, some weeks ago, told her of his intention of holding a dinner party to celebrate his success, saying 'You will be required to act as hostess. I trust you have no objection.'

'I shall carry out my duties,' replied Tam, thinking she might be the paid housekeeper.

Sir William ran through the names: the Cortains, the Marnings, the Carruthers, and others of the hunting fraternity. 'The Dowager Duchess of Carminster, I suppose,' he had added reluctantly. Sir William didn't like the Duchess, and she didn't like him, but not to invite her would be an unforgiveable snub. 'Oh, and your mother and father.'

Tam's hand trembled. He suspected her feelings and was, she knew, asking them only to hurt her. But she showed no sign of emotion now as she carefully wrote down their names.

'Geoffrey, of course, and his mother, I suppose.'

'And Charles?' asked Tam, guilelessly.

'My rival?' asked Sir William.

'But Geoffrey's brother,' said Tam. 'Almost one of the family. It would seem a little ungenerous to leave him out. And we need an extra man,' she pointed out.

Sir William hesitated. It would be fine if he – Sir William – won, he would be able to gloat over his vanquished rival. And surely he would win this time. He had been very circumspect; knowing the outrage caused at the last election by his paid trouble makers, he had made no effort to 'treat' people, or encourage mobs to enter the fray. 'I suppose we'll have to,' he said grudgingly, and Tam wrote 'Mr and Mrs Charles Waring', knowing that Juliet would not come, she never did.

When Sir William lost the election Tam did not commiserate with him. She had the preparations well in hand for the dinner party, and as the guests began to arrive she stood silently with him to receive. She wore an evening dress of rose-coloured velvet, the bodice close-fitting and décolleté to its pointed waist, the skirt extremely full, and she knew, from the hastily veiled expressions in the eyes of the gentlemen as they entered, that she looked beautiful. She received them all with dignity, saving a special smile for the Dowager Duchess, who entered in her usual outrageous clothes and pressed a kiss on the cheek of her protégée, for so she regarded Tam. Annabel and Lord Brooke entered carelessly, with style;

Geoffrey and his family and, behind them, Charles. And Tam's heart beat its usual merry little tattoo and she tried to stop the blush of pleasure flooding her cheeks.

So they sat in the splendid drawing room, carrying on the sort of light conversation Miss Laker had taught so long ago: the weather, the coming hunting season, the London balls. Tam saw her mother sitting with Lord Brooke, saw them glance into each other's eyes, and the same old childish envy asserted itself. Mama had everything: the love of her husband, just as she had had the love of Papa; Mama the successful, who always had her way; Mama, against whom you could never compete. She turned away to find Sir William informing each gentleman which lady he was to take in to dinner, a carefully planned operation which ensured that everyone filed in order of precedence, for which it was necessary to know the precise position of each guest in the social hierarchy. When the butler announced dinner, Sir William led the way with the senior lady – the Duchess – Tam brought up the rear with the senior gentleman, Sir Robert Peel from nearby Tamworth.

The table contained a mass of Fargate treasures and heirlooms: silver candlesticks, crystal glasses, gold flower vases holding late blooming roses and ferns. It was a rich show, but an expected one. The menu was hand written in French, and very long. Two soups, two choices of fish, then venison or chicken lightly cooked in cream. Flancs or side dishes came next, followed by soufflés, gateaux, apricots tossed in brandy and, finally, dishes of fruit.

At last Tam managed the delicate operation of meeting the ladies' eyes, and to signal it was time for them to withdraw. Back in the drawing room, the Duchess patted a seat beside her, and Tam went to her with a smile.

'You should entertain more,' the Duchess said. 'As I'm always telling you.'

'I entertain when Sir William wishes,' Tam replied. 'Apart from that, I don't have much time.'

'Humph. Still working on the canal?' The Duchess frowned, and looked at Tam shrewdly. 'You're not very happy, are you?'

Tam shook her heard ruefully. 'I detest him,' she said candidly.

'Oh well, it happens, not many marriages are made in heaven, not with the system we've got now. Glad I've not got any gels, only sons, and my eldest, the Duke, took a deal of hooking. Oh the anxious Mamas with their dutiful daughters – ' the Dowager gave a raucous laugh. 'All expiring with love – love of a title and a well-endowed estate.'

Tam allowed herself a laugh. 'You are too cynical, Duchesss,' she said.

'I'm old, gel, I've seen too much. But you – and I've never asked you this – why did you marry that old skinflint?'

'I wanted the canal and I had no money,' said Tam, adding, 'And I was pregnant.' She wondered why it was so easy to talk to the Duchess who was far from being a cosy sympathetic character.

'H'm. It's Charles Waring, isn't it?' asked the Duchess, and Tam bowed her head. 'So why didn't you go and live with your Mama?'

187

'Because she was marrying Lord Brooke.'

'And you don't like him, do you?'

'No. Nor do I like the way Mama acted.'

'You're very much like her, you know.'

'Yes, you've told me that before. I hope not,' said Tam. 'The way they live now, always in debt, spending money like water.'

'Maybe not in that way. But you have the same style – and the same courage.'

'Why do you say Mama has courage?' Tam asked, peeved.

'Because she faced the world and went her own way – with Brooke. Tony Carleton he was then, a younger son.'

'But lots of society women had affairs with other men than their husbands. You think it takes courage?'

The Duchess paused. 'Not in all cases. Some were just pleasure-loving. But on the other hand I admire a woman who refuses to accept that her husband can take his pleasures where he will, while she should not. Your Mama was in love, and she defied her father – '

'Yet she married Papa.'

'You mean Jamie Calder? He was willing,' the Duchess said gently. 'He loved her too.'

'But she never stayed with him – '

'Oh Tam,' said the Duchess, 'have you no sympathy for her, even now, when you – ' she broke off.

Tam set her lips mutinously. 'When I do the same thing? No, it doesn't make me more loving towards Mama, in spite of it.'

'Or because of it,' said the Duchess.

The door opened and the gentlemen entered, and soon Tam excused herself from the Duchess in order that she might mingle with the guests. She badly wanted to talk to Charles, and wondered if she dared. And later, when she felt she had done her duty to her guests, she moved away and found Charles beside her.

'Shall we walk a little in the air?' he asked.

She knew she should not, but she took a quick look around the room and saw that everyone was busy, there were no young girls to need a hostess's guidance, no one left alone. She whispered, 'Just for a moment then.'

They walked in the gardens, over the lawns, towards the summer house. His arms were around her almost before they had gone through the door, and she fell against him, kissing him rapturously. His hands grew more bold, and she knew this was what she wanted more than anything else on earth, to lie with him, as she had on that other election night, five years ago.

But she pushed him away saying, 'No, I can't Charles, not here, not like this . . . I have to go back . . . my dress . . .'

'Please, Tam.'

Oh, it was unfair that he should plead so, and she should be so desiring, and have to say no for both of them.

'No,' she said. 'Not here. Not now. It wouldn't be seemly.'

188

He gave a short laugh. 'Since when have you cared about seemliness?'

'If Sir William noticed he would be most displeased.'

Now he drew away. 'And since when have you cared about Sir William – or anyone?' he asked. 'Tam, what is he doing to you? Is he making you afraid?'

'He can be most awkward to live with,' she replied quietly.

He held her away from him, searching her face in the dim light. 'What haven't you told me?' he asked. 'What, Tam?' but she didn't answer, fearing what he'd do if he knew.

She said slowly, 'I suppose I've always been afraid of him since he ruined Papa. Be careful, Charles, I wouldn't want him to harm you.'

'He won't,' Charles said arrogantly. 'Your Papa – ' he echoed the Duchess, 'was a good man, but he had no ruthlessness or cunning, and both are necessary in the business world.'

'And you have?' she asked.

'Enough. Don't worry about me. Don't you think he would have ruined me already if he could. He'd love me out of the way.'

'But a scandal would play into his hands.'

'True. Well, what do you suggest?'

'I want to be with you, Charles,' she said in a low voice. 'You don't know how I've longed to see you, just to talk to you, to be near you . . . I can't let you make love to me, not just because of the scandal, but because of Juliet. She is your wife, she is dependent on you, she cares for you, and she loves the boy. It would seem – disloyal. And I couldn't anyway, not here, not now, Charles.'

'And you would spoil your dress,' he said, humorously.

'No, Charles,' she said, and thought, for I should go back into the room looking as if I'd been to heaven, and all the stars were lit inside my face – it's bad enough when you talk to me, my eyes light up.

He said, 'Very well. We'll meet occasionally, and have serious talks.'

She chuckled, and this was something else he gave her, laughter.

'May I write to you?' he asked.

Her face clouded immediately. 'Oh no, he might suspect. He does suspect, Charles, I know.'

'Then how can I let you know I am coming?'

'You can tell Jerome.'

'Can you not come to London, ever?'

'I never have, I have no excuse.'

'Find some,' he ordered. 'Make more friends, so you can visit. Let me know and I'll be there.'

'Yes, Charles.'

'And I'll let Jerome know when I am coming. I usually do, but in future I'll tell him to notify the lady in charge.'

She smiled and he kissed her again before they walked back to the drawing room. No one seemed to have noticed, Tam thought thankfully. The gentlemen were still talking politics, Geoffrey was discussing hunting with Lady Cortain, the Duchess was with Annabel. Tam joined them unobtrusively, and sat in a happy dream while talk washed over her.

The guests left finally, congratulating Tam on her excellent dinner party. She went upstairs, praying Sir William would leave her alone tonight, let her think of Charles. And surprisingly, he did.

She woke early and went down to breakfast. He was waiting for her. He said coldly, 'Good morning.'

'Good morning.'

He sat silent till the servants had left, then said coldly and brutally, 'Your behaviour last night was inexcusable.'

It was so unexpected. Why hadn't he said something before they went to bed? But then, she realised, he wouldn't, that wasn't his way, he preferred to let the little fox think it's safely home, then rush in for the kill.

'I have no idea what you mean,' she said defiantly.

'I think you have. You were absent from our guests for about half an hour. Yes, I timed you. And you were with a man.' He did not say gentleman, she noticed.

'We went outside for a breath of air, yes,' wondering how much he had seen, if he set the servants to spy on her . . .

'Don't ever let it occur again. As it is, I have half a mind to send you away.'

Her head shot up. 'If you wish – ' she began, thinking there was nothing she'd like more.

'But you forget,' he said, his voice silken, 'I have the boy, our son.'

'He's not – '

'In the eyes of the law he is my son. And in the eyes of the law I would be entitled to keep him, especially if my wife misbehaved with another man. Adulterous women are not now in favour.'

'You mean adulterous women who are found out?'

'Precisely. You are my wife. May I remind you that this was at your wish?'

'Oh, yes, I cannot forget that. It seems a pity to me that adulterous men don't get the same treatment. How many of your maids have you seduced over the years. Before – ' and her voice grew hard, 'before you were unable – '

He stood up, his face livid and his hand raised as if to strike her. He lowered it slowly. Tam did not know that it was the charge of impotence rather than adultery which enraged him.

'Take care, madam. You have had warning,' he hissed and walked out of the room.

Alone, Tam shivered. I wish he were dead, she thought dully.

Tam fled, as she always did, to the canal. Out to the stables to mount the steady mare, then down to the teeming life of the wharf. The rippling water, blue beneath the summer sky, the coloured boats resting on their moorings, or chugging through while the boatwomen called and the boatmen shouted. The packet boats with their happy travellers, the bustle, the passing show. She dismounted and ran to where the *Princess* was tied

190

up, her own boat, her refuge, and where Jim sat on the deck, a thick writing book on his knee.

'Why, Jim,' she said surprised. 'Whatever are you doing? I expected to find you – ' she broke off. Jim was usually to be found on the wharf, sometimes helping load, more often just talking.

He jumped to his feet, embarrassed. 'I'm writing, milady. But it's all right. The horses are groomed and exercised, the boat's all clean.'

'I know, Jim. I just didn't know you could read and write.'

'Mrs Earp showed me,' he said proudly. 'I'm going to write letters for the others soon.'

Tam's face shadowed. 'Yes. I used to do all that. I don't seem to have time now.'

' 'Course you don't, milady.' Jim was loyal as always. 'But I'll get the horses. Was it a little trip you wanted to take?'

'Yes please, Jim.'

'And young Master Jamie? He ain't here today?'

'No. He's doing his lessons.' And I had to be alone . . .

'Along towards Birmingham, as usual, milady?'

'No, Jim. The other way. Towards Cherry Trees.'

He stared for a moment, she had never once been that way since the house was sold, nearly ten years ago. But he said nothing, fetched the shining horses, put them to the boat, and called, 'You'm steering, milady?'

'Yes, Jim. Take her slowly.'

'Hold out then, milady.'

They were off. Away from the wharf, past the 'Anchor' where Car Boswell used to stand; whatever happened to Car? And then the town was left behind, and the scene was purely rural, with cows gazing placidly as they lumbered into the water to drink, fields where heavy carts were already getting in the hay, for it had been a good summer, past oak trees in the fullness of their glory, widespread and green, cornfields where poppies shone red, and the occasional farmyard where geese squawked and chickens grubbed for food. And Tam relaxed, letting the slow movement and the clop-clopping of the horses' hooves drug her senses, watching the water rippling away from the boat till it gently splashed the bank scattered with clover and coltsfoot and lady's-mock.

'We're here, milady. Cherry Trees. Do you want to stop?'

'Please.'

The boat slid to a halt and Jim jumped on to the bank with the rope. Tam helped him and then said 'Wait here, Jim. I'm just going for a walk.'

It stood there, the old house, mellow in the sunshine. How many memories it contained. Mama, dancing in like a bright butterfly, Celia, Juliet with her arms full of flowers. And Papa . . . Would the ache never go away?

She reached the gardens, unattended now, the flowers rioting into a blaze of colour. A lavender bush spreading itself into the rosemary, whose leaves used to wash her hair. The white daisies of the feverfew which cured headaches. The yellow blaze of marigolds, small suns all, tangled pansies, moss roses, and at the back, hollyhocks. She moved past the cherry trees, round the side of the house, peered in through one mullioned window. She could see furniture covered with dust sheets, cobwebs in the corners. And then she passed and was in the orchard where the trees were heavy with apples, red and ripe, some lay on the long grass beneath, already rotting.

She sat down suddenly, and the trees gave welcome shade. What was she to do about Charles? It had all been so innocent . . . though could it stay so much longer? For all her protestations, could they keep on this way?

Sir William knew, that was obvious. Knew who had been her lover, knew where they went. She had suspected for a long time that some of the servants spied on her, reported her doings to their master, no doubt he paid them well for the service, for their loyalty.

Loyalty? What of her own loyalty to Juliet? The little sister who needed protecting. She had been foolish to think she and Charles could go on being friends. They couldn't. The little talks and walks were doubly dangerous now Sir William suspected.

Sir William. He still forced her to undress nightly and heaped indignities upon her, though his attempts at intercourse had ceased. But with the loss he grew more spiteful towards her, as if he couldn't bear her to be young and desirable unless he could possess her. As long as he had the hope of making her his, his malice was kept under control; without that he'd show his hate.

She couldn't risk losing Jamie. Not now. Not yet. And she realised anew that by marrying Sir William she had placed herself and the boy in his power. If she committed adultery, if she left him, he could, and would, claim the boy. Oh, she fumed, that women could be placed in such a position! By having a child outside marriage they were either permanently ostracised, or forced to marry, at which point they became chattels. Had she been foolish to marry Sir William?

But what in heaven's name could she have done, with no money? And she'd thought, in her innocence, that by his saying he wanted her, he loved her. Well, she knew better now, that much she had learned from him.

So what of the future? Jamie would go to school, boys did, however much their unhappy mothers might miss them. And though she wanted to train him for the canal work, his education must come first. And he'd be safer at school. If the worst came to the worst and Sir William made a scandal, forced her to leave, she'd be able to visit Jamie sometimes . . . wouldn't she? And wait till he could join her again.

There was one consolation: Sir William might threaten her with exposure but he would suffer too if the truth came out. She knew he'd enjoyed the local gentry's admiration of his so-called fatherhood, he'd look a precious fool if it were known just what had happened.

I wish Sir William were dead, she thought again, and wondered drearily if she were very wicked. How simple life looked when you were young, how easy to distinguish right from wrong; how blurred the outlines became as the years passed.

She stood up and walked slowly back to the house again, and for a moment she rested her hand on the sun-drenched wall where a clematis climbed, its purple flowers full of drowsy bees. 'Some day,' she promised, 'I'll be back.'

She returned to the boat where Jim waited. He looked up anxiously. He knew – they all knew – their mistress was not happy, they worried about her shut away with that terrible man.

'Everything all right?' he asked.

'Yes, Jim. The house is fine, but it needs people in it again. It's lonely. There are loads of apples on the trees, Jim, go and pick as many as you can, take them back to the boaters.'

'Yes, milady.'

She waited as he took the painted water-can from the boat and filled it over and over again, tipping the sweet-smelling apples on to the deck. She watched as swifts congregated on an old barn, hundreds of them, twittering, gathering for their return to Africa. And when the deck was full of apples she told him to take the boat to the nearest winding hole then turn back.

On the way back, she thought, I'll write to Charles and explain why we can't meet as we said. And in the meantime I'll look after Juliet . . . Maybe it's for the best after all. I couldn't be disloyal to Juliet, Charles. Not Juliet . . .

Chapter Three

'Come along, Amanda,' called Celia impatiently.

The dark-haired little seven-year-old tossed her head but did not move.

'Come, Amanda, Becky will come when I call her,' said Celia.

Amanda gave the docile little Becky a push, and Celia, goaded beyond endurance by her fractious elder daughter, slapped her hard. The baby began to cry.

'Now see what you've done,' cried Celia. 'Poor Amelia.'

'Is anything wrong, madam?' asked a voice.

'Oh, Nanny,' said Celia, thankfully, and the nurse took Amanda's hand forcefully. The child, recognising authority, moved forward with no further protest.

Celia tried to cover her mortification. 'You are a lucky little girl,' she said. 'Not everyone will be going to see the Queen married. It is something you will remember when you're an old lady, Amanda.'

'Is baby going?' asked Amanda.

'Yes, of course, we're all going. Papa too.'

'Baby's silly,' said Amanda. 'She cries all the time,' and Celia sighed again.

'If you'll leave her to me, madam,' said Nanny. 'We'll be along. Come, Rose, bring baby.'

'The carriages are waiting,' said Celia. 'Oh, there you are, Geoffrey. And Mother.' They entered the first carriage and Celia sat back with a sigh of relief. Really, it was too bad of Amanda to make this trouble all the time: headstrong, that's what Geoffrey called her, and darling Becky so sweet, and baby Amelia . . . Celia's feelings towards her youngest were mixed. She had so wanted a son. Geoffrey needed a son for the business, and although she loved her children she didn't really want many more . . . of course it was a woman's duty when she was married, just as it was her duty to submit to her husband's baser instincts . . . Celia sighed again. Marriage wasn't all pleasure by any means, and now her sigh held a hint of martyrdom. Geoffrey looked glum too, and that was another irritation, the way he was always discussing those tiresome weavers with dear Mother, when she herself had so many problems with the children. Lowering wages it had been again last night, it was too bad. Celia's voice these days often held a complaining note, though she did not realise this. It was just that dear Geoffrey never seemed to notice how difficult things were for her sometimes, and if her voice held a hint of reproof at times, well, she was right. So Celia thought virtuously as she grappled with the eldest daughter she couldn't handle.

Celia turned her head resolutely and looked out of the window as the carriage bowled along. 'They seem to be getting on with the railway,' she said, with some satisfaction.

'Slowly,' said Geoffrey. 'At this rate it will be years before it's finished.'

'It runs right alongside the canal,' said Celia. 'And Tam is furious. I wonder if she will be coming to London?'

'Does it matter?' Geoffrey asked ungraciously.

Tam had been undecided about going to London for the wedding of the Queen. Even when the Dowager Duchess invited her to stay and put the question before Sir William in such a way that he could hardly refuse. Or perhaps, dare not refuse, the Carminsters were powerful. So when she said 'Oh, by the way, Sir William, I would love Tam and the boy to come to London for the wedding. She could stay with me. I don't ask you for I know you never go anywhere,' he'd been furious, and said ungraciously, 'Tam can go if she pleases.'

The Duchess had walked with Tam in the garden and asked, 'Will you come?'

'I don't know,' Tam said indifferently.

'Charles will be there,' said the Duchess.

Tam's walk did not waver. 'I don't see him,' she said. 'At least, only to discuss business matters.'

'I know,' said the Duchess. 'Maybe you should. How old are you now?'

'Twenty-nine.'

'Nearly thirty. And you're not happy, Tam, it shows in your face. It always does, you know.'

'I do have a lot on my mind,' said Tam. 'And how can I see Charles when Sir William watches my every movement?'

'Not in my house,' the Duchess pointed out.

'I'll think about it.' And Tam was suddenly filled with longing.

The Duchess departed after dinner, and Sir William went out of the room as he usually did, without a word, leaving Tam alone with her thoughts. She sat in the drawing room, with its small Sheraton tables placed over the vast expanse of carpet, its dark Fargate portraits on the wide expanse of wall, and it was the loneliest place on earth. No sound echoed in the stillness, the servants were far away in their own quarters, Jamie was at school.

She missed Jamie unbearably, but he had seemed quite willing to go. When she'd asked him if that was what he wanted, he'd replied equably that it was. She'd looked at him a little sadly, 'Won't you miss me, Jamie?'

'Of course, Mama. But all the other boys go to school, the Cortain boys went before they were seven.'

195

She smiled a little ruefully. He was so self-contained, so independent. 'Don't you like living here?' she asked.

'I get a little lonely with no other boys. And Papa never seems to bother much about me. I mean, he's more like a grandfather, isn't he?'

Tam gazed at her son, wondering if she should tell him the truth. Would it hurt him? She remembered her own shock, her animosity towards her mother . . . she could not bear Jamie to turn to her with that look of condemnation in his eyes. Yet he might find out from someone else. Sir William might blurt it out in a fit of rage or malice. Yes, the boy was better away from all that. Oddly, Sir William never mentioned the problem of inheritance. His son, Lewis, never communicated; supposing he should be dead? What then? Jamie was next in line, so what would she have to do? Let the scandal come out? Sighing, she had postponed telling Jamie – for the present.

She paced the room restlessly. Other ladies might sit at their embroidery in the evenings, she was too unsettled. She looked round the silent room and it was an elegant prison. What was she doing here? The Manor didn't belong to her, it belonged to Sir William and the housekeeper, for she had no say in its running; she longed for life, for colour and movement, for people.

Turning, she pulled the bell-rope, and when the footman entered, ordered the carriage. Dressed warmly in a fur-trimmed pelisse and matching bonnet she drove to the wharf and alighted. It was a typical January night, frost covered the fields with rime and edged the piles of coal with silver. The canal ran dark between the banks, the boats in the lay-by showed chinks of lamplight between closed doors below merrily smoking chimneys. Tam crunched her way towards the *Duchess* and knocked.

Mirrie's face peered out. 'Why, Tamarisk. Come aboard.' Mirrie never asked questions. And then she was in the cosy cabin, where the big kettle steamed a welcome and the fire glowed redly in the black stove. The lamp above lit up the patterns of roses and castles on the woodwork, and Tam sank on to a seat with a sigh of relief. It was good to be here.

'All alone, Mirrie?' she asked.

'Yes, indeed. Though we have had some pleasant news today. Margery has been selected to teach at the school.'

'That's wonderful. How old is she now?'

'Eighteen.'

'Is it possible? Oh, Mirrie, it doesn't seem five minutes since she was a little girl.' Tam took the proffered cup of tea, soothed, as always, by the warmth and peace in the little cabin, the faint lapping of the water outside. 'Where is Harry?' she asked.

'He's at a meeting at Birmingham.'

'Trouble?' asked Tam.

'He's worried,' Mirrie said. 'There's a deal of unrest in the Midlands and north.'

'I hadn't heard anything,' Tam said. 'But how can I, shut away in the Manor as I am. It's not the same as when I lived down here and talked to people all the time.'

196

'I think,' Mirrie smiled, 'thou wouldst still like to be living on a boat, Tam.'

'I would,' Tam said candidly. 'I thought when I took over the canal I could change it all in a minute. But after seven years there isn't much change. Nothing is happening.'

'Thou hast met some of the representatives of the other companies, Harry tells me,' said Mirrie.

'Yes, and it was an ordeal,' Tam grimaced. 'At first they looked at me as if they couldn't understand what I was doing there, and when I spoke they listened, but as if to a child, and they were humouring me. I said we must have one firm policy, we must reduce tolls. They didn't argue, just smiled patronisingly. It was infuriating.' She stood up, paced around the cabin, then stopped near the table, staring down at the brightly coloured teapot as if it might quiet her unrest. 'So what's this trouble with the work-people about?' she asked.

'The price of bread is too high,' said Mirrie, simply.

Tam sat down. 'I remember now, Charles said something . . . He told me I should visit the cottagers on the estate. I never do, Mirrie. I never go round like a Lady Bountiful offering bread. That's what lady means, did you know? Loaf-giver. And I don't. You think I should, don't you, Mirrie?'

'Thou knowest that I would never tell thee what thou shouldst or shouldst not do,' said Mirrie, gently. 'Thou works hard enough as it is. And I doubt if Sir William would thank thee for starting another fight with him. He orders the estate, does he not?'

She was right, of course. The canal may be hers, but the estate belonged to Sir William. She said helplessly, 'I don't belong there, Mirrie.'

'I know thou art unhappy, Tamarisk.'

'I am. You know I don't care for Sir William. Mirrie – dare I tell you? I love someone else.'

'I had wondered,' Mirrie replied equably. 'But I feel even that is not all of the problem.'

'No? Then what is?'

Mirrie hesitated. 'The canal thou works for – is it to help the people, Tamarisk, or to solve something in thyself?'

Tam stared, agape. And Mirrie continued.

'I feel there is something inside, eating away at thee, it has been there for a long time. And till this is resolved, there will be no happiness.'

Tam was silent, and Mirrie said, 'Forgive me if I say too much, Tamarisk. I wish only for thy happiness.'

'I know,' Tam said. 'But I don't know what you mean.'

Mirrie said no more, and when Tam rose to go she had dismissed her words. What other troubles had she but her unhappy marriage and her longing for Charles? Nothing, of course.

She stepped out on to the wharf. But she did not go straight back to the carriage. She walked down towards the *Princess*, moored well past the lay-by. She wondered, for one mad moment, if she should go aboard, sail away. . . . if that would calm her unrest.

197

She stood, looking towards the boat. And as she did so, a figure emerged, a man who leapt lightly onto the bank, pulled his collar round his face – he was wearing a dark, loose coat, and for a second she thought it must be Jim. But the build was too slight, the coat too stylish for Jim. The moon had risen since she went to Mirrie and by its light she saw clearly who the man was – Geoffrey.

He did not see her as she stepped behind a pile of boxes. She watched him go in sheer amazement, then moved to the boat, went aboard. There was no sign of Jim. She pushed open the door of the nearest cabin. Juliet lay there, on the bed.

Tam took in the scene in disbelief. The girl's state of undress, her hair loose about her shoulders. 'Oh, *no*,' she said.

Juliet sat up, wide-eyed and a little wild-looking, but for once Tam had little sympathy for her. 'You do this?' she asked. 'With Geoffrey? Is it possible?'

Juliet said nothing.

'How did you – ? Where's Jim?'

'I – tell him to go to the "Anchor".'

'Then it has happened before?'

'Yes.'

'How long has it been going on?'

'Just sometimes, when Geoffrey can see me.'

'So that's why you drive yourself to help the poor,' Tam said savagely. 'To ease your conscience.'

'We don't meet often, Tam.'

'But you make love knowing what the doctor said about your having children?'

'Geoffrey is very careful.'

'Careful, pah. You've been very lucky. And what about Charles? If you had another child, would he think it was his?'

'You know he would not, Tam. Charles never touches me.'

'No. He married you to protect you when Geoffrey wouldn't.'

'I love Geoffrey,' Juliet said with dignity.

'It was wrong of you to marry Charles knowing that,' said Tam furiously.

'You persuaded me, Tam.'

Tam sat down. Why did I even bother? she asked herself, wearily. Why did I try to look after them all, why didn't I let Juliet have her baby alone, then Charles and I would be married. She looked at her sister, sitting woebegone on the bed, and asked, curiously, 'Don't you ever think about Celia?' You who were so gentle and good, whom I no longer understand.

'Why should I?' Juliet asked. 'Celia has him, his children, she is his wife.'

'I don't understand you, Juliet,' Tam said perplexed. 'And I am shocked at Geoffrey. How he could – '

'He loves me,' said Juliet.

'Then why didn't he marry you?'

198

'Because Celia would make him a better wife. She entertains his business acquaintances, I couldn't. I wouldn't know what to do.' Juliet twisted her hair round her finger, and Tam asked amazed, 'You accept that?' and knew it was a stupid question. Everyone accepted that, Juliet merely stated the fact.

Juliet stood up. 'I am going home,' she said.

'Wait a minute,' Tam ordered. 'You always go away when things get unpleasant, don't you?' But the look Juliet gave her was so devoid of any feeling at all that Tam was shocked. And, as her sister walked from the cabin, from the boat, Tam wondered what to do, wondered if Geoffrey really did love Juliet.

All this time, she thought tiredly, I've been keeping away from Charles, protecting Juliet . . . Really, I think I'm the one who's innocent . . .

Tam had a memory of the child Juliet running through the meadows, flowers in her hands, her hair . . . and Mama never there . . . Mama should be here now to guide and help, not leave Tam alone, unknowing where to turn, what to do. Should she tackle Geoffrey . . .? The old wound re-opened. Mama was to blame. Mama who always went away leaving her daughter in charge . . . the daughter who looked to Papa, and never held him.

But now there was Charles. And for so long she had stayed away because of Juliet. And now . . . Tam thought, *she's set me free* . . .

Tam was amazed at the opulence of the house in Park Lane. The Duchess had been the daughter of a wealthy marquess, with an excellent dowry, so the family had houses in London and in the country, enough for the Dowager to live in style on her own, while her son, the present Duke, had another superb dwelling in Belgravia.

When she decided to go to London, taking Jamie to see the wedding of the Queen and Prince Albert, Tam had written to the Duchess asking if she could order a new gown. And the Duchess had put her in touch with her own dressmaker, patterns and measurements had been exchanged, and Tam was to visit Madame Clothilde for a final fitting when she arrived, and the gown would be ready the next day, Madame said, omitting to mention the hordes of girls who would sit up all night stitching away. It was all so easy, thought Tam. Now, shown to her room, she turned as a knock came at the door, and the Duchess entered.

'My dear Tam,' and she kissed her. 'Are you well? Are you comfortable here?'

Tam looked round the well-lit, luxurious bedroom, and her eyes came to rest on the huge fire burning merrily in the grate – all the Duchess's rooms were warm, unlike the Manor – and said, 'Dear Duchess, it's lovely here. And the fire . . . do you have any difficulty in getting coal?'

The Duchess laughed. 'Are you planning to sell me some?' she asked.

Tam laughed too. 'I confess that's how my mind works these days. If I see coal I wonder where the person has obtained it, and whether it was brought along my canal.'

'Forget all that now,' the Duchess advised. 'You are here to enjoy yourself.'

'Yes, I know.' Tam's face was glowing suddenly. 'I have ordered a new gown, I must collect it later.'

'You must visit the Great Cloak and Shawl Emporium in Regent's Street too,' the Duchess said. 'They have superb shawls there, all the new styles. By the way, have you not brought your maid?'

'No.' Tam looked at the many travelling cases, as yet unopened. 'I was unsure . . . I don't know how far I can trust them at the Manor. I have decided to look for another maid, one who will be loyal – as Abby was to Mama – ' and again it was there, the old envy of Mama who obtained everything, even loyal maids.

The Duchess eyed her shrewdly. 'Don't worry, I'll find you a maid, send her to you. In the meantime I'll lend you Harriet. Is Jamie comfortable in his little room? It is farther along the passage, but near enough to you.'

'It is ideal, and he is enjoying himself hugely,' Tam assured her.

'Good. Well, you'll want to change, so I'll send Harriet, then we'll eat and have a long talk.'

She left, and Tam determined to enjoy herself for every minute of her stay. It wasn't difficult, London was *en fête*: there were decorations in the streets, the shops in the West End were crammed with beautiful fripperies and rich jewels. She fetched her new gown, took Jamie sightseeing, dined on turtle soup and venison with rich wines, sat in the great drawing room of the Duchess's house with its fan-vaulted ceiling, and met members of London's high society.

On a cold day, the 10th of February, she went, with the Duchess and Jamie, to the small Chapel Royal and watched Albert enter, splendid in the uniform of a British Field-Marshal, and the Queen, small, radiant in white, walking towards the man she loved. Outside, the commoners clapped and cheered as the newly-married couple drove away, the nobility following, and then Tam and the Duchess drove back to Park Lane to prepare for the ball.

The ballroom was filled to overflowing, it glittered and sparkled: coronets and tiaras, men in uniforms, in evening dress, ladies in diamonds and pearls. Tam wore a gown of white crepe embroidered with coloured silks, her waist pulled in tightly, her skirts very full. A blue grenadine gauze scarf draped her bare shoulders. She saw Charles even before he saw her, elegant in black, his hair curling into his neck, a smile on his face. Their eyes met, and the glitter and pomp faded momentarily. She waited as he approached her.

'You came,' he said. 'I didn't know for sure . . .' And then she was in his arms, the orchestra played a waltz, he was looking down at her and whispering, 'You are very lovely,' and she melted towards him, loving his arms around her, smiling a little for she knew, and he didn't, why she was here. The waltz ended, and she saw that the windows at the rear had been opened, showing a brilliant illumination in the gardens, each branch of every tree holding a small lamp.

'I mustn't dance every dance with you, we must be circumspect,' she said, teasing.

'Must we? Shall I take you in to supper?'

She hesitated. 'Well . . . maybe. And later, perhaps we can find somewhere to talk . . .?'

They found a secluded little alcove and she made great play with her jewelled fan. Above it her eyes were glowing as she whispered, 'Are you staying the night?'

He paused, his eyes met hers, and for once she did not look away. 'The Duchess did ask me . . .'

'Then?' she asked, and now the fan covered her face completely.

There was no need to say more. He knew her thoughts, as he always did know.

And that night he came to her. She was waiting dressed in her prettiest nightgown and when he stepped through the door she slowly took it off. He stood before her for a moment and she gloried in her body. Then his arms were round her, he threw off his own clothes, they were together on the bed . . .

'It's been so long . . .' he murmured.

Then he was kissing her tenderly, stroking her breasts, her legs, starting again at the beginning of the long road to fulfilment. Slowly he roused her with delicate little touches and drifts of passion, slowly he moulded her body to his as she cried out for him to enter her, to complete her womanhood. And the night sped by on dappled wings as he re-taught her the meaning of love.

In the morning, when she awoke he was gazing down at her. She glanced sleepily at him as he kissed her shoulders, her neck. 'I must go back to my room,' he whispered. 'The maids will be around.'

She put her arms round his neck, running her fingers through his hair.

'When do you go back?' he asked.

'Tomorrow. In the afternoon.'

'Then I'll come tonight.'

'Yes.' Her lips were on his neck.

'Tam.'

'Yes.'

'Why did you agree – now?'

She sat up. 'Because I found Juliet – with Geoffrey.' He was silent, and she went on 'Esther told me she was going out in the evenings – I did nothing. I didn't realise not even when you asked me if she'd been seeing him. Did you know?'

'No. And you can't blame yourself, Tam. What could you have done?'

'But if people get to know . . . what do they think here in London, about your wife, why she isn't with you?'

'I tell them the truth, that she is not strong enough for the life here.'

'Isn't it a bit unfair, that she couldn't marry Geoffrey because he needs a wife to entertain, yet you – '

'Hush, Tam, don't let's go over all that again. I wasn't in Parliament when I married her.'

There was a little silence, then she said, 'Charles . . . why is Geoffrey seeing her? Is he just using her . . .?'

'I don't know, Tam.'

'But can't you talk to him?'

'No, Tam. I can't order my brother's life.'

'But you told him once before, when they were at the Pick-Nick, that first night when it all started – '

'That was different. Juliet was a young innocent girl. She is not now.'

'But, Charles.' She strove for words. 'Charles ... Is Juliet not *different*?'

He hesitated. 'I think she's different in the sense that if she is attached to someone or something, to take that thing away would upset her beyond all reason – that's if she allowed it to be taken away.'

'If she allowed it?'

'Yes. Remember how she went to see Geoffrey at the Pick-Nick? How she insists on going to the soup kitchen? She always does what she wants.' He paused. 'Was she always like that?'

'I don't know . . . We were away so much when we were children. Juliet seemed so pleasant, so easy to please . . . Though we gave in to her, always.' And Tam remembered it was Juliet's wish to live on the boat that had decided the others; Juliet who, as a child, used to go on the boats with the boatpeople; who insisted first of all she would not marry Charles until she realised it was the only way to keep her baby.

'Are we then to let her have her own way all the time?' she asked.

He sighed. 'I don't think there is anything we can do.'

'So you won't say anything to Geoffrey?'

'For God's sake, Tam. The Midlands is in uproar, and you think I should worry about who my brother is sleeping with – '

'She is your wife.'

'No, Tam, she is not.'

She said in a small voice, 'We're quarrelling.'

'We're too much apart,' he said morosely. 'We can't just meet and kiss as though nothing had happened in between. There is so much to say, so much we haven't told each other.'

'I'll see you more often now, Charles.'

'Yes, Tam, do. I am too much alone.'

And then he was kissing her again, fiery kisses that turned her bones to water. And Juliet faded into a mist.

'Charles,' she whispered, as they lay side by side. 'I love you.'

'I love you.'

'Charles.'

'Yes?'

'Jamie is here. We shall be riding in Hyde Park later.'

'How strange. I thought of doing that too.'

Hyde Park was the rendezvous of smart society. From early morning ladies and gentlemen rode up and down the Row, while in the afternoon the mounts were replaced by phaetons, where a member of the *haut monde* might meet friends and chat pleasantly together before five o'clock when etiquette demanded that handling the reins oneself was out, now it was the turn of state carriages.

So it was perfectly natural that they should meet casually, Tam in her green zephyr cloth habit, trimmed with Valenciennes lace, Jamie beside her on a sturdy pony, and the man in the dark Newmarket coat, with drill pleated trousers, and half boots with spurs. It was quite natural that he should stop, raise his hat, and say with dancing eyes, 'Is it not Lady Fargate? And did we not meet last night at the Duchess's ball?' And when she nodded, 'I believe so,' nothing was more natural than that he should dismount, help her down, and, with Jamie beside them, walk to the side where they could talk as they watched the riders of high birth and breeding compete for admiration with the pretty little 'horsebreakers', the ladies of dubious reputation.

'This is my son,' she said.

They shook hands gravely, the man and the boy who were so much alike.

'How do you do, Uncle Charles?' Jamie said.

Charles smiled as he studied the self-possessed, independent child. 'Strange that we have never met before,' he said.

'But you are busy, and I am away at preparatory school,' said Jamie, reasonably.

'And do you like your school?'

'Oh yes. Very much.'

'It is run by a most excellent man,' Tam said. 'Later he will go to Rugby school. I confess I had been most alarmed by the reports I'd had about various public schools, but I hear there is a new headmaster at Rugby, who is changing the old system, he treats boys as gentlemen and expects them to behave as such.'

'Where did you go to school, Uncle?' asked Jamie, curiously.

'Me? Oh Chilverton Grammar,' said Charles.

'Did you? I suppose that's why you're sending Roderick there?'

'Er, well, yes,' said Charles.

'Mama said he could go with me to school but Aunt Juliet didn't want him to go away. She does rather dote on Roderick.' Jamie paused. 'And Uncle Geoffrey agreed. He said he might find a place for him in the weaving factory when he grows up.'

Tam looked at Charles, startled. 'I didn't know – ' She began, and added in a low voice, 'Can he be accepting his responsibility then? Geoffrey?'

'He needs to accept responsibility for more than that,' said Charles. 'How are things at the factory? Is he cutting wages, like the rest of the country?'

'I don't know,' she said. 'Though Mirrie did say there was trouble brewing – '

'It's been brewing for a long time,' Charles said. 'Bread is too dear, wages too low. And if there's to be another cut . . . I think there will be trouble, Tam.'

'Will it be bad?' she asked.

'Who knows? I hadn't meant to worry you about this, but maybe you should be warned, going to the boats as you do – ?'

'But the boatmen won't – '

'The weavers might, and you go through the town. Take care, Tam, and take care of Jamie. If there is trouble, don't get in the thick of it as you did once before – ' and his eyes met hers as they remembered the night of the election.

She whispered, 'If there hadn't been trouble that night we'd never have . . . there wouldn't be Jamie.'

He grinned then as he whispered back, 'We really cannot have a child every time there is a riot. It isn't seemly.'

Add on that light-hearted note they parted.

Jamie Fargate was a normal little boy with all the usual little boy's likes and dislikes. He had inherited his parents' determination without their tempers, he looked on the world with equanamity. His mother was wont to say he always fell on his feet, and certainly he seemed to attract luck rather than the storms she so often did.

He loved his mother, and liked riding with her, but he looked too for masculine company, not merely boys of his own age, but an older man, a hero. As a small child he'd found this in Jennings, the coachman, but since going to school his world had expanded, and Jennings was no longer quite so satisfactory. Unconsciously, he widened his search. He did not like the man he called Papa, and felt no guilt about this, for he knew Sir William did not like him. The masters at school were all right, but not the stuff that heroes were made of, they dealt with unpleasant things like discipline and lessons. He had met Uncle Geoffrey, but with a child's instinct, felt him to be lacking, sensed his weakness.

Now he had met his other uncle, Charles, and he seemed to fulfil the boy's dream. Uncle Charles was firm and strong, he laughed a lot. Moreover, he was an important man, a Member of Parliament, whatever that might be.

As he returned from London with his mother Jamie talked of his uncle and Tam, eager to talk of him too, let the boy chatter away.

'Why doesn't Uncle Charles come to see us?' he asked. 'He is a nice man, isn't he?'

'Very nice,' said Tam, a smile curving her lips. 'But he is too busy to do much visiting, Jamie.'

'What does he do in Parliament, Mama?'

Tam was about to say she didn't know, but sought a favourable reply. 'Why, he helps the poor,' she told him. 'The weavers.'

'Why doesn't Uncle Geoffrey help them?'

'Oh, you know Geoffrey,' said Tam, impatiently.

Jamie thought this a very unsatisfactory answer. He was a logical child. 'Are they in trouble?' he asked.

'There's been trouble ever since I can remember,' said Tam.

'Why?'

'Oh, too little money, and they don't like the factory.'

'Why did Uncle Geoffrey build the factory then?'

'I don't know. To make money, I suppose.' Tam recollected that she was talking to her son. 'That's enough, Jamie,' she said repressively.

And maybe it would have been enough, but the trouble Charles had warned about burst in the July of 1842, just when Jamie was home again for the summer holidays. He went with his mother to the wharf to hear the boaters report that the storm had broken in Staffordshire, when the colliers, following reductions in wages, marched to every works in the neighbourhood and compelled their companions to come out: those who refused were thrown into the canal. Very soon the trouble spread, and by August work throughout the industrial Midlands and North was at a standstill.

On the Saturday Tam went out to order the pony-chaise. 'Take me with you, Mama,' said Jamie.

She looked at him doubtfully. 'I don't know if I should – '

'I'll be all right, Mama.'

'Oh very well. Come along.'

They drove to the wharf and Jerome came to meet her. 'You shouldn't be here, Lady Fargate,' he said. 'The weavers are out.'

'I came to see how the boats were faring.'

'They can't work, milady. If they go anywhere they can't deliver, they must stay here.'

'But we'll be losing money. Oh well, I suppose it can't be helped.'

'Would you like me to accompany you home, milady?'

'Of course not, Jerome. I'm not afraid.'

'No,' he said, admiringly. 'You have courage. But I beg you to stay at home till this is settled.'

'Oh, Jerome, you're an old fusspot.'

'Someone should take care of you,' he muttered under his breath, but she caught the words and smiled. 'Come, Jamie,' she said.

They returned but Tam, being Tam, did not stay at home. Nor did Jamie. And now there was a lot for sharp young ears to pick up: tales of rioting in the north, policemen killed in Manchester, mobs attacking the military in Preston, Chilverton apprehensive. Geoffrey Waring was hopeless in a crisis, Harry Earp said, he wasn't the man his father was. Harry Earp knew a lot about weaving, and was willing to explain about it to young Jamie. He promised to take him to see a hand loom when they started again. And the factory? asked Jamie. No, he couldn't go in there, but perhaps if he asked Geoffrey Waring . . .

Jamie was a polite little boy, and he wrote a letter to Uncle Geoffrey asking if he could look over the factory. But Geoffrey, not unnaturally, had too much on his mind at this time, and the letter was never answered, and Jamie never heard his uncle's side of the story. Did not know that Geoffrey, like his weavers, could not understand why there should be tariffs on bread but not on silk, that he was desperate for orders. Jamie heard only the weavers' side, they shouted that Geoffrey Waring should not lower their wages again or they'd burn his factory down. Jamie saw Geoffrey attempt to speak to them, saw him fail ignominiously.

And then Uncle Charles came riding into town on a black horse. He talked to the crowds in the street, he promised he'd do all he could to get them cheaper bread, he begged them not to burn the factory or they'd put themselves in the poorhouse. 'Go home peaceably,' he ordered. And they went.

Then Charles rode back to Tam, who had been watching him controlling the crowd. 'Are you going to do something in Parliament, Charles?' she asked.

'Oh yes,' he said savagely. 'This time I'll make them listen. Our Ministers are even now holding their customary fish dinner at the "Crown and Sceptre" in Greenwich, would you believe? But this time I'll make them understand.'

Tam drove away and Jamie asked, 'Why didn't the people listen to Uncle Geoffrey, Mama?'

'I don't suppose he said much to them. He'd as soon talk to the looms – '

'They listened to Uncle Charles.'

'Yes, Charles knows how to handle people.' There was a trace of irony in the statement. 'Come Jamie, let's go home.'

The strike lasted a fortnight but Geoffrey's factory was fortunately not damaged. Troops poured into the north on the new railways, the police arrested the ringleaders. And the strike crumbled. Geoffrey Waring reopened his factory, but the wages were lowered.

Yet the rising had done a number of things. It awakened the conscience of England, leading to Peel repealing the Corn Laws, making bread cheaper, and to Lord Shaftesbury's Factory Act. And it brought Charles Waring to the attention of the House at last, for he spoke long and loudly and would not be silenced. Finally, it changed Jamie Fargate's life. His mother did not know this, and would not know for many years, for Jamie kept his own counsel. But his future course was set, and so, indirectly, was that of many other people.

Tam watched the growing railway with continuing disquiet. It would run in opposition to the canal, and she worried about the outcome. She talked it over with Harry and Jerome in the little office.

'Sir William will no longer send his coal by water,' she said. 'That will mean we lose payments, tolls and so on – '

'The problem will be if others follow his example,' said Harry. 'Because if they do – ' he broke off, but the unspoken words hung on the air. If others did they would have no income, they would be ruined.

'Lady Fargate,' Jerome said, 'if we lost revenue, as we shall, our main problem is that you cannot, as a canal owner, run your own boats. If you could carry freight you could undercut the railways, for their charges are very high. But it's against the law.'

'As well I know,' said Tam.

'The law needs changing,' Harry said. 'It wasn't so important before, but now – '

'Yes, indeed,' Tam said. 'We could run in opposition to Sir William, fight him every inch of the way.' Her eyes sparkled and the two men looked at her somewhat uneasily. They all knew Sir William, but for a woman to so openly fight her own husband . . .

'Sir William is not going to close the Chilverton Canal,' Tam said determinedly. 'Now what can we do to bring in this law?'

'You could bring the matter up at the next meeting of representatives,' suggested Jerome.

So it was agreed, and in May 1844, Tam went to London to the meeting of the United Body of Canal Proprietors, who were increasingly anxious about the encroaching power of the railways. 'They're out to ruin us,' said one man, gloomily.

Tam looked round the room at the middle-aged, bearded men sitting on the leather chairs. She felt some trepidation, she had not been well-received before, yet she was determined to put her case.

The Staffordshire and Worcestershire representative jumped to his feet. 'We must remember we are at war,' he said, and Tam remembered the letter Jerome had shown her from this lively company. They, at least, were alive to the danger.

So was the Aire and Calder. 'We must tell the public that it was we who helped develop the industries of this country,' their representative said. 'And if one canal breaks the chain of waterway links we are finished. Remember, without us to check them the railways companies could bring in any charge they liked, they are too powerful – '

It was the opportunity Tam had waited for. With heightened colour she rose to her feet. 'We need to get a bill passed to enable canal companies to act as carriers,' she said. 'As it is, I own the Chilverton, yet cannot run my own boats, and a railway is opening in opposition. So what do I do? Give in meekly? Oh no, gentlemen. We want a bill, or the railways will ruin us,' and there were cries of, 'Hear, hear,' and even a few cheers.

Tam sat down, pleased that, though a woman, she was now recognised, her words were listened to.

The Aire and Calder man jumped to his feet. 'I propose we draft a bill – ' he said.

'But we're not in Parliament – '

'Then it will be up to us to lobby Parliament – '

There was agreement, a bill was drafted, and Tam reported back to Harry and Jerome.

'We have to lobby MPs,' said Jerome.

'I'll ask Mr Waring,' said Tam. She always tried these days to be very circumspect when Charles was mentioned, referring to him by surname, never meeting him alone when he came to Chilverton. Only within her did she carry the knowledge of their secret meetings at the Duchess's house in London. Such meetings were few at first. From never wanting to go to London she could hardly desire now to be there all the time. Not without careful planning. So she allowed the Duchess to persuade her – before Sir William – to visit for shopping. 'Really, gel, your bonnet is dreadfully out of date. Sir William, how can you let your wife dress so? Can she never come to London to see the best milliner?' And Sir William had no option but to allow his wife to buy a new bonnet in London. Then she needed a dress, and clothes for Jamie, and she confessed that London's shops were really quite reasonable in price . . .

And no one ever knew of the back entrance to the Duchess's house, or the dark handsome man who stole in and out while Tam was there.

She had a new maid now, a London girl who despised Sir William as a country bumpkin and the Manor servants as beneath her notice. She was paid well, and intended to save for her own little business in time, in fact the Duchess had promised something of the kind. So Emmeline accompanied her mistress, and was as silent as the grave.

Yet they were playing with fire, and they knew it. Under the influence of the Prince, the Queen now set the fashion for happy domesticity. He had been shocked by Victoria's giddy behaviour, it was rumoured among the echelons of high society; he did not share her pleasure in dancing all night, late nights upset his digestion. Nor did he care for extravagance, and scandal was abhorred. Respectability became the keyword. Any breath of scandal would ruin Charles now, as it was later to ruin Parnell. And Charles was becoming noticed in government circles, Tory reformers consorted with him, the old Whig aristocracy deigned to look over their pince-nez, while the new liberals welcomed his orations. Charles, the radical outsider of ten years ago, was becoming the new man of the hungry forties, when even the most reactionary realised that reforms were needed. So he'd been right, this young upstart, to warn them about what the people would do; he was a man to watch. And Charles found the new success, and the inklings of what power could mean, a heady brew.

The people of Chilverton worshipped Charles, they waited for him to come, wanted to see him about all their various problems.

But only I, Tam thought, sleep with him. And it was this knowledge that gave her eyes their slumbrous delight, that kept the green lights at bay, that even changed the contours of her face to a softer line. She recognised this change, this effect he had on her, of softening her . . . he who was so ruthless in some ways, yet in others so gentle. And it was the gentleness that captivated her. Sir William might storm and rave, she was unmoved, would never give in. Charles's tenderness melted her completely.

Even now, after being lovers for three years, his name mentioned still had the power to move her. It did so now, and she hoped she was not blushing like a silly girl.

'I will see Mr Waring when I can,' she said. 'Maybe he can advise us about this matter of an act.'

'Yes, put it to him,' said Jerome, thinking how wondrous fine Lady Fargate's eyes looked when they sparkled, and wondering who her lover could be. He didn't doubt that she had a lover, a woman like Lady Fargate. He would have offered for her himself if he thought he ever had a chance. But he was a mere underling, and Sir William was a bad enemy. He wrenched his thoughts back to the canal.

Tam was wondering how she could ever have thought Jerome attractive. Beside Charles he was a candle eclipsed by the sun. 'I'll see what I can do,' she said, and walked outside, to the multi-coloured boats on the blue water, the songs and the shouting on the wharf. Her heart was singing. She was to see him again, and this time she had a legitimate excuse.

But she had to find an excuse for Sir William. She didn't need any new clothes and this pretext, used too often, might make him suspicious. Yet if she waited Jamie would be home for the summer holidays, and she liked to spend as much time with him as possible, taking him to the wharf. And Charles would be here too, they could discuss the matter in the office with Jerome, and that was not what she wanted. Then it would be the hunting season, with Sir William's friends clumping in for breakfast, possibly raising eyebrows if Lady Fargate was away in London. No, it had to be now. So she said, as casually as she could at breakfast, 'By the way I have to go to London. Some more canal business.'

He looked up. 'Not another meeting of your representatives. You're wasting your time,' he said with calculated cruelty.

'A few matters still have to be cleared up,' she said. 'I thought I'd choose a day when you wouldn't require me here.'

'Very considerate of you.'' He stood up. 'I have no plans for next Thursday.'

It was as easy as that. Tam dropped her eyes, exulting.

'You'll have to stay the night.' It was a statement rather than a question.

'Of course. I can't get back on the same day. The Duchess – '

'Yes, I know. But when the trains are running you'll be able to be there and back in a day.' He moved away.

Yet she was a little worried by his very compliance. Much as she loved Charles, and wanted to see him, there were two fears always at the back of her mind: the fear of being found out, of the subsequent scandal and the harm it would do to Charles, to herself and Jamie, and the fear of pregnancy. She remembered Juliet saying that Geoffrey was careful, and wondered what she meant. She couldn't quite bring herself to ask Charles, and there was no one else to talk to about such matters. Yet Charles did know how they were placed, so presumably he was doing the right thing, whatever that might be.

In fact, Charles knew only too well what scandal would do to his career. But he was at the present time on the crest of a wave, he was being noticed in the House, and he had Tam. No man could ask for more. Charles too had a streak of recklessness.

Tam wore a warm dress of merino wool, with a matching cloak, and boarded the fast coach to London. She had written to the Duchess and to Charles, using the new penny post which, she was certain, had been introduced by Charles in answer to her request for cheap postage. Now she had another request for him, and when they met, in a room in the Duchess's house, she put it to him. Was it not time an act was passed enabling canal companies to act as carriers?

'I'll do what I can,' Charles said. 'I've always thought that was one of our most ridiculous laws. But of course, it was brought in to stop canal companies having a monopoly of trade.'

'I know that, Charles.'

'And you know what Sir William would have made of it.'

'He did it anyway.'

'True, but without that law he wouldn't have allowed any other boat on the canal. No, it worked quite well, only the Trent and Mersey managed to evade the prohibition, by forming another, separate company.'

'But the railways don't have this rule, Charles.'

'No, that's why the Canal Act must go, it's hardly fair competition. But it won't be easy. Not when so many people have interests in the railways.'

'Please, Charles, for my sake.'

He smiled at her.

'I'll try. But you won't have Sir William's boats, will you? What is he planning to do with them?'

'I don't know, he won't tell me. Perhaps he'll let me have them.'

'He won't do that, Tam, not to run in competition with his railway. I think – '

'What?'

'I think he'll go all out to ruin you.'

'He can *try*, but he won't succeed.'

He sighed. 'Other canal companies are selling to railway companies. Sometimes I wonder – '

'Wonder what?'

'Why you are so determined.'

'Charles! I'm not the only person to believe in canals.'

'No. But I still wonder why. Is it just to get your own back on Sir William?'

'You do talk nonsense, Charles.'

'But you do want to get your own back.'

'Of course I do. He killed my father. And don't say any more about it, please, I don't like it.' She was angry, her eyes flashing green, and he stared in some amazement.

'Tam, I only – '

'I won't hear any more, do you hear me? Not a word, I won't, Charles.' And when he moved towards her she shrugged him away. 'Leave me alone.' But he held her tenderly as she suddenly burst into a storm of sobs, smoothed her hair without a word. And later, when he came to her room he took her in his arms as if she were a fractious child. She said in a muffled voice, 'I'm sorry, Charles.'

'That's all right.' He kissed her gently on the cheek. 'Sometimes I forget what a heavy burden you've had to bear.' And she was soothed, and clung to him, feeling that only he out of all the world could comfort her.

When, in 1845, the Canal Carriers' Act got through Parliament, Tam was certain that this was all Charles's doing, and she told him so when they met.

210

'Certainly I voted for it,' he said, laughing. 'But as for doing it all myself, it isn't as simple as that. There are six hundred of us in the House, Tam, not just me – ' and he launched into an explanation of the workings of the House of Commons, the different factions. Half-way through a description of Private Members' bills he broke off. 'You're not listening,' he accused.

'What? Oh sorry, Charles.'

'You're not interested, are you?'

'Well, no, Charles. I mean, it is a little boring, isn't it?' And for a moment he was silent. 'Come, Charles, don't be cross,' she coaxed. 'You know how delighted I am about this Act. Now I can act as carrier, own my own boats. That's what I've wanted for so long.'

'There is one snag, Tam.'

'Oh. What's that?'

'The Act also empowers companies to make traffic agreements with railway and other canal companies. And to lease themselves to any other canal or navigation company.'

'Traffic agreements? What does that mean, Charles?'

'Well, that will depend on the agreement.' He paused, thinking. 'Let us hope that the canal companies will be very wary about making any agreements with the railways.'

'Oh I'm sure they'll be very wary, Charles. Why, the representatives were very bitter about the railways at the last meeting – '

'And the railways are very astute,' said Charles. 'Well, we'll just have to wait and see.'

But Tam was delighted. Now, she felt, she could fight Sir William's little railway, and more important she could start fighting *now*, before it came into being.

She asked Sir William if he would be willing to sell his boats to her.

'No,' he said curtly.

'But you won't require them when you have the railway running. You've said so.'

'And they're not going to be any good to you either, madam, I'll see to that.'

'But what will you do with them?'

'Burn them.'

'And what will happen to the boaters?'

'I have no idea.'

'Why are you so cruel?' fumed Tam. 'You alienate everyone. Your son left you. You never repair your cottages or farms – '

'You won't need boats when my railway runs,' he said.

'You planned this from the beginning, didn't you?' she asked. 'You put my father out of business because his idea of making the canals uniform would have made them successful. You knew even then you would bring in this railway. And if the canals became successful your railway would be doomed. Well, you won't stop me. If I can't have your boats I'll buy some from the boatyard – '

'If you have enough money from your falling dividends.'

'I could always borrow from the Duchess.'

That silenced him, as she knew it would. Before the Duchess even Sir William quailed.

He said curtly, 'Buy your boats. In law, I am responsible for my wife's debts.'

She said, amazed, 'You'd buy boats . . .?'

'I am a wealthy man. No one is going to rush me for payment. And when I am dead the debts will be paid out of the money that will come to you.'

Tam pondered this. It seemed watertight. Yet she hesitated. For although she had taunted him with the fact that she'd inherit from him on his death, this had been no more than an angry retort on the spur of the moment, as was her remark about borrowing from the Duchess, she had never thought seriously about either. Now she wondered. It would be a way out. Some of his money must come to his widow. But her innate caution where money matters were concerned overruled any thought of running up debts. Memories of her father dying penniless were too strong. She would buy boats, but would pay cash out of her small capital.

And, as always, he thought of other ways to hurt her, one being through Jamie. When the boy came home for the holidays, and they sat at breakfast the first morning, Tam asked, 'Where will you be going this morning, Jamie?'

'To the stables, Mama.'

She smiled fondly, knowing his love for horses.

Sir William said, 'You are not to ride today.'

Both Tam and Jamie stared in amazement.

'Why not?' asked Jamie.

'Because I say you shall not.'

'But I always ride . . .'

'Not today.'

'Can you tell us why?' asked Tam.

'My dear wife, I can say who shall or shall not ride my horses, I believe.' He looked at Jamie. 'It isn't wise for boys who are heirs to risk their necks.'

'But I am not the heir,' said Jamie. 'Your eldest son inherits.'

'If he can be traced. He may be dead.' Sir William smiled, a thin, cold smile.

'Come, Jamie, we'll go to the canal in the carriage. I assume that we are allowed to do that, or are we to be kept prisoners?' Tam said.

He shrugged. 'Take the carriage if you wish.'

'What does he mean, Mama?' asked Jamie, when they were in the carriage. 'All boys ride, heirs or no.'

'I'm afraid he's just – ' she hesitated.

'Just being unkind,' said Jamie.

She guessed the reason. It was another piece of refined torture. Bring the boy up to think he is the heir, his shock when he found out would be all the greater. And Tam would either have to bear with it, or tell Jamie the truth. She could feel Sir William smiling maliciously. Aloud she said

212

'Lewis is the heir, and when Sir William dies, the lawyers will send to America, put notices in the papers. You will not inherit, do you understand, Jamie?'

'Will you still live at the Manor then?' asked Jamie.

'Oh no, it won't belong to me, it will belong to Lewis. No, I shall go back to the canals. That's why I take you so often, Jamie. The canal will be yours one day. Another Jamie Calder.'

'But I am not Jamie Calder, Mama.'

She could have bitten out her tongue. 'It is the name of the business,' she said hastily. 'I am going to buy boats, so it will be called the Calder Boats.'

'I see.'

Throughout the holidays Sir William refused to let Jamie ride, talking more and more of the danger of losing his heir. And Tam wondered if Lewis really was dead, if Sir William had heard something, and what she would do when the time came and she had to state why Jamie should not inherit.

Jamie said nothing, he simply stared at Sir William with his clear gaze, and this didn't please Sir William either. There was no point in hurting someone if they didn't show they were hurt. But Jamie stayed longer and longer in Chilverton, sometimes overnight with Roddy, or Harry and Mirrie, and Tam saw less of him. She comforted herself with the thought of the day when they'd work together on the canals.

When he returned to school the quarrels between Sir William and herself grew more frequent, he would find fault with every little thing she did, and though she tried hard not to answer he would keep on until, goaded past endurance, she had to retort. She knew he wanted to bring her down, to make her cringe, to beat her figuratively, if not literally, into submission, and it was her refusal to be beaten down which infuriated him. She felt too that he had expected she'd be forced into giving up the canal by this time, and her persistence, together with the fact that she was in business on her own, independent, not forced to beg from him, angered him too. She fled with relief to the canal, and began to dread going back to the Manor, to the life of fault-finding and bickering over trifles. If only, she thought, I were free.

Chapter Four

Geoffrey was right, it was years before the railway was finished. Jamie had started his first term at Rugby, Roderick was in the grammar school and Celia had given birth to her fourth daughter, Beatrice, before the day came.

The Trent Valley line, extending the route from London to Rugby and Stafford had already been opened by Sir Robert Peel at Tamworth, and among the distinguished guests were George Stephenson and George Hudson, the 'Railway King'.

The Chilverton branch line was less important and was opened by Sir William. Tam did not attend, and this brought more quarrelling. It was the first time she had refused to act as hostess or accompany her husband when asked, but she felt that to be with him at this time of his triumph was asking too much. It was open war between them now.

For two years, since the Canal Carriers' Act was passed, Tam had been running her own boats. She had bought two at first, from carriers who were pulling out, and she let it be known among the boaters that she was looking for crews. The result was that Sir William's men defected to Tam and, as she dipped into her reserve fund and added to her fleet, he was left almost without crews, and forced to come to her for transport. He had taken on more, untrained men, who ran into difficulties as soon as they learned how to handle a boat for, oddly, the locks were always against them and when they got stuck in the mud and a boater came to assist they somehow left them deeper in the mud than ever, often forcing them to remain for days. Legends of the ghosts in tunnels were rampant, and one new boater, tied up for the night because he was unable to steer in the dark, found in the morning his whole load of coal had disappeared and was never seen again.

Tam carried coal mostly, much of it from the Milden colliery, owned by Sir John Carruthers, a local squire who had no love for Sir William. So when Tam offered a lower rate he was only too pleased to employ her men. She also took over deliveries of flour, as the flour mill was independently owned and by a man who had suffered from Sir William's bullying tactics.

214

There were other loads too, timber, and stone from the quarry. She even ran occasional trips herself in the *Princess*.

But now the railway was opened. Sir William announced it with a great show of publicity: posters, handbills, advertisements in the local newspaper, all announced that the new travel would be fast and cheap. 'No more perishable goods rotting in bad weather,' cried the advertisement. 'Our railway will get you there in good speed.'

All the town turned out on opening day, to marvel, just as thirty-six years before they had watched the opening of the canal. Local dignitaries were offered a free ride, for Sir William was to run passenger trains too.

Tam sat with Jerome and Harry in the small office, discussing their plans.

Harry said, 'I could not make a trip today, Tamarisk, no one was interested, everybody had gone to see the railway opening.'

Tam snorted. 'They'll be back. By the way, Harry, someone told me in the town that they wanted to get up a party to travel to Coventry and you refused to take them.'

'That is true. They wanted to see the hanging of the woman who killed her uncle. And I'm sorry, Tamarisk, but I do not believe in hanging, public or otherwise, and I could not go against my conscience to take people to gloat over that unfortunate woman.'

'But she was a murderess,' started Tam, who at times wished Harry's conscience did not conflict with business, then she gave a reluctant smile. 'Oh, Harry,' she said, 'if it were left to you the place would be overrun with murderers. Still, it's your boat.'

Jerome interposed. 'Lady Fargate. Let us come to our main problem. How much of our freight-carrying are we going to lose to the railways?'

'That we don't know. We don't know that everyone will desert us. Have you contacted the collieries farther along?'

'Yes. Two have their own boats. Two others are changing to rail.'

'So soon?'

'Yes. We still have the flour and stone.'

'And the Milden colliery'?

'Waiting to see what happens. But they are nearer to the canal than the railway.'

'So are most of the new factories, including Geoffrey Waring's,' said Tam. 'All on the water's edge, built there for the coal deliveries – '

'And because they needed the water,' said Jerome.

'Yes. But, even if they sent their goods by rail, it would not be economical to have coal delivered that way. Yes, I feel that we shall still have markets.'

'There is one other market,' said Jerome. 'Pickfords are pulling out.'

'They've been doing so for years.'

'I know. But they plan to be right out by 1848. We might pick up some of their business.'

'Yes, that's a thought,' Tam said, pondering. 'Now, how would I find out what their markets are?'

'We could go down to their depot in London,' suggested Jerome.

'Yes. We could always pick up some sort of load for the journey down. I'll do it. I'll go to London.'

'Not you, milady,' protested Jerome. 'Let me go.'

'No, Jerome, you have work here. I want to go, I have a plan.'

She went out to the lay-by, where more boats than usual were tied up. 'Josh,' she called. 'Josh Lawson.'

'Yes, Miss Tam. I mean, milady.'

'Miss Tam will do,' Tam said brusquely. 'Have you no orders?'

'No, Miss Tam. We was just going out to look for loads.'

'Right. I want to go to London, Josh. You know the way?'

' 'Course, Miss Tam.'

'Will you take me? I might find us business.'

'You ain't bin to London by canal afore, Miss Tam?'

'No.'

'It's a hundred miles. There's a hundred and sixty locks, and it takes seven days.'

'Will you take me, Josh?'

'Gladly, Miss Tam.'

'Right. You go to Milden, load up with coal, accept whatever price he asks, while I go back to get some clothes. Then we'll go to London.'

'Miss Tam, there ain't exactly room for sleeping – '

'Don't talk so soft,' his wife interrupted. 'You can sleep on top of the coal wi' the lads. It ain't cold, and it won't be the first time. Me and Miss Tam will have the bunks.'

Tam laughed. 'We'll manage,' she said. 'We're off to find new work, Josh.'

They set off. This was not a flyboat with galloping horses and Tam found it very slow going after her own packet boat. The horse, driven by one of Josh's lads, ambled along, nose-bag over his head, the pale autumn sun gleaming on the brasses, as they drifted between hedgerows filled with red haws and purple elderberries, and Tam forgot her worries and gave herself up to enjoyment, watching the water fowl, coots and moor hens hiding in the rushes, swans gliding aloofly by.

Josh and his wife refused to let her steer, so she sat on the top step leading to the cabin, trying to memorise the route. Braunston village with its old weatherbeaten inn, the locks where Josh and his oldest boy had to leg the boat through, after unhitching the horse which Tam took over the road.

Tying up for the night at Stoke Bruerne, where Tam went to the little boaters' shop to stock up, and entered a veritable Aladdin's cave: groceries, piles of crockery, teapots, mixed with herbal remedies for illness, clay pipes, boots, aprons and buttons. Hanging from the ceiling were hurricane lamps, kettles and saucepans.

On again, and Tam let the soothing quality of the water journey envelop her completely. Over the cast-iron aqueduct at Wolverton, seeing the long line of the Chilterns coming into view, up to the summit at Marsworth,

216

and on to the 'Cowroast Inn', where Josh tied up for the night.

'Cowroast?' asked Tam. 'Do they roast cows here then?'

'No, Miss Tam, it's "Cow Rest" really. The old drove road used to come through the gap in the hills, where they brought cattle into the valleys in winter.'

And after that it was the long flight of locks which stepped gradually down to London. They spent their last night at Bulls Bridge Junction, seeing the lights of London below.

They made an early start. Maida Vale tunnel, Hampstead Road locks, Kentish Town. There were buildings now, factories, warehouses, a huddle of houses. Tam thought of her other visits to London, to Park Lane and the Duchess, and here she was now, creeping in the back way, seeing a London she hadn't known existed: City Road Basin and, finally, Pickfords' Wharf. Josh tied up and Tam went into the cabin to change her dress. Then, neat and tidy, she stepped ashore.

The mighty Pickfords had been carriers since the beginning. Tam knew they were a huge concern, but she was amazed at the astonishing activity that awaited her as she passed through a pair of large folding gates into a court. Waggons were pouring in from all directions, laden with goods, and men were unloading them into huge warehouses. She wandered along, past blocks of stables, rows of offices and counting-houses, where men scurried to and fro like busy ants. Tam stopped one clerk, his hands full of papers, and asked to see someone who dealt with the buying and selling.

'Oh, you'll mean Mr Coates. I'll see what I can do. This is a busy part of the day, you see.'

'Yes, I do see that. Have I come at the wrong time?'

'Well, it's in the early evening we get all the waggons coming in. In the morning we send them out with goods just brought in by canal. But I'll see what I can do. Wait here.'

Tam waited, fascinated by the noise, the bustle, and wishing her own business was as flourishing as this one.

A voice in her ear said 'You wish to see me?' And she spun round. 'I am Mr Coates.'

He was a man of some forty odd years, smartly dressed. She replied, 'If you can spare the time. I had no idea you would be so busy.'

He smiled. 'Will you come into my office?'

She followed him into the counting-house, through a large room which contained at least a hundred clerks, all busy scribbling away, into an office which seemed almost as large, its walls covered with folios and maps. She stood before the maps, fascinated anew. 'This is amazing,' she said.

'These are the names of all our districts,' Mr Coates explained. 'We have branches in ninety-seven towns. So you see there is a lot to manage here, all the transactions, respecting the horses, provender, boats and waggons. And now, of course, railways.' He turned from the maps, he was a busy man. 'Now, what did you wish to see me about?'

'I have some coal to sell,' said Tam, baldly.

'Ah. Well, you see we have our own – '

'Yes, I suppose so,' said Tam, who had known all along, but had wanted an excuse to see someone.

Mr Coates was trying not to stare. 'You are, er – ' and Tam hastened to fill the breach.

'I'm so sorry, I was so fascinated by your establishment. I am Lady Fargate.'

Mr Coates was nonplussed. Why on earth should a lady be selling coal? Tam, who had no compunction about using her married name when it furthered her ends, noted his amazement.

'You have the coal here?' Mr Coates asked.

'Oh yes,' said Tam, blithely. 'I brought it down on a canal boat. I am a carrier, you see,' as he looked blank.

'I see.'

'My father owned the boats. And I try to carry on . . .' Tam remembered Charles in the beginning asking her if she intended to fight fair. Well, you couldn't, if you were a woman, you had to use any weapon you had. 'How many times I have seen your boats sailing past,' she went on dreamily. 'I never thought that I would ever be standing here, right at the heart of it all. And to think it is all passing.'

'Only the canal traffic, Lady Fargate. We are changing to rail transport.'

'So what will happen to your boats?'

'Well.' Mr Coates was non-committal. 'We shall dispose of them, naturally.'

'Will you really? Oh, I wish I might buy some of them.'

Mr Coates pursed his lips. 'They are for sale.'

'I could not, of course, offer much of a price. Not when everyone is going into rail.'

'Then, forgive me, Lady Fargate, why do you wish to buy?'

'Sentimental reasons,' said Tam. 'The act of a foolish woman whose father started the Chilverton Canal, who made its prosperity his lifework. He lost his money, but I carry on his work.' She put her handkerchief to her eyes, peeping over it to see if Mr Coates was visibly moved: he looked vaguely uncomfortable. 'I have little money, but I sympathise with the boatmen. What will they do?'

Mr Coates looked distressed. 'We have offered jobs to the men where we can. We have always been good employers.'

Tam knew this was true. 'But these men were born on boats, they want to die on boats, they know no other life. I'll buy the boats and give them the life they prefer.'

'Well, now . . .' Mr Coates considered, and the price he quoted was very reasonable. Tam knew she had enough in her reserve fund to cover the purchase of three boats and went to see them. The bargain was struck, and she threw in the load of coal for good measure, and left, still with the handkerchief to her eyes.

They took their own boat farther along the canal, and woke early the next day. Tam and Josh made their way carefully towards the boats she had bought. The wharf was, if anything, busier than on the previous

218

evening. Waggons were taking out goods for distribution, the boats were being loaded in the half-light.

Tam talked to her new crews before sending them on to Chilverton. From them she obtained the names of all the firms they had previously delivered to. She visited all the firms in turn. And when she went back home she had orders for timber carrying, for iron, for bales of cotton, barrels of ale and cider. Even for coal. She was well satisfied with the result of her mission.

She returned to Chilverton to trouble, both at the Manor and in the town. Sir William was furious that she should absent herself in such a manner, and for so long. 'How do I know where you have been?' he asked.

'I should think it is obvious,' said Tam, pointing to her bedraggled appearance, her mud-spattered, coal-dust-covered gown. 'I hardly look as if I've been dancing with a lover. I've been getting orders for the men you are throwing out of work.'

'Then you should tell me where you go. You should ask my permission before you absent yourself for days on end – '

Tam sighed. Their relations were so strained these days, they saw so little of each other, spoke so seldom, it hardly seemed to make much difference whether she were in or out.

She went to her room, where Emmeline waited on her with solicitude. 'You're tired, milady.'

'A little. And dirty. But it's been worth it, Emmeline. I've got more orders.'

'That's good, milady. I'll get hot water for a bath.'

'Thank you, Emmeline.' She waited as the maid brought in the round tin bath, poured in hot water, then she slowly took off her clothes and sank into its warmth with a sigh of relief. 'So what's been happening while I've been away?'

'Oh, Sir William's been creating something chronic, milady. I told him what you said, but he said you should have asked him first.'

'Yes. So he told me. Never get married, Emmeline.'

'I don't intend to, milady.'

'And what else has been happening?'

'Trouble in the town, milady.'

'Oh. What's that?'

'There's illness in the Patch again.'

'Not cholera?'

'No, they don't think so. But it's a nasty fever. Dys – something or other.'

'Dysentery?'

'Could be that. Some people died, and they don't know the cause of it. There's a meeting in the town today. Mr Waring's coming.'

'Mr Charles Waring?'

'Yes, milady.'

'What time is this meeting?'

'Seven tonight. In the Temple Street Hall.'

'I'll go.'

'But you're tired, milady.'

'I feel better now I'm clean. When I've had a meal I'll be all right.'

She sought out Sir William. 'Will you be going to the meeting tonight?' she asked.

'I shall not.'

'I would like to go.'

'I don't see why.'

'Because I am interested, that's why. If you don't care about people dying – ' she broke off. No point in antagonising him further. 'I'll just call in,' she ended. 'After all, my sister Juliet does take a great interest in the people in the Patch. I wondered if we might have dinner at six o'clock? If not, I'll eat later.'

Surprisingly he agreed. And after their silent meal, Tam called the carriage and was driven to the meeting hall. It had been over two months since she'd managed a so-called shopping trip to London, and she was longing to see Charles, it would be enough just to hear him speak.

The hall was crowded. Geoffrey was there, all the local dignitaries and officials, tradespeople, Mirrie and Harry, who smiled as she entered and beckoned to her to sit with them. She told them of her success with orders, when the chairman called for silence, and Charles walked on to the platform, accompanied by Dr Phillips.

The chairman introduced Charles, who, after mentioning how some of them had tried to get a Public Health Bill through Parliament, and failed, came to the point.

'I called this meeting,' he said, 'because I hope to see something done about the insanitary conditions in the area known as the Patch. Ideally of course, these houses should be removed and new ones built.'

Geoffrey interrupted with a cry of outrage. 'I can't afford to build new houses – '

'If they are not to be replaced,' Charles went on, equably, 'then we must build a completely new water system. New pipes for the sewage, and new separate pipes to install clean drinking water.'

'Whatever for?' asked a voice querulously.

'Take a look at the Patch. Courts of small cottages. One privy for each court, one pump – standing next to the privy. The privy gets full, overflows, water and excrement seep into the drinking water well – '

Tam suddenly felt queasy, a wave of sickness spread from her stomach till she thought she'd have to go outside. It's true, I am tired, she thought. The journey was too much. She bit her lips, clenched her hands tightly and the sickness passed.

'We believe,' Charles was saying, 'such leakages can be the cause of illness, even cholera.'

This was met with hoots of derision. 'Who thinks so?'

'Dr Phillips for one. Dr Phillips – ' and the doctor rose to his feet.

'In London,' the doctor began. 'In one of the poorer parts, Soho, a Dr John Snow, working among the poor, has made a study of these matters. He believes that cholera is spread by the pollution of drinking water by sewage. He will publish his findings shortly.'

'This really is nonsense.' One of the dignitaries of the town was on his feet. 'Everyone knows the cholera is spread by poisoned air. To say the disease is spread by water is really ridiculous.'

'Those open sewers and bad drains are the cause of much illness,' cried the doctor, angry now himself.

'But to install new water pipes . . . Who would pay for all these modern marvels?' asked the dignitary.

'We must all pay – ' began Charles. But this was too much and there was uproar. The meeting wound to its end and nothing was decided, except that no one believed that dirty water caused the cholera.

Outside, Tam said, 'I'm sorry, Charles.'

'We'll win in the end,' he said. 'I only hope that there isn't serious trouble first.'

It was a hot, dry summer, with little rain, and Tam's sickness persisted. At first she thought it was mere tiredness, or simply the smells from the Patch when she went to the wharf. But she didn't go to the wharf every day and still she felt sick, especially in the mornings. She wondered if she should see a doctor.

It was Emmeline who voiced the truth to her, one morning when she refused to go down to breakfast. Her maid took in her pallor, her wretchedness, and asked, 'You wouldn't be – in a certain condition, milady?'

Tam put down the cup of milk she'd been endeavouring to drink. And she knew this had been at the back of her mind all along, and she'd never dared face it. 'Oh, God.'

Emmeline said, troubled, 'Maybe you should go away, milady. That's what ladies often do.'

'Away from him, without his knowing? You know I couldn't, Emmeline. Oh heavens, what am I to do?'

'Maybe you should tell the father,' suggested Emmeline.

'No, it would make too much trouble. Emmeline, I must see a doctor, make sure. Will you ask him to see me?'

'Here, milady?'

'No. I must visit him. See to it, will you?'

Two days later a carriage drew up outside Dr Phillips's dwelling, and a veiled woman, accompanied by her maid, alighted and were shown into a private room. Dr Phillips entered.

'Before I tell you who I am,' Tam said. 'I trust that you will tell no one of my visit, nor of what ensues.'

Dr Phillips sighed. He had heard of wealthy indiscreet ladies who asked physicians this question. 'I assure you your visit is confidential,' he said.

'I have your word on it?'

'I have just given it.'

'Very well.' Tam took off her veil, and told him her symptoms as he examined her.

'I think you may safely say you are enceinte, Lady Fargate.'

'I see.' She re-wrapped her face. 'You understand my concern, Doctor Phillips. I am a busy woman, I run the canals.'

'Well, Lady Fargate, there is no reason why you should stop working for some time yet.'

'You think not?' Tam was surprised. Ladies were usually enjoined to do nothing but rest when in that interesting condition.

She stared, and the doctor, bowing a little, replied, 'If you work on the canals, you may have noticed that the boatwomen work as usual almost to the end. They have no choice, neither do the women in the Patch. If they can do it so can you, your body is exactly the same as theirs.'

Tam suddenly smiled, and the doctor was taken aback. 'You are a man after my own heart,' she said. 'Now give me your bill please, I will pay now.'

The doctor complied, and Tam and Emmeline left.

'Well,' Tam said. 'We know the worst, Emmeline.'

'What will you do, milady?' asked the ever practical Emmeline.

'I don't know yet. I suppose I'll start worrying tomorrow. But now, let's get back to the Manor.'

The scorching summer continued and in August a heat haze lay over Chilverton. Tam rode daily to the wharf, encouraged by Emmeline, nor did she realise for some weeks just what the maid had in mind when she said 'It'll be for the best.' When she finally understood that a miscarriage was considered 'the best', she was momentarily shocked, then wondered if Emmeline might not be right. What else could she do? She could not, dare not, tell Charles, lest in some moment of chivalry he'd leave Parliament and live with her. She was extremely thankful when she heard from Jerome that he'd be delayed in his visit to Chilverton during the Parliamentary recess, he was visiting colleagues in the north. She couldn't let him leave the work he loved, and anyway, what then would become of Juliet? Who would care for her, and Roderick? Would Geoffrey? The man who'd let her down in the first place?

And what of Jamie? As her son came home for the summer holidays Tam knew she feared seeing the condemnation in his eyes. Jamie was a well-grown boy of fourteen now, already showing signs of maturity in his voice and a slight darkness around his upper lip. He was a pleasant boy, Tam told herself, as daily he accompanied her to the wharf, quiet, amenable though only up to a point, for when that point was reached he would be finished for ever with the person who offended him. Since the day Sir William had refused him the stables, he had never spoken to his supposed father unless spoken to, when he would answer civilly but with a veiled insolence in his bearing that Sir William noticed but could not alter, the boy merely turned away. Sir William was infuriated by the same proud independence that he hated in Tam, for Sir William liked people to bend to his will. Tam wondered desperately what Jamie would say, or do, when he found out.

She longed for a confidante, but had no one. She dare not tell Mirrie.

She knew she would not condemn, but she shrank from facing the look in those clear grey eyes. She had, after all, committed adultery, and what did Mirrie know of the dark turbulent passions swirling in Tam's body? Mirrie was happily married to Harry, how could she know of *her* temptations? Tam felt that while the world would punish her for adultery, what they really punished her for was her own nature, for her passion. How much easier to be like Celia, who these days made it plain by her petulance and complaining that she cared nothing for her husband's bed and the continuing child-bearing it brought her. How much easier for women never to know passion – was that why men liked to pretend they didn't?

Round and round in circles went her puzzled mind, befuddled by the heat. One thing was clear though, Sir William must not know. How he would grasp at this chance to triumph over her, finally bend her proud will to his. She wondered sometimes if he guessed why she went to London, made no protest, as if he were waiting . . .

The only possible solution Tam could think of was to go away, have the child and leave it with foster parents. The Duchess would help her. But what possible excuse could she give to Sir William for being away for months . . .?

It was Jerome who reminded her of the meeting of the canal proprietors in Birmingham, asking her if she'd attend. Jerome these days was a little worried about Lady Fargate, she didn't seem well, and there was a strange hunted look in her eyes.

'I'll go,' she said. 'And take Jamie.' She grasped the chance of taking Jamie with her. Partly because she had always intended him to take over the boats when he grew up, partly now, without realising it, she saw it as a means of keeping him with her. Unconsciously perhaps, she also tried to put him in Charles's place.

Jamie was agreeable, he had little else to do in the holidays. Together they set out on the *Princess*, Jim driving the horses, Jamie steering, while Tam sat beside him letting the sun touch her face beneath the sun-bonnet, finding as always healing calm in the placid sailing, knowing a strange joy at the sight of a dragonfly hovering over the water, loving the dark full trees in the distance.

'You've never been to a representatives' meeting, have you?' she asked.

'No, Mama, but tell me all about them.'

'It will be different when you see for yourself. After all, you'll be the representative yourself some day.'

They were nearing the clang and bustle of the city, and she looked round eagerly. Tam liked Birmingham. Its motto was 'Forward', and indeed it forged ahead aggressively to the clanking of thousands of hammers, with smoke and flame pouring from its vitals. Yet it had an intellectual core, and much of the modern thinking had its roots in that city, which produced brilliant scientists, inventors and engineers such as Boulton and Watt, and was breeding great statesmen. It was, in short, a mixture of the new age, as she was herself. So, as she drove through the streets to the meeting hall, she felt revitalised, her tall son beside her. Nothing, she vowed, must interfere with this. Nothing.

The meeting opened. Tam listened with apprehension to the

representative from the Trent and Mersey tell how the opening of a new railway diverted the export trade of porcelain and earthenware from the Potteries to Liverpool. But that was as nothing to the shock the man from Birmingham was to deliver.

He stood up and waited, almost as if he were afraid to speak. Then he cleared his throat nervously. 'We have,' he said, 'made an agreement with the London and Birmingham Railway,' and Tam knew a sense of dread as she remembered Charles's warnings about agreements with railway companies. Someone cried out, 'Shame.'

'It is a good agreement,' the representative said, defensively. 'We subscribe to the new railway, and in return we are guaranteed dividends of four per cent, while the railway will nominate half the Canal Company Committee.'

There were some dubious looks, but the man went on hastily, 'It is water-tight. As long as the Canal Company does not need the guarantee our directors would have the casting vote.'

As Tam struggled to grasp this new development, Jamie got to his feet. 'But,' he said, 'if you at any time did need the guarantee to pay the four per cent, then you would come under railway control.'

There was muttering at this, words of agreement, of the dangerous slippery slope they were treading. 'Make no mistake,' cried one, 'railway control will simply mean the canals being left to decay.'

There was a pause as the representatives digested this, and Tam looked at her son with pride. 'What a good head you have for business,' she said. This was the side she hated, she sometimes thought men liked to make things difficult with their talk of percentages and guarantees and shareholders' meetings, instead of just getting on with things. But men did like to hear themselves talk. Still, they had nothing else to do, they didn't have to wrestle with babies. She'd be glad when she had Jamie with her, to deal with all this nonsense.

Another representative was talking, and she brought her mind back to listen. 'There should be none of this selling out,' he cried. 'We should all act together. We need to form a union, the Merchants' and Manufacturers' Carrying Union, it is the only way to survive. The railway companies are united, let us combine too to meet them as a united body.'

Someone cried, 'Hear, hear,' and the man went on. 'We should link all our carrying operations into one general system, under our own control, not under railway control. We need one Union Carrier, one list of prices and tolls.'

'I agree,' cried Tam.

But the word 'union' frightened many of the representatives. Unions belonged to the new factory workers who were joining together in one body and being penalised for their pains, either by transportation or jail. 'Besides,' said one representative, 'it isn't combination which makes this country great, it is individualism.'

The meeting was adjourned with no motions carried, and Tam and Jamie made their way unhappily back to the boat.

'What did you think?' she asked him as they began the return journey.

'I think,' he said slowly, 'the railways are winning. And the canal men are doing nothing to stop them.'

'Addle-pated fools,' said Tam. 'But I was proud of you, Jamie, you spoke well. You'll be an asset to the Canal Company.' She moved into the little cabin and busied herself making a meal. 'Come and eat, Jim,' she called. 'Tie her up, let's sit here awhile, it's so pleasant.' And they sat as the violet dusk fell around them, and the sweet scent of new-mown hay came from the meadows.

Tam still visited Juliet though their intimacy had been lost. She never asked her sister about Geoffrey, nor did she see him again on the boat. She reflected sometimes that if it hadn't been for Juliet none of the present muddle would have happened, the baby that swelled her waistline would not be in existence, or at least, not in this particular way. Yet she could not blame Juliet, nor ever come to dislike her as she had always disliked Celia. There was still a sweetness about her that disarmed opposition. And she loved Roderick dearly.

September was still hot. Jamie was back at school and as Tam entered her sister's house she saw Juliet was home. They sat down for a few moments talking, then Juliet said in her usual way, 'I'm going down to the Patch.'

Tam sighed, as she studied her sister. She must be thirty-three now, yet there was still a youthful air about her; Tam refused to use the word 'childish'. 'They need me, Tam, there's much illness there,' Juliet continued.

'Still?' asked Tam.

'It's the cholera,' said Esther, who had just come in.

'Oh no. Are you sure?'

'Dr Phillips says so. Two people died yesterday.'

'Then you mustn't go, Juliet,' Tam pleaded. But to no avail. Juliet merely put on her bonnet and went to the door. 'Let me at least take Roderick back to the Manor,' called Tam.

'No, no,' said Juliet, turning. 'I couldn't bear to be away from him.'

She went out, and Esther said grimly, 'She isn't quite responsible, milady. She don't understand.'

'But we can't take Roddy away against her will,' said Tam.

'Nay, she'd break her heart.'

'Maybe it'll soon be over,' Tam said hopefully.

But the outbreak wasn't soon over, it was one of the worst in living memory. Soon every house in the Patch had one or more cholera victims. People were buried hurriedly, at night, in a mass grave. Dr Phillips worked hard, Charles came down, still the disease spread.

'I've stopped running the packet boat,' Harry said to Tam. 'No one wants to take pleasure trips now.'

'The boaters are all right though, aren't they?'

'Yes.'

'I am going to nurse the sick,' said Mirrie.

'Oh, Mirrie, do be careful.'

225

'I shall be most careful. I have seen Dr Phillips, he advises me not to drink water from the pump in the Patch. I shall not do that.'

'But what about our supply on the wharf?' Tam asked.

'That must be all right.'

Tam privately had misgivings about the doctor's thoughts on water spreading infection. Surely it was more reasonable to suppose it was spread through the air, as people said.

'I suppose I should help too,' she said. 'But I've had no experience of sickness.'

'Thou hast enough to do running the boats,' said Mirrie. 'Cargoes still have to be carried. No, Tamarisk, don't try to do too much.' For one moment Tam wondered if Mirrie's words had another meaning, if she could possibly know . . .

'Your children, Mirrie . . .'

'Margery and Ruth are away at school, and Robin is working farther along the canal, overseeing some maintenance. But we are in God's hands,' and Tam envied her her calm.

She was very worried about Juliet and went to her house, finding her absent as usual. Roddie came home from school and sat listlessly in a corner. Tam didn't take much notice, he never did say very much; not until he suddenly ran to the privy out in the yard. And when he came in his face was ashen, he was shivering, could hardly stand.

'Roddy,' cried Tam, her heart sinking, 'are you ill?'

'I've got pains,' the boy said. 'In my stomach.'

Esther came running, between them they got the boy to bed, doubled up now with pain. Tam ran to the Patch for Dr Phillips and Juliet.

She found them both together at the bedside of a dying victim. It wasn't a pretty sight. The room stank of vomit and excrement, the woman was screaming in agony. Her face was pallid, yet beads of sweat were on her forehead, she looked shrivelled, like an old woman. Her limbs suddenly went into convulsions, and the screaming stopped with such a suddenness that Tam stood open-mouthed.

'Is she better then?' she asked.

'No,' said Dr Phillips, curtly. 'She's dead.'

'Please,' Tam said. 'Come with me. It's Roddy.'

Slowly Juliet turned from the dead woman on the bed, her eyes dilated with horror. 'No,' she cried. 'Not Roddy.'

'Oh, Juliet, why didn't you let him come to the Manor?' Tam asked.

Dr Phillips said sharply, 'Hush. I'll come along in a minute. Take Mrs Waring, please, Lady Fargate.'

Tam led Juliet outside. 'Come,' she said. 'It'll be all right, you'll see. Come.' For Juliet seemed as if she couldn't hurry. 'It's been too much for you, all this, you'll have to take it easy . . .' She half led, half pulled her sister along the street, to the wharf where a group of children watched, fingers in mouths. They walked to the doorway, when Juliet collapsed.

'Oh my God,' said Tam. 'She's tired, isn't she? She must be. It can't be the cholera . . .'

'Can't it?' asked Esther, darkly, and she lifted Juliet bodily in her strong arms and took her to bed.

Dr Phillips arrived soon after, and Charles was with him. He looked at both patients, but lingered with Roddy. 'It's cholera all right,' he said. 'Now, who's to nurse them?'

'I shall, of course,' said Esther.

'And I,' said Tam.

'No, Tam,' protested Charles, and Dr Phillips gave him a sharp look, but said nothing.

'If you will tell us what to do, Doctor,' said Tam.

He gave instructions. 'Don't give them this water to drink,' he ended. 'Get some from another pump.'

'But we're not in the Patch,' said Charles.

'Your water may be affected. Get more. Don't use this.'

He went out, and Esther said, 'I can't see that it makes any difference, milady. I don't believe the water has anything to do with it.'

'You heard what the doctor said,' Tam told her sharply. 'You'll have to fetch it from the pump on the wharf.'

'But that's a long walk – '

'I know.'

The next few hours were, Tam thought afterwards, a horrifying nightmare. For years she would remember the boy's cries of agony as the pain in his stomach and limbs increased; remembered his eyes, the look of despair, she had seen that look often when in the grounds of the Manor she'd chanced upon an animal caught in one of Sir William's many traps, and she'd steeled herself to kill the creature to end its suffering.

She bathed Roderick, she sat by his bed, she held his poor shrivelled face as he vomited. She stood up stiffly as Dr Phillips called again, and went to the door because she could no longer stand the boy's pain. When she returned he was lying still. She looked at the still lifeless form, and gasped 'He can't be . . .? Not little Roddy.'

'I'm sorry,' Dr Phillips said softly.

'But so quickly! He was all right a few hours ago – '

'It happens like that sometimes. Now, why don't you go home, Lady Fargate? You are tired – '

'No, not now. I must look after Juliet.'

Then Charles was with her, taking her down the stairs, producing a bottle of brandy, pouring out a small glassful.

She drank it gratefully, and said, 'Will you tell them at the Manor, Charles, I'm staying here still Juliet is better?'

'If you promise you'll rest tonight, Tam. You've had a shock.'

'I promise. I'll sleep in the parlour.'

'Do that. They'll come later to fetch Roddy. I'll be with them . . . I'll see you're not disturbed.'

She nodded, and he left. Alone she stood, then tiptoed upstairs again and stood by Roddy's bed, looking down in bewilderment at the boy's face. How could it be that Roddy, so young, so innocent . . . he'd done nothing, ever, to hurt anyone, he'd just been quiet, sitting with the mother who loved him. The same feeling she'd known when she'd seen her father's grave came over her, so *small*. So too was Roddy small, unnoticed by the world, so too would he go into a small grave. But no he wouldn't, even that would be denied him, he'd be put with the others. Why had he died? And how would they tell Juliet? And suddenly she was weeping, for all the cruelty and sorrow in the world, and the injustice of it all. She stumbled back to the kitchen, made up the fire. There was a harsh knock at the door, she went to open it and found a figure standing outlined in the gloom.

'Can I come in?' a voice said.

She said startled, 'Geoffrey,' and stood back to let him enter. 'You heard?' she asked. 'About Roddy?'

'Charles told me. May I see him?'

Without a word she led him to the boy's bedroom, left him alone and sat waiting in the large kitchen. When Geoffrey returned his face was ravaged with grief, he seemed almost beside himself. He stood, bewildered, and she said, 'Sit down, Geoffrey.'

He stumbled to a chair. Tam took the brandy bottle Charles had left and pouring out a large measure handed it to him. He swallowed it in one gulp.

'I loved that boy,' he said thickly.

'D – did you, Geoffrey?'

'Of course. He was my son. My only son. I was going to take him into the business, you know.'

'I had heard.'

'He was a nice little boy, wasn't he?'

'Yes, Geoffrey.' And now tears threatened to engulf her again, her throat ached.

'Juliet used to bring him to the house sometimes, and I talked to him. My *nephew* . . . I wanted to give them money, but Juliet wouldn't take it . . . it would have looked as though – ' he broke off. 'But I bought him presents.'

'Yes, I'm sure you did all you could,' she tried to reassure him.

'I must see Juliet,' he said.

'Sit for a moment, Geoffrey, you've had a shock. We all have.' Waves of exhaustion were washing over Tam, she wanted to lie down. Yet she could not leave Geoffrey in this state. She handed him more brandy.

'I can't lose her as well.' He looked up at her desperately.

Tam said, amazed, 'Then you do care for her?'

He bowed his head. 'Yes, I care,' he said slowly. Then almost violently, he continued, 'Why shouldn't I care for her? She is the only person who loves me as I am.'

Tam stared, saying nothing, but for the first time in her life she felt pity for Geoffrey, forced to work beyond his capabilities, pressed on by wife and mother – and possibly his father – striving for success in this new world where success was so important. He would perhaps have been happier sitting with the books, the accounts, the ordering, leaving the running of the factory to someone else. *She loves me as I am*. What more could a person ask?

He said at last in a low voice, 'I should have married her.'

Now Tam sat down too. 'I don't think – ' she began.

'Yes, I should. And you know why I didn't? Because I am a coward.'

'Oh, Geoffrey, don't torture yourself this way,' she said.

'Charles married her.'

She moved to him now, touched his arm. 'I don't think Juliet would have married you,' she said, and wondered if it was true, if in the beginning he'd approached her, before Juliet knew Celia loved him . . . She shook her head as if to clear it. 'You know Juliet isn't up to entertaining,' she said. 'It wouldn't have done for you, Geoffrey, you know it wouldn't. Juliet knew that. She knew you'd make Celia happy.'

'Do I? Celia's always grumbling.'

'We all grumble,' Tam admitted. 'But this I tell you, Geoffrey. Celia was happy to marry you, she loved you, she would have been destroyed if you'd not married her. Come, Geoffrey, don't tear yourself apart this way.'

He said unsteadily, 'I didn't really love her at the beginning – not either of them. It was only later, when I saw more of Juliet . . . and she had Roddy.' He stood up. 'Where is she?' And Tam led him to the room upstairs.

After a while Geoffrey came down and Tam saw him to the door. On the step he halted. 'She will get better?' he asked pathetically.

'Yes, I'm sure she will.' And he stumbled out into the night.

When Tam woke in the morning her tiredness had gone, and she ran upstairs. 'How is she?' she asked Esther, fearfully, at the door.

'Not as bad as some,' said Esther.

'She doesn't know about – Roddy?'

' 'Course not. They took him away last night. They were quiet, she didn't hear.'

Nor did I. Tam averted her eyes from the little room that had been Roddy's and went in to her sister.

Tam didn't sleep again. For two days and nights she helped nurse Juliet. Two days and nights of restless fever, of vomiting and pain. Charles came in and begged her to rest, she refused. Somehow it was terribly important that Juliet should live. Dr Phillips came often, tired himself.

'She's holding on remarkably well,' he said.

'She seemed always so frail,' marvelled Tam.

'Yes, well, it's like that sometimes. Big strong people are often the first to go. If she can hold on through another night I think she'll have turned the corner.'

Tam sat that night, with Esther and Charles. Juliet tossed and turned, her fever seemed to mount. Then, as the cold grey dawn began to spread over the sky Esther leaned over the bed.

'This is the time they go if they're going,' she said. 'There's a change.'

Tam touched her sister's forehead. 'She's cooler,' she gasped and, remembering Roddy's pallor, 'Is she – '

'She's breathing easy,' said Esther. 'I think she's turned the corner.'

229

They waited, hardly daring to breathe as the light deepened, and Esther put out the lamp. 'She's getting better,' she pronounced.

Relief washed over Tam. Someone came to the door to fetch Charles, but she hardly saw him go. Exhausted, she went to the door and stood outside, gulping in the fresh air. Below was the clamour of the wharf, the boats working as usual, it seemed incredible that life could go on normally while tragedy relentlessly stalked their lives.

She returned to the room, and now the tiredness was on her again. It's because I'm pregnant, she thought, but I had to save Juliet. She slumped into an armchair.

Esther gave her a sharp look. 'Don't you feel well?'

'I'm all right.' Tam opened her weary eyes. 'You don't seem to get the cholera,' she said in wonder.

'No,' said Esther in satisfaction. 'And I drunk the water too. I told you it wasn't the water.'

'No, we mustn't drink the water,' said Tam. Her head seemed to be spinning round.

'It won't hurt in tea. I fetch water from the wharf pump to drink, but the other won't hurt you in tea. Tea's different.'

Tam hardly heard. She felt a violent constricting pain in her stomach. It must be the baby. And she didn't want to lose the baby. Not now. She'd seen too much death. And it was Charles's baby. She vaguely saw Esther coming towards her. Then she fell to the floor.

'Yes, it's the cholera,' said Dr Phillips when he arrived. 'She mustn't stay here, she must go back to the Manor. Wait, I saw Sir William driving through Chilverton, I'll get him.'

Esther made fresh tea and waited. When a knock came at the door she opened it. Sir William stood there, a handkerchief over his mouth. 'Is she ready?' he asked.

'I'll see. Come in.'

'I don't want to come in. I'll wait in the carriage.'

Esther went back to the bedroom, returned shortly to Sir William. 'She's not ready,' she said.

'What do you mean, not ready?'

'She's being sick,' said Esther, crudely. 'When she's better I'll bring her.'

'Oh all right. Don't be long though, it's getting cold.'

'Wait a minute, I'll fetch you something to drink.' She went back, returned with a cup of tea. 'Here you are, sir, drink this.'

'No thank you.'

'This won't hurt you, it's tea. Tea isn't water.'

'You don't think I believe that tarradiddle about water causing sickness, do you?' asked Sir William. 'Never heard such nonsense in my life.' And he took the drink.

Within half an hour Tam was bundled up and carried out by the coachman. She lay, white and still, until they reached the Manor. The maids scattered as they saw her. 'Oh, sir,' one cried, less terrified of her harsh master than of the dreaded sickness. 'Is it the cholera? Oh, sir, we'll all catch it.'

The coachman, carrying Tam, hesitated, his eyes bulging with fear. 'Will I catch it, sir?' he asked.

'Oh give her to me, you fool. Now, out of my way.' And, shouldering his burden, Sir William carried Tam to her room.

Now the days were a mixture of agony and pain and vile stomach upsets. Tam saw faces vaguely around her, saw Dr Phillips, tense and white, bending over her , and she thought she was going to die. Then the pain returned and with it blessed unconsciousness.

Then the day came when she was quite lucid. 'Why, Mirrie,' she said, recognising the face above her. 'You're here?'

'Yes, Tamarisk.'

'It's the cholera, isn't it? Mirrie, you must not nurse me. Think of your family – '

'I do, dear, but they want me to be with thee. Thou hast done so much for us.'

And Tam sank back. 'Did Charles come?'

'He came to ask about thee,' Mirrie said. 'Sir William didn't think it wise for him to come in.'

'Oh, Mirrie,' she said, remembering. 'Mirrie, where is the doctor?'

'What is it, Tam? Thou art getting better.'

'I want to see the doctor.'

'He'll be coming tomorrow.'

When he called the next day, Dr Phillips said, 'Yes, Lady Fargate, I'm afraid you lost the baby.' He sat by the bedside. 'That's why you were so ill.'

She thought of the worry it had been, Emmeline saying 'It's for the best'. And yet it had been Charles's child . . . Two tears squeezed themselves from her eyes, and she blinked them away and tried to appear lighthearted about it, to pretend not to care, as she always did. 'Oh well,' she said, 'there's always tomorrow.'

Dr Phillips looked grave. 'I'm afraid,' he said, 'there won't be any more babies . . . that's why you were so ill, not the cholera, you tossed that off quite lightly.'

She was silent, and he asked, 'How old are you?'

'Thirty-six.'

'Well,' he said, with an attempt at cheerfulness, 'it probably wouldn't have happened anyway, your having more children, I mean.'

'No, I'm getting to a great age, aren't I?'

The doctor rose. Tam said dully, 'Does Sir William know?'

'No, we thought it better not to tell him in the circumstances.'

'In the circumstances. What circumstances?'

Dr Phillips looked at her. 'Sir William also took the cholera,' he said.

'He did? Then – he's ill?'

'Yes.'

'Very ill?'

'He is dead.'

There was silence now in the room, she could hear the ticking of the clock. She whispered, 'So many times I wished him dead. So often I said I'd kill him. And now I have . . .'

Chapter Five

In the event it was quite easy to trace Sir William's son. Sir Lewis, as he now was, had been wise enough to leave his address with the family lawyer: he now owned a plantation in Virginia, was married, with two sons. He wrote that he would be back as soon as possible, but this would take some time, he would first have to dispose of his property, then wait for a decent ship to bring he and his family home. In the meantime he hoped the Dowager Lady Fargate would carry on as usual.

'My God,' said Tam. 'I'm not going to be called a dowager, not for any money. I don't particularly want to be Lady Fargate, and certainly not *that* . . .'

Nor could life carry on as normal. Outwardly the boats ran as always, Sir William's company ran the railway, but she herself had changed. They all had, the whole family, perhaps the whole town. No one could experience the traumatic events of the last weeks and be no different. Juliet was so utterly shocked by the death of Roddy that they feared for her reason. Tam begged her to stay at the Manor, but she refused to leave the little house on the wharf where she sat, white and silent, no longer even going to the Patch.

Tam had not seen Charles in private since the tragedies. She felt the loss of the baby keenly, far more than she'd expected; she could not share this with Charles, so did not want to see him. When he sent a note through Jerome asking to see her, she refused. She had been left too vulnerable, she needed time to replace her armour, to become again the old uncaring Tam. So she sat alone in her grief, waiting for the new Fargate family to arrive. Spring had come early, cowslips and primroses nestled in the woods, the flag-irises stood tall at the canal edge. And when, in May, Tam heard the nightingales singing, she felt a little of her old energy returning and felt ready to face the world again.

It was nearly a year before Sir Lewis and his family arrived, bringing with them mountains of luggage. Tam welcomed them into the Manor and she took them to the rooms she'd prepared, gave them a meal, then they sat in the drawing room taking stock of each other.

233

Sir Lewis was a tall, clean-cut man in his late forties, with little resemblance to his father. His wife, Georgiana, was a dark southern beauty with a roguish face and sparkling eyes. Their sons, Stephen and Francis, were eighteen and fifteen respectively.

'Well,' Sir Lewis said, looking round appreciatively. 'It's been a long time since I was here.' He turned to Tam. 'What am I to call you? It seems a mite ridiculous to call you Step-mother when I am sure you are much younger than I.'

'It seems very ridiculous,' said Tam. 'And Dowager seems even more so. Please call me Tamarisk.'

She turned to Georgiana. 'And how do you think you'll like England?' she asked.

'It's a little cold,' said Georgiana. 'Whatever is it like in winter?'

'Can be grim,' Tam smiled. 'Snow and frost, at least, some years. You'll soon get used to it. Would you like to look over the estate? I can send for the carriage.'

'I would,' said Sir Lewis with alacrity, and so they bowled along the green park, the villages, the farms and cottages belonging to the squire. Tam introduced the family to the tenants, and the women bobbed a curtsey. 'My oh my, do they always do that?' asked Georgiana.

'Do you find it very different?' Tam asked as they returned to the drawing room. 'What was your plantation like?'

'Very big,' said Sir Lewis. 'The settlers were often younger sons, kinsmen of the gentry, and they wanted to run things as they do here. I was only sixteen when I went, my mother had recently died, and she left me her jewellery, which I sold. So I had a little money and was soon able to buy a partnership on a small plantation, getting a loan too, of course. I prospered, later bought my own place, and – ' he smiled – 'married and settled down. Georgiana was a Page of Virginia, a very well-connected family.'

'It was a lovely life out there,' said Georgiana, a little wistfully. 'Do you have many balls and parties here, Tamarisk?'

'Sir William didn't,' Tam replied. 'But you will be able to please yourself, of course. I suppose you'll miss your home at first.'

'Well, yes,' said Georgiana. 'But we always knew we'd return here, Lewis being the heir. They tell me you have a son,' she ended, curiously.

'Yes,' Tam said, a little abruptly. 'He's at school at the moment.'

'We'll have to send Francis to school,' said Lewis. 'And Stephen to Oxford.' They paused, and Tam gazed at the brothers, both tall, yet so unalike. Stephen resembled his father, Francis was a thin-faced, studious-looking boy with straight black hair and a shy manner.

'Tomorrow,' Sir Lewis said, 'I shall visit the lawyer about the reading of the will. I suppose it's pretty straightforward.'

'Do you think Jamie should be here?' asked Georgiana.

'I'm sure he should,' said Sir Lewis, briskly. 'Shall you send for him, Tamarisk? I'll put the lawyer off till he comes.'

A week later, they sat in the library, the Fargates, Tam and Jamie, facing Mr Benton, the lawyer.

The will was brief. The canal belonged to Sir William's second wife, Tamarisk. Everything else, the estate in its entirety, all the moneys and income, went to his son, Lewis. There was no other provision for Tam and none for Jamie. The lawyer put his papers away and left.

Sir Lewis turned to Tam, a little perturbed. 'I say, I'm sorry . . . it seems very harsh. How could he do such a thing?'

'It doesn't matter,' said Tam, colourlessly. 'After his death the estate ran as usual, you will see the figures. There are no debts.' But she was shocked, even knowing how much Sir William had hated her.

'No, but look here . . .' Sir Lewis seemed more English in his agitation. 'He can't leave you without a penny, and his son. You must let me make you an allowance. Both of you.'

Tam hesitated, looking at the boys. 'May I speak to you alone?' she asked.

'Of course. Jamie, you know the place, why don't you show my boys around? And Georgie . . .?'

'I'll go with them,' Georgiana said, and left in a graceful flurry of skirts.

Tam said, when they were alone, 'I think I should tell you, though I would be grateful if you would treat the matter in confidence . . . Jamie is not Sir William's son.'

'Ah.' Lewis adjusted his cravat, embarrassed.

'Sir William knew,' Tam went on. 'So don't think you're obligated in any way.'

'But – '

'I shall manage,' Tam said. 'I have the boats.'

'The boats?'

'The canal,' Tam explained. 'That's all I wanted, really, so you see I haven't lost out.'

'But where will you live? Of course,' he added hastily, 'you're welcome to stay here till you find a place . . . I naturally thought there'd be an allowance to enable you to find a home.'

'Thank you,' Tam said. 'But I won't need to stay.'

'You see, Georgiana will, I know, plan to start entertaining . . . There doesn't seem to be any sort of Dower House – '

'No,' Tam said. 'Sir William was only a squire, not a belted earl.' She laughed suddenly, and Sir Lewis stared at the sudden charm, previously hidden. 'I'm laughing to think that I'm a Dowager, and a grandmother too.' She thought of the baby she'd lost and the shadow returned to her face. 'Don't worry, we'll be all right.' She was aware that Georgiana had crept into the room, and Tam had no idea how long she'd been there, how much she'd heard.

'I feel,' Georgiana said in her southern drawl, 'we're turning you out of your home.'

'This has never been my home,' Tam said. 'I do not, and never have, liked being here. Forgive me, Lewis, but your father and I weren't exactly happy.'

'I'd have been surprised if you were,' Lewis said candidly. 'I know I

235

wasn't. He beat me so often when I was a child that I never forgave him. He was brutal to my mother. He drove her into her grave, without a doubt. I never forgave him for that, either. When she died I took off for America.'

Tam said nothing. Sir Lewis paced the room. 'It wasn't quite true about the jewellery,' he said. 'My mother did leave it to me, but my father wouldn't allow it – all his wife's property belonged to him. So I stole it, then ran away. I don't know if any fuss was ever made about the loss, he could have branded me a thief.' He smiled sombrely. 'That's why I couldn't ever communicate . . . so do people like my father make criminals of us all. I'm surprised he left me so much money.'

'You contacted your father's lawyer,' Tam said. 'Do you think Sir William ever knew where you were?'

Lewis shrugged. 'I don't know. I asked Benton to keep it secret, but knowing my father, he'd extract it from him if he wished. For though I left my father, I had no intention of giving up my inheritance! The Manor belongs to me, and to my sons and that he could not prevent.'

Tam smiled at him and stood up to go, but Lewis stopped her.

'Forgive me, Tamarisk, but does Jamie know what you've just told me?'

She hesitated. 'No,' she admitted.

'Then – don't you think he should? You must explain why he's been ignored.'

I don't see why . . . let him blame Sir William, she thought, yet she knew he was right. Jamie must know. 'I'll see,' she said. 'Goodnight, Lewis.'

It was the push she needed. As she sat in her room she wondered why she'd waited so long, why she hadn't guessed he wouldn't leave her any money. Why hadn't she suspected that this was behind Sir William's talk of borrowing money for boats against his death? He would have forced Mr Benton to tell him of Lewis's whereabouts, he *knew* . . . She shuddered as she thought of what might have happened. Any debts would have come out of the estate, she supposed, but that would merely have made an enemy of Lewis. Maybe he could have found a way of not paying, she didn't know the law, in which case she'd have been left up to her ears in debt, ruined, as her father had been. As Sir William had intended. She was shocked at his deviousness. Her own mistakes were made out of impetuosity, of hastening into a project without much thought, never from a pre-conceived desire to harm anyone. Now she had to face reality. She possessed the canal, but nothing else. She was back where she started.

She wondered tiredly why he'd even left the canal to her. Perhaps in this alone he had retained some sense of honour. Or was it because he preferred her to lose slowly, to sink into debt, as he was sure she would do. Well, her head shot up, she would *not*. The Chilverton Canal would not close, nor be sold to the railways. She would carry on.

When she went down to breakfast the next day she had made up her mind. 'It's time I went,' she told Sir Lewis. 'I have work to do.'

'But where will you go?'

'For the moment to my boat. It will be like a holiday.'

'What sort of boat?' asked Sir Lewis, dubiously.

Tam laughed, and he was struck by the change laughter made.

'A canal boat,' she said.

'Whatever is a canal boat?' asked Georgiana, curiously. 'I'm sure it sounds most uncomfortable.'

'I assure you it isn't,' Tam said. 'I've lived on it before, we all did when my father died.'

'Please don't rush away,' Georgiana pleaded. 'I feel as though I'm turning you out of your home.'

'But that is part of the English system,' said Tam. 'And you're not turning me out, Georgiana, I want to go.'

'Well, you will come and stay with us, won't you? And Jamie. He must come whenever he likes.'

'Thank you, we will.'

Jamie spoke for the first time. 'What will I do, Mama?'

'We must talk, Jamie. Shall we go outside?'

They walked together down the stone steps, along the path between the carefully tended lawns. Tam murmured, 'Not a single bequest to any of his staff . . .'

'Mama, I must leave school, find work . . .' Jamie said.

'No, not yet. Your fees are paid till the end of the year when you will be sixteen.'

'But – '

'Jamie, I must tell you something first.'

'Yes?'

She walked up and down in agitation. Oh please, don't let him turn away from me . . . 'It is best you know . . . I hope you won't think badly of me . . .'

He stood, a tall handsome youth, hands in pockets, waiting.

She stopped her pacing, faced him. 'You know we have to leave here?'

'Of course.'

'I expect you think Sir William has been harsh to you?'

Jamie shrugged. 'He was a harsh man.'

'Did you like him very much, Jamie?'

'No.'

She drew a breath. 'Then what I am about to say won't perhaps be too much of a shock. You see . . . he wasn't your father.' She looked at him fearfully. 'Do you understand?'

'Of course I understand, Mama.'

'I didn't know how much of these matters you knew.'

'Dear Mama,' he laughed, 'I was running round the stables since I could walk. I know all about mating.'

Tam blinked.

'And I heard the men talking about my – about Sir William. He wasn't well liked, so I can understand your preferring someone else.'

'You're taking it very calmly.'

He shrugged, but didn't speak. And they both started walking again.

'Who is my father?' Jamie asked then.

'Charles Waring.'

'H'm.' The boy nodded as if, Tam thought, he were studying the pedigree of an animal. 'He's not bad, I suppose,' and this, from Jamie, was praise indeed.

'I – I'm sorry, Jamie.'

'Did this happen after your marriage or before?' Jamie asked. 'I know I was born pretty quickly after the event.'

'Before,' she said.

'Then don't apologise to me, Mama, when I was no doubt the cause of your marriage.'

She laughed then, from pure relief. 'Oh Jamie. You take things so calmly. Unlike – ' she broke off, and he did not question her. 'Charles did not know then,' she said. 'And I did not tell him because of harming his career. He had married Juliet out of pity, Roderick is not his child. We have made a terrible muddle. But – we love each other, Jamie, Charles and I,' and he nodded. 'Well,' she went on, 'now to the future. I shall live on the boat for the time being.'

'Will you manage? Do you have enough money?'

'Yes, to both questions. You can see the books at any time. Then later on, when you're finished school, you will be able to work with me.'

'Doing what, Mama?'

'Why, to manage the canal, of course.'

'Will there be enough money to support us both?'

'I have to pay an agent.'

'Mama,' Jamie paused. 'I'm not sure that I would want to work on the canals.'

Tam stopped walking again, and her ready temper rose. At times this son of hers could be too independent. 'You think your Latin and Greek make you too much of a gentleman to work with your hands?' she asked tartly.

'No, Mama.'

'It's what I have planned for us, Jamie. No! No more now, I beg. When the time comes I am sure you will realise that the Calder Boats are as much a part of your heritage as, in other circumstances, a manor might be. You have a good head for business, you'd be of such help.'

'We will wait, Mama,' he said firmly, standing tall and unbending.

Then they walked together into the house.

It was good to be back on the boat, even though she had to leave most of her clothes at the Manor. Jamie was back at school and Tam joyfully sailed along the water, noting the kingcups in the marshy areas, seeing the return of the swallows. Mirrie and Harry welcomed her back, and this brought a temporary shadow to her joy, as she remembered the sadness.

'I visit Juliet most days, Tamarisk, she is very downhearted,' Mirrie said.

'I know. I asked her to come and live with me, but she will not. She still grieves. Oh Mirrie, how can there be a God at all, to act so? To take little Roddy. Poor Juliet, she loved him so . . .'

'Hush, Tam.'

'I wish I could be like you, Mirrie, never questioning.'

'Do you think I never question, Tamarisk? I saw the poor dying of cholera too. But before I blame God, I remember that so much suffering is caused by man.'

'Yes, maybe. But when it harms the innocent – '

Mirrie sat, stroking Tam's hair lovingly. 'In time people will realise that Charles was right about the unclean water,' Mirrie said. 'So good will come in the end.'

'Yes, I suppose so. How are your family, Mirrie?'

'They are very well. Robin is here, as thou knowest, helping Jerome as wharfinger, and in charge of the warehouses.'

'I must see him.'

'Yes. And Margery is getting married. We wondered if thou wouldst like to attend the service?'

'I'd love to, Mirrie.'

'It will be quite plain, the couple just affirm their commitment to each other.'

Tam had never attended a Friends' Meeting House before, and she dressed carefully in her black gown, and somehow Mirrie had persuaded Juliet to accompany them. So they entered the little building where the bride and groom sat surrounded by relatives and friends.

Then the couple stood, and held hands.

'Friends,' said the tall young man who was Margery's affianced, 'I take thee, my friend, Margery Earp, to be my wife, promising, through Divine Assistance, to be unto her a loving and faithful husband until it shall please the Lord by death to separate us . . .'

Juliet was crying, and Tam whispered, 'Do you want to leave?'

'No, it is beautiful.'

Tam thought it must be wonderful to be married to the man you loved, and wondered if that was why so many women cried at weddings. Thinking of what might have been . . .

The next day she walked along the wharf to Jerome's office, and he too welcomed her, noting with relief that she was taking an interest in life again.

'How are things?' she asked anxiously.

'Not bad at all. We're still delivering the Milden coal. Harry's packet boat's doing well again.'

'I wonder,' she said, 'if I should start another packet boat run. Somewhere across country where the trains don't run.'

'It's an idea,' he said. 'Of course you have to remember that things perhaps grew a little slack on the railway with Sir William gone.'

'Yes. And we don't know how Sir Lewis will turn out.'

'They give good reports of him in Chilverton,' said Jerome. 'It seems he's getting all his cottages repaired, all his farms . . .'

'Good,' she said absently. 'Sir William wasn't the best of landlords.'

'And talking of Sir Lewis, I think I can see his carriage pulling up outside the wharf.'

'You do. And – ' Tam craned her neck ' – his wife. I'd better see what they want. I'll talk with you later, Jerome.'

She stepped out of the office and walked towards them, smiling. 'Have you come to visit me?' she asked.

'A letter came for you to the Manor,' said Lewis. 'We thought we'd bring it. And yes, we wanted to see your boat.'

'Come aboard,' invited Tam, and she led them down the steps, into the saloon.

'Well, isn't it just cute,' cooed Georgiana. 'And so tiny! I declare, Tam, this is just the daintiest thing I ever did set eyes on.'

Tam smiled as Georgiana endeavoured to sit down, her ample skirts almost catching on the seat opposite. 'Do you like my new outfit?' Georgiana asked. 'We went to London last week, and I assure you these are all the mode.'

'However do you support them?' wondered Tam.

'The skirt? There is a lining made partly of horsehair, it's called a crinoline.'

'Good heavens.'

'And they say skirts will go wider yet.'

Sir Lewis handed Tam the letter and she put it on one side. 'I've been hearing good reports of your work on the cottages and farms,' she said.

'I was disgusted,' said Sir Lewis, frankly. 'As I am with the conditions in the Patch. I didn't realise things had got so bad. As I remember, when I left, the hand-loom weavers were doing quite well.'

'Yes, much better than now,' Tam said. 'They only earn a few shillings a week. But still they hang on.'

'Their ribbons are beautiful,' Georgiana put in. 'I ordered some immediately.'

Tam had been making tea, and she handed cups to Lewis and his wife, cutting a small cake as she did so.

'What, you do your own cooking?' asked Georgiana.

'For the moment,' Tam said. 'I confess it isn't my favourite pastime. But I might start packet boat services again, then I'd employ a woman.'

'Tamarisk, I have been looking into the business side of things since I've been here,' Sir Lewis said.

'Yes?'

'And that includes the railway.'

'I see.'

'Now.' He cleared his throat. 'We are friends, Tamarisk, and I want us to stay that way. But – and I hope you won't take this amiss – I shall run the railway as before.'

'Of course,' said Tam.

'Which will mean we are working in competition.'

'Yes, Lewis, it will.'

Sir Lewis looked out of the window, watching a boat edge its way out of the lay-by. 'Tamarisk,' he said, 'would we not get on better working together?'

'In what way?' she asked.

'Say, an amalgamation. We could come to an agreement. For example, your company could subscribe to the railway and in return we'd guarantee your dividends.'

'The Birmingham Canal did that,' she said. 'and it was pointed out – by my son – that if they ever needed to use the guarantee the canal would come under railway control.'

He showed his astonishment. 'I see you are a business woman,' he said, and she could read his thoughts, imagine a woman understanding that.

'I'm sorry,' she said. 'I wouldn't dream of it.'

'Then why don't you sell outright? I'd give you a good price. You'd have enough money to buy whatever you wanted. A house maybe . . .'

'Really, Lewis,' protested Georgiana, 'that sounds as if we've turned her out of her home and then forced her into this deal.'

'Nobody's forcing me into anything,' Tam returned. 'I have my home on the boat. There isn't a house anywhere I'd like to buy – except one, and that's not on the market.'

'The competition will be fierce, Tamarisk.'

'I know.'

Sir Lewis's pleasant face looked troubled. 'It's just that I don't like to be hard on you, being a woman – '

'Oh come,' said Tam, 'what has my being a woman got to do with it?'

'But if you lose everything, what will you do?'

She smiled. 'I am not going to lose. My canal will not close. I am willing to wager, Lewis, that in a hundred years' time there will still be boats on my canal.'

'I fear not,' said Lewis.

'And we certainly won't be alive in nineteen hundred and forty-eight to see,' Georgiana pointed out.

'Well,' Sir Lewis rose, 'we must be on our way.' He turned to Tam. 'If you change your mind – '

'I shan't,' said Tam, confidently.

They left, and Tam sat down thoughtfully, her mind on where to start the new run, somewhere the trains would not go to. Eventually she settled on Stratford-on-Avon.

After a while she remembered the letter Sir Lewis had brought, and picked it up studying the handwriting. It seemed vaguely familiar. She tore it open and read in surprise.

'My dear Tam,
'I have not heard from you for so long, and you have never been to see me that I am wondering what has happened. You wrote to tell me of Sir William's demise, and your own illness, and I badly wanted to come to visit you, but alas, I have been ill myself. Nothing to worry

about, don't get alarmed, but I am an old woman now, do you know I shall soon be eighty? And I have been suffering from gout, would you believe such an appalling thing? I am not bedridden, just stuck with a foot that will not let itself be moved.

'So dear Tamarisk, if you can, come to visit. If not, let me know how you are.'

'Your sincere friend, Eleanor Carminster.'

Tam dropped the letter, horrified. The Duchess ill, and she hadn't known. Her dear friend . . .

What have I been thinking about? she wondered. All these months . . . it's as though I were living in a dream.

She went to the deck. 'Jim,' she called.

'Yes, milady?' Jim emerged from a nearby boat.

'I have to go to London, immediately.'

'On the boat, milady?'

'I think not,' she said regretfully. 'It would be too slow.'

'You're not going on they new-fangled trains, milady?'

'I fear I have no choice, Jim.'

'But there's still the coach – '

'I never have cared for coaches. I shan't like the train, either, but I must hurry. My dear friend is ill.'

'I see, milady.'

'Cheer up, Jim. I haven't gone over to the enemy. I'll soon be back, and I'm planning to start trips again. How would you like to go to Stratford?'

His face brightened. 'I'd love it, milady.'

'Good. Well now, I'll have to go back to the Manor to fetch my clothes. Can you saddle one of the horses right away.'

But at the Manor, Georgiana would not hear of Tam's returning to the boat that night: nothing would do but that she stay with them, and in the morning they would drive her in the carriage to Rugby station. So, attired in a warm merino wool dress, covered by a thick black mantle, and accompanied by Emmeline Tam was prepared for the worst the railway might provide. They entered the station, and Tam asked for two return tickets, first class. 'And one for the maid?' asked the man in the office.

'The second is for my maid,' said Tam tartly.

'It is usual for the lower orders to travel third class,' objected the clerk.

'Good heavens,' said Tam, 'I want Emmeline with me, I need someone to talk to.' And she swept on to the platform followed by the man's disapproving stare.

The train was waiting, and Tam gazed at the long engine with its tall chimney and large middle wheel. She walked slowly down the length of the train, stopping to look at the second-class carriages, long boxes with open sides, wooden benches within. Tam sniffed, and moved further along to the third-class compartments, which were simply trucks, and already filled with men and women standing close together.

'Good heavens,' she said again. 'Look at this, Emmeline. Why when it rains you'll all drown,' she told the occupants of the nearest truck.

'No, ma'am, there's holes in the floor to let the rain out,' said a man.

Tam sniffed. 'And you'll be covered in soot from the smoke when it starts. Why don't you travel by canal? It's much more comfortable. And you get meals too.'

'This is quicker,' said the man. 'We get to London in four hours or thereabouts.'

'Come on, milady,' urged Emmeline, who feared her mistress would be removed from the station if she made trouble.

The first class was better, Tam had to admit: leather upholstered seats with arm-rests, covered both at the sides and overhead. She perched on the edge of the seat, fearing the worst, and when a whistle gave a piercing blast, she shuddered. She grimaced many times during the journey at the noise; she watched the black smoke billowing away and wondered about the poor third-class passengers. But when they alighted at Euston, even she had to admit this station was impressive with its great Doric arch flanked by lodges. And the train had been very much quicker.

At the Duchess's house she was ushered into a splendid bedroom, the bed hangings being of cream-coloured silk embroidered with flowers, matching the curtains. But the room was so large it contained as much day furniture as night: sofas, chaise-longues, tables edged with gilt, a Savonnerie carpet on the floor matching the Beauvais tapestries on the walls. Only when a deep voice called, 'My dear Tam,' could she locate the Duchess, lying on a day-bed, her bandaged foot propped before her.

'Dear Duchess,' Tam said. 'How are you?'

'An unsightly mess, as you see,' said the Duchess, whose face, Tam noted, was painted as always. 'But what has happened to you?'

'I am so sorry,' Tam said. 'We had such a bad time. Juliet ill . . . little Roddy died . . .'

'And you were ill yourself, were you not?' asked the Duchess.

'Yes, I had cholera.'

'H'm.' The maid brought in tea and the Duchess turned to Tam. 'Will you pour?'

And she poured from a massive silver teapot into delicate Sèvres china cups. She had fully intended to tell the Duchess about her miscarriage, but somehow she couldn't. They chatted about this and that, and then the Duchess asked, 'What about Charles?'

'I – haven't seen him for a long time.'

The Duchess sniffed. 'Seems like you've not been seeing anyone for a long time.'

'I haven't. But I'm better now. Back on the boat.'

'And do you want to see Charles now you're here?'

Tam looked up, her eyes dull. 'I – don't know.'

'Well, I've asked him to call tonight. If you don't want to see him, you needn't.'

'I'll see him,' Tam agreed reluctantly, but in private wondered if she *wanted* to confront him to tell him about the baby. If we had been a married

243

couple living together, she thought as she changed for dinner, how much easier it would have been, sharing trouble as well as happiness. But they weren't married, and in some obscure way Tam knew she resented his freedom, while she, the woman, had been left to endure her pain alone. Perhaps in the end we are always alone, she reasoned.

And maybe it would have been all right if they'd met first away from the servants. As it was, they had to be circumspect, and their meeting was frustrating; too much had happened. 'I tried to see you, Tam,' he muttered to her, as they went into the large stately dining room.

'I know,' she whispered. 'But I couldn't let you come to the Manor.'

'I don't see why not.'

She didn't answer, and they were forced to make light conversation as the dinner progressed. At last, the servants had gone, and with the Duchess returned to her bedroom, they were alone. He walked over to her and took her in his arms. And for a moment she rested, and when he kissed her the fires were lit again. She knew he wanted her badly, and yet she couldn't fully respond.

'It was bad, Tam, all of it. And worst of all was our being apart. I want to be with you,' he said.

'Yes.'

'All the time.'

'But we can't.'

'We can't go on as we were before, can we? It wouldn't be the same. Besides . . .' he stopped.

'Besides what?'

'You don't give me all of yourself.'

'Of course I do,' she said crossly. 'What more do you want?'

'You, yourself. Not just your body. Tell me, Tam, after all these years, what do you know of me?'

'Of *you*?' she was puzzled.

'You never once ask about my work. You know nothing of it.'

'Oh, Charles, you're always telling me about it. About votes and – cholera – and the Patch.'

He sighed. 'No. We meet, we make love, we part.'

'Then what do you want?'

'I suppose I want a wife.'

'But we can't,' she repeated.

'Why don't you come to London to live? You're free now.'

She stared, utterly taken aback. 'Live in London. Where?'

'You could find a small house somewhere . . .'

She was silent, only her eyes flashed dangerously green. 'Who would pay for this small house?' she asked carefully.

'I would.'

'Then I'd be a kept woman.'

'Nonsense. You'd be no more a kept woman than a wife is. You are my wife, in all but name. I want you with me. I want someone to talk to when I come home at nights.'

'But,' she said, drawing away from him, 'I wouldn't be able to stay with you, go anywhere with you, entertain for you. It would be a hole and corner business, Charles. And besides, you can't afford to run another establishment, nor the scandal – '

'Would you care about scandal?' he asked sullenly. 'Are you not as brave as your mother?'

He could have said nothing worse. To compare her with her mother, when already she was shrinking from the similarity of the thought of being a kept woman. So they faced each other, neither comprehending the other's feelings. His need for a companion to come back to after a hard day, her fear of being like her mother.

'That's unfair, I was thinking about you,' she cried.

'That's unusual then – '

'You'd enjoy a scandal, would you? All of it coming out? Juliet and Geoffrey, Mother and Father – '

'That's it, isn't it. You – your father.'

She looked at him almost piteously. 'There's so much – ' she whispered.

'When are you going to forget it?' he interrupted. 'All this business about running the canal, what are you trying to prove? That your father was right? Yes, but time moves on, you can't live in the past.'

She stood up. 'The canals have a future,' she said. 'If only people wouldn't panic. You're just trying to dismiss it because you can't imagine that a woman wants to work independently. Well, you're wrong. Why should I give up my work to live in a little love-nest with you?'

'Because you're hanging onto the past. To your father. It's been there all along, between us.'

'What has?'

'He has. Your father.'

She said in a low voice, 'He wasn't my father.'

'What?'

'He wasn't my father. Lord Brooke was – is.'

Charles stared, shocked. 'How long have you known?'

'Since – just before I married Sir William. When Mama married *him*.'

'And you never told me?' He was hurt, but she failed to see it in her anger and distress. 'That's what I mean, we are lovers, but we're not close.'

She shrugged. 'I thought you knew. Celia knows,' she went on. 'She'd tell Geoffrey. Juliet knows.'

'Geoffrey and I never have any sort of amicable conversation as you know, we're not likely to share secrets. And as for conversation with Juliet, that is almost impossible.' It was the first time he'd spoken unkindly of Juliet, and she was about to retort, when he asked again, 'Why didn't you tell me?'

She was silent. 'I don't know,' she said at last. 'I just don't know, Charles.'

'Damn it,' he said. 'I thought I knew you, even though you take little interest in my affairs. I thought you told me everything.'

245

'Well, I don't,' she said. And now she wanted to hurt him as she'd been hurt. 'There was only one person I could tell everything to . . . my father. Jamie Calder *was* my father, whatever anyone says.'

'I see.' He took a step towards her, but she turned away.

'I'm going to my room,' she said. Her eyes were dull now, the fires were gone.

'Very well.' He was angry too. 'I'm sorry I'm not your father. I offered you a man's love, not a father's.'

'I shan't come to London again. I shall be pretty busy on the boats,' she said, walking to the door.

Charles let her go in silence.

The May Fair was held and Tam decided to attend, for in addition to the usual cattle market there was, this year, to be a horse fair. With the coming of railways horses were not now quite in such demand, and Tam hoped to pick out one or two bargains, for good, fast horses were needed on flyboats and packets, and if she were to start the *Princess* again then Darkie and Prince would have to go, they were showing signs of age. Since returning from London Tam resolved to turn all her thoughts and energy to her business. For the first time she felt that Charles had failed her, and would not admit, even to herself, that this was unfair when he did not know the cause of her hurt. How different it would have been if he had been by her side when she lost the baby, if he had been her husband . . . But he was not, and could never be, and to be asked to be a kept woman, now, when it was comfort she needed . . . So the gentleness he gave her, that she needed so desperately, was denied her and she buried her hurt beneath a shell of hardness. Charles had failed her, all men failed her, except Papa. And yet even Papa, by preferring Mama, by dying and leaving her alone . . . From now on she would fight them all, she had no need of them.

She called to see Juliet, for she knew that she would always love her baby sister, especially now she too was bereft. Juliet was, as always now, sitting hopelessly by the fire, her hands idle, her eyes dull.

'Come, Juliet,' said Tam, making an effort to be cheerful, 'come to the May Fair with me.'

She thought Juliet would refuse, but she rose without a word and fetched her shawl, stood waiting, and this passivity was somehow worse than if she had protested.

They walked to the fairground, past the cattle market, the boxing booths, the hiring stands. Men and women milled around, shouting, laughing. In the far corner they could see the horses, hear the neighing and braying, see the galloping and the trotting and Tam's heart quickened, and she wondered if Jake Boswell would be there.

And he was, she saw him immediately, together with a group of gipsy men with dark features and gay neckerchiefs, and gold ear-rings. Two of them were riding, long black hair flying in the wind, and as she approached, one leaned back in the saddle until he was lying flat, the other stood bareback, while people cheered.

Tam walked towards Jake. 'Do you remember me?' she asked.

'I never forget a face, Mistress Calder.'

And it gave her a strange sense of comfort to be known by her old name. Calder she was and Calder she would die, she resolved never to call herself Lady Fargate again.

'I'm looking for two horses,' she said, and he smiled.

'I have the very thing. Over here. I bought them for a song.'

'And how much will you sell them for?'

'Twenty pounds apiece.'

She stared at him dubiously. 'Why do you part with them if they're so good?' she said.

He drew himself up proudly. 'Because you are my friend,' he said. 'And the friend of Charles Waring.'

'A lot of water has flowed under the bridges since we met,' said Tam.

'True, mistress, but some things remain the same, and friendship is one.'

She sighed. 'Yes, Jake, I'm sorry I doubted you. I have become a business woman, you see, and too many people are practising too many tricks.'

'It's the way of the world,' said Jake, philosophically.

'But the world never gets the better of you, Jake.'

He laughed. 'No, indeed. But then, I never let go my heart out of my hand,' and she turned away, wondering how much those black eyes of his could see.

But she bought the horses, and Jake promised to deliver them to the boat, so Juliet and Tam walked back to the house on the wharf. At the entrance Juliet halted.

'What is it?' asked Tam. 'Don't you want to go in?'

'Oh Tam,' Juliet said, and her voice was forlorn, 'I'm so lonely without him. The house is so empty without my little Roddy.'

Tam stood, helplessly. 'Don't you see Geoffrey now? she asked.

'No.'

'But – why not? If you want to meet him on the boat . . .' and she knew she'd do anything to take that lost look from her sister's eyes. 'He cares for you, Juliet.'

'I don't want to see him now. Not again. I don't think I have any feeling left.'

'Oh Juliet.' Tam drew her sister into her arms, and knew she was crying.

'The house is so empty,' Juliet said again.

'Come and live with me on the boat,' Tam said. 'It'll be like it used to be.'

'No.'

'That what is it you want?' Tam stroked her hair gently.

'Oh Tam. I want Cherry Trees. I want to go back. Tam, take me back there, take me home.'

Tam put her sister away, and looked into her eyes. 'I will,' she promised. 'I will. Don't cry any more, baby. I'll take you home.'

* * *

She went to see Geoffrey in the office, away from Celia, and put the case bluntly. 'I want Cherry Trees,' she said. 'Juliet wants to go back there, and so do I. You don't live in it now, you don't need it.'

'Are you proposing to buy it?' he asked.

'No. I can't spare the money.'

'The canal still pays good dividends.'

'I need all that to fight the railways.'

'You are proposing I *give* you Cherry Trees?'

'It was our home.'

'Your father lost it – '

'My father was swindled out of it by Sir William, whose henchman you were. It belongs to us by rights. Celia only wanted to buy it because she knew I loved it – if you *did* buy it.'

'I cannot afford – ' he began.

'Juliet needs it,' said Tam. 'She is lonely since Roddy died. She seems to have lost the will to live.'

Geoffrey seemed to shrink into himself, but Tam went on remorselessly. 'I wonder what Celia would think if she knew. There's a lot Celia doesn't know, isn't there, Geoffrey?'

Geoffrey cried, outraged, 'Why, this is blackmail.'

'Yes,' Tam agreed pleasantly. 'I suppose it is.'

Geoffrey slumped over the desk. 'All right,' he muttered. 'You can have Cherry Trees.'

Tam walked away. But there was no joy in her victory.

Chapter Six

The first railways had concentrated on passengers and parcels traffic rather than the less well-paying heavy goods. So for a time the canals held their own, indeed water carriage held advantages over land. But the lack of uniformity foreseen by Jamie Calder so long ago, together with the archaic state of the old river navigations with which the canals connected, now proved to be their downfall. Navigation on the Thames, Trent and Severn was little better than in the middle ages, there were weirs obstructing the Thames, and gravel shoals on the Trent, and had these companies remedied this state of affairs at the time all might have been well. But instead they preferred to muddle along.

Sir William had been one of the first to use his railway for transporting his coal, but others soon followed his example, and now the railways quoted an uneconomic rate for goods, recuperating their loss from passenger traffic. The canal companies panicked; many sold their undertakings to the railways or surrendered the controlling interest as the Birmingham Canal Navigations had, in return for a guaranteed dividend. So in the years up to 1847 the railway companies obtained control over one third of the total inland waterway mileage of the country, including such important ones as the Trent and Mersey, the Thames and Severn. It was the time of the railway mania, new companies sprang up hurriedly, and everyone rushed to join the boom, Geoffrey being one of them. Nor did he ask his mother's advice, for she had never been very enthusiastic about investing in get-rich-quick companies; Geoffrey told himself he'd tell her when he'd made a fortune.

Tam prepared for the shareholders' meeting with a heavy heart. The number of shareholders had dwindled: Mr Snell and Mr Davison had sold their holdings after Sir William's death, no doubt to join the scramble for railway shares. She looked through the window at the December sunset. Low on the horizon colours spilled over the sky in a mass of orange and red, while above a clear blue held the remaining day. Come, Tam cheered herself, I have Cherry Trees, I knew I'd get it back some day. The rest will work out too.

She managed Cherry Trees with as small a staff as possible, a cook-housekeeper, a woman who came weekly to do the rough work, plus little Matty, a pauper orphan from the workhouse, whose status was never quite defined, but whose thirteen-year-old body was for ever running to help Cook, or answer the door, her plain face wearing a permanent smile at being away from the dreaded poorhouse. Emmeline had decided to stay with the Fargates; Tam had no need for a lady's maid at Cherry Trees, and Georgiana had been only too pleased to keep her. All in all, Tam thought, we manage well enough. She drove a pony-chaise herself in place of the carriage, an old man saw to the garden and the horse, helped by young Jim. She had let Esther go now there was no Roddy to be taken care of, nor had Tam ever been quite certain that Esther had not given them water from the forbidden pump, though she said nothing of her suspicions to anyone.

The sunset was paling now to a long bar of orange, and in Chilverton lights were springing up. Tam watched the solitary horseman ride towards the house and wondered who he could be.

Little Matty enlightened her. 'Mr Jerome Randall,' she announced.

'Jerome,' Tam said uncertainly.

'Lady Fargate.' He stood before her, uncertain in his turn. 'I had to tell you before the meeting . . .'

Yes?'

'I don't know how to say this. I feel . . . I am troubled. You see, I have been offered another job.'

'Oh, Jerome.'

'I'm truly sorry. I – ' He was plainly uncomfortable.

'Well, you aren't an apprentice bound to me for life,' she said, endeavouring to smile. 'If you have obtained a better position, well, I must be glad for your sake.'

'You see,' Jerome said, 'I was always Deputy Agent, even though I did the Agent's work, and was paid in full,' and she saw now how this must have rankled.

'Where are you going, or don't you want to tell me?' she asked.

He paused. 'With Sir Lewis,' he said at last.

She was silent.

'I know,' Jerome put in quickly, 'it's like a betrayal. But the offer was so generous, I'd be a fool to refuse.'

'What will you be doing?'

'It's a supervisory position such as I have now. But Lady Fargate,' and the words came in a rush now, 'I thought, well, you know, I've been thinking it over for some time, I thought I might help you.'

'How?'

'I could let you know of his plans.'

Tam stared at the man. That wasn't his reason for accepting she guessed. Jerome was on the make, he saw a better chance and took it. Well, who could blame him? But if he was serious about helping her with news of Sir Lewis's plans, he was hardly the best of employees from Sir Lewis's point. She pondered. Yet why not? Why not use his help in any way she could? The railway companies were as astute and powerful as Sir William had been, there were many secret agreements always leading to the same thing – the destruction of the canals.

'Where would we meet?' she asked practically. 'It would hardly be wise for you to come to the wharf office in full view of everyone.'

'No. I wondered . . . if you still held those afternoon teas, now you live at Cherry Trees, as you did at the Manor? They are mainly for women, I know, but not exclusively so. I might call in occasionally . . .'

Tam's eyes widened. So he wanted to call! He was attracted to her, she knew, was this then simply an excuse to see her? If so, why not? 'I have not started any such gatherings as yet. I have little time . . . or the staff. But I might arrange one every month or so, then if you have anything to impart – ' she tried to keep it on a business footing.

His face lightened. 'I'll help you all I can,' he assured her.

'It will be good to have a friend in the enemy camp.' She smiled. 'Now if you'll excuse me, I have to go to the shareholders' meeting.'

'Yes. You understand I had to see you beforehand. I didn't want to attend a meeting when I'm no longer entitled – '

No longer entitled to find out our secrets. Well, that's something I suppose, she thought and wondered if he knew of Sir Lewis's letter to her, if indeed that might be one of his reason for leaving. 'Your shares – ' she began. 'Shall I take them off your hands?'

It was agreed, and she went to the meeting, breaking the news to Harry and Robin, all that remained of the group.

'So we have to find another agent,' Harry said.

'And that won't be difficult,' Tam smiled. 'Robin, of course.' She looked at him: he was twenty-six now, a tall, upstanding young man, she liked his eagerness, and hoped that soon Jamie would also be sitting with them. 'That is, of course, if he wishes to stay. He too could get a better job, no doubt.'

'Out of the question,' said Robin.

'You still prefer the canals?' asked Tam with a smile.

'I still like canals,' Robin answered. 'Shall I tell thee why? My first memories are of the Patch, and my father's loom clacking away. We all helped with the weaving. Then work dwindled and food grew less plentiful, and then scarce. Then thou came along, Tamarisk Calder, and my childhood was suddenly transformed: I lived on a boat, in a pleasant cosy cabin; I woke to the cries of birds and sailed along day after day. To a child it was a dream, and maybe I'm still a child, but I still like waking on a boat . . .'

Tam smiled. She wasn't sure if that was the best reason for taking a responsible position, she had little use for dreamers, but there was no one else. 'I shall make you Deputy Agent, Charles is still Agent – ' though, since they moved to Cherry Trees, she no longer paid Juliet his Agent's pay, it was not now necessary, nor indeed could she afford it. She went on, 'And Jamie will be coming to join us when he has finished school. But where will you live? I expect Charles would let you live at his house – '

'No, no, I shall live on the boat,' said Robin.

251

'Then that's settled,' said Tam. 'Now to other matters.'

Robin supplied the figures: maintenance had been fairly heavy, the volume of trade had fallen slightly, but the dividend was still six per cent.

At last they came to the most important business of the meeting. 'I have received an official letter from Sir Lewis Fargate,' Tam said. 'This confirms a matter he put to me unofficially some time ago. In short, he makes us an offer for the Chilverton Canal. It is a good offer, running into thousands of pounds, or, if we do not want to sell outright, an amalgation with his railway company, offering us half shares of all combined dividends.' She put the paper down. 'It is a good offer. I welcome your comments.'

Harry spoke first. 'Tamarisk, thou owns practically all the shares in the canal company, it is for thee to decide. Thou art the one who stands to gain – or lose, if that may be the case.'

'My views are unchanged. I want to keep the canal. Nevertheless, I don't want you to continue against your will,' she replied.

'I want to continue,' said Robin, eagerly.

'Harry?' asked Tam.

'I shall stay,' he said.

'Don't stay out of loyalty,' Tam began, but Harry interrupted.

'Tamarisk, what else would I do now? I am fifty-six years old, I think I shall end my days on the canal.'

'It is a final offer, remember,' Tam pointed out.

Harry said, heavily, 'That letter was a declaration of war, Tamarisk. That, and getting Jerome to work for him.'

'I believe so.'

'He will begin to undercut us now. It is being done on many canals by railways in opposition.'

'We can face that.'

'I am just warning thee, Tam.'

'I know, Harry. But what will happen if we sell out? Look what's happening now. The railways are supposed by law to keep the canals they own in good working order, but they don't. They neglect maintenance, they divert water supplies, they raise tolls. Sometimes they close waterways for long periods on the pretext of carrying out repairs. No, Harry, not for us.'

'I don't want to be too depressing, Tamarisk. I just felt it my duty to put the facts to thee. I shall be happy to end my days here as I said. But thou art a comparatively young woman – '

'Heavens, Harry, I shall soon be forty – '

'Young enough to start a new life,' Harry looked at her hesitatingly. 'I do not wish to pry into thy affairs, merely to help, as thou hast no one to advise thee. Dost thou have sufficient moneys in the bank for safety?'

Tam smiled bleakly. 'I saved from the dividends in the good years,' she said.

'And thou hast the upkeep of Cherry Trees, and the care of thy sister, Jamie's schooling,' said Harry. 'Dost that leave enough to draw on for any eventuality for the canal, should it arise?'

Tam hesitated. 'Enough,' she said.

'Consider, Tamarisk. If thou took this money now, thou wouldst be in comfort for the rest of thy life. If the offer is not repeated and money is needed – '

'Then I shall lose everything,' said Tam, quietly. 'I know, Harry, I understand. But I shall continue. I hope Robin will think well about it . . .'

'You have already heard my answer,' said Robin.

Agreement was reached and the offer was formally refused.

Tam went back to Cherry Trees in the boat, as she had come; she always travelled that way when possible. Young Jim, much older now, drove the two horses she'd obtained from Jake, and Tam watched him smiling. So Jerome had left, but there were other faithful employees. At last the boat slid into the mooring at Cherry Trees and Tam stood up. Overhead she had fastened a huge sign: *The Calder Boats*, lit at night by hanging lanterns. She stood for a moment beneath it, with pride. This was what she was fighting for, her boats, her canal. They'd been her father's concern, and after her, they would be Jamie's, and his son's. From here she would run outings to various places in the neighbourhood, usually out of the range of the railways. Sometimes she visited Stratford-on-Avon, a small town with little to offer but memories of Mr Shakespeare. People preferred Coventry at the Corpus Christi Fair in June which lasted eight days with its grand procession including representatives of the old trading companies, mercers, drapers and so on, preceded by St George in armour, and Lady Godiva on a white horse. Tradesmen came from London to display their goods at this great fair, and there was no shortage of entertainments. There were always crowds clamouring to see public hangings either at Warwick or Coventry and Tam, trying to avoid Harry's eye, sometimes took these trips, but keeping well away from the spectacle herself. Hangings apart, Warwick was a pleasant town, though she knew the locals were not particularly interested in its castle or for that matter the castle at Kenilworth; they preferred a good hanging in the present day to tales of battles and killings in the past. Leamington was fairly popular for its spa; there had been a steady stream of invalids taking the waters since a medical man had recommended them way back in 1784; now there were two wells and a range of baths and the town was growing.

Jim tied up the boat and helped Tam alight.

'I wonder, milady, if I might have a word with you,' he said.

'Of course, Jim, what is it?'

'Well.' Jim twiddled his fingers. 'I'm thinking of getting wed.'

'Are you? Well now, and I never knew. Is it anyone I know?'

'Don't think so, milady. Her name's Sally Harris. I've bin writing to her for a long time.'

'Tell me about her, Jim.'

'Well, milady, I first saw her – I often saw her when she was a little kid. Then one day the boat went by and she was steering and she was quite growed up and I thought that's the one for me. So I smiled at her and waved.'

'And did she smile back?'

'I think she did. She did the next time. Then I wrote my initials underneath the bridge and waited; sure enough she wrote hers underneath.'

Tam nodded. That was the true sign of courtship.

'So then we was all set, milady. I wrote to her. We sometimes had the chance to talk. I axed her to marry me – '

'Good.'

'Yes, milady. But when a boater marries he allus gets his own boat. So I was wondering – '

'Oh I see. Well would she be willing to live on the *Princess* with you?'

Jim beamed. 'If that would suit you, milady?'

'Yes, indeed. Perhaps we could start refreshments as we used to do. She could see to that, and I'd pay extra, of course.'

'That'd be lovely, milady. But there's one other thing – ' Jim hopped from one foot to the other. 'The boat. We allus dresses the boat up for a wedding, you know. Then we has a party at the "Anchor".'

'Well, you can dress my boat up, Jim,' she reassured him.

He beamed again. 'Thank you, milady. And will you come to the wedding?'

'I will indeed, Jim. And I'll try to persuade Miss Juliet to come. It would do her good.'

She walked up the path to the house, wondering if Juliet would be waiting up for her. But Matty informed her that she'd gone to bed hours since. Tam sighed. She had hoped that the return to Cherry Trees would bring her sister back to life, find new interests, but still she sat, passive, in the daytime, retiring very early to bed. If Tam asked her to do anything she would, willingly, but she never made any suggestion herself, it was as though some spring had been broken inside her and could never be repaired.

Sometimes Charles came to visit, and would sit with Juliet, for Tam showed him no more than the bare civilities. She was still angry that he should have asked her to become a *kept woman*. All her days now were spent in carrying on the fight for the canal, nothing else mattered, except Jamie. She knew that something had been lost, that even Cherry Trees did not mean quite as much as formerly, but would not analyse the reason, she pushed all deep feelings aside. So they lived, Juliet in a passive dream, Tam working and fighting. Neither allowing their innermost feelings to be touched.

In 1849 Mrs Waring Senior died suddenly. In her early sixties, she had seemed hale and hearty, and her death was a shock to Geoffrey and Celia, who both mourned her sincerely. Tam attended the funeral. Charles was there, and though he spoke to her civilly, he did not seek her out nor ask to be alone with her, nor did Tam wish that he would.

Charles's success in the House was growing, and had he been a member of the main parties he would undoubtedly have been made a minister. Since the cholera outbreak he had renewed his attacks on the insanitary conditions in the Patch and elsewhere, and was joined by others. Disraeli wrote of alleys streaming with filth, doctors made reports of towns in the north which made horrific reading. And it was not only the poor who suffered. The Queen's apartments at Buckingham Palace were ventilated through the common sewer, London streets were ankle deep in horse dung. In the Houses of Parliament the stench from the river was unbearable.

So Charles was praised in the House, and could not help but be flattered by the notice he received. And when several prominent Whigs made overtures to him, asking why he did not stand as a member of their own party he was thoughtful. An independent member did not get very far, and after all some of these new liberals were progressive, reform was in the air on both sides of the House. He pondered his future, and when one member asked about his wife, was she very ill, he realised what was meant. A minister needed a wife, to entertain, to act as hostess. Because of his quixotic action he could never marry Tam, even should Juliet die. For the first time he asked himself if today he would marry a girl out of pity, and knew he wouldn't. Then he'd been a boy, now he was a man, and he sighed for the passing of youth's ideals.

But the Public Health Bill was passed, and Charles hoped the Chilverton dignitaries would show some enthusiasm, for although new inspectors had been appointed he doubted their ability to galvanise the local worthies, who were, after all, unqualified, part-time amateurs chosen at the local Vestry Meeting.

Geoffrey was far from enthusiastic about the new reforms. Ten Hours Act for Women and Young Children, Lord Shaftesbury thundering in the House, Charles Dickens and his novels, Geoffrey hoped the inspectors wouldn't be in too much of a hurry to get to his factory. He was a worried man. The money he'd speculated in the railway mania had been lost. He had taken most of the spare capital from the weaving business and placed it in a high-dividend railway company which had subsequently crashed. His only income now was from the still safe Chilverton Railway shares and his house rents. If his workers decided to do something silly like going on strike he would be in trouble.

Geoffrey missed his mother and turned to his wife for consolation, but she was wrapped up in the girls, and his other sense of grievance, that she'd never given him a son, came to the fore. He thought longingly of Roderick, he would have taken Roddy into the firm, done so much for the lad . . .

Celia's voice interrupted his reverie. 'Dear,' she said, 'Sir Lewis has invited us to the Manor.'

'Oh?'

'I was thinking . . . Amanda is sixteen now, not out yet, I know, but she soon will be. She should be presented, Geoffrey. Do you know anyone who could present her?'

'No,' said Geoffrey, shortly.

'I don't, either. I mean, not well enough. I thought of Mama, but no one is allowed at Court these days who has been involved in scandal. I can't think of anyone else. No one at Sir Lewis's is sufficiently interested – ' Celia broke off, she had been about to say *interested in us*. 'Really,' and now her voice took on the self-pitying whine it so often held these days. 'He might ask us there more often, I think.'

'Why should he?' asked Geoffrey. 'It was his father I worked for – with – not him, he manages his own affairs.'

'Well, it doesn't seem right. It's a pity you let Cherry Trees go to Tam, Geoffrey, I never could understand what you were thinking of to sell it to *her* – ' Celia never knew that Tam had not paid for Cherry Trees.

'Oh heavens, what does that matter now?'

'It matters now, Geoffrey dear, because it would look well if we had another country place. Why, I'd like to go there myself occasionally, you know I am often unwell.'

Celia had had a miscarriage before the birth of her last child, Beatrice, and another two years ago, when she was indeed quite ill. Since then she had refused Geoffrey her bed. 'I'm in a delicate state of health, Geoffrey, and I assure you there can be no more babies, not at my age.' And there was some truth in her statements about poor health. Because she had followed the fashion of the day and took no exercise or fresh air lest her skin turn brown, and she had with her contining pregnancies lost her figure and was now completely shapeless, much overweight. This made her breathless, the stuffy rooms gave her headaches, then she became alarmed, had attacks of the vapours, and grew convinced she was very ill indeed.

Geoffrey only grunted, and Celia rose with an air of martyrdom and went to look in on her daughters, working with their governess. She walked over to Amanda, who stood up as her mother entered. At sixteen Amanda was developing rapidly, her figure filling out, and her face was quite beautiful in repose, though her whole bearing was one of impatience.

'Amanda dear,' said Celia. 'I was just saying that you will have to be presented.'

'Presented where?' asked Amanda.

'At Court, where else?' asked Celia.

'Oh, Mama, don't be stupid. That's far above us.'

'What can you mean?' asked Celia, bridling. 'Above us, indeed!'

'We may have a large house and we have money,' said Amanda, cruelly, 'but in the eyes of the aristocrats we are *nouveaux riches*, Mama, almost as bad as Americans.'

'Really.' Amanda's outspokenness was a sore trial to Celia. 'My mother is – '

'Yes, I know, the daughter of an earl. But I don't particularly want to be presented.'

'You want to get married, don't you?'

'Not particularly.'

'Amanda, sometimes you are quite stupid,' Celia said. 'What do you want to be, an old maid?'

Amanda sniffed. 'Aunt Tamarisk isn't married. Well, she was, I know, but she isn't now, she lives alone and works. She doesn't live at all like a widow in a black cap.'

'The Queen,' said Celia, coldly, 'very much disapproves of women taking any sort of activity – '

'Oh, pshaw, Mama.'

Really, thought Celia, sometimes Amanda is quite like Mama. 'We are invited to Chilverton Manor shortly. Another few years and who knows . . .' her voice trailed off.

'You mean you want me to marry one of the Fargate boys,' said Amanda, frowning. 'Well, Stephen's all right, I suppose, though I like Francis best.'

'He is delicate,' said Celia, dismissively.

'And the younger son,' said Amanda with a grin.

Celia moved away.

'Mama,' cried Becky. 'I have worked my sampler, do see.'

'Yes, dear, and very pretty it is too. What have you been doing, Amelia? And Bee?'

Amelia shyly presented her own neat work, and Celia moved towards Beatrice, whose sampler was sadly crumpled and very grubby. Celia, though she never admitted it even to herself, did not like her youngest child. At seven, she was short and stocky, with a habit of stomping around as though she wore heavy boots. Little Bee was exactly like Jamie Calder, and Celia did not like to be reminded of her father's humble beginnings. Besides, short stocky girls were not really presentable, and there were hints from little Bee's roguish smile that she would become another Amanda, though without Amanda's looks. Celia sighed, 'Oh Bee,' and moved back to the safety of Amelia and Becky. Her two middle girls were entirely predictable, entirely what daughters should be. Quite pretty – resembling their father – but with little personality, they would never kick over the traces, never want to do unmentionable things such as work; looking at their faces it was easy to see their whole lives, marriage no doubt with a presentable young gentleman, pretty children like themselves. She loved Amelia and Becky wholeheartedly.

Celia returned to Geoffrey just as the butler entered.

'Mr Jamie Fargate to see you, sir,' he said.

'Jamie, what's he want?' Geoffrey wondered.

'I don't know, sir, he said it was private – and important.'

'Really, some of these young people get very uppity,' sniffed Geoffrey.

'What can you expect from one who's been at Rugby?' asked Celia, who eyed all young men, even sixteen-year-olds, as prospective husbands, and Jamie Fargate would not do. He was a cousin – Celia did not know that he was related on both sides – and quite penniless. Celia, like the rest of Chilverton, had been amazed at Sir William's leaving both Tam and Jamie unprovided for; of course, Sir William had always been a difficult man, but it made one think that Tam must have offended him deeply.

'Show him into the library,' said Geoffrey, rising.

'I've come to see you, Uncle Geoffrey, on a matter of business,' said Jamie, and Geoffrey eyed this young nephew with distaste. He was so

257

self-assured. Came from his early upbringing, he supposed, at the Manor, the Squire's son . . .

'What is it?' he demanded testily.

'I would like you to take me into the firm.'

'You'd what?'

'Yes. I've thought about it for a long time. It is what I want to do.'

'Why?' Geoffrey asked curiously.

'Well.' Jamie paused, as if weighing up his uncle. 'You could say it started years ago when there was that big rising in the Midlands, and the weavers joined in. I was there.'

Geoffrey remembered seeing the pony and trap; Tam, the little boy. 'So,' he said truculently, 'you were there, eh? And immediately you thought Ah, I shall go into this business.'

'Yes,' said Jamie, simply.

'Why?' Geoffrey repeated.

Jamie hesitated before saying, 'I think I have something to offer.'

'Really.' Geoffrey's voice was dry. 'What?'

'I have a theory, Uncle, that if people are happy they work better. That's why so many cling to their hand-looms, they like that life, they don't like your way.'

'You know all about it, do you?' Geoffrey asked sarcastically. 'And you'd make them happy, would you? How?'

'Some of these Quaker owners are dealing well with their hands. There are some people in Birmingham called Cadbury, they give them milk and buns in the morning, tea in the afternoon.'

'Cadbury? Never heard of 'em.'

'They make chocolate.'

Geoffrey snorted. 'And they'll be out of business within a year if they give tea and buns away.'

'I talk a lot to Harry Earp, and he is not a fool by any means – '

'He's a radical rebel.'

'Uncle, he believes in bettering conditions. Factories are new, we haven't learned yet how to manage things, *we* have to learn as well as the hands.'

Geoffrey stared at his nephew. *We* have to learn. And yet he was, he knew, quite unable to deal with the hands if they rebelled, if they joined one of these wretched unions springing up everywhere. With his mother to advise him he had managed, alone he was lost, with no idea . . . He needed someone to discover what was wrong in the factory. 'What position had you in mind?' he asked cautiously.

'I'd start in the factory, serve my apprenticeship – '

'I don't do it that way now.'

'I know. You put young lads on looms and give them half-pay. You employ women and children as cheap labour. And by doing so you upset the weavers – '

'I can't run my factory to please the hands – '

'But you can't just ride roughshod over their beliefs and feelings, and

258

the Guild rules they made years ago and kept. That way you antagonise them and make them bitter, then they go on strike and burn factories – '

Geoffrey nodded. Having his factory burnt to the ground was an ever-present worry. It had happened to so many.

Jamie went on, 'So I wouldn't want to start off on the wrong foot. I want to learn the job properly, then I'd know what they're talking about. Warp and weft, winding and weaving. Besides – I'm interested in weaving.'

'Are you?' Geoffrey asked curiously .

'Surely you served a full apprenticeship, Uncle Geoffrey?'

'Yes. My father saw to that.' And for a moment Geoffrey's mind went back. His father's face, kind but firm. His saying 'Fast and true, like Coventry blue – ' the dye used for ribbons which became a watchword. His father, standing before him, 'Fast and True, Geoffrey.' Geoffrey blinked. His eyes seemed to be deceiving him. He almost thought it was his father standing before him now. A trick of the light. Yet there was a likeness, to his father, to Charles . . .

Charles . . . Surely this boy couldn't be family, after all? Wanting to come to *him*? Him, instead of Charles? Like most weak men Geoffrey craved affection and approval, he sought it everywhere, from women, from his betters, he would like it from his hands . . .

'And supposing I decided to give you a try. I don't promise, mind . . . are you proposing tea and buns for my hands?'

'First of all you must bring piped water into the Patch,' Jamie started.

'Hey, wait a minute. That's nothing to do with the factory. Besides, there's this new Health Act, the town is responsible – '

'With a lot of chivvying they will put in a main pipe from the reservoir. But to put it in each house will take years, with them all bickering and squabbling about it – '

'But I can't afford it. I've had losses recently.'

'They are your houses,' said this strange young man. 'I have been reckoning your rents. You must have been getting a hundred pounds a year from your properties. You must pay from that.'

Geoffrey blinked. He had always regarded his rents as pure profit. 'What would I gain from it?' he asked.

'You would have fewer people dying, like poor Roderick,' said Jamie, with unconscious cruelty, and Geoffrey stared at him with horrified eyes.

'Are you saying that I killed Roderick?' he asked.

'No,' said Jamie, wondering why his uncle seemed so upset suddenly. 'But the cholera did, and the cholera came from the Patch.'

Geoffrey was clutching at the table. 'It was an Act of God,' he said. 'An Act of God.'

'No, Uncle Geoffrey, it was the cholera, caused by bad water. Because the cesspools drain into the drinking water . . .'

'That's enough. You're young, you think you know it all.' Geoffrey rose to his feet and paced up and down. Certainly this boy was cock-sure, but he talked a lot of sense. And by God, he needed someone.

'When do you leave school?' he asked at last, weakly.

'Now. I'm sixteen – '

'Too old for an apprenticeship – '

'No, Uncle, listen to my suggestion. I'll serve my seven years. Three on the looms when I'll get half pay. Then I'll go in the office and study accounting, and finally the import/export side. By that time I shall be earning more, and when I'm fully trained we will negotiate again.'

They shook hands in agreement and Geoffrey watched the boy walk out of the room. He was filled with a strange sense of gladness. It was as if the son he'd always wanted had come to him. As if Roddy had come back.

'You want to work for Geoffrey?' Tam asked, amazed. 'But you're still at school.'

'I intend to leave, Mama.'

'Your education is not finished, Jamie. I won't hear of it.'

'Mama, I shall leave,'

They were sitting in the pleasant drawing room, Jamie home for the Christmas holidays. She turned to look at her son in perplexity: so tall, so handsome, so determined in his quiet way. She asked, 'Why?'

'I have all the education I need. It is a waste of money to carry on further.'

'Jamie, please, think well. I can manage about the money. You should go to university.'

'I don't wish to, Mama.'

'But I wish it, Jamie.'

There was a pause. 'Mama, you cannot have your own way all the time. Not in this – '

'Whatever do you mean?' She stood up, angry now. 'I have always let you do whatever you wished to do. And where your future is concerned surely you agree I know better than you.'

'What do you want for me, Mama?'

'You know what I want: you are to work with me on the canal. I've always planned it. We have need of educated men to deal with the lawyers on the other side, the crooked deals, the lobbying of Parliament – '

'I'm sorry, Mama, but I have not the same interest in canals.'

She felt a sharp, almost physical pain but tried to keep calm. 'I appreciate your wanting to leave school but you can still work with me.'

'No, Mama.'

'Suppose I refuse to hear of it?'

'I shall still do it.'

'Oh.' She bit her lip in rage. Yet she knew he would. And what would that mean? That he'd leave the house . . . leave her? That she could not bear: the rage left, bewilderment took over. 'But why *Geoffrey*?' she asked. 'Why?'

He repeated his story of the troubles he'd seen. 'I want to help,' he said simply, and she thought about how like Charles he was. But to work with Geoffrey. To lose her son was bad enough, after all her hopes and plans, but to lose him to Geoffrey . . .

260

'Why not become a doctor?' she asked. 'You could help the people that way.'

'I don't want to be a doctor, Mama. This is what I want to do. I've thought a lot about it, read about the new laws being brought in.'

'But how, when?' she asked, perplexed that she hadn't known.

'Harry Earp used to tell me a lot about it,' he said. 'You remember when I used to stay with them, when Sir William wouldn't let me ride?'

'I remember.' And she thought about how pleased Charles would be.

'And you see, Mama, my family are weavers. I am related to many of them in the town. There aren't many Warings, but the Jacques . . . my grandmother was a Jacques.' And Tam stared, wondering who he meant, until she realised it was Charles's mother. And she saw she faced the strongest opponent of all, one that could not be beaten, the sense of family, of a craft that had been handed down for hundreds of years, the sense of belonging. And she had none of that feeling; as it was, she was a hybrid, with a father who wasn't a father, and a mother who had never been there, never belonged to them. As Jamie had never belonged to the Manor. She saw that giving Jamie to the Warings was the best thing that could happen to him. But it left her bereft.

Jamie saw her distress, and wanted to comfort her. 'I think I have persuaded Uncle Geoffrey to put new water pipes in his houses,' he said.

'You have?' she asked in astonishment, and moved to the window. Dusk was falling, a mist rose from the canal. It would soon be Christmas, the boaters would be celebrating in wayside taverns, dancing and singing to the strains of a fiddle. 'It would have been so good, our working together,' and her tone was wistful.

'I'm truly sorry, Mama, I know you work so hard. But you must see there's no point in forcing me into something I don't want to do.' He came to her, putting his arm around her shoulder. 'I think we can persuade the town to run the main water pipe from the reservoir,' he said. 'Your reservoir, the Canal Company's. They will have to pay you. And I'll see Uncle Geoffrey carries on having his coal delivered by water.'

Tam smiled ruefully. How like a man, to cover a betrayal with a gift.

'I think I should notify my father,' Jamie said then, and she was surprised at his easy use of the word, his acceptance.

'Do you? Why?' she asked.

'Well, he has been clamouring for this to be done, hasn't he? Clean water in the Patch. So I think he should know. He doesn't come here now, we haven't seem him for ages, have we?' He paused. 'Have you quarrelled with him?'

She answered in a low voice, 'Yes, I suppose I have.'

'Well, I shall have to tell him.'

Long after he'd gone to his room Tam sat staring into the fire. Did Jamie want them to be together then, she and Charles? What did she know of her son, after all? How could she know, when he'd been away so much? Poor Jamie, there'd not been much of a home-life for him at the Manor. Although Sir William had relaxed his rules on Jamie not riding, the

261

damage had been done, the boy had spent more and more time away from home, staying with the Earps. She'd been glad he was on the canal, and all the time he must have been talking to Harry about the weaving . . .

They all tell me I want my own way, she thought bitterly. How seldom I get it . . .

In his room Jamie sat, pen in hand. 'Dear – ' he almost wrote 'Father' but who knew who might open the letter addressed to the House of Commons, and he didn't know his private address. So he started 'Dear Uncle Charles . . .' and paused. 'I thought you might like to know that I shall be working with Uncle Geoffrey in his business in future. I have already persuaded him to install water pipes in the Patch, and hope to carry out other reforms if necessary.' Jamie hesitated, gnawing his pen. 'I hope you will come down to see us to talk about it. Mother would like to see you too. Yours affectionately, Jamie.'

Charles was dining with colleagues. John Barnes had been a friend for many years. Not particularly radical in his stand, he and Charles spent many hours putting their differing views to each other. Charles found himself at times even accepting the other's reasoning, to his own surprise. He often dined with the family, and envied John his pretty wife, their children.

This evening there were a number of guests, and Charles was introduced to his partner for the evening. 'This is Mrs Mary Travers,' said John Barnes. 'A staunch liberal supporter, she knows more about the House than we do ourselves.' And in a hasty aside he added, 'She is the daughter, niece, and widow of prominent men, Charles. You would have known her husband, of course, Hugh Travers. She has been mourning him – until now.'

Mary Travers was not particularly attractive, but she had a pleasant quiet voice, and was remarkably intelligent. As the night wore on Charles found himself still at her side, listening with awe as she touched on all the issues of the day. No need to explain Parliamentary procedures to her, she knew all about them. She talked too, quite naturally, about her late husband.

'You have children?' Charles asked.

'Two boys. And you?'

'No,' he said, hating himself for the lie. He had the letter from Jamie in his pocket, and he wanted to acknowledge him, to say 'Yes, I have a son.' And knew he could not. Not to Mary Travers. Yet he enjoyed talking to her. She listened so carefully to his own ideas, criticised when necessary, in a reasoned tone. Yes, she was a remarkable woman to be able to understand so well. He hoped he would see her again.

But first he had to see Tam.

And this time Charles found her alone: Juliet always went to bed early, Jamie, who saw his father arrive, sped to his room. Tam, in the library, was gloomily looking over the canal accounts, and when Matty announced,

'Mr Charles Waring' she was thrown into confusion. She stared down at her serviceable gown of black alpaca, wondering if she had time to change. But he was already in the room. He came towards her, hands outstretched, and as she touched him he drew her into his arms, then let her go.

'I'm sorry,' he said. 'I should have known you wouldn't want to live like that.' He had, in the months they hadn't spoken, begun to realise his mistake. Had he told her the truth of his need for her, to be with him, waiting for him . . . but he hadn't, and she was too unversed to know how difficult most men find it to describe what they feel is a weakness. She knew none of this, so said grumpily, 'It's taken you long enough to tell me.'

'I know, I know. But you didn't want to see me, you made that plain – '

'Sit down,' she said. 'Please. I – ' she tried to arrange her hair. 'You caught me unawares,' she said. 'I must look a fright.'

'You look beautiful.'

She tried to compose herself. 'I expect you heard from Jamie,' she said.

'Yes. He wrote to me. I hadn't intended to come to Chilverton till after Christmas, but when I got his letter I came immediately.'

'You shouldn't let Jamie spoil your plans, even if he is your son. Do sit down, Charles. You must need some refreshment.'

'That can wait. We must talk first.'

'Yes.' She sat opposite him, away from him. 'Did Jamie tell you about his plan to work with Geoffrey?'

'He wrote some amazing tale about how he's persuaded him to install water pipes. How on earth has he managed that when I've been ranting and raving for years?'

'I think he just walked in and told him that's what he should do.'

'Well, I'm damned.' He stood up. 'I think we've produced a decent son, don't you?'

'Yes, Charles.'

He was near her now, holding her hands, pulling her to her feet. 'Oh Tam,' he said, 'how could we have been apart for so long?'

'Because I wished it,' she said candidly.

'I've told you I'm sorry.' He took a step back, still holding her hands, searching her face. 'And now, Tam?'

Was the hardness she had encased her heart in beginning to melt? She hardly knew if she dare let it.

'We can be friends, Charles.'

'Just friends?'

'It's better that way.'

'Why, Tam?'

'I'd prefer it, that's all.'

'Oh come on, Tam, don't pretend you're one of those cold ladies – '

'People change – '

'Not you. Remember I've seen you crying in passion – '

She said angrily, 'I might have known that's all you want – '

He said, angry now in his turn, 'It's not all I want. Dammit, I can obtain that anywhere – '

'It's all most men want. It was all Sir William wanted – ' she said sullenly.

He interrupted. 'Sir William? But I thought – '

'You never knew,' she said, with unconscious cruelty. 'What I had to put up with from him. The degradation. He treated me like a whore.'

'You should have told me.' Now he was sullen too. 'I knew there was much you didn't tell me.'

'I didn't tell you I had a miscarriage.'

'When?'

'When I had the cholera.'

'Then it was mine?'

'Of course it was yours. I'd been so worried, wondering what to do. And then – '

'Oh Tam,' he said. 'You make me so ashamed.'

'I wanted to tell you,' she said. 'I was so alone. So ill. And then when I saw you, you asked me to become a kept woman.'

He let her go then, stared in something like horror. And in that moment it seemed that she was the stronger of the two, she who had been through so much while he wasn't there.

He said humbly, 'I'm sorry.'

'It doesn't matter now,' she said.

'But I came to the Manor. First Sir William turned me away, then when he was dead, you wouldn't see me . . . Is that it then? You were worried about having another child?'

'No, I can't have any more.'

'Oh Tam.' It was a cry of pain, and again she found herself the stronger, found herself comforting him.

'Don't worry,' she said. 'It's probably too late anyway, I'm nearly forty.'

'So,' he said. 'Is it over then? Is that what you're trying to tell me? I think I understand – '

'No, you don't understand.' How can you when I don't understand myself? she thought. I still love you, Charles. She walked round the room and he watched her. 'It's not that I don't want to – But I couldn't let you make love to me. Not here, not now, not while Juliet's in the house.'

'But – ' He was about to reiterate that that wasn't all . . .

'It can't be right, Charles. Not my own sister. Do you understand? I mean, it's almost regarded as incest.'

All thoughts of telling her that didn't matter, of saying how members were trying to get a bill through Parliament enabling a man to marry his deceased wife's sister, flew away. He said heavily, 'There's always something between us, isn't there, Tam?'

'What do you mean?'

'What I say. You didn't have to bring Juliet here, or to live with her.'

'She wanted to come. She was unhappy. And you know how much I love Cherry Trees.'

'I know all that. I might have understood if you were different.'

'And what does that mean?'

264

'You aren't the most unselfish person, are you, Tam? So why do you always put something or someone between us?'

'And that's not true. Or I wouldn't have had Jamie – '

'We were both carried away that night – '

'Well! Is that all it was?'

'You know what I mean.'

'And I stayed with you at the Duchess's house, if you remember, when if Sir William had found out – '

'Yes,' he said. 'We were happy then.'

Yes, thought Tam. There was no thought of the future. Except that when you're young you think the future's bound to come right. No thought of losing a baby I was afraid to have, the guilt, the grief . . . and you not there. She said, angry again, 'You call me selfish. Yet I'm the one who had to look after everything, everybody. I've had to be selfish, to survive. And I've had my own work, you never thought of that. Tell me, Charles. You say I never ask about your work, and maybe that's true, but I know we can never marry. And supposing, in the future, and God forbid that anything should happen, but just supposing that you were a widower and I'd left my work, my son, to live in a little house in London to be near you. What then? What if you had a chance of high office? You'd need a wife. So what then would become of me in my little house, had *you* thought of that?' And he was silent, wondering how she could put an unerring finger on his dilemma.

She continued, 'So I'm selfish. By God, Charles, women have to be. Do you ever think of my work? The work I'm pledged to do?'

'For your father,' he said. 'Maybe that's the trouble.' He turned away from her. 'Leave it now,' he said. 'I won't bother you again. You must come to me if you want me.'

She said stiffly, 'I'll order your refreshment. And send Jamie down to you.' She left the room.

He stayed two nights, walking and talking with Jamie. But Tam did not see him alone again.

Chapter Seven

At first Jamie was eyed with mistrust at the weaving factory. Wasn't he Sir William's son? And a boss? At best he would be one of the do-gooding people who brought tracts round to the poor and were always telling them to behave. But he bought a gallon of ale as all new apprentices were obliged to do, and drank his share without hesitation. Jamie, for his part, was surprised. He had expected to find a group of downtrodden, weary people. Weary they often were, for they worked long hours, but they were still able to laugh and even sing, though some of the songs they sang were hardly flattering to his uncle. Jamie learned more from the songs – when once he could hear above the noise of the looms – than from the weavers' talk. He painstakingly learned the weaving trade, never taking time off because he was the boss's nephew. He made it plain – for Jamie was a truthful lad – that he would not stay with them, but that he wanted to learn about the work and conditions, and this went down well.

In truth Jamie did not feel half so confident as he appeared. His knowledge of Latin and Greek was no use to him here, neither were mathematics or English. All he needed to know was how to use a loom, and that wasn't as easy as it looked. Jamie, for all his education, knew less than the lowest child in the weaving shed and the weavers knew it. But he didn't hesitate to ask advice; nor did they refuse to tell him. Gradually, a grudging admiration was built up. 'Aye, well, he tries, give the lad his due,' they said to each other. And to Jamie, 'Aye, we'll mek a weaver of you yet, lad,' or, 'Aye, we'll have you on a Jacquard loom, weaving all the fancy patterns.' And a final word of advice, perhaps the most sound of all: 'You have to like the weaving really. You have to have the knack. It'll come in time . . . but you have to like it.' Like the colours and the patterns and the making a thing of beauty out of long strands of silk. It came easily to these people, born of weavers, helping since childhood; to Jamie it was at first a nightmare. But he persevered, remembering that he, too, was of weaving stock, that he was not a Fargate, but a Waring.

He never told the weavers that he was responsible for the new water pipes even now being laid in their homes; after all, Geoffrey was paying. But

266

he listened with pleasure to their cries of wonderment. 'This water's coming out pure as the driven snow, not mucky like the last. It's a marvel.'

And yet somehow they did find out, no one quite knew how. No one ever has found out just how knowledge sometimes gets more quickly to people who can't read or write than to those who can. Perhaps a chance remark, fastened on by those whose senses are often more alert to things not put on paper, perhaps an inspired guess, whatever it was, someone approached Jamie.

'I hear it was you arranged for the water pipes.'

'I did suggest it, I'm not paying for it.'

'Who is then?'

'Mr Geoffrey Waring.'

'I'm surprised he's paying for owt, old skinflint that he is.'

'I don't think,' Jamie said carefully, 'that he quite realised how much damage dirty water could do.'

'You think it caused the cholera, then?'

'That's what Dr Phillips thinks and he got it from a Dr Snow in London who's just published a paper about it.'

'Aye,' the men said among themselves, 'he's a clever young lad, no doubt about it. And he's really going to do summat for this place.'

'Can't believe it really, and him Sir William's son.'

'Ah. Meks you wonder if he is.'

'What do you mean, Amos?'

'Well, he's very thick with the Warings. It was Charles Waring's idea in the first place about these pipes – '

'So?'

'Meks you wonder if he's Charles's son.'

There was a pause as people thought about it.

'If you see 'em walking together you'll notice how much alike they are.'

'Aye,' ruminatively. 'His mother always did see a lot of Charles Waring – '

'Did she?'

'Oh aye. Old Joe used to tek the ribbons down the wharf and he saw 'em talking together.'

'That don't mean nowt – '

'No. It were just the look of 'em, old Joe says. Mind you, she's a good sort, she is, working on the boats. Still, it could be, I suppose.'

Nothing more was said. No one bothered very much. The weavers didn't really care who Jamie's father was, they merely put the point they'd noticed. But it did become an accepted fact. When, perhaps months later, it was alluded to again, it was, 'Ah, they say he's Charles's son . . .' The weavers were fond of Charles and Jamie, none would wish to hurt them. But the talk had begun.

Had Jamie and Charles ever stood side by side before a mirror they too would have noticed the resemblance, but they never did. To Tam the likeness had become dulled by familiarity: her eye, without knowing it, looked for the difference in each, not the resemblance. So Charles Waring and

Jamie Fargate walked about Chilverton, often together these days, talking about the new water system, dreaming of plans for better houses in the future.

It was, surprisingly, a full year before Sir Lewis started the war of the canals, a year which to Tam, in retrospect, seemed a welcome calm, a lull before the encroaching storms.

She worked on the boats as always, running trips to the Midland towns. She went to the wharf, though she was content to leave the administration to Robin. She ignored the fact that Charles never came, she had other visitors. True to her promise to start her afternoon teas, she put the word around, and found to her surprise that she collected a vastly different set of people than at the Manor. The Cortains and the Marnings were no longer interested now she did not hunt, Celia was aloof, Georgiana came only very occasionally. The few people she knew in the town were unable, for various reasons, to socialise, the Vicar's wife was an elderly invalid, and the doctor had a growing family and little money. So the crowd who turned up were a motley crew, the sort of people, Tam knew, her mother would never have dreamed of entertaining, and Tam disliked them, not because of their lack of social standing, but because they were so obviously trying to ingratiate themselves with Lady Fargate. Unfortunately there were few men, so, to make it appear normal for Jerome to appear, Tam asked the curate to call, and he, a bespectacled, intensely shy bachelor of some forty-odd years, would sit, quite silent, a cup balanced on his knee, looking so absolutely petrified that Tam was quite sorry for him, and even wondered if he thought she had designs on him, which sent her into fits of laughter once he had gone, and made her wish she had someone with whom she could share the joke. But she carried on with the teas, in the hope of gleaning some information from Jerome, and they all sat chatting in the garden. They sat in the spring as the cherry blossoms covered the trees and the boaters painted their boats for the new season; in summer, while heavy bees hummed among the lavender and honeysuckle, and the cherry petals drifted down around them; in the autumn as the birds prepared for their migration and the mists spread over the water. And as it grew colder they moved to the house and sat in the drawing room watching the canal grow dark with heavy waves blown by the gales.

Christmas came and went, Jamie worked at the weaving factory, and in January, when a film of ice was forming over the water, Tam's calm was shattered.

She had written regularly to the Duchess, and when in January she received no reply she was alarmed. The Duchess, although seemingly indestructible, was almost eighty, she could not get about much, and when Tam wrote again and still had no reply, she took the train to London, and found her old friend in bed with bronchitis.

'I'm glad to see you,' the Duchess wheezed. 'I'm not going to live for ever, don't know that I want to. Now sit and talk to me.'

And, after a certain amount of catching up with the news, the Duchess said, 'I must ask you – what about Charles?'

'Charles?' Tam asked uncertainly.

'You see him?'

'He visits Cherry Trees occasionally. We talk.'

'Just talk?'

'What do you mean?' Tam asked, more puzzled than ever.

'You know very well what I mean,' the Duchess retorted. 'Let me put it more crudely as we did before everyone became so mealy-mouthed. If you don't sleep with him, someone else will.'

Tam flushed. 'Men do,' she said. 'It doesn't mean anything.'

'Have you quarrelled?'

'No. But we do seem to be at cross-purposes lately.'

'Do you still love him?'

'Yes, of course. I've never loved anyone else.'

'And you expect him to be always waiting for when you're ready to see him?'

'If he wants me,' Tam said, still sulky.

'You see him as the same eager youth always waiting to pick you up when you fall? No, Tam, that's an old maid's dream. People change. Charles is ambitious.'

'He never used to be,' said Tam.

'Oh, I think he was, a little, right from the start. And with no family to divert him, he has nothing to do but further his career.'

'What's all this to do with what you were saying about other women?'

'Ah. You said it didn't mean anything. But this time it might.'

'Who is she?'

'He's been seen around in public with a quiet widow named Mary Travers.'

'But – he's married. People will talk.'

'It's not people's talk that worries me, it's the man himself. He's alone, he's been alone for many years. This particular friend of his moves in his circles, has friends who could help him – ' the Duchess broke off at the look on Tam's face.

'What can I do?' Tam cried. 'Juliet is living with me. How can I possibly – '

'You can still come here. Maybe I'm a meddling old woman, and maybe I shouldn't advise you as I do. But he's loved you for years, Tam, yet love can die if it isn't nourished, if someone comes along who's willing to give him what he wants.'

'But he can't marry this Mary Travers.'

'Not at the moment, no. How is Juliet?'

'She is – well. She seems happy.'

'Is she really? Really well and happy? Sometimes it seems, from what you've told me about her, from what you write, that she is just sitting around waiting to die.'

'Oh!' Tam's hand flew to her face.

'I'm sorry,' the Duchess said again. 'But in some ways, Tam, you're so honest, so far-seeing, and in others always ready to turn a blind eye. Ah well, perhaps we all do,' and she lay back on her pillows, her wheeezing increased, and a nurse bustled in and ushered Tam from the room.

Back at Cherry Trees Tam paced around her room. She was consumed by an overpowering jealousy of the unknown Mary Travers. She knew that the Duchess was right, she *had* expected him to be there, waiting for when she chose to join him, as he had years ago when she'd run to him for help. She'd been hurt and angry, but she'd thought the anger was all on her side, that he'd come when and if she beckoned. And there was Juliet; what was this about her waiting to die? Tam studied her sister and thought there might be some truth in the statement, and tried to urge her sister into action.

'What would you like to do, Juliet? Shall we go out? Would you like to come on the boat?'

And to everything Juliet replied quietly, 'If you wish, Tam.'

'But what do *you* want, Juliet?'

'I'm all right, Tam. I am happy at Cherry Trees.'

Sometimes Tam thought her sister was back in her childhood, that she hardly knew the difference between then and now. Times when she'd walk round picking the flowers, letting them drop where she picked them, or as now, in winter, simply staring into the rain and snow. Why hadn't she noticed all this before?

She decided action must be taken, she would go to London again and see Charles. But before she could put her plan into operation she received news that the Duchess had died. She mourned her old friend sincerely, but knew this was the end of any plans to visit Charles in London. And it was precisely this moment that Sir Lewis chose to strike: he reduced the charges for freight on his railway.

Jerome told her first. He came on a day when there had been fewer visitors than usual and they had left early, so Tam was alone. He was always very circumspect, he never stayed more than a few minutes, so was it merely chance that, when she handed him tea, he touched her hand? He withdrew it hastily and no word was said, yet Tam knew instinctively that someday, perhaps soon, Jerome would declare himself. Not yet, she prayed, I haven't time to think about him.

'I thought he'd be satisfied with transporting his own coal,' she said to him now. 'What more does he want?'

'I fear he is after other freight,' Jerome said.

'Our freight?'

He shrugged without answering. And when he left she drove down to the wharf and went into the little office where Robin was working to tell him what she'd heard. 'We can't afford to lose the Milden colliery,' she said. 'And all the other business I've worked for.'

'No,' Robin said, and Tam studied him. She liked Robin, he was a good worker, yet now, in a moment of crisis, was he perhaps too young, too inexperienced? She could not put a finger on anything wrong. He tried, he was always willing . . . did he perhaps try too hard? And she wondered why he did not use the thees and thous of the Friends now. Oddly, it was this latter which disturbed her.

She longed for Charles, to talk to as in the old days, to pour out her troubles . . . and realised ruefully that it was precisely that he had wanted from her: a listening ear. For the first time she understood.

In the end she decided to talk to Harry, listen to his wisdom. So she waited till he brought the *Duchess* back and tied her up, watched the passengers disembark.

When Harry joined them in the office she commented, 'Not quite so many passengers today.'

'They've been dwindling a long time,' he said.

'But I will have a full load on my trips – '

'Yes, Tamarisk, because they are trips. Excursions. For daily travel now they go by train. In fact, I've been wondering just how long I can carry on.'

'You don't mean give up the boat?'

'Oh not yet. But I'm getting to be an old man, Tamarisk, and our daughters are in Birmingham.'

'Yes, of course. Ruth – ' Tam tried to reckon up the age of the youngest girl.

'Ruth has been teaching in the school for many a year,' said Harry with a faint smile. 'Now she too talks of marriage, and would like us to go and live there – '

'Oh, Harry, no. You can't leave me.' Tam was horrified. 'Not after all these years. Why, I've just lost the Duchess – '

'It is one of the penalties of getting older,' said Harry. 'That we lose our companions. But we're not thinking of leaving yet.'

Tam remembered Abby's voice from the past, talking about her husband. 'He can't stand much more, out in all weathers, and he has the rheumatics bad . . .' She looked at Harry, noticed his white hair, his stooped shoulders. It was a hard life on a boat.

'Well, we'll talk about it later, Harry. In the meantime, what do we do about Sir Lewis's latest move?' she asked.

'What dost thou think?' asked Harry in turn.

'I think we'll have to cut the tolls.'

Harry rubbed his forehead. 'Think well, Tamarisk,' he said. 'Canst thou afford to cut any further?'

'I don't think I have a choice. If I don't cut the tolls I'll lose freight.'

'That is so. Well, then, how much shalt thou cut?'

'A penny a ton to start with?' hazarded Tam.

'I think so.'

'I'll have posters printed,' Tam said. 'Display them everywhere: "*The Chilverton Canal cuts its tolls. Cheaper travel.*" And I know what I'll do: when I am not running trips on the *Princess* I'll take her along and look for other cargoes, things I can carry in her, local trips.'

'The weather's getting bad,' said Harry, dubiously.

'But that might help us,' said Tam.

That night Tam went over her accounts. So much had to be held in reserve for maintenance, there were wages to pay, clerks, engineers, the crews, as well as the more humble tasks. She had to find more markets.

January was cold, there was a bitter wind blowing from the east when they set out and Tam wrapped herself in a warm shawl. Sally was well able to steer, so she left the girl to it while she studied the wharves they passed. And when they came to the little farmers' stations she had her idea.

'Farms,' she cried excitedly to Jim. 'Unhitch the horses, we're going to ride. You stay here, Sally.'

Over the cold fields they rode, calling in at each farm. And they were quite successful: many farmers could not get their produce to the railway, were still producing small amounts, sufficient for their immediate use and that of their village.

'I could grow ten tons of potatoes,' said one farmer. 'But who's to buy 'em?'

'I will,' said Tam. 'What have you surplus now?'

'Oh, apples in store. They'll all rot soon, or I'll give 'em to the pigs.'

'I'll buy them,' said Tam. 'What's your market price?'

He hesitated, then quoted a price. She immediately offered half. The farmer took it gladly and lent a cart to take his apples to the boat.

'Oh, milady, what have you done?' asked Jim, horrified.

The apples were piled on to the boat, in the saloon, in the cabins, their sweetness penetrating the air. And they took the boat to Birmingham.

'You'll never sell these in the market,' said Jim, aghast.

'I don't intend to try,' said Tam, and as the boat tied up she piled her water can with apples, hitched up her skirt and stood beside the boat. 'Cheap apples,' she cried. 'Who'll buy my lovely apples?'

Apples were scarce in January, only those with lofts to store them being able to keep them through the winter. In less than an hour the apples were gone. Tam had found a new market.

It wasn't always so lucrative. But word got around that the Calder Boats would take any small load and soon farmers were waiting at their tiny wharves with their leftover produce, and the boats did a brisk trade in potatoes, swedes, turnips, butter and cheese, sides of bacon. As always, business led to more business: sometimes a satisfied farmer would give her boats a full load perhaps going to London. 'Why not?' he asked. 'It's not that much cheaper by train, and I have to get them to the station. You can pick them up here, and these things will keep a few more days.' And occasionally it worked the other end; a hotel might ask if she could bring some butter, and somehow she'd obtain butter from a farmer who knew she'd do him a favour by taking his surplus bacon, as she had in the past. Tam found her new venture an exciting challenge. Those who said the canals were doomed were too pessimistic. All you had to do was keep trying.

In the spring of 1851 Tam and Celia heard from Annabel that Lord Brooke was dead, and they were invited to the funeral.

Tam stared at the letter in her hand with mixed feelings. She could not pretend to feel any sorrow, Lord Brooke had always been a shadowy figure, the one who took Mama away from them all, from Papa. As long as she was away from Mama she need not think much about her, seeing her would bring back all the old animosity. Yet she must attend: however unconventional she might appear to be, the old proprieties asserted themselves. So when Celia called, resplendent in a black crinoline, Tam said grudgingly, 'I suppose we'll have to go by train.'

'Of course. I'm glad you realise it, Tam.'

'I've never disputed the train is quicker. For passengers, anyway.'

'Will Juliet go?'

'No, better not. She doesn't really want to go. I think she would be wiser to stay here. Jamie will, of course.'

'Yes. My girls too.'

'All of them?' asked Tam. 'They are not really related.'

'They may not be, as I was not illegitimate,' snapped Celia, 'but Mama would wish it.' Celia liked to visit Greytowers and felt it was a pity her mother did not invite them more often; she had met Lord Brooke's son only once, but she knew he was married to the daughter of a peer, knew they had children the same age as her girls . . .

'Whatever are you going to wear, Tam?' she asked. 'Not that dress, I hope.'

Tam looked down at her serviceable alpaca. 'I suppose not. I have some good clothes brought from the Manor.'

'Heavens, they'd be long out of date,' said Celia. 'Have you no crinoline?'

'I have – an old one,' said Tam, shortly. 'I'm thinking of getting some bloomers.' She couldn't resist teasing Celia.

'Tam, really,' Celia cried.

'Why not? They'd be ideal for the boats,' said Tam, trying to keep her face straight.

'All this selling on boats. At your age,' disapproved Celia. 'You should have sold the canal when you had the chance. Geoffrey says you couldn't sell it now even if you wanted to.'

She rose to go and Tam watched her sister depart: how plump she was, she absolutely waddled. And once she was so thin. Tam went to the mirror and studied her own face and figure. She wasn't fat, nor likely to be, all the rushing around she did. But her complexion was not so clear as in girlhood, it was sadly burned by wind and sun . . . Oh, what did it matter? Though Charles still visited, very occasionally, she was often out when he came . . . no, it didn't matter now. The wild jealousy she'd felt for Mary Travers had given way to a dull ache. She didn't know if he still saw her, tried not to care. It was over, she told herself, all the wild joy, the desire, gone with the wind of her youth. So she hadn't asked him about Mary Travers, knowing deep inside that if she did he might ask why she was interested, why she herself held aloof, and this she did not want to answer.

They rode together in the train, Tam and Jamie, Celia, Geoffrey and their three eldest daughters. Amelia and Becky sat quietly in one corner, Amanda pouted in the other.

273

'Really, Mama,' she said. 'I do so hate wearing black.'

'You have to wear black at a funeral,' said Celia, shortly.

Amanda fluttered her eyelashes. 'Do you like wearing black, Cousin Jamie?' she asked.

Jamie smiled. 'I don't mind.'

'Amanda,' Celia snapped repressively.

'What?' asked Amanda, all injured innocence. 'I'm merely talking to my cousin.'

Celia frowned, and Tam hid a smile. Amanda was flirting with Jamie, the minx, and Tam knew Celia's feelings well enough. Jamie – even if he were not a cousin – wouldn't do for Amanda; Celia was setting her sights high.

The train rumbled into the nearest station, and they piled into the waiting carriage. Celia noted the almost dilapidated state of the carriage, the shabby uniforms of the coachmen. Not much money to spare here, but what could one expect when he and Mama had been so extravagant?

The carriage drew up at Greytowers, and as they were ushered inside Celia noted the same air of shabbiness everywhere, there were even gaps on the walls where paintings had been removed, probably for sale. Celia pursed her lips.

'My dears,' said Annabel, who, even at sixty plus, still looked stylish, though Tam noticed she wore a little more pearl powder on her face than usual. 'Dear girls,' she said. 'And dear grandchildren. How good of you to travel so far. Now, have we all met?' She made the introductions, her stepson, the present Earl, his Countess, the Lady Jane, a cool beauty with ice-blue eyes, and their children, Lord Cravenfield and Lady Caroline, who was, Celia noted with pleasure, just the age of her dear Amanda.

In the large bedroom she was to share with Geoffrey, Celia said happily, 'I was right. The Brookes are quite poor. Not surprising when you think how the late Earl spent so much time at the race track, Mama accompanying him from all accounts. I wonder if the present Earl is such a spendthrift?

'Does it matter?' asked Geoffrey.

But Celia was sitting on the bed, a thoughtful frown on her face. 'I think,' she said enigmatically, 'there may be a way our two families can help each other.'

Celia kept her ears and eyes open, and when the funeral was over and they sat together in the drawing room she knew this was her last chance to operate her plan, for they returned home tomorrow. 'What will you do now, Mama?' she asked Annabel.

'I hardly know,' said Annabel. 'There is no dower house here.'

There was a short silence, neither the Earl nor the Countess spoke. Then Celia asked, 'What of your father, Mama? Is he still alive?'

'Heavens, no, he died years ago,' said Annabel.

'But you didn't tell us,' said Celia, taken aback.

Annabel shrugged. 'What was the point? He never forgave me.'

'And your brother?'

274

'He cares nothing for me. If you are asking why I don't go to live with him, Celia, the answer is that he has never asked me.'

'I was not asking that, Mama. If you have no home now you must come to us.'

Annabel hesitated and looked at Tam, who turned her head away: no, she could not have Mama with her, could not bear it . . .

Annabel said graciously, 'Thank you, Celia. I accept.'

Celia said to the Countess, 'Your Caroline is the same age as my Amanda, I believe?'

'Yes, indeed. She was to make her debut this year, but we shall postpone it now for another season.'

Celia said wistfully, 'I would so love Amanda to have a season in London.'

'Well, you have a town house,' said Annabel.

'Yes, indeed.' Celia noted the enquiring look the Countess gave her. 'And very pleasant it is too, in one of the best areas. Of course, we hadn't thought about presentation – ' she paused, delicately.

'Caroline is to be presented,' said Annabel. 'Why don't you two get together as some mothers do, share expenses?'

The Countess's eyes glittered momentarily and Celia knew her guess had been correct, the family were poor. Then the Countess said coolly, 'That might be an idea. Whose house would we use?'

'Why, mine of course,' said Celia.

'An idea, certainly. And your – er – Amanda could be presented with Caroline.'

Celia clasped her hands in ecstasy.

'I don't know that I want to be presented,' said Amanda.

'Of course you do,' said Celia sharply.

Summer was well on its way before Annabel settled in with Celia, and almost immediately she came to visit Tam. The old house was at its best. Honeysuckle twined over the porch and sent its heady perfume into the air. Roses massed in the gardens, where an aged gardener tried to get some order into the riot of marigolds, snapdragons, pansies and lavender. Out in the fields beyond, poppies flamed in the corn, the trees were full of birds. Annabel cried wonderingly, 'Why, it's just the same.'

'Yes, Mama, what did you expect?' Tam asked.

'And where is dear Juliet?'

'I'm here, Mama. Sitting in the garden.'

'How are you, my sweet?'

'I'm quite well, Mama. How are you?'

'Oh.' Annabel shrugged. 'As well as one can expect at Celia's. In truth, I miss dear Tony more than I thought possible.'

Juliet looked blank as if she could not remember who Tony was. Tam turned impatiently to Annabel and said, 'Mama, I hope you don't mind, but I have to go.'

'Go? Go where?' asked Annabel, vaguely.

'To work,' Tam said curtly.

'Oh, you mean the boats. Are you still playing with them? Well, don't worry about me, I'll sit with Juliet.'

Tam walked down to the *Princess*, and as they sailed away to the nearest farm where she was collecting butter and eggs, she hoped her mother wasn't going to make a habit of visiting Cherry Trees. But Annabel did, and the next time she came she brought Amanda and Bee with her.

'Tell me, Tam,' said Annabel, 'isn't Bee the most delightful child? Come, Bee, say hello to Aunt Tamarisk.'

Bee stomped forward with no trace of shyness, and Tam looking down at the small girl couldn't help smiling. Somehow she looked so odd; nothing seemed to fit. Her dress with its flounced skirt was pretty, but far too long, almost to the ankles, and her white drawers showed underneath. Tam decided it was because Bee's legs were too short and no effort had been made to make the dress fit. No small girl could go out without a hat, but Bee's was large, too large, it slipped askew, hiding her front hair completely. Her face was round and plain, yet she had an engaging grin as she stood before Tam, hand outstretched.

'Tell me,' said Annabel. 'Don't you think she's just like your Papa?'

For an instant Tam stiffened, then realised that Annabel meant Jamie, and she said, 'Yes, she is,' and added in a whisper, 'but why should you care?'

'Mama thinks Bee is troublesome,' said Amanda. 'But then, she thinks I am too.'

'Oh, Celia always was a fool,' said Annabel, and Tam gave her mother a warning look. What mischief was Annabel up to now?

Amanda sauntered round the gardens, looking at the flowers, returned to Tam. 'Is Jamie in?' she asked casually.

'No, your cousin is working,' Tam replied. 'He always does in the daytime.' The girl's a flirt, she told herself. She needn't cast her eyes on Jamie. And hoped her reply would warn her off, that Amanda wouldn't want to come again. But she did, almost daily, together with Annabel and Bee.

Tam worked as always, leaving them in the garden. But when she was at home she soon realised that Amanda was interested in herself as much as Jamie.

'Tell me about your work,' the girl demanded.

'You mean the boats?'

'Of course. How long have you been doing it? Mama never will talk about it.'

Tam gave her a brief outline, expanding on what she was doing now.

'The Calder Boats,' said Amanda, dreamily. 'I do think it's marvellous, I think you're marvellous, Aunt.'

'Why?' asked Tam.

'Why, to work, of course. Don't you think it's good for women to work? I'd love to.'

'It isn't easy,' said Tam. 'I was more or less thrown into it when my Papa died.'

'But you married, and then came back here,' said Amanda. 'Though I

276

understand Sir William left you quite poor. Or shouldn't I say that?'

'It's true?' said Tam, indifferently.

'But if it hadn't been true, I mean, if he'd left you well off, what then? Would you have given up the boats?'

'No,' said Tam shortly. 'They were my father's, now they're mine, and the canal too. The Calder Boats,' she added proudly.

'I think it's wonderful. And Grandmama used to be an actress, didn't she?'

'Yes.'

'I think I'd like to be an actress.'

'Oh no,' said Tam. 'I'm sure you don't, Amanda.'

'Mama wants me to be presented, and I don't want it at all.'

'What do you want, Amanda?'

'To *do* something. I don't know what. I wish I were a man. Men are more free, aren't they?'

'I suppose so,' said Tam.

'I was always a tomboy when I was a child,' said Amanda, reflectively. 'Perhaps I should have been a boy. Mama thinks I'm quite ridiculous, but Grandmama says I'm sensible.'

Later, Tam said to Annabel, 'What are you doing with those girls, Mama? You know Celia doesn't like Amanda talking about freedom and work and so on.'

'Celia's a fool,' said Annabel, blithely.

'Oh, Mama, you're outrageous, you really are. Are you encouraging Amanda to want to be an actress too?'

'No,' said Annabel, her eyes wide with innocence.

'Really, Mama, I wish you wouldn't bring them so often.'

'Worried about Jamie?' asked Annabel with a wicked grin. 'Amanda does cast her eyes over every man in sight.'

'Like some others I could mention,' Tam retorted savagely.

'The girl's wasted with Celia, Tam. She has great potential.'

'That is as maybe, but I don't want to be drawn into it. I have enough on my hands as it is.'

'But Bee, Tam, you must like little Bee.'

And Tam had to confess she did. She liked to see the child stomping purposefully around the garden, though she did wonder sometimes how much schooling she had these days, and why Celia didn't put her foot down. But Celia couldn't afford to quarrel with Annabel, her link with the Brookes and Amanda's London season. So the three continued to visit Tam.

And then it was August, the Parliamentary recess, and Charles came to visit. Now there were six of them sitting in the garden – when Tam could spare the time from her boats which wasn't so often these days – and she watched in growing annoyance as Annabel talked to Charles: how was London, the House, what had happened to Lord Palmerston, was it true that the Queen disliked him, indeed had insisted on his dismissal? How ridiculous, he was a brilliant man, why she remembered him as a young Regency buck dancing at Almack's with the Countess of Lieven. He had so many love affairs . . . and then married Lord Melbourne's sister, Lady Cowper, and they were so happy, he loved her devotedly. So Annabel chatted vivaciously, and Charles responded. Tam gazed at them with gloom. The old pattern re-emerging: Mama carrying off all men, even Charles. Grudgingly Tam admitted that her mother still had the same stylish air as always, but even so . . . When Annabel hastened away to fetch Bee and Tam was alone with Charles, she said caustically, 'Mama flirts as if she were a young girl.'

'Some women never grow old,' said Charles.

'But she is old, Charles, she is over sixty.'

'Your Mama will be able to charm men when she's eighty,' said Charles, and Tam was furious. Was it always to be thus? And in her rage she said, 'And you will always be susceptible, won't you? I hear you are taken with Mary Travers – ' and broke off, appalled.

'Mary Travers is a friend,' he said quietly.

Tam was alarmed now. 'A friend? Is that why you are so often around London together?'

'In London, yes. I need a partner, Tam. I am not the green youth I was when I first went to London. I attend political parties, balls, it is expected of me. Sometimes I have to entertain in return and I need a hostess.'

'How old is she?' asked Tam.

'About your age.'

'Then surely people will gossip. Surely you should have found an older woman – '

'People will not gossip. Mrs Travers is from an impeccable family, her morals are impeccable. Everyone knows this. They know too that my own wife is ailing. So nothing is said. There is nothing to say. It is a purely business arrangement.'

'Is it? And does Mary Travers know this?'

He was silent.

'Suppose you were a widower, what then?' she asked.

He moved away from her. 'Why look to the future?'

'Because no doubt Mary Travers looks to the future. Oh, Charles, I don't understand you.'

'You never did, Tam. I am ambitious.'

'That's what the Duchess said – '

'And it's what you never understood.'

She stared, knowing she'd sensed a ruthlessness within him, but had preferred to see only the gentle side that looked after people.

'I think you've changed.'

'Maybe I have. We can't stay the same all our lives. I've been alone a long time, Tam,' and there was a hint of reproach in his voice that angered her. 'So I had nothing but my career. And it has come to mean more and more to me. More than I dreamed possible.'

'So you want high office?'

'Yes.'

'And Mary Travers will help you to this end?'

'Yes. She is of an old established Whig family, related to many ministers.'

'Then,' Tam said, 'they will expect marriage when you are a widower.' And he didn't deny it.

Amanda begged Tam to take her to the wharf.

'Oh very well,' said Tam, at the end of her patience, tired of her whole family; of Mama, of Celia, of Amanda. 'But if your mother is annoyed don't blame me.'

They drove down in the pony-chaise, and Amanda cried in delight as she saw the wharf, its loads of coal, the farm produce. They went to the little office where Robin sat alone at his books as always. Tam introduced the two.

'Why, how nice to meet you,' said Amanda, fluttering her eyelashes as he took her hand. 'It must be such an interesting job you have here.'

Tam groaned to herself; Amanda was at her tricks again, and she hoped Robin would dismiss her with a flea in her ear.

But Robin was not a worldly young man. Brought up strictly by his parents, he knew nothing of girls. Perhaps his over-zealousness sprang from the fact that he had no outlet for his animal spirits. Instead he became a shade too self-righteous, too serious. He had no experience of women whatsoever, he hoped that someday he'd marry, when the right girl came along. So far she hadn't and the girls his parents knew seemed somewhat dull. So when Amanda appeared in the dusty office, wearing a blue silk dress, cut daringly low for such a young girl, he felt a thrill run right through his body. And when she swirled her full flounced skirts, and fluttered her eyelashes at him, Robin was lost.

With the winter Annabel and Amanda ceased coming to Cherry Trees, for which Tam was heartily thankful. She didn't want to see her mother, the animosity was still too strong, and she was a little tired of Amanda and her bold looks and fluttering eyelashes. She had seen the girl trying her tricks with Jamie on the few occasions he was home, and had said to her son in private, 'You are cousins, you know, Jamie. More so than Amanda realises.'

'Yes, I know. Why?'

'I just don't want you falling in love with her, Jamie. Aunt Celia would never allow it.'

'I haven't fallen in love, Mama.'

'Good. Coming here with her frills and flounces . . .'

'She's a pretty girl, Mama. A little like you.'

'Flatterer.' Tam eyed her son fondly.

'And as I'm only eighteen, and not earning much money at the moment, I can hardly think of marriage.'

'Good, I'm glad you're so sensible. Amanda seems so wild, as if she'd run off with anyone.'

'I don't think she's very happy at home.'

'Well, we can't help that.' Tam dismissed Amanda from her mind, now she knew Jamie was not in thrall. 'Tell me, how is your work going?'

'Very well. I'm in the office now, studying accounts.'

'And are they in good order?'

'Oh yes, Uncle Geoffrey knows about figures.'

Tam grunted. She didn't altogether like the idea of her son helping Geoffrey to make money. 'What are you going to get out of it?' she demanded.

'I hope a partnership in the end.'

'Does Geoffrey know this?'

'Not yet.'

Tam smiled. He was her son, after all. 'I thought you were going to help the weavers,' she said.

'I have. We have a ten-hour day now, strictly adhered to. We pay more than we did. And later, I hope to persuade Uncle Geoffrey to build new houses – '

'New houses for the weavers?'

'Yes. In place of the Patch. Some people do it, Mama, some employers are beginning to build model villages for their workers. Not many, there are still too many slums – '

'Yes,' she said, 'I remember Charles – your father – talking about it.' She smiled. 'I still wish you worked with me, Jamie.' Yes, it was still a sore point, she thought, as she watched Jamie leave the house, how sad it was that children seldom seemed to do what you planned for them. Oh well, she thought, I didn't do what my mother wanted . . .

And if Mama and Amanda stopped coming to Cherry Trees, there was still the occasional visitor, and one of these was Jerome. He walked in one Thursday and her heart sank. She knew when he came it was usually to bring bad news. But she made a pretence of welcoming him, for Matty's benefit. Tea was brought, cakes, and they sat talking of trivial things till they were at last left alone. Then Tam asked, 'What is it, Jerome?'

'Sir Lewis is cutting his freight rates again.'

'Oh no.'

'I'm sorry, Lady Fargate . . . Tamarisk. May I call you Tamarisk?'

'Yes – ' she replied indifferently. 'I always call you Jerome.'

'He's a determined man, Tamarisk. I wonder sometimes – '

'Yes?'

'If it's worth it from your point of view. Why you want to carry on. Or is that a too personal question?'

'No. People are always asking me that. And I always give the same answer. I shan't give up because I want to keep the canals open. Too many are being left to decay, not used. They know the remedy, they won't do anything.'

'And the railway companies offer them good money not to do anything,' said Jerome, shrewdly.

'So everyone is mad for the railways now. How do we know that something else will not turn up in the future and put the railways out of business?'

'What else can possibly turn up, Tamarisk?'

'Oh, I don't know. Perhaps we shall fly in the air.'

He laughed. She laughed too at the absurdity of people flying through the air. And when they stopped he stood up and took a step nearer to her and suddenly the air was charged.

'I am doing well in this job, Tamarisk. I have been promoted again. I have a higher salary.'

'Good,' she said.

'I can afford to marry, Tamarisk. I know I am bold, and in the old days I could never dare to approach you . . . that is the real reason I left, I wanted to improve my status . . .'

'Hush, Jerome.'

'I love you, Tamarisk, you must know that. Will you marry me?'

'Oh, don't spoil it all, Jerome. Why, even if I accepted, we'd be in the same position as I was with Sir William, fighting my own husband.'

'I am sure we could come to some agreement.'

She said shrewdly, 'You think I'll be forced out of business, don't you?'

'I fear so,' he said. 'Canals will soon be finished.'

'You're wrong,' she said. 'Some may have given up, but not all. And not mine. *My* canal will never close.'

'Leave that for the time being,' said Jerome. 'Just say you'll think it over, my proposal, that you won't turn me down out of hand . . .'

'I'll think it over, certainly,' she said, and as he bowed and left she watched him a little sadly. She did not love Jerome as she had loved Charles, but she was lonely. She admitted there was a great gap in her life and she needed a friend, a lover, a confidante . . . Yet it seemed that her work prevented her from marrying, she knew she would either have to sacrifice her boats, or stay as she was. And she would not give up the canal.

She prepared for her visit to the wharf to take the bad news to Robin and Harry. It was a dreary day, murky, with mist rising from the canal, and with a raw cold that ate into the bones. She walked into the office, Robin was there, Harry had just returned from his trip. She told them the news.

'And,' said Robin, 'the dividends will be down this year, too.' He seemed somewhat distrait. She frowned, and he went on, 'And if Sir Lewis is cutting his freight rates again – '

'He can afford to, he makes it up from his passenger traffic,' Harry pointed out.

'Well, we'll just have to cut our tolls again,' said Tam.

Harry looked worried. 'Can we afford to?'

She said heavily, 'I don't see what else I can do. Will there be much maintenance this coming year, Robin?'

'We have to dredge, it was left last year, to save costs.'

'Well, it must be done, we can't have the canal silting up.'

'And the Passmore lock gates need repairing.'

'That means traffic will be held up. Can it be done on Sunday?'

'No, it's too big a job.'

'Leave it to summer then, the nights will be shorter.' She paused, pondering. 'I could always cut wages.'

'I couldn't agree with that, Tamarisk. We've had enough trouble with that sort of thing,' Harry said.

'But bread is cheaper now . . . ' She looked at his closed face and knew she couldn't afford to upset Harry. But Jerome would have agreed, she thought resentfully, and for the first time knew a moment's impatience with Harry.

'Very well. But I shall allow Sunday working in future. I know you won't approve, Harry, but you needn't work. I can't help it, I must keep going.'

'And thou wilt drop the tolls too?'

'I must.'

When she left them she was concerned. She wished Jerome was still working as agent, he'd been a good man. Harry was getting too old, and Robin was somehow absent-minded these days. But where would she get another good man now? All the bright youngsters were going on the railways.

Celia and Amanda departed to London at Easter where they entertained on a lavish scale. Lady Jane showed a ruthless determination to make their reception a success, and though they never managed to entertain the Queen, they were among the guests at other functions where she and Prince Albert appeared. They went to the opera, they heard Jenny Lind and Henrietta Sontag, they listened to the works of the young Italian, Giuseppe Verdi, and those of the young and handsome Mendelssohn, the Queen's favourite composer.

Celia hoped Amanda realised just how much she had done for her, but the girl seemed sullen with her mother, and in company alternated between high spirits when she danced all night, and strange moods when she insisted that she'd like to go on the stage. Celia bore with her unruly daughter as best she could, and prayed that some nice young gentleman would turn up to take her off her hands. So after every ball she would question Amanda: who had danced with her? Was that young Lord X? What did he say? And Amanda would pout and say he was as dull as ditchwater. Then she'd burst out laughing and say that she'd told him her father was in trade, and he had been quite put off. And Celia gritted her teeth and bore it all with what little patience she could muster. It would be worth it in the end, she thought, if Amanda managed to carry off one of the season's prizes, even a younger son would be acceptable. After all Amanda, for all her faults, was an attractive girl . . . if only young men didn't think her too bold. Daily Celia impressed on Amanda the correct behaviour for young ladies, the modesty of bearing, the downcast eyes, that is how the dear Queen liked girls to be. 'Pooh,' said Amanda. 'The dear Queen throws her weight about enough, and did when she was a girl, from all accounts.' Celia sighed again, and longed for her troublesome daughter to be safely married.

After a bright spring it rained, and carried on raining for two months. Tam eyed the canal anxiously, she could not afford any hindrance to her boats. She went to see the engineer.

'We can't let it overflow,' he said. 'It will go over Sir Lewis's land and there'll be all hell to pay.'

282

'Are the reservoirs full?'

'Yes. All of them.'

'Great heavens. Even the weather's against me.'

'We have no flood paddles, Miss Tam. I did mention it – '

'So what will you do?'

'I'll draw the lock paddles, let the water run down into the lower pound, it'll drain off easier there.' We hope, he added mentally.

Tam returned home and squelched her way into the house. She was, she knew, a sorry sight. Oilskins over her clothes dripped water in the hall. Her hair was soaking wet.

'Matty,' she called. 'Where are you?'

Matty ran in, her eyes wide with fright, and behind her was Celia, hovering like an avenging angel. Tam blinked, wondering if her eyes were deceiving her. 'I thought you were in London,' she said.

'Where is she?' Celia cried.

'Who?' Tam asked blankly.

'Amanda, of course.'

'How should I know where Amanda is? Isn't she with you?'

'She ran away,' said Celia, brandishing a note. 'She left this.'

'Well, what does it say?' Tam asked impatiently. 'That she is coming here?'

'She said she is running away with Robin Earp and going on the stage. Who is Robin Earp?'

'Robin *Earp*? Amanda?'

'Will you tell me who he is.'

Tam's heart was sinking suddenly. 'He's Agent of the canal.'

'The canal. I might have known. I might have known. And who introduced her to this – this Agent, may I ask?'

'Well, I did – '

'And who are his parents?'

'They live on a boat – '

Celia moaned, and made as if to faint. Tam watched her unmoved. She wanted to get out of her sopping clothes, at least dry her hair. She was sorry for Celia, and furious with Amanda. And Robin Earp ... dear heavens.

'You did it,' Celia said. 'You always were against me. You deliberately took my daughter and introduced her to this – this – fortune-hunter, who can only be after her money – '

'Just a minute,' Tam interrupted. 'He is not a fortune-hunter, the Earps are a respectable family and not concerned with money, we'd better go and see them. I did not encourage her to come here at all, Celia, she was a bit of a nuisance, but Mama brought her – ' And it struck her. Mama, she thought, I might have known.

'Where's Geoffrey?' she asked.

'I haven't told him yet. I came straight here.'

'Let me get dry, Celia, then we'll go.'

Matty was despatched to fetch Geoffrey, and he arrived at the wharf at the same time as Tam and Celia. Jamie was with him. Celia told him the details and together they went to see Harry Earp.

The Earps were shocked. They had no idea Robin was gone. Yes, he had got up early this morning, but then he always did. He had said nothing . . . A visit to the office proved that Robin was not there.

'I am grieved,' said Harry. 'That a son of mine should so deceive us – '

'*You're* grieved!' shouted Celia. 'How do you think we feel? That my daughter's good name should be besmirched.'

'He's after her money, no doubt,' said Geoffrey. 'But not a penny of mine will he have.'

'But where are they?' wailed Celia. 'We must go to London to find them.'

'And where would you look?' asked Tam. 'In the whole of London?'

Celia rounded on her. 'It's all your fault. You introduced her to this – this *fellow*, she must have been meeting him before we went to London. And he persuaded her to run away – '

'Damned canting hypocrites, that's what I've always said,' Geoffrey blustered. 'Pretending to be so good and all the time seducing innocent girls – '

'I blame Tam,' said Celia.

'Don't talk to my mother like that.' It was Jamie who spoke and they all turned to him in surprise. 'I didn't know she was meeting Robin, but one thing I can tell you. It wasn't his fault.'

'What?' Celia gaped.

'Oh, he was quite innocent, you must know that, Mama. Amanda persuaded him somehow to run away with her – '

'How dare you say such a thing?' squealed Celia.

'Because she tried to persuade me,' said Jamie, calmly. 'She was after anybody – '

'Oh.' Celia put a hand to her brow. 'How can you let him say such things, Geoffrey?'

'She wanted to get away from home,' Jamie went on. 'She told you she didn't want to be presented, Aunt Celia, I think really she wanted to do something useful with her life – '

'Useful? Going on the stage?'

'That was all the work she could think of – '

'Robin has never been near a theatre in his life,' said Harry.

'I told you she was headstrong,' said Geoffrey. 'And I told you where she gets it from. Certainly not from my family!'

Celia was led, weeping, from the boat. There seemed little more they could do.

'We'll go too,' said Tam. 'I'm sorry, Harry, Mirrie, about it all. If I was the unwitting cause – '

'No,' said Harry. 'Robin is not a child, he is old enough to know right from wrong – '

'He obviously thinks he's in love with Amanda,' said Tam.

'Then he should have come to us and to her parents in the correct manner,' said Harry. 'I shall not easily forgive him.'

'Harry, please,' pleaded Mirrie. 'He is thy son.'

'Is he? How can he be, to act thus?'

'We are all human,' said Mirrie.

But Harry was unbending. His face, in the dim light, looked old suddenly. He said, 'Tamarisk, he has let thee down badly. What wilt thou do now for an agent?'

'I don't know,' Tam said. 'Let the wharfinger try his hand I suppose. He hasn't Robin's qualifications, but I cannot afford another man just now. And that would mean hiring another wharfinger. We could manage in the past with extra men, but now money is so tight – '

'If thou approves, I could try,' said Harry. 'I'm not an expert at engineering or even accounts, but I could keep my eye on things, and if thou explained to the men, we could try to work together – '

'But what of your packet boat?' Tam asked.

'There is little enough trade now, as I told thee.'

'And you wanted to go to live with your daughters,' said Tam.

'That can wait. I am responsible for Robin. I will do what I can.' He turned to Mirrie. 'Thou agrees?'

She nodded her head slowly, 'I am willing.'

'Very well,' said Tam. 'But a temporary measure only. Perhaps Robin will soon be back, married . . .'

'I do not wish to see him,' said Harry.

In September Amanda wrote home. She was married, and she was happy. But did not give any address.

Robin also wrote to his parents in the same vein. He was sorry for the distress he must have caused them all, but he loved Amanda desperately. He had no idea that such love could exist. He had found work, and they lived in rented accommodation. He too gave no address.

Chapter Eight

Charles won his elections so easily now that Tam took little notice when they occurred. But when, in 1852, his majority dropped alarmingly, she asked Jamie what had happened.

'I think it's because he's against war, Mama.'

'There isn't going to be a war, is there, Jamie?'

'I hope not. But there has been a lot of trouble.'

'Charles did win, even so.'

'Only just. And what made it worse is that his opponent is so unimportant. If there had been a good man against him he wouldn't have done so well as this.'

'Oh, it's just temporary,' Tam dismissed the election. 'Why, look what he's done for the people of Chilverton.'

'I do know, Mama.'

'He's devoted his life to them.' More than you know, she added mentally. Well, we chose our own paths, she thought to herself. He still escorted Mary Travers around London, it was all very circumspect: he visited Juliet when in Chilverton, and at election celebrations Juliet was nominally hostess – with Tam's help – Mary Travers was never asked here. Jerome still called occasionally, still waiting patiently for Tam to change her mind and marry him.

'Yes, Mama,' Jamie was saying, then, instead of going off to the factory, he walked to the window. 'By the way, Mama, I'm going to London next Friday.'

'Are you? On business?'

'Yes. I'm learning the import side now. Did you know, that there is a difference between Bengal and China silk? Chinese silk is more expensive.'

'I did not. Are the silk worms better fed there?'

He laughed and she asked, 'Where will you be staying?'

'At the Warings' town house.'

'Yes, I remember, I went there once. In fact, that was where I first met your father. In a muddy dress, trying to be ladylike.' She smiled at the memory.

'You – do not see Father now?'

'No.' She wondered if she should tell him about Mary Travers, if he knew.

Jamie did seem to know most things even if he didn't talk about them. Better say nothing. So she changed the subject, 'I'm surprised Geoffrey doesn't sell that house, Celia's always saying how poor they are.'

'It wouldn't really help, Mama. All it would mean is that we'd have to pay hotel bills, and they can be very high in London.'

'Yes, I know. Well, enjoy your trip.'

'Thank you, Mama.'

It was the first of many such journeys to London, and often Jamie would go on the Thursday and stay the whole weekend. When, some months later, he started buying new clothes, including an evening suit, Tam chuckled.

'My, my, you are growing up. How very smart you look. Mind you, men's clothes aren't what they were when I was young, much too dull. Heavens, I sound like the Duchess. But you look fine. Have you met many people in London, then?'

'As a matter of fact Uncle Geoffrey introduced me to a number of people. There are silk merchants in London, Mama. And others we deal with, lawyers, and so on.'

'Well, that was kind of Geoffrey,' Tam said. 'He seems quite fond of you. So you visit these people's homes then?'

'Occasionally, Mama.'

'Meeting young ladies, I'll be bound. Just be circumspect, Jamie.'

'In what way, Mama?'

'Don't do anything silly, like your cousin Amanda and young Robin Earp. Oh dear, I'm thankful I haven't any daughters. You haven't seen anything of Amanda in London?'

Robin had written to his parents several times since his disappearance. He begged their forgiveness, but he loved Amanda, and knew her parents would never agree to their marriage, and he'd been doubtful of his own parents. He never sent any address.

'I haven't seen anything of either of them,' Jamie said. 'But London is a big place.'

As Jamie left, she turned her thoughts to the canal. They were managing – just – mainly by operating services railways could not supply. They still paid a five per cent dividend. But other canals were in disarray. There was squabbling between the Midland companies. And, as Tam had warned, the railway-owned canals, no longer forced to be kept in repair and supplied with water, were often left to decay.

Tam had to work hard now. Harry carried out duties of Agent by generally supervising the maintenance and running of the boats. But he had, as he said, no specialised knowledge either of engineering or of accounts, and Tam was obliged to oversee these herself. She put the facts baldly to the engineer and told him just as frankly that if things went wrong he would lose his job.

Sir Lewis had not lowered his prices again as yet. Tam hoped he'd realised he couldn't go on throwing money away. Rich he might be, but there was a limit. She herself had one great worry: that some serious fault might develop which she could not possibly pay for out of her reserve fund. As it was, she poured all her dividends back into this, keeping the bare minimum for herself and for Juliet. Jamie was now supporting himself. Yet year after year, some improvement had to be made, or there was a weather problem, either of drought or flooding, which meant more expense. She felt as though she could never quite catch up.

As she rode to the wharf she saw Harry talking with one of the boatmen and she was struck by his stooped shoulders, his air of weariness. He is too old for this, she thought, he should retire to his daughters, instead of bearing this burden he felt his duty since Robin left. But what would I do then?

She talked to Harry, to the boaters, and had a word with Mirrie, welcoming as always, but quieter these days, her hair white. But the little cabin was peaceful and cosy as ever, and Tam, as always, felt heartened when she left.

It was in the winter of 1853 when Jamie asked Tam if she would like to accompany him to London.

Tam looked up, putting down the newspaper she had been studying. 'Me? I don't know, Jamie. What had you in mind?'

He seemed ill at ease. 'I thought, Mama, you would like to look round the large emporiums, and then we could visit some of the people I know.'

'But I don't know them, do I? Have they asked me to visit?'

Jamie looked uncomfortable. 'Well, you see, Mama, I told them you might come to London, so they – '

'Jamie, what are you up to?'

'Nothing, Mama.'

'Come, now, I know that butter-wouldn't-melt look. Who are we to visit, and why?'

'Their name is Bradford, Mama. Mr Bradford is the senior partner of a law firm we've had dealings with.'

'And – ?'

'And what, Mama?'

Tam was trying not to smile as she watched her son fidgeting. 'Why am I to be dragged to London to meet a lawyer, when I am perfectly able to meet lawyers here?'

'It's just that – they are a nice family.'

'They?'

'There is a Mrs Bradford,' said Jamie, with as much dignity as he could muster. 'And they have one daughter, Catherine.'

'Now we're coming to it,' said Tam. 'How old is this daughter?'

'I believe about eighteen, Mama. She is out.'

'And you want me to meet her?'

'Yes, Mama. It seems the only way. The Bradfords have relatives in Leamington Spa, and Catherine will – sometimes visits in the summer. Maybe she would like to visit us, but of course you have to meet them first.'

'So this Catherine likes to visit Leamington Spa, does she?'

'Yes, to take the waters.'

'Does she suffer from rheumatism then, the poor old lady?' Tam was

288

smiling broadly now. 'Jamie, you're a cunning rascal. This is a plot worthy of a politician.'

'What else can I do, Mama? We cannot issue an invitation to Catherine and her aunt until you meet her – '

Tam stopped her teasing. 'All right, I'll come. But you're far too young to be serious about young ladies, Jamie.'

'I am nearly twenty-one, Mama.'

'Not for some months. And I'll warrant the Bradfords think you far too young to pay court to their daughter yet. Especially if she is their only daughter.'

'They do.' Jamie looked disconsolate.

'I'm not surprised.'

'I am in love with her, Mama.'

'And you'll be in love a hundred more times before you marry, I promise you.'

'But you will come, Mama?'

'I suppose it will be all right to leave Juliet,' Tam pondered. 'She seems so lethargic somehow.'

'But there is Matty, and the servants. And Aunt Juliet isn't ill. You sometimes take up burdens that aren't there, Mama.'

'Maybe I do. I'm so used to carrying them. All right, I'll come. I suppose it is difficult for you here, I hadn't thought. I don't entertain, and Aunt Celia isn't exactly friendly with me at the moment – not that she ever was – so she doesn't invite you there, that's if she entertains now. But it wasn't my fault Amanda ran off.' Tam sighed. 'But you do get the occasional invitation to Sir Lewis's, to the Manor, don't you meet people there?'

'Yes, Mama.'

'But you're in love with Miss Catherine Bradford. Very well, let me meet this young lady.'

'Be nice to her, Mama,' he pleaded.

'As if I would be anything else,' said Tam. In truth she thought she'd enjoy the trip to London, it would make a change from wearisome work.

As the day approached, Jamie, the self-assured, seemed sadly agitated. 'Whatever ails you?' Tam asked crossly. 'You're on pins the whole time.'

'Do you have everything ready, Mama?'

'I'm just sorting out my clothes, I only hope they're not too much out of fashion.'

'I was going to say I'd like to buy you a new gown, Mama.'

Tam sat back and stared with amusement at her son. He really did seem to be very much in love. 'Well, I don't know – ' she started.

'You must know a dressmaker in London. You could send your measurements, choose a design. Then we could go the day before for a final fitting – '

'Very well,' she said. 'Maybe it is time I had a new gown . . .'

She set off with Jamie on the train, he thanking his stars she hadn't insisted on going by boat, and she saying, 'Well, I must say the trains have improved since they first came out. Tell me, Jamie. Will your – will Charles be there?'

'No. I thought it better not – at first.'

'They don't know then?'

'Not yet.'

'There's no reason for them to know at all,' Tam said. It was very pleasant to stay at the Warings' house, to be able to relax and do nothing. She went for the fitting for her gown, and when she finally put it on she was pleased with the effect. Black velvet, low cut, with tight-fitting bodice, it showed up her still reddish hair to perfection. She threw a shawl around her shoulders and, with Jamie, was driven to the Bradfords' house.

And it was a handsome house, showing a certain solid wealth in its furnishings. Mr Bradford was a man in his early fifties who looked as well-built as his house, and his wife, the daughter of an admiral, was obviously a gentlewoman. But it was Miss Catherine Bradford Tam was interested in, the young minx who was trying to snare her son. She had expected a flibbertigibbet, instead she met a tall, stately girl, pretty certainly, but with a calm, unruffled air. There was no coy flirtatious look in her eyes, merely the certainty that she was . . . Was what? Loved?

'My mother, Lady Fargate,' Jamie said, and Tam saw that this was well received and was amused at the effect a title had on people. She offered Mr Bradford her bewitching smile and he blinked. Tam was used to summing people up: he was no fool, this Mr Bradford, and he wouldn't let anyone fool him. She set out to charm through dinner, and when the ladies retired she talked sympathetically with Mrs Bradford. When asked how she could bear to live in such a dull backwater as Chilverton she smiled as she remembered the boaters, the riots, Sir William, Amanda . . . 'Oh, it's not too dull,' she said.

Later as they drove away, Jamie, in an agony, burst out eagerly, 'Well, Mama, did you like her?'

'Very well, Jamie. She is a nice girl.'

'I am serious about her, Mama.'

'Yes, Jamie.' Tell me that in six months' time, she thought, he is so young still.

But in six months' time the country was almost at war.

'Will there be a war?' Tam asked Jamie, in February. 'The papers say the Czar is a menace to liberty abroad.'

'Lord Aberdeen says war is not inevitable,' said Jamie.

But Chilverton did not agree. Charles presided over an angry meeting in the town, where he was asked if he still preferred peace, and when he said he did a voice demanded why.

'Because our army is not fit – ' he began, but was forced to stop with the explosion of angry shouts.

'What do you mean? We have the best army in the world. Didn't we beat Napoleon?'

'That was forty years ago. Our army today knows nothing of fighting.

290

The coasts are defenceless, the navy's growing rusty, the best part of the battle fleet is laid up at anchor. And our guns are out of date.' He was shouted down again.

'Radical coward.'

'We aren't going to let that tyrant down us.'

'We'll fight and win.'

At the end of March 1854, the Crimean War began.

'I had hoped to invite Catherine here in the summer,' said Jamie, disconsolately.

'Well, no doubt she will be able to come, there isn't going to be a war in Chilverton,' Tam replied.

But it wasn't the war that stopped Catherine coming to Cherry Trees, it was Juliet.

It had been a cold winter, and Tam was tired as she came home one day in early April. There was no sign of spring as yet, and as she entered the house she looked for Juliet. 'Where is she?' she asked Matty.

'In bed, Miss Tam.'

'In bed, why? Is she ill?'

'She says she's tired, Miss Tam.'

Tam sped to Juliet's room, where she lay, eyes closed.

'Juliet, what is it? Are you asleep? What's the matter?' Tam was alarmed.

'No, I'm not asleep, and there's nothing the matter. I'm just tired.'

'Won't you come down now, for dinner?'

'I'd rather stay in bed, Tam.'

It was so unlike Juliet to refuse to comply, that Tam was even more alarmed. 'Do you feel ill?' she asked.

Juliet insisted that she was not ill, just tired. Tam went downstairs, telling the already overworked Matty that she'd have to take up a tray. 'Maybe she'll feel better tomorrow,' she said hopefully.

But the next day Juliet was still tired, still in bed. Another day and Tam sent for Dr Phillips.

He examined Juliet, then beckoned Tam downstairs. 'There's nothing too seriously wrong,' he said. 'Her chest is not strong, but I believe she's always been delicate in this way.'

'Yes. Always. But why should she be tired, Doctor? She does nothing but rest all the time. And the air's so fresh here at Cherry Trees?'

'Well, I'll give her a tonic, and we'll see what happens.'

Juliet took the tonic, but it had no noticeable effect. Then she developed a little cough.

'It isn't much,' Tam reported. 'And she often gets coughs in winter. When she was a child she always had bronchitis.'

Dr Phillips prescribed something for her cough. But still Juliet did not recover. She lay in bed, sometimes getting up to sit in the garden, she coughed a little, but as the summer brought warmer weather and gentle breezes she seemed to rally, and Tam was heartened, thinking she was simply run down. She turned her attention again to the canal, noting wryly that the war brought an increase in trade: the Milden colliery, for whom she still delivered, had a large order for coal for Birmingham, where factories were manufacturing guns. Geoffrey's weavers were working fulltime too, though Tam was a little puzzled as to who might want ribbons in a war. But trade improved, and she allowed her hopes to rise during the placid summer, she even persuaded Juliet to take a trip on the *Princess*, where they drifted along through a heat haze, and Juliet lay back with eyes closed. 'I knew,' Tam said, 'the summer would make everything all right.' She forgot the winter was to come.

The winter was one of the coldest in human memory. The canal froze over, the boats were iced up. News filtered through from Sebastopol where British troops had landed in the autumn and it made sad reading. The charge of the Light Brigade in Balaclava was admired as an inspiring feat of gallantry, until it was learned that someone had blundered and only one third of the men came back alive.

Celia was celebrating the engagement of her second daughter, Rebecca. Not for Becky any presentation; after the fiasco of Amanda's debut, Celia had been left to bear most of the costs of the season, with no rewards, while Lady Caroline, who'd shared with Amanda, promptly became engaged to a young nobleman. Celia felt she could not hold up her head for a long time, and though she gradually recovered, she made no excessive plans for Becky. There would be parties and balls, but all at home. Celia did not let the Crimean war trouble her unduly, it was a minor irritation, no more. And when dear Becky found favour with a young lawyer by name of Dawson, Celia was pleased; not overjoyed, he had no title, nor had his family, but at least he wasn't in trade. Her musings were interrupted by the maid.

'Excuse me, madam, Lady Fargate to see you.'

'Lady Fargate. Oh . . .' For a moment Celia's face showed delight, Sir Lewis's wife did not call very often. Then the maid said, as though apologising, 'Lady Tamarisk Fargate I mean, madam,' and Celia's joy turned to fury. How dare she come here? And the maid went on anxiously, 'She says it's important, madam.'

'Of course it's important, why else would I want to come here,' said Tam, who had followed the maid and now brushed her impatiently aside. 'I've had a letter, Celia, from Amanda, and she asked me to show it to you.'

'What is it? Is she all right?' cried Celia, forgetting her histrionics momentarily in anxiety over her daughter. 'And why has she written to you and not me?'

'She asked me to show it to you and to Robin's parents,' said Tam. 'I think you'd better read it.' She passed the letter over, and Celia began to read:

'Dear Aunt Tamarisk,

'I write to you because I feel you might understand perhaps more than most. I came to London with Robin, as you know, and I was entirely to blame. I was a silly and wilful girl, though I sometimes

292

think that the way girls of our class are brought up these days is most at fault. I never wanted to live what I thought was a lazy life, I wanted to do something, I used to envy those women who worked – even the boaters' wives – and I envied you, Aunt Tamarisk.

'I persuaded Robin to take me away, it was my idea. I had some stupid notion of going on the stage – oh, I didn't know what I wanted. I didn't love him, not then, though he loved me, I don't know why. But gradually I came to love him, he was so good and kind to me always.

'At first I was unhappy, I didn't see that being married made any difference. Robin said that the Quaker women always work anyway, and wanted me to help the poor or nurse the sick. Well, that wasn't what I had in mind at all.

'Then this war started, and Robin went to the Crimea. He does not fight, as Quakers are pacifists, but he went to help nurse the sick. And oh, he writes me such dreadful letters. How the poor soldiers lay without tents or food or warm clothes in blizzards, how they died of cholera and dysentery. Robin was so down-hearted, he had no proper medical training, he felt he could not do enough. He managed to get his letters to me through a correspondent from *The Times*, and he says how a woman named Miss Nightingale has gone out and is organising a hospital. He admires her so much, and I feel so useless, that I can do nothing of the kind.

'I have been so worried about Robin, I wanted to see him, to tell him how much I loved him, for I'm sure he never knew how much. And now, the man from *The Times* just came to see me, he said Robin is dead, he died from the cholera . . .

'I am so unhappy. I did love him.

'Your niece, Amanda.'

Celia stood up quickly and rang for the maid. 'Send someone to tell Mr Waring he is needed here,' she ordered. 'Then pack my clothes and call the carriage.'

'Yes, madam.' The frightened maid ran out of the room.

'Where are you going, Celia?' asked Tam, gently.

'To London, of course,' said Celia. 'To my daughter.'

Celia and Geoffrey travelled to London by train, and they found Amanda, a changed Amanda, one whose face was more mature and was washed with tears. She greeted her parents gratefully, but refused to come home.

'I am working here now, Mama,' she said. 'I have found something to do.'

'What is that?' Celia asked suspiciously.

'I am learning how to nurse in a hospital. I think Robin would have approved of this. I hope in time to be able to join Miss Nightingale . . .'

Celia stared at her daughter in horror. 'Nursing in a hospital! But only the lowest women do that sort of thing.'

'It will change, Mama. Miss Nightingale is gently born. I think this dreadful war will do one good thing, it will give women a new status.'

'But, Amanda – '

'Robin would have wished it,' Amanda said firmly. 'The Friends always believed in equality for women. And though I have not embraced their faith, I have met, and still meet, some of their women, they too work at the hospitals.'

'It must be so degrading,' cried Celia.

'I found it so at first. I was quite literally sick. I think the smells are the worst. But I'm getting used to it now.'

'There are no children of the marriage?' Celia asked.

'No, Mama, and this was a great grief to Robin. I confess I didn't mind then. Now I wish – ' she broke off, her eyes wet with tears.

'Well,' Geoffrey said gruffly, 'you have a home whenever you want to come back . . .'

'Thank you, Papa, I will come and see you soon, I promise.'

Geoffrey and Celia returned home, wondering at the change in their wayward daughter.

In the terrible winter of 1854, while British troops still died for want of medical supplies, Tam was forced to face the fact that Juliet was not getting better. Tam had had a bad day, there was ice on the canal, the boats were waiting for the ice-breaker, but in the meantime they were stuck fast in the ice. It was nearly Christmas and as she left the wharf she saw that Charles was holding what seemed to be a meeting. It was but poorly attended and did not seem to be going too well. She drew the pony-chaise to a halt and stood waiting till the meeting dispersed and Charles walked over to her.

'Are you going to Cherry Trees?' he asked.

'I'm going to fetch Dr Phillips first. I'm very worried about Juliet.'

'Is she no better?'

'No, Charles. I can't understand it. I get her the best food, she rests . . . yet she is losing weight, she seemed so thin this morning, I went into her room before she was in her dressing-gown and I was shocked.'

'Come then,' he said. 'Dr Phillips must see her.'

They drove in silence. Dr Phillips promised to come immediately, and they all returned together to Cherry Trees. After an examination he went in to Charles and Tam who were waiting in the drawing room. They said nothing, waiting for him to speak.

'I hardly know what to tell you,' Dr Phillips said with a sigh. 'On the surface there seems little wrong. A certain delicacy which she has always had, a slight cough, a general lassitude. I have tried tonics as you know. I could try other remedies, but I fear they will have little result. I can bleed her, if you wish, but I would not advise it – '

'What do you mean, have little result?' demanded Tam. 'Is she – is she going into a decline?'

The doctor paused. 'I suppose you could call it that,' he said at last.

294

'Then can't you *do* anything?' Tam was agitated.

'When the patient doesn't want to live, nothing I can do will help. I think she has never recovered from the loss of her child.' He turned to Charles. 'Is there nothing you can do to help her, nothing you can provide?'

Charles said heavily, 'I think you should know, Doctor, that Juliet never loved me, except perhaps as a brother. There was – someone else who was the father of her child.'

'I see. And can this other not come to her?'

'She doesn't want him now,' Tam said. 'I have asked her. She never has wanted him since Roddy died. It was as though all her love died with him.'

'And, I fear, her life,' said Dr Phillips.

'But,' Tam cried in horror, 'you can't mean that there's nothing we can do. That she is to die . . .' her voice cracked ominously.

'I am sorry,' Dr Phillips said. 'I know you must find it difficult to understand, you who have such a firm grip on life. Try what you will, by all means, but I can do no more.'

As Charles saw the doctor out, Tam stood staring through the window at the icy ground, the bare stark branches, the dead flowers. And suddenly it was all too much, the endless striving, the fight for the canals, the shortage of money. And now – this . . . She began to cry.

Charles returned and took her gently in his arms. He held her while the storm subsided, and she stared at him. 'It's the first time I've cried since – ' she began, ' – since my father – '

'And you still mourn for him?' he asked. 'Why, Tam?'

Her defences were down. Gone now was the bold, uncaring Tam. She said. 'His little grave . . . no one cared for him, really . . .'

'But you did.'

'Yes. But did he ever realise? I was away so much. And Mama had – that other man.'

'You think you failed him?'

'I don't know. Yes. Yes, of course.'

'And you're still trying to show him – ' he broke off.

She said wildly, 'I loved him. But he never knew. And anyway, he only cared for Mama. Not me.'

'Of course he did, Tam.'

'How could he, when I wasn't even his child?'

Charles said, 'But I loved Roddy, and he wasn't mine.' Yet she would not be comforted, and he sighed, wondering how he could help her.

Christmas was a quiet time for all of them, Celia and Geoffrey grieved for Amanda, the Earps mourned Robin, while Tam tried hard to rally Juliet, she even went to see Geoffrey at the office and asked him to see her.

Geoffrey hesitated. 'I will,' he said. 'But she cares nothing for me now.'

'You can try – '

'Yes.' He sighed again. 'But love dies, Tam. Once there was something fine between us, but after Roddy died she refused to see me, and now I find there is little feeling in my heart for her. But I will see her.'

295

He was right, he could do nothing for Juliet. She merely smiled at him as though he were some friend from a faraway past who meant nothing to her now. She only said, in a low whisper, 'I dreamed of Roddy last night.'

'Oh, Juliet,' said Tam, who was in the room.

It was obvious now that Juliet would not recover. Charles stayed at the house, and in January Annabel came down.

'I have been away,' she said. 'Visiting friends for Christmas. Where is she? Where's Juliet?'

'I'll take you to her,' said Tam.

'No. I'll take you,' said Charles, and he led the way upstairs. Outside the room he paused. 'I think you can help her,' he said.

'Of course I shall help her. My poor Juliet.'

'No, not Juliet. Tam.'

'Tam? Is she ill too? She always seems so strong.'

'Yes, she does, doesn't she? So we've all put too great a burden on her.'

Annabel hesitated. 'Maybe. But she was always the one who could do everything – '

'She's suffering, Lady Annabel, and only you can help her.'

'In what way?'

'Talk to her. About her father. Oh no,' impatiently as he saw Annabel's questioning look, 'Jamie Calder, the man who, to Tam, was her father. She thinks first that you failed him, and that he didn't love her.'

'Tam thinks that?'

'Yes. Put her right, Lady Annabel. I don't care how, but do it.'

Annabel stayed at Cherry Trees too. And as Juliet weakened she and Tam sat by her bedside together.

Outside the frost thickened, branches straggled, covered with rime, icicles hung from the roof. Inside a bright fire glowed, and Juliet seemed to sleep.

Annabel said in a low voice, 'I have lost several people who were dear to me, Jamie, Tony, but the saddest thing of all is to lose one's own child.'

Tam moved restlessly. 'Yes, Mama. I know you loved Lord Brooke, but you didn't love my father.'

'Jamie? Of course I did.'

'Oh, Mama.' Tam was disbelieving.

'I've never talked to you about him, have I, Tam? Maybe I should have, though you never seemed to want to listen.'

Tam knew this was true. But it was different here, in this quiet room, with the ice and snow outside, it was an oasis in a wild world. 'Tell me,' she said at last.

'How can I ever make you understand the passionate affair between Tony and me,' Annabel said. 'The love that flamed . . . the walk along the beach beside the tamarisk bush, that was the night we realised we could not part, even though he was married. Then you came along . . .' She paused, Tam said nothing. 'My father was a hard man, he told me I'd have to go . . . I was young then, Tam, I didn't know what to do. I had met Jamie, I knew he loved me, though he'd never declare himself, feeling our positions would not sanction any liaison. He had come to ask my father's help with the canals. So I approached him.'

'But you did not love him, Mama.'

'Not then, maybe. Maybe not for some time. I was wild, I wanted to go on the stage. But he was a good man, he was always so kind, how could I help but regard him highly?'

'But you went back to Lord Brooke, Mama. After Celia and Juliet were born . . .'

'True, I did. But Jamie knew.'

'He knew? And he didn't mind?'

'Well, he knew of our love, Tam. He knew why I'd married him.'

'And he got the house and boats for his bargain.'

'It was what he wanted, Tam.'

'So you lived with him for a few years. And after Juliet was born you went back to Lord Brooke. So what was for my father then, you were no longer wife to him, he would be so lonely – '

Annabel hesitated. 'Oh yes I was wife to him,' she said. Tam was silent, and Annabel went on. 'Jamie was happy, Tam, that I assure you. He loved me and he loved his daughters.'

'Only I was not his daughter,' said Tam, bitterly.

'He loved you as a daughter,' Annabel assured her. 'In fact sometimes I think he loved you more than the other two.'

'But how could he when I was not his?'

'Oh, pshaw,' said Annabel, with a return to her old style. 'Love is not as you read it in novels. Jamie always looked on you as his own. And at first I think the reason you held a special place in his heart was because you were the reason I married him. Later though he loved you for yourself – and because you were the one who was most like me.'

And somehow this did not bring the old envy, but in a strange way drew them together, Annabel and Tamarisk, both loved by Jamie.

Then Annabel added, 'He once told me that we should have named you Joy, because you brought him great joy – '

'He said that, Mama? Truly?'

'Oh yes, I remember well. It was when you were a baby and he talked about the day you were born, the day the canal was opened. "Morning of Joy," he said. "The canal – and my little girl. Both brought me great joy." And of course you always loved the canal, as he did. I should have let you work with him. I should not have named you Tamarisk – I was selfish – naming you after a bush – '

But Tam was no longer listening. Something had burst over her like a great light that swamped her completely. She felt light as air, as though some heavy weight that pulled her down had been removed, she was free now, she could love . . .

They returned to Juliet. She lay asleep, a soft smile on her face, and they watched her gently. And it was not till morning dawned and they went to wake her that they realised she would never wake again. This was her last sleep.

Tam had no chance to talk to Charles after the funeral, he was recalled immediately to London. And she had to turn her attention to the boats; she had lost a great deal of money while they'd been iced up. Somehow she had to find more money, soon she would have to replace Harry, for though he never complained, she saw how difficult it was for him to walk these days; rheumatism, the scourge of men who work outdoors, had placed its relentless hand firmly on him. Mirrie too, though still quite well, had lost some of her agility, and Tam worried that she could not spare them to go to their daughters in Birmingham.

She mourned Juliet sincerely, she missed the little sister, yet she had been for so long merely a pale shadow, that her presence was hardly missed in the house.

'It is better so,' Mirrie comforted Tam. 'She was never meant for the hardships of this world.'

'No,' said Tam. 'But how do I know where she is now? You know I haven't your belief, Mirrie. Why, I never go to church, I work on Sundays, sometimes I think I'm little more than a heathen.'

Mirrie smiled. 'But a nice heathen.'

'Oh, you always see the best in people, Mirrie. But I must get on, I want to see Harry about some new ideas for – ' she broke off. She had been about to say for making money, but changed this. 'For helping the canals,' she ended.

'He's here now,' said Mirrie. 'Coming for a hot drink I wouldn't wonder.'

'Aye, having thy home so near is very handy, ' smiled Harry.

'I've had an idea,' Tam said. 'It came to me when Jamie was talking about water. Did you know there was a shortage of water in the town?'

'No,' said Harry, with the glimmer of a smile. 'There seems plenty of rain.'

'Yes, indeed, I was surprised. It seems Geoffrey needs more for his factory, he plans to expand. And then, with all the new water pipes everywhere, water is needed.'

'And?' asked Harry.

'Water is the one thing we have,' said Tam, triumphantly. 'I shall sell it to industry and to the local authority.'

'What a good idea,' said Harry. 'I never thought anyone would want to buy water.'

'We'll have to make sure we keep enough for times of drought,' said Tam. 'I thought we might enlarge the reservoir . . .'

'Would it cost?'

'Yes, but it would be worth the extra expense.'

'I see.'

'So, if Sir Lewis does not lower his charges yet again, we should do well out of this.'

'I see thou hast not heard,' said Harry.

'Heard what?'

298

'Sir Lewis is not likely to be bothering so much about the canals in future – '

'Why not?'

'He is standing for Parliament at the next election.'

'*Is* he? Then if he won he'd be in London . . . he'd probably leave the canal alone.'

'*If* he won,' said Harry. 'For that would mean that Charles lost.'

'Oh, good heavens, yes. And that's unthinkable. Charles won't lose.'

'It will be quite a battle,' said Harry.

'They couldn't not vote for Charles. Not after all he's done. Why, it would break his heart.'

'Yes. But the one thing he wanted to do, help the weavers by higher protective tariffs, he has been unable to carry out.'

'You don't think Sir Lewis has a chance, do you, Harry?' she asked anxiously.

'I don't know,' Harry said heavily. 'He is far more popular than Sir William ever was, he has been a good squire; his tenants speak very highly of him. He repairs their cottages, improves the farms. Lady Fargate is well liked too. The people think she's more democratic; it's being American, I suppose. "She don't act high and mighty as if we're dirt," I overheard one cottager say.'

'I didn't know that,' said Tam.

'And finally, Tamarisk, there is the war. Charles was always against it – '

'And with reason, everyone knows now – '

'Don't be too sure, Tamarisk. Whenever there's a war people get very nationalistic. They think Charles is unpatriotic.'

'But that's not true – '

'I have heard,' Harry went on, 'that if Sir Lewis should win the election he'll leave the running of the railway to his deputy, a man named Greatrex. And I have also heard that Mr Greatrex does not believe in cutting freight charges, in fact he may well raise them.'

'I see. But he won't win, surely.'

'Don't underestimate Sir Lewis,' said Harry. 'In some ways he is as hard as his father, thou knowest he was with the railway battle. And I think Lady Fargate would dearly love to be the wife of an MP.'

Tam returned home, her thoughts in a turmoil. Victory for Sir Lewis would mean salvation for the canal. But it couldn't be . . . not if it meant Charles losing. It was unthinkable. If only it weren't Charles, then she could go all out for Sir Lewis to win. If only it weren't Charles.

But supposing there was another way. Supposing Charles was not so keen on opposing Sir Lewis, who knew? Supposing, when she told him what she'd been waiting to tell him since Juliet died, he'd be willing to give up? After all, hadn't he said, 'I'll wait for you to come to me'? And she never had, had hung back, had let him run around with that stupid Mary Travers simply because he was lonely, because she hadn't wanted him. All she had to do was tell him that she loved him, wanted him again . . . She had thought often how she would do this, how she would whisper to him on some twilit night . . . perhaps wait till spring when the cherry blossoms were out. For Juliet's death had set her free in more ways than one, or perhaps it was Annabel who had set her free when she told her of her father's love for her. Now, for the first time she felt loved. And wanted to share that love.

She pondered on going to London, but decided against, it would be so much nicer to see him here, at Cherry Trees. And then the candidates for the election were announced, and it was true, Sir Lewis was standing. She hoped she hadn't waited too long.

She must see him. He'd come to her first, of course he would, but just in case he was afraid of sullying her good name she told Harry casually to tell Charles when he came that she wanted to see him about the canal business.

And then she waited eagerly, as breathless as a girl. She felt like a girl again, the girl she had been when they'd sailed on the boat those first times and he'd held her hands. When she saw him approaching she was glad that Jamie worked such long hours. And when Matty showed him in she stood before him, wondering if he could hear her heart beating.

He came to her, held her briefly, kissed her lightly. 'You wanted to see me?' he said.

'I thought maybe you'd like to stay at Cherry Trees,' she said in reply.

'Oh no, Tam, that wouldn't do, would it? Not now you are alone. No, I'll be at the wharf house.'

'But – '

'Anyway, it's nearer town.'

'But you'll stay for a meal, at least.'

'No, Tam. I'm too busy.'

'But, Charles, I want to talk to you,' she cried.

He looked at her, and she hesitated on the brink of a declaration, thinking of nights they could share, being together always . . . and while she trembled on the edge of the tender dream that had filled her waking days since Juliet's death, he cut in briefly. 'I must go, Tam.'

'But you don't know what I have to say – '

He still looked at her, and his eyes were remote. 'Maybe I don't want to hear,' he said.

It was like a slap in the face. She stood quite still for a moment while her dreams crumbled around her. Then her chin came up in the old remembered way. 'Oh go to hell!' she cried.

He turned then towards the door. And she watched him leave, eyes smarting. 'I hope you lose the election,' she called after him bitterly. 'See if I care.'

Chilverton Manor was a much more pleasant place under the new squire. No longer did it look like a museum, no longer was it bare and cold. Georgiana had brought some of the comfort of her Virginia home into its portals: there were comfortable chairs and sofas in each room, hanging silks and brocades at the windows. Above all, it was warm. Huge fires burnt in each room, and in addition, a method of heating the whole house had been installed, working from a vast range in the kitchen. 'If boats can have warm pipes,' said Georgiana after seeing the *Princess*, 'then I'm sure we can, Lewis. I shivered all through the first winter here, it seems the regular thing in England, to be *cold*. I can't see any merit in it myself.' Lewis, who too had grown accustomed to warmth and sunshine, agreed.

Sir Lewis also kept his tenants' property in good order; he was an orderly man and had been horrified at the state of some of the cottages. 'I just want to look after my cottagers the way I looked after my slaves in Virginia,' he joked. He enjoyed being the Squire, walking round his estate, being kind to people, and as the people benefited from his enjoyment, they bobbed their curtseys, touched their forelocks and thanked him kindly. Georgiana too liked being Lady of the Manor, she saw that no child went hungry, that the sick were cared for. The Fargates became very popular.

And there was nothing more natural in this pleasant English rural life than that he should wish to stand for Parliament. Sir Lewis judged the mood of the country astutely, radicals were out of favour, with their talk of peace, the country was wrapped in a cloak of patriotism, and who better to serve his country than a good old local squire? It wouldn't be easy, not against Charles Waring, but it could be done. Sir Lewis laid his plans, and arranged a large dinner party.

'An invitation to the Manor,' said Celia, pleased, and bought new crinolines for Becky and Amelia. Sir Lewis had two sons, still unattached, dear Amelia was eighteen now, just the right age for Stephen. Bee was a problem as always, nothing ever seemed to fit Bee. She was still small, she still clumped about, and no amount of deportment and dancing lessons made the slightest difference. Sometimes Celia thought her youngest daughter did it all to annoy her, and sighed deeply, Bee was a constant thorn in her flesh. But dressing such a child didn't matter too much, so she was put in white organdie, with a frilled skirt, which made her look quite comical. Bee didn't seem to mind.

Tam received her invitation, and Jamie's, with surprise.

'You will go, Mama, won't you?' asked Jamie.

'I don't know, it's ages since I went to the Manor.'

'You see, I thought we might invite Catherine here. We did promise.'

Catherine. Catherine Bradford. 'Oh, Jamie, of course,' Tam said. 'Why is there always so much else to think about?'

'Don't worry, I know you've been distressed about Aunt Juliet, I told the Bradfords, they understand. But I have been seeing her all the time I was in London.'

'You are serious then?'

'We are practically affianced. In fact, we only waited because Aunt Juliet was so ill. We knew you could not visit, or entertain.'

'Mr Bradford has no objection?' asked Tam.

'No. Why should he have?'

'You are so young.'

'I am nearly twenty-three,' said Jamie, with dignity. 'And Mr Bradford thinks my prospects are good.'

'Does he?'

'He thinks I am likely to succeed, and is willing to give Catherine a handsome dowry.'

'Good heavens,' said Tam. 'I really must congratulate you, Jamie.'

'And Mama – I have told them about my father. I thought it best they know the truth.'

'Yes, of course. And what did they say?'

'They were pleased I'd told them.'

Not for Jamie the deceptions and subterfuges, Tam thought, and said aloud, 'I'm glad that's all sorted out.'

'So I thought, if we invited Catherine here for a few days, she would get to know you, and we could take her to the Manor.'

'I see.'

'Will you ask Sir Lewis, Mama?'

So Tam wrote hurriedly to Sir Lewis, and to the Bradfords. Catherine arrived almost by return, as if, thought Tam, amused, they had it all planned, and the girl was waiting by the door for her invitation. But she made the girl welcome, wondering what it would be like to be a mother-in-law. Strange, she had believed Jamie would not marry for years. Next thing they'd be making her a grandmother!

Catherine talked about her life, and it seemed very sheltered: a governess, a quiet home life. Tam, remembering her own turbulent girlhood, wondered if this peaceable couple would have quiet children, or if there would be a throwback to Tam herself, and she hid a smile.

They set off for the Manor, Tam in her black gown, Catherine in pale blue, her fair hair taken back and tied with a ribbon, covered with a lace scarf. And Jamie said proudly, 'I am escorting the two most beautiful women in the county.'

As they entered the Manor Tam thought he may well be right. Georgiana still had a lovely face but she was inclined to plumpness, while Celia was quite definitely fat these days. Both Becky and Amelia were pretty but dull, and a little overdressed, while Bee never had any pretensions to beauty. Celia's eyes swept over Catherine with what Tam termed her sniffy look, seeking faults and reluctantly finding none. Sir Lewis was affable, Georgiana pleasant and welcoming, Catherine was made to feel at home.

Sir Lewis had brought some American friends, and Tam sat next to a Mr Nathaniel Hawthorn at table. 'He is consul at Liverpool,' said Sir Lewis, introducing them. 'And be wary of him,' added Georgiana, 'he is already writing home about England. And he plans to write books.'

Mr Hawthorn was not in the least flattering in his writings about England, Tam learned. He thought Liverpool was quite dreadful, so much poverty and dirt, so many beggars, so much squalor.

'And what do you think of the aristocrats?' asked Tam.

'I admire them as a class. But they are doomed. This Crimean war will

302

put an end to aristocratic privilege. They made such a mess of the war they'll never be allowed to command again. Yet it's a pity, they are honourable and highly cultivated.'

'You make it sound as if we were at the beginning of a new world,' said Tam.

'You are, dear lady, you are.'

Tam supposed an outsider saw more of the game than others. Yet hadn't Charles said the same thing? She said, 'I used to laugh at Charles, Mr Waring, running on about votes. I suppose he's really – '

'An innovator. As you are.'

'Me?' Tam wasn't sure what an innovator was.

'You work, do you not?'

'Yes, and for that I walk in a cloud of disapproval. I'm what they call a black sheep.'

'You are ahead of your time, you and he both,' said Mr Hawthorn and his voice was tinged with admiration.

'You should meet Mirrie Earp, she wants votes for women,' said Tam.

But his neighbour had asked him a question and he was forced to turn away. Tam was left suddenly aware of time passing, of *change*. Would Charles and his innovations alter people's lives? Would she? And Mirrie? And all those who wanted votes? You didn't know. You worked in the present, weaving your little pattern, but the finished work belonged to the future. Because other people bought it and wore it, but you wove it, you put in the strands, each one representing someone: Mama, Papa . . . She smiled at her fanciful notions, and looked around for Catherine and Jamie.

Amelia was not, to Celia's chagrin, placed next to either Stephen or Francis: Georgiana had put them on either side of Bee, and the young men watched with amusement as Bee plodded her way through course after course, teasing her gently. 'You eat well for a young lady,' commented Stephen.

'But I'm not a young lady,' said Bee.

'You're not a young man,' said Francis.

'I wish I were,' said Bee, darkly.

She amused them with her down-to-earth comments, and when the meal ended and they had moved to the drawing room – Georgiana refused to allow the ladies to leave first – they were still with her.

'You look completely square in that dress,' said Stephen. 'And is your hair supposed to be long or short?'

'It's supposed to be long,' said Bee. 'But it won't grow. Mama thinks I'll make a dreadful debutante, and I expect I shall,' she ended complacently.

'Do you go to school?' asked Francis, tweaking her maligned hair.

'No, I wish I could. I have a governess.'

'I'll warrant you drive her wild,' said Stephen.

Bee grinned. 'I do, too. She says I'm the most unladylike creature she's ever had the misfortune to teach.'

'What does she teach you? Drawing? Music? Painting?'

'She tries,' said Bee. 'They all try.'

'I reckon you do it on purpose,' said Stephen.

Bee smiled.

Celia strolled over to them. 'Bee, I am sure you are being a nuisance to these young men. Stephen, Amelia would love to have a word with you, she does love the Manor so,' and she shepherded the hapless Stephen over to Amelia, who simpered at him, and Bee stood up.

'I'd better go,' she said. 'Mama will be furious.'

'Why should she be?' asked Francis.

'She always is.'

'Don't go,' he said. 'Stay and talk to me.'

'All right, if you like,' and Bee sat down again. As she said, whatever she did would be wrong, so she might as well do what she wanted to do. It was her philosophy.

'You don't seem shy or anything,' Francis said.

'No, I don't think I am.'

'I am. I get nervous when I have to make conversation.'

Bee studied him. He looked nervous, with his thin dark face, his long tapering hands. Bee, who didn't know what nerves were, smiled, and her face was transformed.

'I'm not nervous with you,' Francis said. 'I hope you'll come over again.'

'Well, I will if you ask me.'

'I'll see what I can do,' said Francis.

Sir Lewis was talking to Geoffrey. 'How is the weaving?' he asked.

'Oh, doing well. We took some of our stuff to the Exhibition, you know, at Crystal Palace. Now we have orders pouring in.'

'Good. I was thinking I might send some of your silk to Virginia when I write, you'll have to let me have samples. I'm sure there'd be orders.'

'Why, that's very kind of you,' said Geoffrey, pink with gratification.

'Maybe in time you'll be able to expand the factory.'

'Why – yes. Though it wouldn't be easy.'

'Oh? Why's that?'

'We have no room on our present site. We'd have to move, and that would mean a big outlay.'

'Of course. Are you so hemmed in then?'

'There is the road in front and to the side. The canal is at the back.'

'And the other side?'

'That is your land, Sir Lewis.'

'Is it really? Oh yes, Jenks's farm. Well, I'm sure something could be arranged.'

'Really?' Geoffrey was overjoyed. 'I'd be very pleased if we could have just a small piece – '

'Of course, I'll make it right with Jenks. Can't do anything at the moment, I'm afraid, I'm too busy now. It will have to be after the election.'

'Oh yes.' Geoffrey hesitated. 'If there's anything I can do – '

'Thank you for offering. You are on my side, I take it?'

'Oh, definitely.'

'And your workers? You have influence with them?'

'There aren't many who vote, of course. But the ones who are able will do so for you, I'm sure. Except – ' Geoffrey hesitated.

'Except?'

'Well, Jamie Fargate. Your – stepbrother.'

'Oh yes, young Jamie. Well, he doesn't have a vote either at his age so he's no problem.'

'No. Except . . . he does usually work with my brother,' said Geoffrey, unhappily.

'Does he? Well, never mind.'

'As long as you realise that I have nothing to do with it – '

Sir Lewis placed his hand on Geoffrey's arm. 'I do realise. And as long as I have your support?'

'Of course, Sir Lewis – ' Geoffrey replied fervently.

Sir Lewis smiled, and moved on.

'I'm not at all sure why we were all invited,' Tam said to Jamie as they rode home.

'I think he was preparing for battle,' said Jamie. 'Sorting out his supporters.'

'Did you enjoy it, Catherine?' asked Tam.

'Oh yes, indeed.'

'Good. Well, we must show you a little of the countryside. Has Jamie told you about the boats?'

'I've told her all the secrets of our strange family,' Jamie smiled.

'Father thinks you are brave to carry on the business yourself,' said Catherine, and Tam looked suitably gratified.

'We must take you on a little trip,' she said. So the next day Catherine was duly escorted to the *Princess*, and they sailed to Warwick. Throughout the whole excursion she and Jamie held hands, and Tam, watching them, felt unbearably lonely.

Jamie accompanied Catherine back to London and stayed for a week. Then he wrote to his mother, telling her they were now officially betrothed, and enclosing an invitation from the Bradfords for the next weekend. Tam went down and they celebrated the betrothal of the young couple.

There were no treatings or fighting mobs in this election, as in the bad old days, but Sir Lewis made his presence felt. Daily he addressed meetings, and Tam going to the wharf would often stop and listen. He talked of the war. 'Let tyrants tremble,' he roared. 'We are the sons of liberty, the freemen of the West,' and the people cheered.

But Charles held his own. 'We weren't ready for war,' he said. 'Poor commanders, not enough equipment. I warned you how it would be.'

So they thundered, and it seemed fairly equal. Jamie talked too. 'Who insisted you needed new water pipes and improvements?' he yelled. 'We've never had the cholera in Chilverton since, have we? Charles Waring has served you well over the years and don't you forget it.'

'Look what Sir Lewis has done for his tenants,' cried Sir Lewis's supporters. 'Has he not made Chilverton a better place to live in? And he gives money to good causes in the town. To soup kitchens for the weavers . . .'

The townsfolk, in uproarious mood, enjoyed themselves hugely: men shouted election slogans, women danced in the streets, even the boaters joined in the fun, bringing their fiddles. The children played an old game. 'We don't care for the devil nor you, we are the English.' There hadn't been so much merry-making since the passing of the Reform Bill.

No one knew when the rumours started. Tam certainly didn't know a thing about it until Jamie told her. 'There's talk, Mama,' he said one night.

'Talk? What about?'

'About you – and Charles Waring.'

She was alarmed. 'What sort of talk?'

'They say that you're lovers.'

'We're not,' said Tam, flatly.

'No, but they say he's always visiting here – '

'For goodness' sake, Juliet lived here, didn't she? He had to come. And nothing happened in this house.'

'They don't know that, Mama.'

'Not all the time he came here.' Tam was furious. 'There was nothing, not for a long time – '

'I know, Mama.'

'Who says these things? Can we stop it?'

'Not now. It's gone too far.'

'But for heaven's sake, all the years before no one bothered – '

'Maybe they didn't know. And that's not all – '

'No?' She looked at him, with dread.

'They know about me.'

Tam sat down. 'How?' she asked.

Jamie shrugged.

No one ever knew how the rumours started. But no one was surprised, the weavers had always known. Perhaps they talked among themselves, as always, and one of Sir Lewis's men took it up. Tam blamed Sir Lewis, for he knew, indeed she herself had told him, and certainly his supporters made the most of it. It was the talk of the town. The respectable burghers thought it monstrous that a well-known figure should carry on in such a manner. And with his poor wife's sister! But then, Tamarisk Calder was a wild one and no mistake. Look at the way she worked on those boats. Working! It was disgraceful. She was not a lady. She should be thrown in the canal and Charles Waring with her. So said the burghers self-righteously, and they were the ones with the votes.

Tam, who had vowed not to help Charles in any way, who had half hoped Sir Lewis would win, now swung violently to Charles's side. And when one morning she found a note pinned on the *Princess* saying baldly 'Charles Waring's Harlot', her anger knew no bounds. Enraged, she went to one of the meetings; a large crowd was gathered, waiting for Charles to arrive. Tam stood up.

'I have something to say,' she called, and there was a shout. 'Silence for the lady. Come up on the platform then.'

She went up, quailing, but she faced them bravely. 'This note,' she said, holding it up. 'I think it is despicable. I think you are despicable to repeat gossip. What has Charles Waring ever done to harm you? Nothing. He has always worked for you, sacrificed more than you can ever know. You took everything from him, you voted for him, said how fine he was, let him work and worry for you. And now, what? A breath of scandal and you shout him down. What do you know of him?' And to her amazement and disgust, just as Charles himself entered, tears filled her eyes, ran unheeded down her cheeks. 'If you let him down,' she ended, 'you'll be the biggest traitors the world has ever seen.'

There was a silence, and a voice then piped up, 'Do you deny it?' Tam shouted, 'I do not hold myself responsible to you!' There were more cries, and she shouted, 'Judge him on his record as Member of Parliament, that's all I ask!'

Charles had reached the platform, and she turned to go. The crowd went wild. 'There they are then,' and Charles thundered, 'Silence!'

Tam didn't wait to hear any more, she left the hall, wondering drearily if she'd made things worse. She found her pony-chaise and drove home.

When the results of the election were declared Tam sent Jamie to find out who'd won. But even as he left the house they could hear cries outside, 'Sir Lewis is the man for us.' When Jamie returned, one look at his face told her what she dreaded most to hear.

'He lost,' Jamie said.

'Oh, poor Charles. Where is he?'

'I don't know.'

'What do you mean, you don't know?'

'He heard Sir Lewis was in, thanked us, then when I turned to see him, he'd disappeared. So I came to tell you.'

'I'll go and find him,' she cried.

'Do you want me to come with you?'

'No. Stay here, Jamie, in case he comes.'

She took the pony-chaise and drove into town. The crowds were celebrating. Everywhere were people, shouting, singing, dancing: men waved mugs of beer, children ran around, dogs barked.

She pulled the pony to a halt, unable to take him through the throng. So, instead she tied him up and carried on on foot, thinking dully, it's like that other time, the first time, when he won . . . that night . . .

The night that Jamie had been conceived.

Where would he be in all these crowds? Someone shouted, 'Sir Lewis!' And they took up the cry. 'Sir Lewis. He's the man for us. He'll see us through.' No, Charles wouldn't be with these people. They didn't want him now. Surely he wouldn't leave without a word to her?

She was on the wharf now, making her way to the *Duchess*. She knocked on the boat and Mirrie's head appeared. 'Why, Tamarisk,' she said.

'Is Charles with you?' Tam asked, her voice desperate.

307

'No. But come in.'

'Thank you, no. Is Harry there?'

Harry came on to the well-deck. 'I don't know where he be, Tamarisk. Shall I come with thee?'

'No, Harry. I'm all right.' And she turned away. She retraced her steps, halted before the house on the wharf. His house. It was dark; she knocked and getting no reply entered, stumbling into the living room, where she lit the lamp.

He was there, sitting, his head in his hands.

For a moment she stared. It was the first time she had ever seen him bowed. Always he'd been the bold one, arrogant, a winner.

She went to him and put her arms round him. He turned his head slightly towards her, she clasped him to her breast. So they remained, wordless, for a long time. At last she broke the silence saying, 'How could they let you down? After all you've done for them.'

'It's the way of the world,' he said.

'It's monstrous, that they should turn on you.'

'The worst times are over now, they don't need radicals. They have more work, better living conditions – '

'The hand-loom weavers don't have more work – '

'They are an anachronism, like me.'

'Will you stand again?'

'I don't know.'

'Charles,' she said. 'You told me to come to you, that you would wait for me . . . Here I am. I love you. I want you.'

He said dully, 'Don't say that.'

She drew away, a finger of fear touching her. 'Why not?'

'It's too late.'

'But – '

'I asked Mary Travers to marry me.'

'Oh. But you don't love her?'

'Of course I don't love her. But – '

'But it will help your career. It will help you get back into Parliament.'

'Oh Tam, we're not young lovers now, we are in our forties . . . First I loved your body, I went mad to touch you, kiss you . . . Then I wanted your companionship – that I would have had if we could have been together . . .'

'And I refused you.' She thought dully of the Duchess's warning.

'It couldn't be helped. We couldn't be together. But Mary Travers has helped me.'

'I see.'

'I am promised, Tam.'

He stood up, held her in his arms and kissed her, crushing her till she was breathless . . . and then he let her go.

She watched him walk to the door, mount his horse . . . saw him ride away at a gallop . . . away from Chilverton, and from her.

* * *

Two weeks later Harry said, 'Things will be easier now, Tamarisk. Sir Lewis has ceased competing. Greatrex has put up the freight fares. It won't stop those who want speed, but it's a help to us.'

'Yes,' she said colourlessly.

He went on. 'Tamarisk, I wonder now . . . couldst thou look for another agent? I find it harder and harder now to walk . . . I cannot keep up the pace,' and she was filled with remorse.

'Of course, Harry,' she said. 'I'll find someone.' Of course I will . . . Tam will do everything . . . run boats, find new agents . . . they all depend on you, Tam.

She drove home to find Jamie waiting for her.

'Back from your weekend in London?' she asked. 'How was Catherine?'

'She is well.' He paused. 'I have news for you, Mama.'

'Yes?' She sat down, wearily, hoping it was not bad news.

'We have set a date for our marriage.'

'When?'

'In the autumn. And I have decided to take the name of Calder, if you don't object.'

'It will start people talking again, Jamie.'

'Maybe. But I am not a Fargate, and I do not wish to bear the name.' Then he said, a little hesitantly, 'I want to invite my father to the wedding, Mama.'

'But we don't know where he is.' For they'd not heard a word since the election.

'No, I thought of that. We shall, of course, put the usual announcement in the newspaper. *The Times*, perhaps, would be best. And I thought, if we added a rider saying "Friends and relatives welcome", he'd read it, and understand.'

'You won't put the change of name in *The Times*?' asked Tam.

'No, Mama, I wouldn't want to embarrass you.'

'Well, if that's what you want to do.' She knew very well that if that was what Jamie wanted to do, then that would be done. She began, 'Jamie – ' but broke off. No, she wouldn't tell him that Charles was going to marry Mary Travers. She wouldn't spoil his wedding. But she doubted if Charles would come.

Charles sat in his room in the London square reading the announcement. Jamie was getting married. His son. He understood the meaning of the words, it was an invitation – to him. He picked up the letter he'd received that morning. He'd read it over and over till he knew it off by heart. Members of the Liberal Party, she said, led by her father, Lord Packworth, and her uncle, Sir Hubert Graves, would like him, Charles, to stand when the next seat became vacant. But there was a problem. He would be obliged to curb his more radical views, the constituency they had in mind was very mild – Charles smiled at the word – in the south of England, so he would in effect be making a fresh start. She herself could see no problem in this. And if he agreed, why then, they could be married, and she would do all in her power to help him, and to influence her father and uncle in any way she could. If he chose not to stand she would be sorry, and would understand that he did not wish to be re-elected, that he no longer had any desire to stand for Parliament. She would be sorry to lose him, but he would understand that she was too involved with the Party to wish to leave, or to work in any other field . . .

Charles dropped the letter and looked again at the newspaper announcement. Then he stood up. What did his ambition mean to him now? How long had it meant so much? For years? Always? Even at the start when he'd told everyone – including himself – that he wanted to help the poor, hadn't there, even then, been a touch of arrogance in the statement, a hint underneath that it was power he wanted? Power he'd never had as a younger son. Or had his ambitions started when once he was in Parliament? Or when, alone far too long, denied a family life that other men had, he'd turned to his career for solace? Who knew? But when Mary Travers first came along he knew then. He knew he wanted power, just as he knew Mary Travers wanted to be the wife of a powerful man. That's why she'd waited . . .

Now he had a choice: power and a loveless marriage, in a mild constituency, given the sort of help he'd never had; or – to spend the rest of his life with the woman he had always loved.

Had loved. Did he love her now? He thought of the girl she had been. The laughter, the passion. The way she'd shouldered her burdens without complaint, taking care of her family . . . If she was wilful, if she made a mistake in marrying that old skinflint, wasn't he, Charles, to blame for taking her, and leaving her with a child?

But they'd been apart too long. Was any love left? And if not, did he not owe her something?

Marrying Mary Travers would mean saying goodbye to Jamie as well as Tam. He knew well what the words *a fresh start* meant. Mary Travers knew nothing of Tam, and she wouldn't want to know. If she guessed there were indiscretions in his past she would expect them to be put behind him if he married her, they would belong to his past, he would start afresh, a newly married man.

He had to sacrifice Tam – or his career.

He had to choose. And it was the hardest choice of his life.

Tam had bought one of the new crinoline cages for her gown for Jamie and Catherine's wedding. At first she'd demurred, but Jamie had insisted, insisted on paying for her outfit, so, as they were staying with the Bradfords the week before the wedding, she'd allowed herself to be persuaded.

'Tut, milady's skin,' admonished the dressmaker. 'Milady rides a lot outdoors, maybe?'

'Maybe,' said Tam, feeling more gipsyish than ever against the pale London faces. She looked at her reflection in the long mirror. She was still slim, her waist was quite tiny, her hair as rich in colour as ever. I just need a new face, she told herself wryly, and allowed herself to be treated with egg white and lemon, cucumber and oil of rosemary. And when the day arrived she surveyed herself with a fair amount of satisfaction. The crinoline, of finest blue silk, billowed out below the waist in flounces, and Jamie had presented her with a fine silk shawl, specially woven for her.

The bride was enchanting in white, a veil covering her face, and as she entered the fashionable church on the arm of her father, Tam was aware that someone had slipped into the seat next to hers. She half-turned. It was Charles.

And after that the ceremony passed in a blur. She admitted to herself now, that she'd hoped he'd come, that his coming meant he'd stay.

But they had no chance to talk. At the wedding breakfast they were not together, and as the bride and groom left for their honeymoon in France, the fashionable crowd filled the room with well-dressed bodies and high-pitched talk until Tam's ears reverbated, and her eyes were dazzled with sound and colour. So that when Charles came to her and spoke she could hardly take in what he was saying.

He was talking about Jamie. How surprised he'd been to hear the news, what a nice girl Catherine seemed, the Bradfords were well-to-do and well-connected. And when he stopped talking the high-pitched sounds seemed even louder around them, and he said at last, exasperated, 'We can't talk here. Where can we be alone?'

'In my room,' she answered. 'I'm staying until tomorrow.'

'Come then, lead the way.' And she wondered then, again, if he had come to stay with her, for there was no sign of Mary Travers . . .

He said, reading her thoughts, 'We have broken it off, Mary and I.'

'Oh Charles.' And she hadn't known till that moment how thankful she'd be. But it didn't stop her asking curiously, 'Who broke it off, you or she?'

He hesitated. 'I did,' he said.

'Oh Charles. And you've come to me. But your career . . .'

'Is over.'

She searched his face. 'Are you *sure*?'

'I have thought well about it. I have decided not to stand for Parliament again.'

'And Mary Travers wished you to,' she said shrewdly.

'Not as an Independent. I told you before, Tam, times are changing, many reforms have been carried out. There will be a surge now for votes for more people . . .'

'I still have a fight,' she said softly.

'Tam, listen to me. You always were headstrong, rushing into things without careful thought. What do you want of me? That I come back to Chilverton?'

'Of course.'

'But I have no work now. And precious little money, for what my father left has mostly gone on expenses . . .'

'Oh, Charles, there is your old job, Agent on the canal. I need someone

311

desperately, Harry wants to leave, and he never did the work properly anyway, he couldn't, he wasn't trained . . .' She paced up and down, thinking. 'I need you, Charles. It's been hard for Harry and for me, too, since Robin left. If you were there I needn't work so hard – '

'I see,' he said, with the glimmerings of a smile. 'You just want me to take over the work – '

'Of course,' she said, smiling in turn.

'And where would I live?' he asked, turning to face her.

'At Cherry Trees, of course. With me.'

'Tam, think well. We can never marry. You are my wife's sister. The act allowing it has never got through Parliament . . .'

'Then we shall live without marriage,' she said.

'That wouldn't be easy for you,' he told her. 'You'd be the one who'd be slighted – '

'Oh, pooh, do you think I care? I've never done the things I'm supposed to be doing, anyway. It's all so stupid. A couple dare not live together openly, yet they have all sorts of liaisons, as – as my mother did. If my mother dared, then so dare I.' And she marvelled that she should finally align herself with her mother. 'Anyway we've had our own backstreet liaison for years, haven't we? Because we loved each other. So what difference does it make if an act is passed saying we can do so legally? Except to prove that all morals are man-made.' They were but a step apart now, staring into each other's eyes. 'Besides,' she said wistfully, 'I'd like to live with you, as if I *were* a wife. I never have, you see.' Still he stood, a step away, and she said, a little quiver in her voice, 'Don't you care for me any more, Charles?'

'I never stopped caring for you,' he said, and now his eyes held the old remembered look, the possessing look, that forced her to drop her own glance, that made her breathless suddenly, a girl again.

'Jamie is taking the name Calder,' she said, inconsequently, as Charles still stood on the brink.

He did it deliberately, he thought. Forcing my hand. Letting everyone know that Fargate wasn't his father, that the gossip was correct. He wants us to be together, so he's finished me in Parliament . . . So why not? . . . Tam, whom I loved, love . . . wouldn't I have longed for her even if I'd had Mary Travers in my bed . . .?

He took the step forward.

He kissed her. He held her and the torrents of passion were unleashed. They clung to each other as though they could never get close enough, they gasped and shuddered with longing. And when he led her to the bed she removed her clothes without qualm. The noise below was blotted out as they entered their world, their very own world, and she felt she was one with him at last, part of him, whole, because he was there.

312

PART FOUR
1855–1906

Of all the seasons I most love winter

Coventry Patmore

Chapter One

People did talk. Chilverton reverbated with talk. So it was true then, Charles Waring had been carrying on with his dead wife's sister all these years. Poor Sir William, he must have had to put up with a lot. And young Jamie, announcing to the world that he wasn't Sir William's son, or why else would he want to take his mother's name? It was shameful. Sir William, in death, became a much better figure than in life, remembered as a poor old man, cuckolded by his flibbertigibbet wife. Men cut Tam, and in the street women drew their skirts aside as she passed as if she had some loathsome disease.

She did not go into Chilverton often, but there were times she needed to visit the shops, and on one of these occasions she bumped into Jerome Randall.

Tam stopped, forgetting for the moment that she was in disgrace. 'Jerome,' she said with pleasure. 'How are you?'

He raised his hat stiffly. 'Lady Fargate,' he murmured, and she had the impression that he would have passed by had she not stopped.

'I haven't seen you for some time, I wasn't able to tell you – '

He cut in. 'I must confess, I had no idea that while I was paying court to you, Lady Fargate, you were consorting with Charles Waring.'

'I wasn't at the time,' said Tam, her colour dangerously high.

He bowed awkwardly, clearly disbelieving. 'I'll bid you good day, Lady Fargate,' he said, and passed on.

Tam held her head high and tried not to care. But it was difficult to act as a normal wife when no one would speak to her. Celia made it plain that she could not possibly associate with a sister who so flouted conventions. Georgiana had never visited very often, she was busy as an MP's wife, and often in London. Jamie and Catherine had had a house built quite near to Tam, a square, modern dwelling on top of a hill, called Four Winds, and they visited, though Catherine seemed a little put out, Tam thought. Being a Londoner, Catherine deemed provincial society too funny for words, the serious way they took themselves – yet her own family had been highly respectable, fitting in with the mores of mid-Victorian society.

313

And almost immediately after her marriage Catherine became pregnant so she could no longer be seen in public.

But Annabel called, and for once Tam was pleased to see her mother. Annabel was over sixty now, yet her stylish air remained, and though she refused to wear a crinoline cage, her skirts were wide and flounced, her face covered with pearl powder, and still beautiful.

'So,' she said, sitting down. 'You have upset Chilverton yet again, Tam.'

Tam rang for tea. 'Is this what you had to put up with for so long?' she asked.

Her mother smiled. 'It was indeed. It isn't easy, Tam.'

'It's so stupid,' Tam said. 'Who are these people to sit as my judges?'

'People love to judge others,' said Annabel. 'Especially those who dare things they're afraid to do themselves. But you're happy?'

'Yes, I am happy.'

'Then,' her mother said. 'You can't have everything, can you?'

Tam supposed not. Yet she had never been a rebel from choice, rather had she been thrown into rebellion, partly because she did like her own way and did not see why she should let public opinion dictate how she should live. She wanted to work on the canals, she wanted to live with Charles, and rather than give up the idea because of any code, she would defy and become a rebel. But for all that, she had always wanted to live with Charles as his legal wife, and it seemed hard that she could not. She knew that he was not ostracised as she was, and that he refused invitations simply to stay with her, and for this she was grateful, and wanted to please him in return.

She'd said at the start of their life together, 'You've never had a wife, Charles. Not really.'

'No.'

'And I never had a real husband. So – you see to the canals, I'll stay in home.'

'Yes, Tam, I'll be able to take all the hard work off your shoulders.'

She showed him the books, the accounts. 'This is the amount I keep for maintenance, this the floating fund, and so on. And this – ' she brought out another book, 'is my own profit. I have now divided this into two separate accounts and we will do so in future.' What might have been an awkward moment passed, as Charles chortled with laughter. No one but Tam would divide money so equally. But Tam hadn't forgotten when she had to account to Sir William for every penny spent, and Charles, being a man of his time, did not oppose having his own account, he would not easily have come cap in hand to her for money.

So they assumed the normal husband and wife roles, each thinking this was what the other preferred. Tam too had at the back of her mind the ever-present worry that he might still wish he were in politics – that he'd lost his chance now, living with her, and might someday regret it. But she said nothing of this.

Nor did Charles ever tell her just what had transpired between Mary

314

Travers and himself. But he missed politics more than he thought possible, missed his fellows in the House, the debates at which he had excelled. Missed the hurly-burly of London, the lights of the city in the dusk, the slow-flowing river, the sheer exuberance of it all. He tried not to feel any sense of grievance towards the citizens of Chilverton who no longer desired him to act for them, and indeed, some of them made glowing overtures towards him – too glowing, he thought suspiciously, while others were shame-faced. It all made it easy for him to turn down their invitations, knowing Tam would not be accepted.

Both had to make adjustments in living together. Both had been accustomed to being alone, pleasing only themselves – Tam more so than Charles. Both had a ready temper, and arguments were plentiful in the early days. Then he would hold her and kiss her and her body would first clamour and then melt in the old remembered way. At least we have this, she marvelled. Nights when they didn't have to part, when he could hold her, when they made love and it was magical as always, perhaps better even, as each learned to please the other. He, experienced, had always known how to please her, now he taught her ways of pleasing him.

She told herself she was happy in the home, she was a wife, whatever the law may say. She supervised the cooking, the housekeeping. But the staff, used to managing on their own for so long, did not take kindly to her ministrations, and as they did not entertain she knew her supervision was hardly necessary. Matty, now a woman grown, loved her mistress and Cherry Trees. But she was, in her own way, as self-willed as Tam herself, and would not change her own somewhat awkward ways for anyone. When Tam suggested they get another small girl to help her, she was affronted, and refused point-blank to hear of it.

So Tam would stand for hours gazing wistfully at the canal, then with a sigh turn away. She listened eagerly to what Charles had to say when he came in, and was pleased to see that things were brighter than for some time. Sir Lewis no longer had the time or the inclination to care too much about his railway, and certainly was not willing to run freight at a loss; so long as Charles could undercut, he was assured of cargoes. And as so many of the new factories had been built alongside the canal, it was more convenient – prices being right – to have coal delivered by water. So Charles kept things going: orders were chased, men kept on their toes, maintenance kept up. Dividends actually rose. They said a fond farewell to Mirrie and Harry, and Tam asked Charles what he would do with the *Duchess*.

'We still have the *Princess* running as a packet boat,' Charles said. 'There aren't enough passengers for two boats now. Occasional trips, yes, but to get round the country people go by rail.'

'Can't we sell the *Duchess*?'

'No one would buy.'

So the *Duchess* stood rotting in the lay-by.

One morning Charles had a letter from London, and he took such a time reading it that Tam was curious. 'Is it bad news?' she asked.

315

'What? Oh no. It's from John Barnes, a colleague in the House. We were good friends – ' he broke off.

'And?' she asked.

'It's nothing, Tam.'

'It is something, Charles. What does he say?'

'He wants me to visit, that's all.'

'Then you must go.' She was firm.

'But, Tam – '

'I know,' she said. 'I could not go along with you. Well, for heaven's sake, Charles, I don't expect you to drag me along on your coat-tails everywhere. Anyway, it would bore me, politics always does. And I suppose that's all you'll talk about.'

'Yes,' he said, relieved. 'But I can't leave you, Tam.'

'Why not? I shan't disappear.'

'I would like to go,' he said. 'I like John Barnes, and his wife – ' and he could have bitten off his tongue.

But she was unperturbed. 'I do know other people are married,' she said. 'You must go, Charles.'

'We – ell.' Charles tried to hide his pleasure. 'As long as you realise it's only business, and not another woman.'

'Men are so conceited,' she returned equably. 'They think women are always ready to run after them. I recollect I told you something of the sort the very first time we met. But you're not a handsome young dandy now, Charles, and who would want an ageing *roué*?'

He laughed. 'And here am I thinking all the maidens are swooning for my favours.'

But it wasn't women Tam feared: her rival had always been his work. And at times she was afraid.

Charles went to London, and it was one of many such trips. John Barnes was a Liberal, and, knowing nothing of Tam, he tried to persuade Charles to stand for Parliament again. 'So you lost one seat,' he said. 'There are others.'

'It wouldn't be quite the same,' Charles replied. 'I felt myself a representative of the people of Chilverton – '

'As you were – '

'Because I know them, I worked for them.'

'And what are you doing now? Working on your old job as canal agent. I'll wager it is not too well paid, and if the canals finish you'll have nothing.'

And Charles still said nothing about Tam, telling himself it was for her sake, wondering if indeed it was. Should he not have taken Mary Travers's offer, to stand as a Liberal, when with the aid of her relatives he would have been helped to power – provided he did the right things, and kept free from scandal. He would have had the power he craved, and Mary Travers would have had what she requried, to be the wife of a powerful man. He went to the House, in the public gallery, and wondered if he'd been a quixotic fool.

★ ★ ★

When Jamie's first son, Richard, was born, Tam hastened to Four Winds to see the young mother. Catherine was well, and the baby thrived. She was soon pregnant again, it was the age of big families, and again Tam spent much time at Four Winds. Ian, the second boy, like Richard gave little trouble at birth, but he was a more fretful baby, and often Tam could soothe him when no one else could. The third pregnancy was disastrous from the start. Catherine was irritable and unwell, as if she knew something would go wrong. And it did. In her eight month, hurrying to the door of her room, she tripped and fell heavily. She was put to bed, but immediately labour pains started.

Jamie was sent for, and the doctor. Tam, too, hurried to Four Winds, and stayed for two days and nights, while the young mother moaned in agony, and the babies were left to their nannies. Richard, three years old, was happy enough during this turmoil. But Ian, just twelve months, could not understand what was wrong. He cried, was fretful, and only Tam could quieten him. She nursed him night and day. She stayed with the Calders, sleeping in a bed in the nursery because Ian's fretful wails disturbed the whole house. And when Catherine was out of danger, and the third son, Henry, was born, she took Ian to Cherry Trees, where he settled happily and stayed for three months, until Catherine was on her feet again. Then he went back to Four Winds, but a bond had been forged. Ian was Granny's boy, and as soon as he was able, he trotted down to Cherry Trees on his small pony.

But in the meantime he was home again, and Tam missed him sorely. She was back to having nothing to do, to staring out of the window at the canal, watching the boats, waiting for Charles to come home . . .

And then Amanda came to visit.

She had written regularly to her parents and to Tam, and occasionally Celia and Geoffrey had visited her. She wrote of the founding of the Nightingale School at St Thomas's Hospital, how she had met Miss Nightingale and had been accepted for training as a nurse.

She burst into Cherry Trees like a breath of fresh air. Twenty-five now, Amanda looked both well and happy.

'Dear Aunt,' she said, kissing Tam. 'How wonderful to see you.'

'And you too. Sit down, Amanda, tell me all your doings.'

Amanda talked. No, she didn't particularly want to marry again. She was happy in the new improved training for nurses, so why marry? There was a group of enlightened women in London who thought there were other things in life than marriage, and that women should have rights of their own.

'Like votes?' asked Tam, with the glimmering of a smile.

'Why not? But certainly independence. Our own money, our own work.'

Tam said nothing.

'But you, Aunt, what happened to you?' Amanda asked. 'You were the one who – who inspired me. And now you sit at home like a good little wife, doing nothing.'

Tam moved restlessly under the younger woman's direct gaze. She said, 'I think Charles prefers it.'

'Does he say so?'

'I don't know.'

'You mean you don't ask?'

'Oh – ' Tam stood up in order to avoid that direct gaze, those far-seeing eyes. 'What would you have me do?'

'Oh, Aunt, you are bored to tears, you don't have to tell me. You want to be with the action, where you always were. On the canals. Don't you?'

'I have my grandchildren. They come to see me often.'

'But they'll go to school. You worked all your life, you shouldn't stop now.'

'You think I should go back to the wharf again?'

'Of course. You'd love it.'

When Amanda went back Tam spoke to Charles. 'Amanda thinks I am vegetating at home,' she said.

'Oh.' He strode across the room. 'And are you?'

'I confess I miss the canal.'

'Then come back,' he said.

'May I? Truly? You wouldn't object?'

'And what,' he asked teasingly, 'would you do if I did?'

'Charles.' She stood, serious now. 'Are you happy?'

'Of course.'

'You don't regret giving up politics?'

He paused, and she noted the hesitation. 'No,' he said.

She knew that was what held her back. The fear that she'd lose him. And she couldn't bear to lose him now. She said wistfully, 'If only we could work together, it would make me so happy . . .'

'I didn't know – ' he said. 'You told me you wanted to live as a wife.'

She hung her head. 'I know. And I did. I suppose I meant I wanted you. If you prefer me to stay in home –'

He shouted with laughter. 'No,' he said, and, sobering, 'not with the population of Chilverton refusing to visit. I thought you'd be happier in home, away from people – the risk of meeting . . .'

'The boaters won't care whether we're married or not,' she said.

So Tam went back to the canals. And she changed again. If society disapproved, then let it. She'd tried staying at home, being a Victorian wife, it didn't work. She would not grow into a wilting lily afraid of wagging tongues, she would meet society head on as she always had, and defy it to do its worst. She would not grow into a delicate old lady, as Celia was ready to do, but a fighter for what she believed in.

The weaving trade still fluctuated. Jamie was now a junior partner, having put Catherine's dowry into the business, with both Catherine and her parents agreeing to this move. The Bradfords were wealthy and Catherine was their only child. Geoffrey, who had never recuperated his losses from the railway mania, had been glad of his help, and had learned to rely on

Jamie's judgement. But of late, Jamie had been worried about his uncle. He seemed to act in an irrational manner; without telling Jamie, he had squandered much of their capital on speculation and shares in worthless companies in an effort to recuperate his new losses. Jamie took his family to London to visit the Bradfords, and discussed his worries with his father-in-law.

'You know what you should do, young man,' Mr Bradford said. 'And that is break away from your uncle and set up on your own. I'd finance you. You're a sound fellow.'

'I hardly like to do that, Mr Bradford,' Jamie said. 'Uncle Geoffrey did give me my chance at the start.'

'And from what I can gather you've been more help to him than he is to you.'

'I do feel that, left on his own now, he'd just go to pieces,' Jamie said.

'Then you could pick up the pieces.' Mr Bradford smiled. 'No? Oh well, I admire your loyalty. But the man's a fool.'

Jamie paced up and down. 'I am worried, I'll admit. Things aren't too good on the weaving front at all.'

'Is it the old problem of prices?'

'Yes. As always. They want us to pay piece-work rates, that's like the List Prices of the hand-loom weavers. They prefer it to a weekly wage.'

'And are you going to pay?'

'I think so – in the end.'

'It does seem that silk weaving is beset with troubles, at least the ribbon trade. Could you not branch out into other things?'

'I'd like to, but – '

'But Geoffrey Waring won't. Well, think over what I've said. You'll not get far with him. But I'll not put another penny into the business while he's there.'

'I'll see what happens,' said Jamie.

Charles and Tam visited Jamie and Catherine every Sunday. Four Winds was a pleasant house, well-furnished and comfortable. And this particular Sunday they entered to a surprise guest in the morning room.

'Amanda,' cried Tam. 'You are here and didn't come to see me?'

'I'm only here for two days,' said Amanda. 'I came to see Jamie.'

'Did you indeed?' asked Tam.

Amanda was chuckling. 'Remember when I was eighteen, and chasing every man in sight? I used to chase Jamie too, but he wouldn't have me.'

'Well, don't start again now,' said Tam. 'Not with three babies upstairs.'

'I was a minx,' said Amanda, ruefully. 'Catherine, you don't know how awful I was. But I didn't know what I wanted. Or at least I knew I wanted to work, but work wasn't done by young ladies – still isn't. I saw Aunt Tam and her business, and she seemed like some shining star, and as remote, Mama saw to that. Then my Grandmama came to live with us.'

'My mother,' said Tam. 'I knew she had something to do with it.'

'In a way, yes. She talked about when she was an actress, and I thought, well, women can work, so I'll be an actress too. That's when I persuaded poor Robin to take me to London. But when we got there things changed. I grew fond of him, there was the war, and then I became interested in nursing.' She was silent. 'All that trouble and heartbreak would have been avoided if only I could have done that at the start.' Again she paused. 'But we are going to change things, you know, make life better for women, so they're more free . . . But listen to me running on, when I came to talk about Father.'

'Geoffrey?' asked Tam in surprise. 'He isn't ill?'

'Not exactly, but I am worried about him. There's a look of strain in his face, I've seen it so often in my work. I don't like it.'

'But what can Jamie do?' asked Tam.

'I wondered if he might buy him out of the factory.'

Tam looked at Jamie. 'Would you want to?'

'Oh yes,' Jamie said. 'I'd get on much better. Uncle Geoffrey is – well, his judgements aren't always of the best. I mean where money's concerned. He – speculates, and I can't always stop him.'

'I think he should leave,' Amanda said. 'He and Mother could sell the Grange House, buy a small place, it would be ideal.'

'But would he sell?' asked Tam. 'And would you,' she nodded to Jamie, 'be able to buy him out?'

'Oh yes. Mr Bradford would be only too willing to help in that respect.'

'It just remains to persuade Father,' said Amanda. 'And I'm not altogether sure he'd be willing. He isn't sixty yet, he'd think people thought of him as a failure. Oh dear, sometimes I think it's as bad to be a man as a woman. Men are supposed to be hard and fierce, and I fear poor Father never was.'

Talk turned to other things, and Tam went to the nursery to see her grandsons. Richard, dark and imperious, fat little Henry in his cradle. But she stayed longest with Ian, her own, her baby. And when they returned to Cherry Trees she had dismissed Amanda's worries about Geoffrey from her mind.

It was a warm day in 1860 when Tam sat in the little office. Charles was on one of his visits to London, and she expectd him home that evening. He had stayed overnight with the Barnes, as he usually did, and Tam let him go without a word of protest. Only underneath did the niggling worry remain, that he regretted giving up Parliament, that someday he might want to return.

She did not hear the wheels of a cab above the noise of the wharf, and when the door was flung open to admit Charles, she gasped, 'What's wrong?'

'I've had some rather bad news,' he said. 'I must go and tell Geoffrey. I thought I'd let you know where I am.'

'What is it?'

'About the weaving. It seems that Cobden has been negotiating a secret treaty with France. He plans to take off the last remaining duty on silk, abolish tariffs completely.'

'But – ' Tam was astonished.

'I must go, Tam.'

'Wait for me, Charles. I'll come with you.'

They bowled along to Geoffrey's factory, and into the office where he was talking to Jamie. They looked up, surprised at this sudden entry, and Charles repeated his news.

'But we knew nothing of this – ' Geoffrey cried.

'No, it's all been very secret.'

'But,' he wailed, 'we want the tariff increased, not taken off.'

'It's going through,' said Charles. 'Gladstone is for it.'

'This is monstrous,' said Geoffrey. 'I shall be ruined.' His hands were shaking.

'What can we do?' asked Jamie, practically.

'There's little time to do anything,' said Charles. 'Except protest.'

'Really, so secret,' said Geoffrey, pulling at his thinning hair, a recent habit when troubled. 'And it couldn't have come at a worse time. Just when the spring stocks are completed. We've no more orders . . . whatever shall we do?'

'Calm yourself, Uncle Geoffrey,' said Jamie. 'We will protest.'

Coventry and Spitalfields and Chilverton made their protests known, but in vain. Gladstone secured a large majority in the House of Commons, and with it the death blow to the already weakened silk industry. Within a few weeks English ports were flooded with duty-free silks from France and Switzerland, the weavers were submerged, and the factory owners faced bankruptcy. Thousands of weavers were out of work within weeks. In July many of the silk manufacturers withdrew from the List Prices. The weavers threatened an all-out strike.

'I must withdraw from the List too, Jamie,' Geoffrey said, his face creased with worry.

Jamie walked to the window. He saw a group of weavers talking in the yard. 'If we can hold on maybe trade will improve,' he said, with little conviction.

'With our tariffs off, and America putting high tariffs on?' growled Geoffrey. 'We can't sell here and we can't export – '

'We must turn to other things. I've said so all along – '

'But we couldn't do so in time, Jamie. It's now I need orders. It's now I need money. Damn it, I'm not at all well-placed at the moment. That damned Chilverton railway isn't paying so much this year, some people are even going back to canal transport, and that's all I have to live on, apart from my rents – '

'Won't the banks help?' asked Jamie.

'Not now. They think we're ruined. And I have so much expense. Two daughters to support, a wife who is extravagant – '

'I know,' sympathised Jamie. 'I am married too.'

'You don't know. Your wife brought a dowry with her, mine didn't.' Geoffrey broke off as he wondered what use Celia's aristocratic connections had ever been; times had changed, it was the industrial men who were in charge now. 'We have to cut wages,' he said.

'The men won't stand for it, Uncle Geoffrey.'

'Damn it, they have no choice.'

321

Jamie tried to persuade Geoffrey to wait, but his uncle was adamant. He posted a notice outside his factory, saying he would no longer adhere to the List Prices. The weavers joined Coventry in an all-out strike.

It was an unhappy strike, with much bitterness and poverty, for there was no longer any strike fund. It was a miserable and violent time, and Geoffrey trembled lest his factory be burned to the ground. The soup kitchen was opened again, and pale women queued for food. Many of the weavers left the town, some emigrated to the United States and Canada, some went to Birmingham and Leicester. Almost daily it seemed a group of sad people with little bundles would wend their way to the wharf and board the packet boats. And Tam, hating to see their dejected poverty, would take them free of charge. 'You can pay me when you have work,' she said.

After one such emigration she returned home late to find Charles sitting with his head in his hands. Tam asked worriedly, 'What is it, love?'

'It grieves me to see the weavers broken, and I have done nothing to help,' he said.

She sat beside him, and voiced the fear she had held for so long. 'You wish you had stood for Parliament again?'

He looked at her. It was the time for truth. He said, 'Oh, my Tam, I never told you the whole truth. How Mary Travers offered me the help of her relatives provided I took their views.'

'I see.'

'Do you? Yes, you know how many times I've vaguely regretted not taking it on. I wanted power, of course I did. High office . . .' She said nothing, and he continued. 'I see now it would never have worked. I could never have belonged to the main parties, never voted with them. I didn't vote for war when all wanted it, and I could not, in conscience, have voted against my own people. I may be wrong, but I could not have done it. Not to see them thrown out of work.'

She put her arms around him, comforting.

'They *are* my own people,' he said. 'And it's impossible to take that feeling away. I belong to the weavers, my parents, their parents, my brother, my son . . . I could not have done it. So now, I'm glad I turned her down.'

'And the power?'

'I would simply have been there to say yes to all her relatives' suggestions. And that isn't power, Tam, it's being in someone else's power. And I might have done it and gone on and on until it was too late and I had nothing of myself left at all.'

Tam, who would never have voted for anything she did not whole-heartedly believe in, only half-understood the depth of his feeling. She said, 'The people who voted against you must now realise their mistake.'

'No, Tam. They did what they thought was right at the time. That's the whole point, don't you see? I wanted them to have votes, I should not complain if they use them as they will.'

She stroked his hair. 'It was bound to happen,' she said. 'You once told

322

me hand-loom weavers were an anachronism, don't you remember?'

'Yes. Like me, I said. We've seen too much, Tam, in our lifetime. Factories, trains . . .'

'And you think the canals are an anachronism too,' she said equably. 'But they're still going, Charles. And they will. You'll see. People will still ride on packet boats when they're tired of trains.'

'Oh my Tam,' he said. 'You never give up, do you?'

'Never,' she said.

The strike went on for three long weary months. At the end of that time the Price List was abandoned. The weavers came back to the factories.

But it was too late. There was no work. Geoffrey faced bankruptcy.

Tam was awakened in the night by someone thumping at the door. Charles jumped out of bed and ran downstairs, she followed. It was Celia's coachman.

'It's Mr Waring,' he said. 'Can you come?'

'Is he ill?' asked Charles.

'He's dead.'

They dressed hurriedly and drove to the Grange. Celia was crying hysterically, Amelia was with her. Bee was holding smelling salts, and Tam tried to grasp what had happened. The doctor enlightened her. It was a heart attack: he had died immediately.

The funeral was carried out with great pomp, for Geoffrey had been a respected businessman. Celia wept at the graveside then went home with her daughters. A week later she sent for Jamie.

'What am I going to do?' she wailed. 'The lawyer tells me we have nothing. We are ruined. How can this be?'

'I've been going into things,' Jamie said. 'Uncle Geoffrey had no capital left. It is true the factory has nothing – '

'But can't you do anything?' Celia asked.

'All I can do, Aunt Celia, is offer to take the factory over.'

'But how can you? Have you any money?'

'My father-in-law will finance me. This means I will pay our debts, the debts Uncle Geoffrey left, but there will be nothing left, Aunt Celia, for you. I'm sorry, but it's the only way Mr Bradford will help.'

'You mean you are going to carry on making ribbons?'

'No, there are no orders. I shall turn to other things.'

'But won't you have to pay for my share of the factory?' Celia asked.

'Yes, Aunt Celia, but the money will go to paying the debts.'

'Then I'll have nothing? Nothing to live on?'

'You have the income from the railway shares, and the houses.'

'Oh, oh,' wailed Celia, when Jamie had gone. 'Whatever shall we do? And what a hard young man Jamie has proved to be. As hard as his father.'

'Nonsense, Mama,' said Bee. 'He is paying our debts.'

'We'll be all right, Mama,' said Amelia. 'We can sell Grange House. We'll have enough for our needs.'

'But who will marry you now?' Celia cried. 'You are twenty-three,

Amelia. I can't understand how it is that no one has offered for you. We have met people, had many balls and parties,' and she stared at her pretty, placid, unwanted daughter.

'I am getting married, Mama,' said Bee.

'Oh, Bee, don't talk nonsense.'

'But I am, Mama.'

Celia turned to her youngest daughter. At seventeen Bee was just as clumsy as ever, she had none of the graces of a young lady: her clothes still didn't fit, her body was too long for her legs, her face beneath its straight black hair was square. But her eyes lit up when she smiled, and she had the same roguish smile, but Celia took little heed of that. She had long ago relegated Bee to the shelf, who in heaven's name would want to marry Bee? If dear sweet Amelia couldn't find a husband, what chance had this ugly duckling?

Celia sighed. 'What are you talking about?' she asked.

'I'm going to marry Francis Fargate.'

'Bee, please. I suppose you would like to. And heaven knows I've done all I can . . .' Taken the girls to visit whenever possible, had the Fargate boys to Grange House in the hope that Stephen would take a fancy to dear Amelia. But Stephen remained obstinately single, helping his father with the estate, hunting, shooting, fishing . . . 'Don't say any more,' Celia begged Bee. 'You might want to marry Francis Fargate, but to think he'd look at you . . .'

'*Mama*, how can I convince you? We have agreed to marry since we were children.'

'Oh, children's nonsense,' dismissed Celia.

'No, Mama, not children's nonsense. Francis and I are going to be married.'

'Then how is it he has not declared himself? How is it no one knows of it? Amelia has visited there as often as you . . .'

'Because Amelia can sometimes be a fool,' said Bee. 'She can't see what's before her nose. How many times over the years we've slipped away, Francis and I. First it was to see the birds and let animals out of the traps. Later it was to kiss.'

'To kiss?' said Celia faintly. 'You and Francis have been kissing?'

'Yes, Mama, and we enjoyed it so much we decided to get married.'

Celia stared at her youngest daughter in utter amazement, yet with a dawning hope, as though before her eyes a peculiar chrysalis was beginning to show faint signs of becoming a butterfly.

'But what on earth does he see in you?' she asked.

'He just likes me, Mama, he always has. He's very shy, you see, he likes me because I'm not.'

And all the years Celia had tried to make Bee into a shy refined young lady, the same as Amelia . . .

'Then if you are getting married,' she said tartly, 'you'd better tell your prospective bridegroom to call on me.'

Francis called the next day. And Celia, overcome, agreed to an engagement.

'We c – can't marry for a year, I know,' said Francis. 'But I hope that then you will allow Bee to marry me.'

'Does your father know?' asked Celia, faintly.

'Yes, of course. Mama will be calling on you.'

Celia gave her consent. And exactly one year later Bee was married.

It was a large affair, Celia saw to that, even Tam was invited. She would show her sister that her daughters could do well if they tried. Bee was dressed in white, and though she didn't look beautiful, because she never would, happiness lit her square face and shone out of her eyes. And Francis looked every inch a gentleman.

And exactly six months later to the day, Stephen was killed in a hunting accident. Francis was now heir to Chilverton Manor.

Chapter Two

The next few years were the happiest of Tam's life. The canal still carried her boats, she had Charles, her son, and grandchildren. Jamie's factory, after a hesitant start, was doing well. Two daughters joined his family, Vinny and Cathy, and another son, Robert Nicholas. The hand-loom weavers were practically extinct, the final blows being a disease of silkworms, and high tariffs put on American imports. The death of the Prince Consort added the finishing touches, when the Queen's protracted mourning killed the market for coloured ribbons. A few remained to weave tartans and other types of ribbons the larger looms could not do.

The young Calders had lacked for nothing, thanks to their Bradford grandparents. They had ponies to ride, and when they were home from school they'd all trot down to see Tam and Charles. But Ian remained Tam's favourite, he'd always been Granny's boy, had accompanied her to the wharf from babyhood, had sailed on the *Princess* – run now by young Jim's son – and he loved the canals. He was more like Tam in looks than any of the others, with the same reddish hair, and a fascinating smile which would, she felt, break quite a number of hearts in time.

Tam's only regret now was that time would not stand still. The years whirled past like the cherry blossom petals in a storm, only a few lingering as memories.

There was the sad year of 1870 when Annabel died. Tam, who had grown closer to her mother during the last years, mourned her sincerely, and saw that her body, at her own request, was buried beside that of Lord Brooke. Sir Lewis died in the same year, and Georgiana, after visiting her parents in America, wrote that she would not be coming back, she preferred the warmth of Virginia.

Francis and Bee were now Sir Francis and Lady Fargate, and Celia basked in their reflected glory, and spent as much time as she could at the Manor. She lived in straitened circumstances, with Amelia, and bemoaned the fact often to Bee, but Bee had no intention of having her mother live with them. She did help her, and invited her to the social gatherings which pleased Celia so much. Francis did not care for hunting, he liked such odd pastimes as painting, music and writing, and though these pursuits were more respectable than formerly they were still unconventional, and at first Celia eyed his art colleagues and friends askance.

But when she learned that some of them were related to aristocratic families her misgivings were allayed, and she learnt from them all the gossip about the big world of London society. There was the romance of Lord Randolph Churchill, son of the Duke of Marlborough, who announced his intention of marrying a Miss Jennie Jerome, an American, to the horror of his parents, the Duke saying that he could not contemplate an American connection.

'But they're determined to marry,' said Dorothea Varden, whose husband, was a well-known artist.

And marry they did, even though the Duke and Duchess refused to attend the ceremony. But the Prince of Wales liked Jennie Churchill, and the Duke and Duchess gave way in the end, for her son, Winston, was born at their home, Blenheim Palace.

Celia was utterly shocked at the behaviour of the Prince of Wales. His affair with the beautiful Lily Langtry – the Jersey Lily – was quite dreadful. And as for his being involved in the Mordaunt case – Celia could not bring herself to say the word divorce, it was a word too bad to be spoken.

There were other tales of love and passion among the wealthy. And so Celia sat, over the years, working at her embroidery, listening to gossip, wondering why her dear Amelia could never find anyone to marry, welcoming her grandchildren, Bee's three sons, Becky's five girls and boys – dear Becky was not too well off these days, such a pity she could not have married a richer man. . . . Life was so unfair: Bee was no prettier than she'd ever been, but it was obvious that Francis thought the world of her. She was well liked on the estate, and her sons adored her. As for Amanda . . . Celia would sigh. It was true what dear Geoffrey had said years ago that Amanda was like Tam, and Celia had to accept the fact that part of her family was a little odd. Take Tam: still running the boats, at her age, so indelicate . . .

Tam was accepted now in Chilverton as a character, and admired as such. 'Oh yes, she's a one,' said Chilverton. 'She don't care for nobody, not her,' and following Bee's example, they vied with each other to invite her to their parties and soirées. Somehow, living in sin didn't seem to matter so much when you were older, a fact which set Tam to laughing heartily in her own home.

For it was too late. Tam no longer cared for the society of Chilverton, and in spite of this, perhaps because of it, they asked her all the more. Tam took pleasure in turning down their invitations.

Charles too, found a measure of content he had not thought possible. He had missed so much of his own son's company, he was now able to make it up with his grandchildren, and especially Ian. Ian had stayed with them so often, having his own room, they hardly noticed when he moved in for good.

'I like living here,' Ian told them. 'Families are all very well, but when you're in the middle, as I am, you're neither one thing nor the other.'

'Not exactly in the middle,' said Tam.

'Richard is the eldest, and doesn't he let us know it. He can be really overbearing. And Henry's so serious, thinks of nothing but his books. He's had to wear spectacles now, I'm not surprised, but they make him look like an owl.'

'Poor Henry,' said Tam. 'He's a nice lad.'

'He's a dull clod. Then the girls, oh, yes, they're all right, but *girls* . . .'

Tam smiled, and Ian came to her, putting an arm around her waist. 'You want me to stay here, don't you, Grandmama?'

'Go away with you, wheedling around. Of course I want you to stay, but you must finish school first.'

So Ian carried on at school, but he spent all his spare time on the canals. And when Tam asked Jamie if he minded, she was told, 'You wanted me to work on the canal and I refused. So take Ian in my place.'

And perhaps 1873 was the best year of all. The Indian summer which lingered, like a ripe apple, before falling beneath winter snows. Tam was sixty-two now, still slim and supple, her hair only just beginning to grey. Her complexion was not, unfortunately, so white and flawless as those of the ladies who carefully shaded their skins with parasols every time they went out, and there were wrinkles, especially around the eyes when they crinkled with laughter, but her mouth was still firm. The crinoline had disappeared in favour of the bustle, though Tam had never worn either on the wharf.

Ian was fifteen now, nominally still at the town grammar school; in reality he was working with Charles. And seeing his eagerness, Tam no longer went to the wharf every day, she knew Charles loved the company of his young grandson, so she was content to leave them to work.

It was early in the year when Ian came home full of excitement. 'We've got some more orders, Gran,' he said. 'And there will be more.'

'Really?' Tam smiled at his eagerness.

'Yes. People are grumbling about the high cost of railways.'

Tam, who had been reading newspaper articles about the same thing, feigned surprise, and Ian went on. 'They are holding meetings too. And you know what? They want an act passed through Parliament to control the railways.' He turned to Charles. 'Grandfather, you must do something.'

'I'm not in Parliament now,' said Charles.

'No, but you know men who are. We must lobby, Grandfather.'

'We?' asked Charles, grinning.

'Take me to London with you,' begged Ian. 'Please . . .'

Charles hesitated. He had never, in all his many visits to London, mentioned Tam or his family. And Tam, gazing at him, guessed his dilemma. There was a brief silence. Charles looked at his young grandson, the pleading eyes so like those of Tam, and said, gruffly, 'I'll take you.' He turned to Tam. 'How about you? Will you come?'

She shook her head. 'No, Charles. You know political talk bores me.'

Charles took Ian to London. They stood outside the Houses of Parliament, went inside. He met his friends, and introduced Ian,' This is my grandson,' proudly, knowing a sense of satisfaction that he had, at last, acknowledged his family.

And when Ian asked awed, 'You really were important, weren't you, Grandfather?' Charles was gratified.

But his friends promised to help, for there was much concern now about the railway influence over canals. And in 1873 the Regulation of Railways Act was passed, appointing Railway Commissioners who were to see that through rates were fair, and to be the guardians of public interest. The railways were forbidden to acquire a controlling interest in a canal unless approved by the commissioners, and the act stated that those railways who did control canals must maintain them, so that the canals be kept open at all times.

'No more leaving canals to fall into disuse,' chortled Ian, gleefully. 'We're winning, Grandmama.'

'I always said we would,' she replied complacently.

They spent Christmas at Four Winds. Presents were exchanged, carols sung, they went to church on Christmas morning. Tam held Charles's hand on the drive home, and thought they were closer than they'd ever been.

But the Indian summer was nearing its end. The ripe apples began to fall.

Ian had left school at sixteen and started his training proper. Tam still left the running of the canals to him and Charles, going to the wharf occasionally, at other times content to wait for them to come home. She waited now, watched them enter, Ian running ahead, Charles more slowly. And after dinner they sat in the drawing room, watching the trees blown by the wind, and Ian said excitedly, 'There's talk of building a big canal in the north, the Manchester Ship Canal they'll call it.'

'A ship canal?' marvelled Tam.

'Yes. They're wanting to make one at Birmingham too.'

'That's a bit far inland for ships,' said Tam.

'Yes, but they want one. It would be cheaper than rail, you see. And this Manchester Ship Canal would connect Manchester to the sea . . .'

'It's only talk as yet,' Charles warned. 'They'll have to get acts passed, and the railway companies oppose it.'

'Oh well, they would,' snorted Tam.

'It'll come in time,' said Ian, his eyes shining.

'Maybe in your time if not in mine,' said Charles, and Tam turned to look at him a little worriedly. And when he went to bed early, saying he was tired, she turned to Ian. 'Is your grandfather all right?'

'Yes, of course. Why shouldn't he be?' asked Ian.

'Oh, I don't know. Just a feeling I have,' said Tam. 'It's not like him to feel tired.'

'But Gran, he's nearly seventy.'

'Yes, I suppose so,' Tam said, marvelling. Nearly seventy. Was it possible . . .?

Ian went to work with the engineers, and Tam watched Charles closely, as the summer progressed. He seemed to get tired easily, but perhaps that was natural when the weather was hot. And if he seemed preoccupied, well, there was something bothering him, as he told her.

'I'm worried about Snell,' he said.

George Snell was the son of the Mr Snell who had once owned Canal Company shares, and who was beginning to make himself known in Chilverton as a businessman. Francis Fargate was completely uninterested in business matters. He left the running of the railway to his agent, which benefited the canal, as there was no longer the cut-throat competition; he still owned the pits, but he sold the quarry to George Snell.

'Why are you worried?' asked Tam.

'He's taking it too near the towpath,' Charles said. 'It could be dangerous if he goes too far.'

'In what way?' Tam asked.

'Well, if the worst came to the worst, there could be a breach.'

Charles wrote to George Snell, but received no reply. And for the moment he let the matter rest. And Tam could not help but contrast this lassitude with his former energy. Once he would have ridden immediately to Snell, confronted him, taken him by the scruff of the neck and forced him to behave reasonably. She pondered on seeing Snell herself, but as Charles had always dealt with the maintenance work she failed to see how she could without humiliating him.

She waited patiently for Ian, but he was not back long before he was away again, finishing his course. 'I'll see to it when I'm home, Gran,' he promised. 'There isn't much I can do now, after all, Grandfather is in charge.'

Tam asked Bob, Jim's son, to take her for a trip in the *Princess* when he wasn't busy. She often did this, so it caused no comment. They sailed to the quarry, and Tam asked him to stop. She gazed at the yawning chasm in consternation. 'Good heavens,' she cried. 'It's nearly on the canal.'

Back home she told Charles, 'I had no idea it was so bad,' she said. 'Can he do this?'

'I've been to the lawyer,' Charles replied.

'And what's he doing?'

'Writing to Snell.'

Tam snorted. 'And they'll be writing for years. And in the meantime the canal is threatened.'

'He's on his own land,' Charles said. 'Not on Canal Company land. He's within his rights.'

'I think we should see Snell again, Charles.'

'It won't do any good, Tam. But you go, by all means, if you wish.'

Tam's blood was up. So, with Charles in agreement, she went to the quarry and confronted Mr Snell in his office. He faced her, unsmiling, a thin, long-nosed man in his forties, and he listened as she told him her grievance. He then repeated Charles's words, he was on his own land, he was within his rights.

'But surely, in common decency – ' Tam began. 'You would not wish to damage anything, or I will sue you.'

'There is no danger of damage,' said Snell.

'There is much danger,' cried Tam. 'And of hurt to my employees if the towpath is breached.'

He gave a thin smile. 'I assure you that will not happen.'

'If it does,' Tam said, 'I'll make you suffer.' And she flounced out of the office.

With September the gales began, and they were stronger than usual. Tam took another trip and saw the gaping hole of the quarry creeping ever nearer, and fumed at her helplessness.

The winter brought snow, deep snow that lay for weeks over the fields. The canal was frozen, the ice-boats pushed their cracking way through, only to find the water freezing again almost as soon as they'd passed. Boats were laid up, Christmas came and went with Ian home, and parties at the Calders' and at the Manor. And still more snow.

It did not thaw until February. Then there were floods. Water lay over the fields, the canal was high. Charles and Ian rode daily to find places where it had burst its banks, luckily in spots where little damage was done.

One cold dark night a gale blew up and Charles looked worriedly into the roaring blackness outside. Ian had ridden miles away to the other end of the canal where the bank had given way. Charles said, 'I think I must go – '

'Go where, Charles?'

'I'm worried about the towpath near the quarry.'

'But, Charles, it's ten o'clock. You've been out all day.'

'It's dangerous, Tam. There are boats nearby.'

'Don't go, Charles.'

'I must, Tam.'

He put on his coat, and she noted how tired his face seemed. She went to him and put her arms around him. 'Take care, my love,' she said. 'You mean more to me than the canal.'

And suddenly his old smile was there, and the dancing merriment in the black eyes. 'I never thought to hear you say that,' he said. He kissed her, and was gone.

She sat in the drawing room with Matty. The wind raged, rain beat against the panes. 'Oh my dear lord,' Matty said, as the wind shrieked. 'The house'll fall around our ears.'

'I think I'll go and see what's happening,' said Tam.

'You will not, Miss Tam. Not in this weather.'

'Charles is out in it,' said Tam. 'I want to see him, Matty. I'll take the carriage.'

'And who's to drive it, old Banty's long abed.'

'Young Ben can drive it as well you know, Matty. Go and call him.'

Matty still stood, and Tam said. 'I'm worried about Charles, Matty.' And Matty went.

331

Young Ben was one of the Lawson tribe, and he brought the carriage round, helped Tam inside, and she pulled her heavy cloak tight round her body for the wind penetrated every corner. The carriage plunged into the darkness, slowly, because Ben dare not take the horses at a gallop for fear they'd stumble over broken branches of trees that littered the roads. There was water in some places, from the still melting snow. 'Oh Ben,' Tam cried. 'It's a terrible night to be a boatman,' and knew that Ben would not hear a word against the raging wind.

She had directed him to drive to the nearest opening to the quarry. And when he stopped he tied the horses and accompanied her to the slippery, waterlogged path leading down to the canal. Then they were on the towpath, muddy, awash with water, tramping through as if in a nightmare, feet lifting heavily, unable to hurry. Ahead she could see lights from flares, could hear shouting even over the wind, and she stumbled on till she was near enough to see where the towpath adjoined the quarry.

A terrible sight met her eyes: men shouting, straining in the darkness, Charles, he was there, and there were boats, seemingly unable to pull away because the fast flowing water, driven by the wind, held them back, even with the horses straining with all their might. The canal was swollen, it washed over the towpath until it was impossible to see which was path and which canal. She could see now what the men, with Charles shouting orders, were doing. Trying to shore up the towpath. Trying in vain against the raging wind, the implacable water which forced away everything in its path. Before her very eyes she saw the towpath give way, yards of it, and the water pour into the breach . . . Saw a narrow boat go with it to be broken like matchwood. Saw another, with a man on board, coming close, saw Charles running to stop it . . . what could he do? Heard herself screaming helplessly, 'Charles!'

It was too late. His body went over into the quarry, together with the boat.

Chapter Three

Tam turned back to the canal. It had always been there, through losses, troubles, death. Even the fact that the water had taken Charles did not make any difference to her love. She knew that Charles had been ailing for some time, she often wondered if that last mad dash were deliberate . . .? In his place, she would have done the same.

She went back to work, for she had no choice. Ian still had much to learn, but he was learning fast. Even so, she was needed now in the office, so daily she went to the wharf. And when Matty remonstrated she said dully, 'What else can I do now?'

She redoubled her fight against George Snell, helped now by Jamie, who, shocked by his father's death, backed her with all the money at his command. 'Why didn't you tell me?' he asked Tam, but she shook her head.

'I couldn't, Jamie.' Couldn't let Charles know that he was failing before our eyes, that we had to force him into a back seat while others fought his battles. Not Charles.

George Snell, to do him justice, was quite appalled at the damage he'd caused, and rebuilt the towpath, shoring it up on the quarry side, stopping any more work on the nearside of the canal.

Tam worked, eyes bleak. She missed Charles: missed his dear face beside the fire, his kiss when he left, the warmth of his body beside hers. Without him she had never felt complete, now she was like an engine with some vital part missing, but still forced to carry on. She wondered why she had been so foolish as to stay away from him for so long, wondered why there had always been so much between them, wondered too if perhaps in another life they would meet again, love again . . .?

'But I can't come yet, Charles,' she muttered. 'Not until I see the canals are right. The Calder Boats is still a going concern, canals haven't been wiped out as so many said they would be. But we haven't won the battle yet.'

Ian bore out Tam's prophecy of becoming a heart-breaker. He fell in love with a rapidity that was disconcerting, he would talk of the latest love, of Susan or Pamela or Jenny, how they'd met at one of his parents' gatherings, or at Bee's, how he'd sit and gaze with longing at the charmer, hold her hand, arrange to meet – duly chaperoned of course. And how, just as the luckless young lady thought he was ready to approach her father, he would fall for another, and wonder whatever he had seen in Susan or Pamela or Jenny.

In 1876 Amanda came home with the startling news that she was going to attend the School of Medicine for Women that had been opened two years previously.

'But, Amanda,' protested Tam, 'you're not a young woman.'

'Over forty,' said Amanda. 'But I've been nursing for years, Aunt Tam. I know a good deal now. And many young ladies won't want to become doctors, you know. I do.'

Over forty, Tam thought, as Amanda went back to London, face glowing. Jamie the same age. Young Ian growing up, he'd soon be looking for a wife. Indeed, he needed a wife, as she pointed out to him in no uncertain manner. 'Running around with all these girls is very well,' she said. 'You must marry.'

'Now why do I need a wife?' Ian teased. 'When I have a grandmother like you?'

'Because you won't have me for ever, and you need a son,' said Tam.

'Ah, I see what you mean. A son for business, not because of my own comforts.'

'Of course,' said Tam, equably. 'I'm not going to die till you have a son.'

'Don't talk that way, Gran. I don't want you to – '

'I know, and you're a good lad. But I'd love a great-grandson. One who looked like . . . Charles.' And Ian was silent.

Tam, in the years that followed, turned more to her grandchildren, seeking the one most resembling her lost love. She studied them in turn: Richard, like his mother Catherine, tall and stately, who walked among her brood with a calm, unruffled air; Ian, like herself; Henry, serious, even smug, so obviously cut out to be a lawyer like his grandfather Bradford, so obviously unlike Charles; little Robert Nicholas, a mischievous little monkey, and the girls, Cathy, with her heart-shaped face, quiet, almost secretive, Vinny . . .

Vinny, dark and tempestuous. Surely this was the one.

Tam said to Jamie, 'I think Vinny resembles your father, don't you, Jamie?'

'She's a wilful little madam. I think like you, Mama, but then you and Father were alike in some ways.'

She was silent, and he added gently, 'You miss him, don't you, Mama?'

'So much, Jamie. When he was alive, even when we were apart, still I knew he was *there*, somewhere. But death is so final.'

'Don't you believe you'll meet again, Mama?'

She hesitated. 'I don't know. Sometimes I think we *must*. But I've never been a religious person, Jamie. I find it difficult to believe in heaven. Perhaps because I feel that I wouldn't get in.'

He touched her hand. 'I think you would, Mama.'

She laughed shortly. 'After the life I've led? Marrying Sir William for the canal? Living in sin with your father? Working on the canals?'

He smiled. 'Most of our marriages are arranged for prospects and money, as well you know, Mama. As for living in sin, you loved him, didn't you? And when the bill is passed allowing men to marry their wives' sisters, then it won't be a sin, will it? And I doubt if working for a living would keep you out of heaven. Just out of Chilverton society.'

She smiled. 'You are a comfort, Jamie. Do you believe in an afterlife?'

'Yes, Mama.'

'What a nice boy you are. Your father said that once. And it's so surprising after the life you had. Your supposed father, Sir William, so unkind to you. Being turned away from your home. Then my life with your real father, being ostracised. By all accounts you should have turned out a dreadful rogue, instead you're the nicest son a mother could have . . . But enough of compliments, I'm getting soft in my old age. We must find a wife for Ian, Jamie.'

'I'm sure he's perfectly capable of finding one for himself, Mama.'

Tam snorted. 'Too capable. I want to see him settling down, with a son.'

Jamie smiled. 'All in good time, Mama.'

Tam snorted again, but knew that Jamie had never been hurried or persuaded against his will. Nor, it seemed, would Ian.

In the eighties, matters between railways and canals changed radically. People were beginning to understand the dangers of a railway monopoly. Tam, in her delight, forgot that Ian still hadn't chosen a bride, as she chortled, 'Listen to this, Ian. "For the first time since the Industrial Revolution foreign manufactured goods are seriously competing with our own in the home market because of free trade. So cheap transport is vital, and on the Continent both railways and waterways are cheaper than in Britain".'

'We can't lower the canal charges any more, Gran. We're cheaper than the railways.'

'Yes, yes, they are wanting canal transport. Listen to this, written to the Secretary of the Royal Society of Arts, "Sixteen years ago anyone advocating water transport was promptly accused of galvanising a corpse." Ian, you're not listening.'

'I am, Gran. But I have a message from Father. Vinny is getting married.'

'Is she? Vinny? Good heavens, how old is she now?'

'Twenty, Gran.'

'So many weddings,' Tam said. 'They're all married now except you, Ian.'

'And Cathy and Robert.'

'Bee's sons are married.'

'Only Stephen, Gran. Not Frederick or Kit.'

'No, well. You met such nice girls at those weddings too. What are you waiting for, a princess?'

'Are you going to Vinny's wedding, Gran?'

'Of course I'm going to Vinny's wedding. She's a lovely girl. Who's she marrying?'

'You know well who she's marrying, Gran. Alex Macdonald.'

'He's Scottish, isn't he? My Papa was Scottish.' She hesitated. 'No, he wasn't, was he? I always forget.' And for a moment she looked so lost that Ian went to her and took her hand.

'Alex is Scottish, Gran, and he's an engineer.'

Her face brightened. 'Papa always wanted to be an engineer.'

Vinny was married in the spring of 1881 in Chilverton Church. Tam, wearing a royal blue gown, saw the wedding, then drove to Four Winds for the wedding breakfast. She enjoyed these family gatherings. Jamie, was it possible he'd soon be fifty? Catherine, flanked by her sons, Richard, Ian, young Robert and Henry . . . even Henry was married now. Cathy, like her mother, a graceful eighteen. Bee and her family. Celia did not come, she had been ailing for some time, and seldom left the house. Amelia looked after her. Poor Amelia, the Victorian old maid, the spinster aunt . . . If only Charles could have been there; strange, sometimes she could go for quite a long period without thinking too much about him, then, at a time like this, the loss would strike again, the loss, and the pain. Little things would trigger it off, a trip to the wharf, seeing a place where he'd always stood, every time she sailed past the towpath where it had been breached . . .

She came back to the present with a jerk. No point in going back to the past like this. Sign of age. Age? Ha! She'd show them yet, as she always had. She had to wait for Ian's son to be born. Ian. Where was the boy? Talking to a girl, as usual. Who was it this time?'

'Who's that?' she asked her neighbour Frederick, Bee's son.

'That's Anne Macdonald, Alex's young sister. She was a bridesmaid.'

'So she was. Only a child.'

'A pretty child, Aunt Tam.'

Tam snorted. And went over to Vinny, kissed her and said with a rough catch in her voice, 'I wish you all the happiness in the world, Vinny.' She turned to Alex, tall, reddish-haired, with startling blue eyes. 'Be good to her, Alex.'

'I will,' he promised in his soft burr.

Tam smiled. 'Where's that young sister of yours? Anne. Ah, there she is. Come and talk to me, my dear.' She patted a seat beside her. 'How old are you?'

The girl looked surprised. 'Fifteen.'

'Humph. Far too young.'

'Too young for what, Lady Fargate?'

'Heavens, child, don't call me that.'

'Too young for Ian, she means,' chuckled Frederick, at her side. 'Aunt Tam, you are outrageous.'

'Live in Scotland do you, Anne?' asked Tam, no whit abashed.

'Yes, in Edinburgh.'

'So you'll not be down here again for a long time.'

'Not unless I visit Alex,' said Anne. 'He's going to live in Stratford-on-Avon while he works round here. But I'm afraid I shan't be marrying your grandson. If I marry, it will be to a fellow Scot.'

'Humph,' said Tam, and turned back to watch the bride and groom walk to their carriage, to be whirled away to Scotland for their honeymoon. And Ian, returning home that evening, was strangely quiet. When Tam, in the next few weeks, teased him about his lack of young lady friends, he confessed shyly that he had fallen in love with Anne Macdonald. But she was too young, she would have none of him.

'Nonsense,' said Tam, robustly. 'You'll just have to chase her.'

For five years Ian chased Anne Macdonald. When she visited Vinny and Alex, he went there too. When she went home he wrote to her. And in 1886 Anne gave way. She agreed to marry Ian.

She came to see Tam, and faced the formidable old lady with quiet composure. Tam studied her. At twenty Anne was dark and lovely, yet with the same blue eyes as her brother, and there was always an aloof air about the girl, contrasting well with Ian's extroverted ways. 'So you've finally given in,' Tam said.

'Yes, I have . . . er . . . what do you wish me to call you?'

'Gran, of course, what else? Well, I hope you'll be happy here, at Cherry Trees. I believe in marriage myself, though I never was married, at least not what you could count. Jamie was Charles's son, you know, not that old skinflint's, Sir William, I wouldn't want to have a son of his.'

'No, Gran,' said Anne, a little faintly.

'We couldn't marry, Charles and I. Couldn't wait for Parliament to make up its mind about that bill . . . humph. Are you going to have children, Anne?'

'I hope so,' said Anne.

'Yes, you must. Provide the Calder Boats with an heir.'

'Gran – ' protested Ian, but Anne merely smiled.

They were married in 1887, and one year later their first child, a girl, was born. Tam strove to hide her chagrin that it wasn't a boy as Ian said, 'We thought to name her Tamarisk, then decided against it, there can only be one Tam. So we thought Annabel would be admirable, for your mother, and it is Anne's name too.'

'Just so long as it's a boy next time,' Tam said. 'It don't matter what her name is.'

Yet she loved the baby, and came to admire Anne too, without ever quite loving her. Anne was kind, thoughtful, pleasant – but always a little reserved.

As little Annabel grew and began to stagger around on sturdy legs Tam said to Ian, 'Remember the talk about the canals by the Royal Society of Arts?'

'Yes, Gran.'

'They're holding a two-day conference in London. I want to go.'

'Oh Gran . . . it's a long way. Is it wise?'

337

Tam smiled. 'I never in my life did things that were wise, and I'm not going to start now.'

'Then I'll come with you.'

'I'm going by boat, Ian.'

'But – '

'By boat, Ian.'

Tam went to her room. At seventy-seven her hair was still not quite white, there were, incredibly, touches of colour which led people to assert untruthfully that she dyed it. Her face was wrinkled, but her eyes still gleamed green when she was angry. Rheumatism in her legs prevented her walking far, and she used a stick. For the rest she was as spry as always, and more determined than ever to have her own way. When in a temper she would bang her stick on the floor or on any luckless person who happened to be in the vicinity. Ian laughed at her and loved her, but he knew how far he could go. He knew that if Tam wanted to go to London by boat, then by boat they would go.

They journeyed on the old well-remembered route, Tam smiling with pleasure. 'Look, Stoke Bruerne,' she said. 'The little shop's still here . . . And Cowroast. Did I ever tell you about the time I came down here to Pickfords?'

'I think so, Gran,' said Ian, who had heard the story fifty times.

They slept in the little cabins, waking each morning to the sound of water gently lapping the sides of the boat, bird cries, sometimes the patter of rain on the roof. On again, Tam watching the water voles swimming across, the occasional otter, the swarms of tiny minnows.

'We should have brought Anne,' said Tam. 'There's no nicer way to travel than by boat. Now, where are we? Coming into London yet? My goodness, there are more buildings than when I was here last. We'll stay at a nice hotel. I might not have made a fortune, but I'm not short of a penny. And I did what I wanted to do. That's the secret of a long life, you know. Do what you want to do.'

'Yes, Gran,' said Ian.

'We'll stay at the Piccadilly,' said Tam. 'I remember coming here with Mama and the girls, years ago, when we bought our dresses for Celia's wedding. Poor Celia, been dead now for five years. And that simpering Amelia gone to live with Becky, acting as an unpaid drudge for the family. More fool her. Amanda wouldn't have. Nor Bee.'

'We're here, Gran,' said Ian, and he helped her on to the towpath, to the street, where they called a hansom cab. And she marvelled at the busy roads, the horse-drawn omnibuses, gaily coloured, with their passengers crowded inside. 'Not very comfortable,' she snorted. 'They'd be better on a boat.'

'Or a bicycle,' said Ian. 'Do you know, Gran, they're talking of putting a little engine on to bicycles now?'

'Really?' Tam sniffed.

They went to the hotel, and Tam was glad to rest, though she would have died rather than admit it. And she insisted on hiring a cab later and

338

touring the streets, where the Jubilee decorations of the previous year still lingered. 'Fifty years a queen,' marvelled Tam. 'They say the procession was a wonder. Exotic Indian cavalry, kings and princes from abroad, Scottish pipers . . . one woman ruling a great Empire. Ah well, let's go to the conference.'

The conference was crowded, and leading waterway engineers and managers read papers on the revival of the waterways. A discussion followed and Tam listened eagerly to the speakers.

'Firms are having to move to the coast to avoid the high rail charges – '

'All they need to do is send their goods by water – '

'The railway people are such powerful opponents – '

'We must amalgamate and modernise. We need uniformity of gauge on the great through routes – '

'I've heard all this before,' Tam said loudly. 'My father was saying it back in 1816, and I've been saying it ever since. And everybody just talks and talks and does nothing.' She banged her stick on the floor.

'We need steam haulage,' another speaker said, with an apprehensive look at Tam and her stick.

'And who,' asked a voice, 'is to pay for all the improvements needed?' And there was a pause.

'There is so much needs to be done. We couldn't possibly raise the necessary capital. So why don't we ask the government to take over?'

There were dubious looks, and another man rose to his feet. 'We know the traditional independence of Englishmen is opposed to government interference, yet the descendants of Englishmen in Canada and the United States are now enjoying the benefits of artificial waterways provided by their governments.'

'Yes.' It was General Rundall speaking now, and his voice carried authority. 'I propose there should be a Water Commission. A Royal Commission.'

After the discussion the following resolution was carried:

> 'That the legislature should seriously consider the necessity of encouraging and assisting the improvement and extension of the canal system, by State acquisition or otherwise, and that meanwhile the Conference urges the Council of the Society of Arts to petition the House of Commons for the amendment of the Railway and Canal Traffic Bill by authorising local authorities to constitute Public Trusts, for the development of the existing system of canals.'

Tam said doubtfully to Ian on the way home, 'Is this the best way? I don't want to lose my canal.'

'You won't,' said Ian in his usual blithe, carefree manner.

Too blithe and carefree perhaps. For the very optimism which had endeared Ian to Tam in the beginning now seemed a drawback. He was so young . . . She longed for Charles, his sound advice. She decided to talk it over with Jamie.

Jamie pondered when she asked him.

339

'I think you have no choice, Mama,' he said at last. 'You cannot possibly make all the improvements needed without help, and you need the Government to overrule the railways, for they won't want to improve the canals they own, they just leave them to decay.'

'I will ask for a Royal Commision,' she decided.

'Ask by all means,' said Jamie.

'You think I might not get it,' she said, with the glimmer of a smile. 'Don't you know me yet, Jamie?'

'At the very least,' said Jamie, 'you will have done your share. You have kept your canal open against all opposition. Future generations will thank you, Mama.'

'Humph,' said Tam.

The arguments and discussions went on, but there was no Royal Commission. The Manchester Ship Canal was being built, but was not finally opened until 1894, with a procession of boats headed by the *Norseman*, carrying the directors, and followed by a trail of merchant ships, seventy-one of which entered the docks. And on May 21st, the formal opening took place by the Queen herself.

'I'd love to see it,' said Tam, wistfully.

'No, Gran,' Ian was alarmed.

'I'm not too old to travel,' she said belligerently. 'I'm only eighty-three.'

'I know, Gran, but Anne's baby is due in May, and I don't want to leave her. Why not wait till there's a Ship Canal in Birmingham?'

Tam snorted. But she did not go. In the six years of marriage Anne had been unlucky, and had had two miscarriages, though the doctor said there was no reason why she should not have another full-term pregnancy. Now, pregnant again, and near her time she was forced to rest as much as possible. Tam was hoping that this time it would be the longed-for son, but alas, again her hopes were dashed. The baby was healthy – but a girl, Elizabeth.

Amanda asked, why a son? Could not a girl run the canals as she, Tam, had done? Women were breaking away from the restrictions of Victorian home life . . . Tam smiled, but did not tell the real reason she longed for a boy.

Tam did not get out much these days, she spent her time writing letters to newspapers, following the arguments which still raged about canals versus railways. She asked for a Royal Commission, and bemoaned the fact that the much talked about Birmingham Ship Canal had not materialised.

'Come, Gran, it's getting cold, come to the fire,' said Ian. 'We don't want you getting pneumonia.'

'Don't worry about me,' said Tam. 'I'm not going to die till we've had this Royal Commission. And until you have a son.'

But alas, the son did not materialise either. In the next ten years Anne gave birth to another daughter, Grace, and had a number of miscarriages. One small son was born in 1899, lived two hours and died, and Tam sat grieving over the tiny form, feeling the loss as keenly as the mother.

* * *

In the spring of 1906 Tam sat in the drawing room of Cherry Trees. Outside the blossom petals drifted down like a small snowstorm, blown by high winds. She said, 'I remember seeing them once before like that, when Juliet was a small girl, and Mama said, "Always take care of Juliet, Tam." Well, I did.'

She was huddled by the fire, for she felt the cold sorely these days. Beside her sat her great-granddaughters, and upstairs Anne lay in the throes of labour.

'I hope it's a boy this time,' said Tam. 'So many children born all the time. They tell me Bee's eldest boy – what's his name? Stephen, I think – has a son now. He's Sir Stephen of course, poor Francis is dead. He always did seem a sickly boy, though likeable. I never knew him very well.'

Ian came in, and Tam looked up. 'How is she?' she asked anxiously.

'Not well. Not well at all, Gran. Oh dear,' and Ian wiped his brow. 'This will be the last, the doctor said. Anne's forty now, you know . . .' He broke off, remembering he was talking before his small daughters.

'Sit down,' said Tam. 'Talk about something else, take your mind off things. You can't hurry nature, you know. How's the canal?'

'Oh, everything's fine.'

'I don't mean in Chilverton. I mean what's the Government doing? All these resolutions passed, everyone pressing for a Royal Commission – '

'Gran,' interrupted Ian, conscience-stricken. 'I forgot to tell you, I was so worried – ' he wiped his brow again. 'They're appointing a Royal Commission at last. All the pressure's worked. Now they're going to do something.'

Tam smiled. 'I knew it,' she said triumphantly. 'I knew if I wrote enough letters to newspapers someone would take notice – '

'Yes, Gran.' And indeed Tam was known now. Her letters were published in newspapers all over the country. And when one enterprising reporter learned her age he had hastened over to see her.

'I wonder,' he said, 'if you'd tell me your story.'

'Why?' she asked in the old direct manner.

'Why? Because I read all your letters, and I had no idea that you were an old lady of ninety-five.'

'What do you mean old?' asked Tam, bridling. 'Oh, I've seen a lot of changes in my time. I saw the Queen married, now she's been dead for . . . how long?'

'Five years, Mrs . . . er – '

'Miss,' said Tam. 'Miss Calder. They tell me that an act allowing a man to marry his dead wife's sister is going through Parliament, will be made law next year.'

The reporter wondered what that had to do with anything, and asked what she thought of the new horseless carriages.

'They'll put the railways out of joint,' chuckled Tam. 'Sit down, young man, and I'll tell you my story. And that of my Papa.'

Tam knew the value of publicity.

341

She chuckled as she remembered. It was so easy to talk about Papa, sometimes it seemed only yesterday that she was riding with him to the wharf, that she'd promised to help him . . .

The nanny fetched the girls, but Tam hardly noticed. She walked to the window in order to see the petals falling. 'It's a strong wind,' she said. 'And the water's up. I hope the boat's secure. Jim's away. Is it Jim?'

A maid brought her a meal, and she moved away from the window. 'Don't draw the curtains,' she said. 'I want to see the water. It's rising.'

'Yes, ma'am, it's been raining a lot,' the maid said.

'I hope the boat's secure,' Tam said. 'Where's Ian?'

'Here I am, Gran,' and Ian burst into the room. 'Such splendid news. A boy, Gran. A boy.'

And then the nurse entered, carrying a tiny bundle. Tam gazed at the little face in awe. 'It's him, Ian,' she said. 'It's Charles, in miniature.'

'Yes, Gran. We're going to call him Charles James.'

Tam wiped away a tear. 'How is Anne?' she asked.

'Weak, Gran, but fine. I'm going up now. Will you be all right?'

'Of course I'll be all right. I'm not in my dotage. Is the boat secure, Ian?'

'Which boat, Gran?'

'The *Princess*, of course. Jim's away.'

'Oh Gran, the Lawsons have all gone now, don't you remember? We don't use the *Princess* now. At least not very often.'

'Oh,' she said. 'But it's still there.'

'Of course. Now I must go back to Anne. Do you want me to send anyone to you, Gran?'

'Of course I don't, what for? You go to Anne, and give her my love.'

'I will, Gran.'

He left, and Tam listened to the howling wind. It was going to be all right now, everything would be all right. Little Charles was born, and the Government was going to do something about the canals. At last. She would like to tell Papa.

How the rain poured down. The canal was rising fast. She couldn't see well now, it was getting dark, but she knew from past experience how the water rose, so fast sometimes it was frightening, she had watched it many times creeping over the garden . . .

If only the boat was secure. It had stood there so many years, the *Princess*, it had been Papa's gift to Mama, and though it was old now, it had always been kept in good repair, been repaired so many times it was like a new boat, Ian said. So it mustn't break away, or it might be smashed to pieces down a quarry like that other one . . . she couldn't allow that to happen . . .

Why didn't Ian come back? No, he must stay with Anne. And Ben would be in bed. And the maids. No, the maids were around, but they didn't know anything about boats. Not like she did. She'd have to go and see to the boat herself. Make it secure. It was a long way to walk all down the garden, but she'd do it.

She hobbled to the door, stick in hand, pulling her shawl round her shoulders. She opened the door and the wind slammed it shut behind her, yet no one inside heard over the raging wind.

She saw in the half light that the water was still rising, coming up the garden. Could she reach the boat? Make it fast?

She made her way down the garden and the wind hit her, carrying the rain in its arms. It knocked her breath from her body, and she gasped in shock at the cold. But still she hobbled on.

The boat seemed very near now. The wind played strange tricks and the darkness too, she thought she could see Mama on the deck, Mama as she used to be, with little Juliet and Celia. Over on the other bank a dark handsome fellow rode on a black horse, laughing down at her . . . Charles. She must get to the boat . . . For there . . . was that Papa . . . ?

She must tell him that she had kept the canal open, she'd fought them all, kept the boats running. She walked on eagerly. And she didn't feel cold when the first water washed over her.

Her body was never found. She joined the legends of Spring-heeled Jack and the lady who is seen in tunnels. Boaters swore they'd seen old Tam when they were going through a bad patch, perhaps in a tunnel, when she'd rise before them and guide them through. She always helped.

'No, she ain't dead, not old Tam,' the boaters said. 'We see her often, and she always helps us.'

The *Princess* had pulled her mooring. She was swept downstream by the wind and smashed into the hump-backed bridge near the 'Anchor'. Then, helplessly broken, she drifted to the bottom.

Epilogue

The Royal Commission of 1906 presented its report in twelve volumes in 1911, the most comprehensive study of the waterway system that had ever been made in the British Isles. They recommended improvements which would result in a saving of transport costs. But railway supporters were against it, and against a state system of waterways, although this was the usual practice on the Continent. When the First World War broke out, canals were put immediately under control of the state through the Railway Executive Committee, together with the railways themselves. Nothing was done to control the independent waterways, however, and in 1920 canals reverted to private control, and the time between the wars was one of steady contraction, though motor boats were working now as well as horse-drawn boats.

In 1939 railway-owned canals again came under the control of the Ministry of Transport as part of railway undertakings, and the government felt that the greatest use was not being made of canals during the war, and in 1941 a report was commissioned. It was recommended that the government should assume responsibility for them. Efforts were made to put as much traffic on to the waterways as possible, but a number of factors made this difficult. Canals suffered from the poor standard of maintenance as previously, and from the drain of skilled men and women from boats and boat-building and -repairing yards.

Since 1888 there had been serious debate about state ownership of the waterways, and the Transport Act of 1947 brought this into being almost without controversy. There was talk then, as there is still occasionally today, of the benefits of waterway carrying; how, if the canals had been widened, they could take much of the congestion from the roads. For now the long war between the railways and canals was drawing to a close; competition would in future be from motorways and juggernauts.

But people refused to let the canals die. In 1951 a commission report classified waterways into three groups: those that offered scope for commercial development, for example the Aire and Calder; those that should probably be retained in the waterway system, like the Leeds and Liverpool,

345

Birmingham, Coventry, and so on, and the rest which might be useful for pleasure boating.

Passenger carrying restarted in 1957, and by the sixties canals were again popular. A few, which had been left to fall into decay, were opened by enthusiastic volunteers. A new canal age began.

The Chilverton ran working boats until the fifties, and when finally they were finished, Charles James Calder started his popular passenger boats. They are not unlike Tam's old packets, they float along to well-known beauty spots; American tourists love them. Tamarisk Calder would have been delighted, though not surprised, for she never doubted that boats would always run on her canal.

As the boaters say, 'Old Tam still lives.'

Bibliography

Anon, *Nuneaton – A Local Diary 1810–50*

Eliot, George, *Collected Works*

Gayford, Eily, *The Amateur Boatwoman*, David & Charles

Gladwin, D D, *British Waterways*, Batsford; *Canals of Britain*, Batsford; *Pictorial History of Canals*, Batsford; *The Waterways of Britain: A Social Panorama*, Batsford

Hadfield, Charles, *British Canals*, David & Charles; *The Canal Age*, David & Charles; *Canals of the West Midlands*, David & Charles

Hanson, Harry, *The Canal Boatman*; *Canal People*

Hart, Roger, *English Life in the 19th Century*

Plummer, Alfred, *The London Weaving Company 1600–1970*

Priestley, Joseph, *Priestley's Navigable Rivers and Canals*, first published 1831, reprinted by David & Charles

Rolt, L T C, *Inland Waterways of England*, Allen & Unwin; *Narrow Boat*, Eyre Methuen

Seaman L, *Victorian England*, Methuen

Skipp, Victor, *Making of Victorian Birmingham*

Smith, Donald, *The Horse on the Cut*, Patrick Stevens, Cambridge

Thurston, Em Temple, *Flower of Gloster*, David & Charles

Veasey, *Nuneaton: History and Industry*

Windsor, David, *The Quaker Enterprise*, Muller

BIRMINGHAM PUBLIC LIBRARIES
HOUSEBOUND BORROWERS RECORD SHEET

1	2	3	4	5	6	7	8	9	10	11	12	13	14	15	16	17	18	19	20	21	22	23
24	25	26	27	28	29	30	31	32	33	34	35	36	37	38	39	40	41	42	43			
44	45	46	47	48	49	50	51	52	53	54	55	56	57	58	59	60	61	62	63			
64	65	66	67	68	69	70	71	72	73	74	75	76	77	78	79	80	81	82	83			
84	85	86	87	88	89	90	91	92	93	94	95	96	97	98	99	100						

101	102	103	104	105	106	107	108	109	110	111	112	113	114	115
116	117	118	119	120	121	122	123	124	125	126	127	128	129	130
131	132	133	134	135	136	137	138	139	140	141	142	143	144	145
146	147	148	149	150	151	152	153	154	155	156	157	158	159	160
161	162	163	164	165	166	167	168	169	170	171	712	173	174	175
176	177	178	179	180	181	182	183	184	185	186	187	188	189	190
191	192	193	194	195	196	197	198	199	200					

201	202	203	204	205	206	207	208	209	210	211	212	213	214	215
216	217	218	219	220	221	222	223	224	225	226	227	228	229	230
231	232	233	234	235	236	237	238	239	240	241	242	243	244	245
246	247	248	249	250	251	252	253	254	255	256	257	258	259	260
261	262	263	264	265	266	267	268	269	270	271	272	273	274	275
276	277	278	279	280	281	282	283	284	285	286	287	288	289	290
291	292	293	294	295	296	297	298	299	300					

301	302	303	304	305	306	307	308	309	310	311	312	313	314	315
316	317	318	319	320	321	322	323	324	325	326	327	328	329	330
331	332	333	334	335	336	337	328	339	340	341	342	343	344	345
346	347	348	349	350	351	352	353	354	355	356	357	358	359	360
361	362	363	364	365	366	367	368	369	370	371	372	373	374	375
376	377	378	379	380	381	382	383	384	385	386	387	388	389	390
391	392	393	394	395	396	397	398	399	400					

401	402	403	404	405	406	407	408	409	410	411	412	413	414	415
416	417	418	419	420	421	422	423	424	425	426	427	428	429	430
431	432	433	434	435	436	437	438	439	440	441	442	443	444	445
446	447	448	449	450	451	452	453	454	455	456	457	458	459	460
461	462	463	464	465	466	467	468	469	470	471	472	473	474	475
476	477	478	479	480	481	482	483	484	485	486	487	488	489	490
491	492	493	494	495	496	497	498	499	500					

(11/89)